Sensitive Content Advisory

This book contains mature themes, which is a lovely warning that tells you absolutely nothing. Unfortunately, more explicit warnings risk providing spoilers: insight into story details that, if previously known, may reduce surprise or suspense for a first-time reader. If you'd like to discover the story along with Becca, the main character, you can stop reading this section now.

If you're more comfortable hearing about how I handle certain sensitive subjects before you come on this journey with me, the following two pages are for you. While I obviously hope you do decide to enjoy the book, informed consent is a key value for me. I provide this information to help you decide whether you wish to engage with the story.

Consent: Let's admit this up front: Becca is bad at consent. Everything is new to her and she doesn't yet have the experience to know whether she'll like it. More than once in the story, she says 'yes' when she probably should have said 'no'. Both Morgan and Lynn have more experience; they recognise the problem and work hard to keep Becca as safe and comfortable as possible while she learns how to give good consent.

> *"Okay," Lynn said. "So your words are telling me that you're curious and you want to learn something new. That's fair. So why is your body language screaming that you're terrified?"*
>
> *"I'm sorry," Becca said. She made an effort to sit up straighter. "I know I'm being unreasonable. I apologise for my reactions." Morgan squeezed her hand under the table. It helped.*
>
> *"I don't want an apology," Lynn said. "I want to know that you're making a choice to be here. I want to know that you'd feel safe, saying no, because if you're saying yes because you're afraid of the consequences, that's not a yes we should be taking."*
>
> *"You said you won't hurt me," Becca said. Lynn nodded.*
>
> *"That's true," they said. "And as long as you know that applies to saying no, as well as if you say yes, I'm happy to help."*

Kink: Morgan and Lynn both enjoy BDSM; safewords are a normal part of their interaction with one another. Becca explores kink for the first time during the story. Several chapters focus on shibari rope bondage. These progress from demonstration to instruction to an actual 'scene' in which Becca is tied to the mast of Morgan's and Lynn's boat. Other kinks mentioned or explained include impact play with whips, puppy play, and pursuit and take-down. All of these are presented as having been consensual and rewarding for the people participating.

> *"I do have whips," Morgan said. "And other things. I never said that I don't hurt people. I have, and I will. People who enjoy it, who want to engage in that sort of play with me." Morgan took a breath. "You've <u>known</u> that about me, as you say, and you're right that it wasn't something that was relevant to our friendship. What I'm telling you is that it still isn't. I won't hurt <u>you</u>."*

Gender: Morgan and Becca are female; Lynn is nonbinary. None of them 'used to be' a different gender. If they were assigned to a different gender in the past, that error does not negate the reality of their identity.

> *Becca had heard about Lynn, of course, but had never met her friend's partner, or even spoken with them online. She knew they were nonbinary — Morgan referred to 'them' rather than 'him' or 'her' — and that they did something with computers, but that was about it.*

Sexual Orientation: All three of the main characters are queer. Morgan sometimes describes herself as a lesbian for the sake of simplicity, but may be better described as a skewed pansexual; heterosexual, cisgender males rarely appeal to her. Lynn is also pansexual, but slower to leap into relationships than their partner. As for Becca, her life experiences will suddenly start making more sense to her if somebody explains what it means to be asexual and demiromantic. Right now, not having words to understand how she's feeling is more than a little scary.

> *"I never felt this way in high school." she said.*
>
> *"What, no crushes on a cute guy?" Morgan teased gently.*
> *"Or a girl?" Becca shook her head again.*
>
> *"I mean, I knew I was supposed to. I thought about it, I guess. Like this guy might not be awful, if I had to be with somebody. But it wasn't something I really wanted. Nothing like ..." she waved her hands vaguely. "I want to do stuff with you. Even if it seems scary, but I know you like it, I kind of want to at least try it? Because if you like it, then it can't be that bad?"*

Relationship Models: Morgan and Lynn are in a stable, committed relationship that is not monogamous. The dynamic they have allows them to explore potential new relationships independently without violating their existing relationship agreements. Things that impact the other person (e.g. risk of disease transmission from sexual activity, or even needing to prepare more food for dinner because somebody will be visiting) require discussion, but flirtation and even dating do not. In practice, of course, new people are exciting and they will often talk with existing partners about that excitement.

> *"I promise it's okay," Lynn said. "I told you before that she won't offer you anything that would hurt me if you accepted. That's still true."*

Bigotry: All of the above are potential axes of discrimination. While the events of this story do not include bigotry, its effects have shaped Morgan's and Lynn's lives. The UK's now-repealed Section 28 was active while they were in school. The legal status of LGBTQIA+ people in certain Caribbean countries affects where they can safely dock their boat or resupply. Unpredictable treatment by staff and patrons has made Lynn more hesitant to try unfamiliar restaurants or entertainment venues. Morgan and Lynn discuss some of these risks with Becca because they see her as being newly vulnerable to anti-queer bullying.

> *"Yeah, I definitely want you two to stay safe," [Becca] said. Lynn looked at her.*
>
> *"Has it occurred to you, yet," they asked, "that this applies to you, too?" Becca blinked.*
> *"That's," she began. "Umm. Yeah. I guess that is a thing."*

Missing the Boat

Missing the Boat

Heather W Adams

BOOKWYRM

MISSING THE BOAT

Cover illustration © 2021 by Emiliano Figueroa Falcón
Emoji illustrations by Sajeela Kiran

ISBN: 978-1-7776330-4-2 (hardcover)
       978-1-7776330-1-1 (large print)
       978-1-7776330-2-8 (paperback)
       978-1-7776330-3-5 (ebook)

*For Linny, without whom
much of this book would
have been impossible*

*And for Tammy, without whom
nothing would be meaningful*

One

"But we were here for the *last* boat, and *it* was too full!" Becca had to shout to be heard above the diesel engine. On the other side of the barrier, the man in the ferry company uniform shrugged.

"You weren't here when we started loading, and now this one is full," he told her.

"But we were just over at the picnic benches!" Becca argued. "For four hours!" The man shrugged again. "Seriously? How long do we have to wait now?"

"Next ferry's at nine," the man said.

"So only another hour?" That was something, at least.

"Nine in the morning," he clarified. "Sorry about that."

"What?" Becca yelled at him, but he had already turned his back on her and jumped the gap that was opening between dock and boat. "But what am I supposed to do?"

It was too late. He was no longer even looking in her direction, and the ferry was steadily pulling away from the dock, disappearing into the glare of the setting sun.

Morgan stepped forward to put a hand on Becca's shoulder, but the shorter woman shook it off.

"I can't believe this!" Becca turned to her friend. "How can they just ... strand somebody on the island? They brought us here; shouldn't they have to take us home?"

Morgan nodded sympathetically, and Becca followed her back to the seating area.

"I just, I don't know what I'm going to do now," Becca said. "I thought I'd planned for everything, but this ...." She shook her head.

"You were so insistent that we be back here for four," Morgan agreed. "I thought you were being overcautious, then."

"So did I," Becca admitted. "But now? I just don't know."

"What are your options?" Morgan asked. Becca took a deep breath, trying to steady herself.

"I mean, I guess I'm stuck here for the night," Becca said. "Umm. I know there are campsites. We passed one of them on the lighthouse trail. I think I saw that there are some in the southern nature area, too, when I was planning this trip." She shook her head. "But I don't have anything I'd need to camp — I don't even have what I'd need for a night at a hotel. All my things are back in my room on the mainland."

"We passed a couple of hotels, I think," Morgan suggested.

"Yeah," Becca said. "I guess if I can find one with a vacancy, it would be better than nothing. Though I hate to pay for another night's hotel room when I have a perfectly good room already. Do you have any idea what you're going to do? I thought the last ferry from the other side of the is-land left at quarter to."

"Lynn and I anchored around the south side of the island, off the nature reserve," Morgan said. "I left the dinghy up at North Island Marina." She hesitated before offering, "If you don't want to rent a room here, or if you can't find one, I could take you home. I mean, if you wanted."

"Could you?" Becca grasped at hope. Maybe she should have been more hesitant; after all, she technically hadn't even seen Morgan in person un-til the other woman had been waiting to meet her when Becca stepped off the ferry that morning. Years of online chat and weekly gaming sessions weren't nothing, though. Their friendship had transitioned seamlessly from text and role-playing games to a realspace connection, exploring the is-land together as if they had known each other for years. Which they had.

"Of course," Morgan said, already tapping a message into her phone. "I'm not going to just walk off and abandon you. I wouldn't do that to anybody, let alone somebody as lovely as you are." The device in her hand chimed, and she looked back down at it; her partner had replied quickly. "Yeah, Lynn says it's fine. We'll have a bit of a hike to get back to the marina, but taking you home is no problem at all."

"I mean, we meant to spend a lot of the day hiking," Becca said, trying to be positive. "How bad could it be?" Morgan consulted her phone; Becca saw a map come up on the screen.

"About 7.2km," Morgan reported. Becca winced. "I know," Morgan said. "Maybe there's a taxi service?" She flipped between apps again, tapping at the screen. "Rideshare has nothing."

"There is, but I think it's limited hours," Becca said. "I can walk, though I wish now we hadn't returned the bikes."

"Wouldn't have worked, I'm afraid," Morgan said. "The bike rental place is here, and they don't have a drop-off or pick-up location at the marina."

"You mean you had to walk 7.2km even before you met me, this morning?" Becca asked.

"You were worth it," Morgan said with a grin. Becca just shook her head.

"I don't see how," she said, "but okay."

"It wasn't exactly my first plan," Morgan sighed. She picked up two plastic shopping bags that she had been carrying since they had gotten lunch at the bakery. "Older charts show a marina right at the ferry docks. I was hoping to tie up there, even if the marina wasn't quite in service any more."

"I don't see anything," Becca said, peering into the water to either side of the docks.

"Yeah," Morgan agreed, turning left from the ferry ramp onto West Shore Road. "No such luck, obviously. Even most of the pilings have been cleared away, and the rest are too rotten to trust. I had to go all the way up to North Island Marina, then walk back."

"Are you going to have enough gas to get home?" Becca asked. She didn't know how dinghies worked, she realised. "Do you even use gas? It would be worse if you had to row, I guess."

"There's an outboard motor," Morgan smiled. "It uses diesel but, yes, I did use more than expected going all the way around the island. I refuelled when I got to the marina, though, so at least that chore is done already."

Past the visitors' centre, the tavern, an ice cream shop, and the bike rental place — all of them now closed — the distance between buildings increased. The night was warm, but not hot enough to make the walk unpleasant. To their left, Lake Erie lapped at the crumbling edge of the island, sometimes threatening the road itself. Becca and Morgan kept to the right-hand side, despite the lack of sidewalk. Walking facing traffic might be safer in theory, but falling into the lake or twisting an ankle on crumbling asphalt was not a preferable risk.

As the sky grew darker, the last of the light slipping into the lake, Morgan transferred both her bags to her left hand and took Becca's hand in her right. When Becca looked over at her, a little uncertain, the other woman smiled.

"I don't want us to get separated," Morgan explained, and her voice was even warmer than the summer night. "I'll just hold on to you, for now, if you'll allow it."

Becca found herself blushing, though she wasn't sure why. Morgan's presence beside her was comforting, though. Walking through darkness, only rarely lit by the headlights of a car passing them on the road, it almost felt like they were alone in the world.

For Morgan, the pleasure of Becca's company made the walk easy. It took almost an hour and a half before they reached North Island Marina, but Becca's silent presence and her hand in Morgan's made the time seem short. When they finally reached the lights and activity of the marina, Morgan was almost disappointed that their shared isolation was ending.

Lights illuminated the parking lot as Morgan led Becca through it. Several of the docked boats were cheerful with deck lighting and people socialising, but the office was dark and the fuel bar was locked up. Morgan led Becca to the end of the floating fuel dock, where she had left the dinghy that morning. There were several T-shaped cleats available at the edge of the wooden platform, but *bash* floated alone, waiting for them.

"Could you hold these, please?" Morgan asked, passing Becca the bags; they were not at all heavy, but they were a bit too bulky for her to manage easily while also messing with the security cable and painter line.

"Sure," Becca agreed, taking one in each hand and standing back far enough to give Morgan room to work.

Morgan fished a key from her pocket and unlocked the stainless steel cable securing *bash* to the dock. She unthreaded the cable from the cleat's uprights mostly by feel, leaving the painter line to hold *bash* alone, then stepped into the boat. Sitting on the middle bench, she continued guiding the security cable out of the armholes of her own life jacket and freed one of the two buoyancy aids they kept in *bash* "just in case". She tossed the buoyancy aid onto the dock in front of Becca; even in the limited light of the marina, the bright yellow nylon of its shell was clearly visible. Finally, Morgan unlatched the lid on the picnic cooler that stayed in the dinghy and removed the battery-operated navigation lights.

"I'll take the bags now," she said, once she had clipped the lights to the bow and stern of *bash*'s white fibreglass hull.

"Okay," Becca said, taking a hesitant step towards the edge of the dock. Was she uncomfortable around the water? She had seemed fine on the beach.

"Thanks," Morgan said, as she deposited the bread and pastries in the insulated and watertight container and latched the lid. She pulled on the painter line, drawing *bash* against the dock so Becca wouldn't have as far to stretch when she boarded. Unfortunately, this didn't seem to help much.

Even with the relatively flat bottom of its modified tri-hull design, *bash* was less stable when empty than an inflatable would have been, and Becca was clearly unfamiliar with boats at all.

While Morgan kept pressure on the painter to keep *bash* close to the dock, Becca's first step left the small boat rocking wildly and the woman herself pulling her foot back in consternation. Her second try had even less confidence behind it and a corresponding lack of success.

"It's okay," Morgan told her. "You won't tip it. Just step into the middle and sit down quickly."

"I'm sorry," Becca said. She was standing further back from the edge now, clearly uncomfortable. "I'm not trying to be difficult. I just don't want to fall."

Morgan nodded, considering options.

"Okay, first thing? Put on the buoyancy aid, then pass me your phone and anything else that couldn't survive a dunk."

"This doesn't sound like a plan that involves me not-falling," Becca objected, but she was already shrugging into the yellow buoyancy aid and zipping the front closed. She took her cell phone, keys, and wallet from her pocket, passing all three to Morgan.

"You've heard the saying that the stuff you're prepared for never happens?" Morgan said, and Becca nodded. "Okay, so we're preparing for you to actually fall in. That means you're safe."

"I'm not sure it actually works like that," Becca said dubiously as Morgan added her things to the picnic cooler.

"Well, it's what we have," Morgan said, "so it's worth trying."

"I suppose," Becca said.

"Okay, now that everything will be fine even if you did fall in, why don't you go ahead and sit on the edge of the dock?" Morgan suggested.

Becca did as she was told, eyeing the dark water warily.

"You're sure about this?" she asked.

"It will be fine," Morgan promised, offering a hand. "Now just slide over, right into the boat." She tugged gently, helping Becca make the transfer. The small boat rocked as Becca's bum hit the seat, but it settled quickly, and eventually Becca's death-grip on her hand relaxed. Morgan gave her friend a few more minutes to settle before untying the dinghy from the dock and moving past her to sit on the rear starboard seat and start the outboard motor.

Bash's motor made it faster than walking, but the trip back around the island still meant almost an hour on the water. Maybe it would have been better to have asked Lynn to bring the *C Shell* around to the north side and re-anchor there, earlier in the day, but Morgan hadn't thought of that at the time. It was too late, now; it was safer to work around an inconvenient mooring location than to risk sailing near an unfamiliar shoreline after dark.

The motor's noise prevented much conversation, but Morgan kept an eye on her friend as well as minding the navigation. Becca seemed comfortable enough once they were moving, and when Morgan was able to point out the glow of the *C Shell's* mooring light, as they came around the south end of the island, she relaxed even more. It would be good to get her home and settled in for the night.

Lynn had evidently heard the motor as the small craft approached the *C Shell*, and they were ready to catch the painter line Morgan tossed. In deference to Becca's discomfort, Morgan carefully nosed *bash* up against the swim step at the stern of the larger vessel, but did not cut the motor. Positioning *bash*'s port side against *C Shell* so that her own weight would help balance it, Morgan kept the motor on low to hold it tightly against the larger boat. She leaned a little further over the starboard wall of the dinghy to help balance it as Becca awkwardly reached over the narrow swim step to take hold of the raised ladder, trying to use it to steady herself as she stood. Seeing what was happening, Lynn quickly grabbed the top of the ladder to prevent it from swinging down, holding it steady through Becca's transfer onto the step.

"Just a moment," Morgan said, and Becca hesitated on the ledge just above the waterline. Morgan opened the picnic cooler and returned the woman's keys, wallet, and cell phone.

"Thanks," Becca said, maintaining a one-handed grip on the ladder even as she slipped her things into the right side pocket of her jeans. Lynn unclipped the lifelines across the rear of the deck and reached out a hand to redirect Becca from the more precarious support of a ladder that was designed to descend from the swim step into the water, not rise to the deck. Becca struggled a little with the larger step, to get over the transom, but

Lynn was there to steady her. With Becca sorted, Morgan killed the motor and passed the two bakery bags up to her partner before transferring to *C Shell* herself.

It was so nice to come home to somebody she knew would be willing to help with whatever needed to be done, Morgan reflected. The day on the island had been lovely, but it was good to be home.

Becca had heard about Lynn, of course, but had never met her friend's partner, or even spoken with them online. She knew they were nonbinary — Morgan referred to "them" rather than "him" or "her" — and that they did something with computers, but that was about it. She glanced sideways at the person who had helped her into the boat and was now sharing the cockpit with her as they waited for Morgan to join them.

Lynn was probably about the same height Morgan was, but they were more solidly built. Their red hair had been cropped short on the left side of their head, but the remainder was long enough to brush their right shoulder, and they were wearing a faded navy blue t-shirt with a penguin on the front. Lynn moved easily through a space that seemed to be formed of white moulded benches topped with wooden planks. Becca found herself shuffling awkwardly, trying to be out of the way, until she found herself backed into the space where one bench met the waist-high barrier of the cabin wall.

Moving any further towards the front of the boat would have meant climbing onto the top of the cabin, under a structure of metal tubes and canvas that seemed almost like a three-sided tent. There were horizontal grab bars on the cabin roof, flanking the open hatch down into the interior, so Becca supposed climbing on top of it was *possible*. Still, it would probably be overkill, just to stay out of Lynn's way. Warm light shone upwards through the hatch, illuminating the blue canvas of the cover and reflecting off the flexible vinyl windows sewn into the front of the awning.

The cockpit itself was also well lit, but beyond its benches and the recessed area into which Lynn had helped Becca climb, the deck was dark. The single white light on the mast had made the boat obvious as they approached it in the dinghy, but it did nothing to actually illuminate the deck. Becca could just barely make out clothing, maybe a shirt and a pair of shorts, hanging from the lines that fenced off the right hand side of the boat. The water surrounding the boat was dark, and even the island was only a shadowed mass in the distance.

Becca wondered how long they'd need to stay before Morgan took her home. She heard the motor from the dinghy cut out and watched Lynn reach down to accept the bakery bags from Morgan before they moved to the side.

Morgan, of course, moved from the dinghy to the bigger boat's step and climbed into the cockpit as if it were nothing. She seemed just as comfortable on the boat as she had been hiking the lighthouse trail or, for that matter, veering off the trail

because she had spotted a patch of ripe raspberries. Becca wished she had even half her friend's
confidence.

"Well, this is home," Morgan announced. "Lynn,
I would like to introduce you to my friend Becca.
We managed to miss her last ferry, so I offered to
bring her home for the night."

"Pleased to meet you, Becca," Lynn took a step
towards the woman, offering a hand in greeting.
"You just had too much fun together to part, did
you?"

"Likewise, I'm sure," Becca said, taking the
proffered hand in a rather less than certain hand-
shake. She looked at Morgan. "I'm sorry; I thought
you had offered to take me home?"

"Well, and I have," Morgan said. "Lynn and I live
here."

"Oh," said Becca faintly. Lynn gave her hand
what was probably meant to be a reassuring
squeeze before releasing it.

"I think she may have thought you'd be going
back to her place, not ours," Lynn suggested, when
Becca didn't say anything further. Becca nodded,
reclaiming her hand and fiddling with the buckles
at the front of her PFD.

"Please leave that on while you're on deck,"
Morgan said. Becca quickly dropped the buckles,
keeping her hands carefully at her sides, and nodded.

"I'm sorry you misunderstood," Morgan continued. She gestured around the boat, at the darkness
Becca had already noticed. "It's ... really not prac-

tical to try to take a boat into a strange harbour after dark. There are no lamp posts out here, we don't know the landmarks, and it's too late in the day to arrange a transient slip."

"It's nothing personal," Lynn offered. "It really is just a navigation issue. Morgan texted me before bringing you home, but she didn't have to. She pretty much does what she wants, where her partners are concerned."

"I don't have any of my things," Becca worried out loud. Lynn's tone had sounded like they intended to be reassuring, but hearing Morgan had a habit of just doing what she wanted, even with those she loved, wasn't exactly comforting. "Not even a change of clothes. This was only meant to be a day trip." She hadn't even brought a purse; she'd just stuck her wallet and keys in the pockets of her jeans, the better to be able to traipse about the nature trails.

"It will be okay," Morgan told her, taking control of the situation. At least that was better than it being completely out of control, Becca supposed, and Morgan was good at finding solutions on the fly. "I'm sure we can make you comfortable here. You'll probably fit one of my nightdresses. We'll wash out your bra and knickers in the sink and hang them on the lifelines, so they'll be dry by the time we're ready to go in the morning." She gestured to the clothing Becca had already noticed, on the lines around the deck. "Lynn did that with their swimwear after they were in the water, earlier, and it's nearly dry already."

"I suppose ..." Becca's head was still spinning, but at least it was a plan. She didn't resist as Morgan guided her over to the cabin hatch and below deck.

The companionway consisted of two wooden steps set vertically against the rear wall, leading down to a wider, carpeted surface and then one more step to the floor. Sturdy metal grab rails ran up the wall to either side of the steps, providing handholds after the sides of the hatch ended, and it only took Becca a moment to figure out how to back down the ladder into the cabin.

Rather than watch Morgan's backside as the other woman descended, Becca turned to survey the room. To her left, a small built-in desk featured a bewildering console of dials and switches; to her right was a tiny kitchen complete with a small oven beneath a two-burner stove; a pair of sinks on the counter protruded almost to the centre of the cabin. Moving forward to be out of Morgan's way brought Becca into what she supposed was a dining area. A drop-leaf table supported by a floor-to-ceiling pillar at the far end filled most of the right side of the boat, surrounded like a restaurant booth by a blue padded bench on two sides. A laptop computer sat closed on the table, with a couple of hardbound journals, one with a pen holding it open.

"Welcome to our home," Morgan said, behind her. "You can take off the buoyancy aid while you're inside, but we prefer that guests keep them on while above decks, especially outside of the well, and keep one of us with you if you're not comfortable with boats. Are you okay with that?"

"Sure?" Becca agreed, still looking around. "What's the well?"

"Sorry," Morgan ducked her head, slipping off the black harness she was wearing and hanging it on a hook beside the ladder. "It's that recessed area, around the cockpit, between the stern and the cabin hatch. Even the benches are lower than deck level, so there's minimal chance of falling off." She shrugged. "It would still be better if you wore the buoyancy aid and had supervision, but we're not going to be as strict about it."

"Not pulling out the whips to enforce that one?" Becca tried to joke, removing the PFD and passing it to her friend.

Morgan laughed and hung it beside her own harness. "Not unless you ask nicely!"

Becca flushed; she hadn't actually been considering that aspect of visiting Morgan at home. Not that she had actually planned this visit at all. It didn't matter, though; she and Morgan were friends, but not the sort of friends where ...

Becca very deliberately decided to stop thinking about Morgan's sex life. It was nothing to do with her. Besides, Morgan was still talking.

"The head — the toilet — is in here behind the nav desk."

Becca nodded, but Morgan was steering her into the small cubicle.

"Look, I trust you to be able to go potty on your own," she said, "but boat toilets are a bit different from those with which you're familiar. We're not exactly hooked up to city pipes out here."

Becca nodded, trying not to crowd Morgan in the cramped confines.

"Okay, so you see the pump handle here? And the switch is all the way to the right? That lets you flush out the toilet." Morgan demonstrated, pulling the handle mounted beside the bowl up — it seemed to be on a rod — and pushing it down again several times as the water left the bowl. "It might take ten or fifteen repetitions when you've actually used it, of course."

"Okay," Becca said. It didn't *seem* complicated, but not remembering it later would be embarrass-ing.

"Once you've emptied the bowl, you flip this switch to the *left*," Morgan demonstrated. "That opens the valve so that now you're pumping water *into* the bowl." She paused and looked at Becca, as if she didn't expect her to understand.

"The important thing," Morgan emphasised carefully, "Is that when you're done, you flip the switch back to the *right*." She waited for Becca's nod, then explained further, "If you leave the valve open, since we're below the waterline, it will slowly siphon water in from the lake when we're not looking. If we're affected by a wave or something, we might have half the lake flooding in through the toilet and onto the cabin floor."

"I understand," Becca promised. Needing help flushing the toilet would be embarrassing, but flooding the boat would be worse.

"We lock the door when the head is in use," Morgan moved on, indicating the latch. "The door will be closed whether it's free or not, because even minor motion on the water makes unlatched doors swing annoyingly."

"Okay," Becca said again, grateful that Morgan hadn't actually sealed the door as part of the demonstration. The space seemed very small, and very much full of Morgan.

It wasn't that being full of Morgan was a bad thing, of course. It was just the way Morgan took control of situations, her certainty. It was nice to know that somebody was in control, but sometimes Becca felt like she was barely able to keep up with her friend. Other times, she didn't feel able to keep up at all, and it was hard to understand why Morgan would be willing to wait until Becca caught her balance.

She did, though.

Whether in the game, pointing out that the Polyhedra web interface they were using let you just click on the skill you were rolling rather than rolling physical dice and doing the math yourself, talking about why one would sail south to Africa and then across to the Carribean just to get from

Scotland to Canada, or explaining how a boat toilet worked, it seemed like Morgan always just *knew* stuff. And she did take the time to make sure other people understood it, but sometimes Becca felt a little small.

Like now.

Morgan was looking at her, assessing her understanding, and Becca blushed.

"I'm sorry," Morgan said, seeming to recognise how overwhelmed her guest was. "I know it's a lot all at once, but ... it would be more awkward if we didn't tell you until after you needed it?"

"Yeah," Becca said, looking at her feet. "I get it. I'm sorry."

"It's okay." Morgan still seemed concerned, but she didn't push the issue. The sound of Lynn descending the companionway drew her attention, and she finally moved out of the toilet room.

"You do have a perfectly good cabin," Lynn commented, as Morgan emerged. "You don't have to sneak off to snog in the girls' bathroom."

Becca felt her face burn, and she hung back.

"Pfft," Morgan dismissed them. "I was just explaining how to use the toilet. Not all of us want a guest scratching at the cabin door in the middle of the night because he needs to go potty."

"I really should have made good on my threat to just take him out on a leash," Lynn laughed.

"Or actually explained the head to him before he needed to use it," Morgan countered.

"There is that," Lynn allowed. Becca was pretty sure she didn't want to know what they were talking about.

"Are you coming out?" Morgan asked, "Or do I need to let you shut the door so you can use the toilet?"

"Umm, if you don't mind?" Becca blushed. If nothing else, it would give her a chance to get her face under control.

"Of course," Morgan said, moving out of the way to let the door swing shut. "I'm sorry." Becca latched it, as she had been shown, and sat down on the toilet. Maybe by the time she was done in the bathroom, the topic would have moved on.

"Did you have dinner?" Morgan asked Lynn, as Becca latched the door behind her.

"Yeah," Lynn said. "I did up some puttanesca for myself. I assumed you two would have eaten?"

"We spent a few hours over lunch," Morgan said, reclaiming the bakery bag from her partner. "And we stopped for dinner at a tavern near the docks, after the first ferry was too full for us." Lynn nodded.

"So what's this?" they asked, peering into the bags.

"There was a bakery on the island. The cheddar bread looked really good, and I got another loaf of white." Morgan passed the bread to Lynn, letting them decide where would be best to store it. "And when I admitted to not knowing what butter tarts were, Becca insisted I get half a dozen."

"Are they any good?" Lynn asked, putting away the bread.

"I haven't actually tried them yet," Morgan admitted. "Pass a plate, please?" Lynn passed over a small wheat straw plate.

"They had some local cheese, too," Morgan said, arranging three of the tarts on the plate and passing the box with the remaining three to Lynn. "Though I admit we ate a lot of that ourselves, at lunch."

Lynn peered into the bottom of the bag, fishing out half a packet of a semi-soft golden cheese and about a quarter of the pack of black-rinded white goat cheese. They transferred the cheese to zippered plastic bags and moved it into the refrigerator that was set beneath the counter.

"I guess that explains why you didn't get to the sweets," they said.

"There were sausage rolls, too," Morgan said. "But yeah. The cheese was good. The company was better."

Lynn grinned, "It's like that, is it?"

"I value her friendship," Morgan said primly. "Besides, she's not interested. I can still daydream, though."

"She was interested enough to follow you home," Lynn pointed out, finding a plastic container to hold the remaining butter tarts. Morgan shrugged, but Becca's emergence from the head prevented her from saying anything more on the topic.

Actually, Becca had been a fairly long time in the head. Was she okay?

"I was just setting out some dessert," Morgan told her friend, gesturing her deeper into the cabin. "Find a seat at the table?"

Becca eyed the computer and notebooks on the end of the table nearest the kitchen, then edged through the narrow aisle past the table to perch on the bench that wrapped around the far end. Morgan smiled at her reassuringly.

"Lynn, can I get your laptop off the table?" Morgan offered, setting the plate of butter tarts in the limited clear space near Becca.

"Oh, sure," Lynn said, glancing up from re-arranging things in the depths of the refrigerator. "Just throw it on the nav desk." Morgan moved the laptop, plugging it back in at the outlet by the radio and satellite systems. She stacked the books carefully beside it.

"Did you get much done today?" Morgan asked her partner.

"Eh, submitted a pull request," Lynn said, finally satisfied with the way the refrigerator was arranged. "And I got the hull scraped, of course, but I finished that before you left."

"Thanks for that," Morgan said, slipping into the bench surround and sliding down to be closer to Becca, leaving room for Lynn on the end. "I'll make it up to you tomorrow?"

"I'm sure you will," Lynn slid in beside her. They grinned, "One way or another, you'll pay for your time off gallivanting." Morgan laughed, but Becca still looked a little overwhelmed. Morgan reached out to pat her hand, but it didn't seem to help much.

"For tonight, though," Morgan tried to refocus on what Becca needed to feel comfortable, "we need to figure out sleeping arrangements."

"I figured she'd sleep in your cabin," Lynn sounded surprised.

"That works for me," Morgan said, "but then I need to sleep somewhere else." Becca blinked, looking surprised, but she seemed a little less tense.

"Why is that?" Lynn asked.

"I invited her to my home," Morgan said, trying to keep an eye on Becca's reactions even as she addressed Lynn. "That's a bit different from asking her into my bed. The fact that she said yes to the first when she didn't have a great deal of choice ...." Becca shifted uncomfortably on the bench, and Morgan trailed off.

"I mean, you're always welcome in my bed," Lynn smirked. "But I don't want to deprive Becca of your time and attentions."

"It's okay!" Becca said quickly. A bit more quickly than Morgan would have preferred, to be honest. She took a butter tart, passed a second to Lynn, and nudged the plate with the remaining tart towards Becca.

"It is okay," Morgan said, taking a bite. The tart's filling was sweet, a creamy golden gel studded with plump raisins. "I want you to be comfortable; while I would certainly be willing to share a bed with you, I don't want you to feel like it's a requirement." Becca nodded, nibbling the edge of her butter tart. It was hard to read her expression.

"That's very kind of you," she said. "I don't want to put you out, though." Becca looked around the cabin, but even she must be able to see that putting her up on one of the narrow benches wasn't a viable option.

"It's no trouble," Morgan assured her. "Lynn is willing to let me sleep with them, so it's easy enough to sort out."

"Though the bow cabin — Morgan's cabin — does have the skylight with a view of the mast," Lynn put in, looking past Morgan to Becca. "If you'd been in there last night, you might have gotten an interesting view of what we were doing. Or you might have slept through it, but Morgan was making a fair amount of noise."

"Lynn," Morgan said warningly, but her partner continued.

"I suppose you're right, we could have pulled out the ball gag," they said. "Though that muffles your words, rather than sound entirely, and there would still have been the thumping you were making on the cabin roof."

"I don't really think this is the time to discuss it," Morgan said. Becca was looking distinctly uncomfortable, and shifted away when she caught Morgan looking at her.

"Am I embarrassing you in front of your friend?" Lynn teased, though Morgan was quite sure that was the intent.

"You're making our guest uncomfortable," she said. It wasn't that she minded Lynn's teasing, usually, but this wasn't an aspect of her life she'd ever really discussed with Becca, and she had the impression that Becca preferred it that way.

"Am I making you uncomfortable?" Lynn asked Becca directly. Becca froze, her shoulders hunched.

"It's your home," she demurred. "I ... you're welcome to discuss whatever you want?"

"That wasn't exactly the question," Morgan pointed out gently. She didn't like the way Becca seemed to be trying to hide behind the mast that extended through the table. "How do you like the butter tart, Lynn?"

"It's good," Lynn said. "Nothing like a butter pie, though."

"What's a butter pie?" Becca asked, and Morgan was a bit relieved at the safer topic.

"It's a Lancashire thing," Lynn said. "Blackpool, and thereabouts?" Becca looked blank.

"It's mostly onions and potatoes," Morgan offered. "We should make that again, soon, actually."

"I think it was a Catholic thing," Lynn said. "Sometimes they call it Friday pie?" Becca still shook her head, but Lynn shrugged. "It's nothing like this, anyway. More a dinner than dessert."

"Okay," Becca said. "I'm sorry?"

"No, it's fine." Morgan patted her hand. "These are good. It's nice. We're sitting and chatting and it's just a nice discussion of different foods."

"Okay," Becca said, still sounding unconvinced.

"We do need to grab some more groceries, tomorrow," Lynn said. "You could add it to the list."

"That's not a bad idea," Morgan agreed, pulling out her phone. She fiddled with the screen a bit. "Should we do the version with apples and cheese?"

"Would the cheese you got today work in it, do you think?" Lynn asked. "It looked a bit mild."

"No, we'd need a strong cheddar or something," Morgan admitted.

"Old cheddar is easy enough to get," Becca said tentatively. "It's nothing fancy, like what we got today, but it's what I usually buy. Somewhere usually has it on sale for a decent price."

"Sounds reasonable," Lynn agreed, and Morgan tapped it into her phone.

"Okay, so pie crust, cheddar, thyme, and a couple of apples," she said. "How are we for butter and potatoes, Lynn?"

"I think we're okay for butter," Lynn said. "You should probably get a small bag of potatoes, if you can."

"Okay." Morgan added it to the list. "Lemon juice and flour?"

"I think we have enough," Lynn said. "But we're low on eggs." Morgan added them to the list. A glance at Becca revealed that this interlude of domesticity had been somewhat effective in taking the edge off her nerves.

"Are there any other Canadian dishes we need to try, Becca?"

"Poutine?" she suggested. "That's the obvious one. Umm. Coffee Crisp bars? Aero?"

"We know Aero," Morgan smiled. "What's Coffee Crisp? Is it like a stroopwafel, or biscotti?"

"It's a chocolate bar," Becca said. "Wafers inside, like a giant KitKat, but somewhat coffee flavoured, like tiramisu? But crunchy."

"Okay," Morgan said, adding it to the list. "I think I've heard of poutine."

"It's sort of famous," Becca admitted. "French fries with cheese curds and gravy?"

"That sounds ... different," Lynn commented.

"It sort of looks like a mess, too," Becca grinned. She was definitely looking more relaxed. "But it tastes better than it looks, especially when you're really hungry."

"Sounds worth trying, at least," Morgan said, and added oven chips to the list.

"If it makes you happy," Lynn said. "Can you at least get a vegetarian gravy mix? It's a bit much to make from scratch."

"I'll do my best," Morgan promised.

"Are you vegetarian?" Becca asked.

"Pescatarian," Lynn corrected. "Though not much of that; generally just the fish we catch or seafood we forage."

"But ... the sausage rolls?"

"I'm pescatarian," Lynn clarified. "Morgan eats what she wants, outside the kitchen we share."

"Oh," Becca said. "That seems ..." Morgan didn't give her a chance to put into words how it seemed.

"It works for us," Morgan said. "The food we share fits both our diets, and if I have a craving for something more carnivorous, I can always go ashore and find something."

"Part of the issue is how small the fridge is," Lynn explained, "And the way it's sunk under the counter. There's really no good way to keep meat products separate, and they're prone to leak or spoil or otherwise be unpleasant to handle."

"It's not a huge sacrifice," Morgan grinned. "I mean, part of the deal is that Lynn is an excellent cook, to the point where I don't miss the meat in dishes they make."

"That might be because meat isn't actually a necessary component for food to be tasty," Lynn pointed out.

"Pfft," Morgan said. "Take the compliment."

"Thank you for the compliment," Lynn said grudgingly.

"Good enby." Morgan patted Lynn on the head. Lynn glared at her.

"Watch it," they said. "I'm perfectly willing to turn you over my knee and spank you, whether Becca's here or not." Morgan laughed and was about to tell them to bring it on, but a motion in the corner of her eye caught Morgan's attention.

Becca's response to their easy shift into their accustomed switchy dynamic was ... not easy at all. The woman looked actively frightened, as if the threat had been directed at her. Morgan reached out to touch her arm gently, and Becca flinched away.

"There's no use trying to hide behind her," Lynn laughed. "You know you have it coming."

"I'm not trying to hide behind Becca," Morgan said quietly. "I'm holding the space so that she can hide behind me."

"Then maybe you shouldn't make yourself a target when you're trying to be a shelter," Lynn said.

They were still playing, but looking at Becca ... she wasn't.

"Lynn," Morgan said, "Red."

Immediately, Lynn's teasing good humour evaporated. "I heard red," they said. "What's wrong?"

Morgan looked at Becca and bit her lip. "We need to talk," she said. "Will you be okay down here, Becca, if we go up on deck for a few?"

"I guess?" Becca replied uncertainly. It would have to do. Morgan led her partner onto the deck to try to do damage control.

Three

Lynn followed Morgan up through the hatch, and Becca tried not to eavesdrop. Words carried, "What do you think you're doing?" as they moved away from the hatch, then isolated snatches, "ferry" and "dinghy" and her name made it clear they were talking about her, but they clearly didn't want her to be hearing it, so she tried to concentrate on her phone, instead, tucking herself into the corner of the bench around the table. The boat Wi-Fi was too slow for video streaming, but she was able to catch up on unread chat messages.

Lynn returned to the cabin alone.

"Where's Morgan?" Becca asked.

"Still on the deck," Lynn said. "I ... owe you an apology. Do you need her to be here for it? Would you feel safer?"

Safer? Becca hadn't felt *safe* since she'd realised she wasn't making it home tonight. None of her advance research, none of her careful scheduling, none of the steps she took to control the situation had been enough. All she could do now was trust Morgan's judgement, and Morgan trusted Lynn.

"It's okay," Becca said. It had to be. She didn't really have a choice.

Lynn watched Becca's answer as well as listening to it, the way the woman shrugged as she spoke and turned away, avoiding Lynn's gaze. Becca *said* she was okay, but everything in her posture suggested otherwise. And Lynn didn't have standing to argue.

Looking around the cabin, trying to see it from Becca's perspective, it wasn't the cosy space Lynn knew as home. The woman was huddled in the corner of the settee, and there was nowhere Lynn could stand without being between Becca and the exit. Even with one leaf of the table collapsed, as it was now, the aisle between the table and the port bench was too narrow to pass another person without contact.

Lynn stepped into the galley, which at least took them out of the direct path and offered a buffering counter between them and the obviously terrified woman.

"Can I get you anything to drink?" they offered. "Coffee? Tea?"

"I don't want to be any trouble," Becca demurred, still not looking directly at them.

"No trouble," Lynn assured her. "How about some hot chocolate? We should have milk left, and I was thinking of making one for myself." Maybe it was a British thing. On a warm night, a hot bever-age might not make sense to a Canadian. Still, it was the ritual Lynn knew to take the edge off sharp emotions.

"If you're sure you don't mind," Becca said. She still wasn't looking at Lynn, and they worried a little that she was accepting to please them rather than because she actually wanted the drink, but having a mug of hot chocolate in front of her was unlikely to harm the woman. She could always choose not to drink it.

Lynn lifted the lid off the refrigerator, retrieving a two litre milk carton from the depths before re-placing the countertop. The carton was lighter than they had remembered, but they poured the last of the milk into a small pot. Lynn lit the hob, adjusting the flame low and putting the empty milk carton in the trash before they returned their attention to Becca.

Even the brief respite from having Lynn's focus on her seemed to have helped Becca relax. Her shoulders were no longer hunched up around her ears, and she was watching Lynn move around the galley as if she were interested in their work rather than evaluating a threat.

That incremental relaxation was good, but it also meant that Morgan had been right: Becca was at least a little afraid of Lynn, personally. Damn.

"An apology," they began again, trying to keep their voice gentle. "Morgan explained to me that I had ... misunderstood the situation."

Becca nodded cautiously.

"I knew how much Morgan was looking forward to spending time with you," Lynn continued, "and I was happy for her to have the chance. Knowing Morgan, I figured she had spent the day flirting with you, so when she brought you home ..."

"She wasn't flirting with me, though," Becca interjected. "We were just hanging out."

Lynn blinked. They *knew* Morgan, and how flirty she was. Aggressively, toppily flirty. That was why they had tried to undercut the toppiness, when Becca seemed uncomfortable after arriving: they had assumed it was just that Morgan was coming on too strong, and reducing that power differential would help.

What Morgan had told them, on the deck, was the opposite. It wasn't fun, toppy power exchange that had her leading and Becca following, but somebody who didn't see herself as having another option. Becca, Morgan argued, wasn't reacting to her coming on too domme; she was reacting to being trapped in an enclosed area with a stranger who was threatening the only person she knew to trust.

Morgan didn't hesitate to admit that she would have played with Becca, given a chance. That just wasn't what she was doing tonight. Having spent all day flirting without getting any interest in return, Morgan was resigned to her fate.

Apparently, Lynn wasn't the only one who misunderstood the situation.

"Becca," Lynn said carefully, "I just spoke to the woman. She was *definitely* flirting with you."

Morgan had been flirting with her? Becca couldn't believe it. Surely she would have noticed something?

But Lynn seemed completely certain, and they had known Morgan more closely than Becca did, for years.

They had to be wrong, though. Morgan would clear it up. Almost automatically, Becca reached for her phone.

Wait, no. Messaging Morgan with Lynn right there would be rude.

Becca glanced at the other person, hoping they hadn't noticed her lapse of manners.

"Go ahead and ask her, if you want," Lynn said. They didn't look offended. They were smiling, looking almost amused at Becca's reaction.

There was no way they could be right.

```
<Becca> Morgan?
<Becca> Are you okay?
<Morgan> Yeah, just taking a
         few minutes on the
         deck.  Lynn wanted a
         chance to apologise to
         you alone, so you'd
         know it wasn't just me
         making them say it
<Morgan> How's that going?
<Becca> They seem to think you
        were flirting with me,
        today?
<Morgan> Well, yeah.
<Morgan> It's fine that you
         weren't interested,
```

> but I was *definitely*
> flirting.
> <Becca>

"Umm," Becca said, looking up. Lynn was still calmly stirring the milk on the stove. "I ... hadn't realised." Lynn smiled and shook their head.

"Poor Morgan." they said, turning off the flame and measuring brown powder from a purple canister into the hot milk.

"So yeah," Lynn said. "With you having spent the day together, I was thinking more that you wanted to extend the engagement, have a sleepover. It never even occurred to me that you might really have felt like you didn't have any other options, that you might feel trapped here. It wasn't until Morgan pointed out that you literally can't leave without her help or mine that ..." Lynn trailed off and shook their head. They poured liquid from the pot on the stove into two mismatched mugs, and walked over to set one on the raised table leaf in front of Becca before taking a seat on the opposite bench.

"I'm sorry," Lynn said, and they sounded sincere. "I see how, with you already feeling trapped and out of options, my teasing Morgan in front of you might have made you feel less safe. Not just in the situation, but with her. And that was the last thing I wanted."

"It's okay," Becca said, taking a sip of her hot chocolate. The warmth and sweetness of it were surprisingly comforting, but what Lynn had said about Morgan looking forward to seeing her?

Becca hesitated before asking, "You really thought she was interested in me?"

"Is that so hard to believe?" Lynn sipped their own hot chocolate and glanced pointedly at Becca's phone where it sat on the table. "She *did* admit that she was flirting with you today, didn't she?"

"Well, yeah," Becca admitted, looking at the phone herself. The lock screen showed another message from Morgan, but she just shoved it back into a pocket. She didn't know how to deal with this, right now.

"So why *wouldn't* I think she fancied you?" Lynn asked reasonably. "It was your disinterest, where I went wrong."

Her disinterest? Becca could feel herself blushing and looked down at her mug, trying to at least partially hide her reaction behind loose strands of hair. She'd never even realised there was something there in which to *be* interested. "It's never happened before," she explained clumsily. "Nobody's ever been interested in me before."

Lynn looked at the woman in mild disbelief. Becca was still in her thirties, and even with a certain tiredness in evidence from the day and her loose brown hair dishevelled from the wind, she was far from unattractive. Of course, she had also managed not to notice Morgan flirting with her all day, and Morgan was not exactly subtle.

"So far as you've noticed," Lynn suggested.

Becca shrugged self-consciously. "You know what they say. Boys don't make passes at girls who wear glasses."

"I'm pretty sure Morgan isn't a boy," Lynn pointed out. "I have checked, you know." They watched Becca's flush deepen, and couldn't help but smile. "You really didn't notice she was flirting with you?"

"No," Becca said, eyes still on the contents of her mug. Lynn hadn't thought the woman could get any redder, but somehow Becca managed it.

"How would you have felt, I wonder," Lynn speculated, unable to resist the impulse to gentle teasing, "if you had realised that she was flirting with you, if *you* thought she fancied you?"

"I ..." Becca squirmed, unable to find words, "she ...." She took another gulp of her hot chocolate. "I mean ..."

"Yes?" Lynn prompted, a gleam in their eye.

"Well, she's in a relationship, isn't she?" Becca managed. "So it doesn't really matter."

"I do believe I knew that about her," Lynn allowed. "I'm rather close to her partners, you know?"

"But," Becca was still not doing well with words. "You ..."

"I am one of them, yes." Lynn grinned. "And I have rather better access to her than my metamours, given living circumstances." Becca's shoulders were rising towards her ears, again; she was clearly struggling. Lynn sighed, and dropped the teasing. "You knew we were poly, right?"

"I ... guess," Becca said. "I always figured it was none of my business?"

"Because she wasn't interested in you?" Lynn asked.

"Yeah," Becca agreed, and Lynn could see the realisation spread across her face. "Uhhh ..."

Lynn nodded. "But if she is interested in you, it might be relevant, and you should probably figure out how you feel about that."

"Oh," Becca said. How she felt about it? How should she feel about it? Morgan was her friend. She knew how to be friends with Morgan. Don't worry about her personal business, because that's personal. It would never involve her. Why would it? Morgan was *Morgan*, and Becca was just ..."

"Right now, though," Lynn's request interrupted Becca's circling thoughts, "could you let her know she can come back inside?"

Becca nodded. Okay. This much she could do. She pulled out her phone again, and winced at the waiting messages.

```
<Morgan> How does *that* make
         your head explode?
<Morgan> Hello?
<Morgan> Are you okay?
```

She really should have mentioned it before putting the phone away.

```
<Becca> Sorry.  Yeah.  I'm
        fine
<Becca> Lynn made hot
        chocolate
```

<Morgan> Okay?
<Becca> I put the phone down
        to talk to them more.
        I'm sorry I was
        ignoring you
<Morgan> It's okay. I just
        worried I'd offended
        you or something
<Becca> No, no. Nothing like
        that
<Becca> But yeah
<Becca> Lynn said to tell you
        you could come back
        now

Four

"You could have opened with that," Morgan said, sticking her head through the hatch. Lynn was sitting on the port side settee, across the aisle from the table where Becca sat with her hot chocolate. It looked like Lynn had given her their favourite mug, the colour-shifting "Six Stages of Debugging" one.

"Sorry," Becca mumbled, looking at her hands.

Morgan swung down the ladder into the cabin and slid the door panels into place to fill the hatch. Peering at the pot on the hob, she asked, "Did you save any for me?"

"There's *some* left," Lynn said.

Morgan swished the remaining liquid in the pot dubiously before pouring it into a mug of her own. With her cup two thirds full, and with the inevitable lumps from the bottom of the pot floating near the surface, Morgan slid onto the opposite end of the settee Becca occupied and set her own mug on the table.

"We ran out of milk," Lynn explained sheepishly.

"I could have gotten some on the island, if you'd said," Morgan commented. The hot chocolate was nice, even if there were lumps.

"You could have," Lynn agreed. "In fact, I think you were the last one to use the milk this morning, so ..."

"Oh, right." Morgan took another sip of lumpy hot chocolate and sighed. "I guess I should have thought of it."

Lynn shrugged, "It will be fine. We don't *have* to eat cereal for breakfast. We've bread for toast, and some of those maple beans we picked up." Morgan nodded.

"Did you have a good talk?" she asked. It wasn't really any of Morgan's business what had been said, but who could blame her for being a little curious? She looked at her friend.

Becca didn't say anything, but she blushed and examined the chocolate residue at the bottom of her cup. *That* was an interesting response.

"I think so," Lynn said. There was a finality of their tone that suggested they had caught Morgan's curiosity and did not suggest following up on it.

"Well," Morgan said. "Good, then." The silence stretched uncomfortably, though Becca's blush was fading. Morgan still wasn't sure what to say.

It was Lynn who finally sighed, complaining, "I'm not good at awkward."

Becca looked up from her mug when Lynn spoke. They continued, addressing her directly.

"Okay, no, I'm very good at awkward," Lynn said. "It comes naturally. I'm not good at getting out of it fluidly. Small talk seems to have failed us. So ... cards?" They reached into the cabinet behind their seat and came up with a standard sized deck. "Do you play rummy? Poker?"

"Go Fish?" Becca suggested. "I've never played poker. I don't know how."

"It's fairly simple," Lynn offered. "We could teach you?"

Morgan appreciated their effort to reach out, but at the same time, it was getting late.

"Actually, if we're going to wash and hang her things with enough time to dry, we'd better get started on that," Morgan said. "We can play afterwards."

Lynn grinned and their tone turned teasing again. "Is it really fair to get all her clothes off before you even start playing poker with the girl?" they asked Morgan.

Becca squirmed a little in her seat, her face crimson. Morgan glared at her partner.

"I thought you were going to stop doing that," she said.

"Surprise," Lynn grinned unrepentantly. "We talked. I did apologise for getting it wrong, but I think both of us understand the situation better now." They smiled at the still-blushing Becca.

"Umm," Becca hesitated, looking anywhere but at Morgan. "You said I could borrow a nightgown?"

"Of course," Morgan made her voice as reassuring as she could. "My cabin is the bow one, just behind you there. You should find a clean nightdress hanging in the wardrobe on the port side."

"Port?" Becca asked, as she scooched herself sideways, out from behind the table. That it added more space between her and Morgan was purely a coincidence.

"Left, when you're facing forward," Morgan clarified. "You can leave your outer clothes on the bed, and just bring out anything you'd like washed for tomorrow."

The door to the cabin was right behind Becca, as she slipped off the end of the bench. She hid her face against the door. Thankfully, the handle turned easily, and she was able to slip inside.

The space wasn't quite what Becca had expected. The cabin was roughly triangular, with the walls coming together to form a point at the front of the boat. Other than a small bit of floor where she was standing, the entire room was filled by a waist-high, cushioned surface that stretched between the walls. Sheets formed a sort of nest on top of the cushions, and she supposed it was a functional sleep surface. At least she wouldn't be at risk of falling out of bed if the boat tilted in the night.

Regardless, she was here for a nightgown.

To her right was a small washstand with its own sink; on the left was the promised cabinet, with its key left in the lock in lieu of a handle. As she opened the cabinet door, a snarled mass of rope fell at her feet.

Stooping to pick it up, Becca saw that the rope wasn't as tangled as she had thought; it looked like somebody had begun to crochet with it, but hadn't gotten beyond a single chain. Macramé, maybe, or some sort of traditional sailing handicraft? She set it on the sleep surface and returned her attention to the closet.

There were more empty hangers on the closet rod than full, but Becca did manage to find an oversized pink cotton nightshirt hanging as Morgan had promised. Down the front of the garment, large metallic text proclaimed, "Sleep. Relax. *recharge*. Love." Soft pink and 'inspirational' wording wasn't really what she would have expected of Morgan's style, but it was here and it was clean and she needed to stop dawdling.

Becca checked that she had locked the cabin door behind her, before slipping out of her jeans and blouse. It wasn't that she expected Morgan to burst in if she didn't, but she felt oddly self-conscious about changing in somebody else's space. Through the walls, she heard her hosts talking, but their voices were low and she couldn't make out words.

The nightshirt was tighter on Becca than it would have been on Morgan; the metallic text urging Sleep and Relax showed horizontal puckers over her chest, but it did come down to her knees. She was properly covered; it was fine. It wasn't as if she were going to be parading her body in front of a couple of men. Morgan was a woman; Lynn was nonbinary; nobody *cared* about how she looked.

If only she could stop thinking about Lynn's claim that Morgan fancied her. And their suggestion that Becca needed to consider how *she* felt about Morgan maybe fancying her. Becca did not feel remotely prepared to consider that, at this time. Maybe if she ignored it, it would go away?

Enough, she told herself firmly, roughly folding her jeans and shirt before setting them in a corner of the room-spanning mattress. She was being silly.

Becca looked at the rope she had set aside on the bed. It was tempting to just shove it willy-nilly back in the cabinet, but that seemed potentially rude. She didn't know if it had been on a shelf, originally, or one of the hangers, or in the bag of laundry that filled the bottom of the cabinet. Why did she feel like she wanted to hide it, as if she had done something wrong? This too, she reminded herself, was silly. She was far better off just admitting it had fallen out than risking it unravelling or getting lost by putting it somewhere it didn't belong.

The soft click as she unlocked the cabin door sounded loud in Becca's ears, especially as Lynn's and Morgan's low voices fell silent at the sound. Balling up her bra and panties in her left hand, Becca returned to the main cabin with the rope mass in her right. Morgan and Lynn were both looking at her as she emerged, and she suddenly felt less covered by the sleep shirt than she knew she was.

"This, uh, fell from the cabinet when I opened it," Becca said awkwardly, setting the rope on the edge of the table. "I didn't mean to knock it, or anything."

The corners of Lynn's eyes crinkled and there was a grin playing about their lips as they looked at Morgan; Morgan was ... did Morgan's pale skin actually turn somewhat pink in response?

"Is it, um, some sort of craft project?" Becca asked in a rush. "Are you making a floor mat or something?"

"Not exactly," Morgan said, speaking at the same time as Lynn said, "Not quite." She looked at her partner, yielding the floor.

"A warning, Becca," Lynn said, but the tone sounded more like they were teasing Morgan than like they were making a threat. "If you ask that question, Morgan *will* answer it." They looked pointedly at their partner, adding, "*Won't* you, Morgan?"

"Is it ...?" Becca felt the blood rising to her cheeks, and she couldn't bring herself to finish the sentence.

Morgan nodded, and it was strange to see strong, confident Morgan become a little flustered, herself. "You don't have to ask, if you don't really want to know," she offered.

Becca nodded, hesitated. She probably *didn't* want to know, judging by Morgan's response, but she was curious now. Becca looked at the rope on the table, glanced at Lynn, risked another brief look at Morgan, then back to the rope on the table.

"It ... looks like crochet," Becca said, almost managing to keep her voice steady. She took a breath, and braced herself for the answer.

"Okay," Morgan said, taking a moment to steady her own nerves, before replying. She could do this, she reminded herself; she'd given introduction-to-rope lectures with less notice. "First, I need to apologise for not having the rope stowed properly. It should not have been able to leap out of the wardrobe and attack you." She grinned, trying to reduce tension with the lame joke, but it didn't seem to register. Becca's shoulders were rigid, her eyes on the rope, and she was anxiously rubbing a bit of the nightdress between her fingers. It looked as if asking the question had taken every bit of courage Becca had.

Morgan reached out to snag the chained rope with a finger, drawing Becca's gaze with it as she pulled the rope across the table. She traced the line of it with her own fingers, *willing* Becca to relax. Lynn was right; she did need to answer the question, but she so very badly didn't want to scare Becca away. Even if Lynn was wrong, if she didn't have a chance with the woman, Becca's friendship was important to Morgan. She didn't want Becca scared or disgusted, but how do you tell a vanilla that they've been handling used rope without that sort of reaction?

"You're right that it's basically finger crochet. This is the rope Lynn and I were using last night," and that brought a deep blush to Becca's face, but Morgan continued. "We chain it after use so that it doesn't get tangled. We'll keep it like this — see the way the chain is loose enough that water can get at the whole thing? We'll be keeping it like this until it's been through the washing machine, next time we're at a laundrette. After it's clean and dry, we wind it back into a hank. That way, too, it's easy to tell which lengths need washing and which are clean."

Becca nodded, and the blush on her face was fading with the matter-of-fact explanation, but she was still standing with her back against the cabin door. She looked as if it were taking real effort not to bolt through that door and escape, even knowing there was nothing but a closed-in cabin on the other side. Hide, maybe, instead of escape. Her knuckles were white around the mass of fabric in her left hand, and Morgan remembered why she had sent her friend off to get changed in the first place.

"Speaking of laundry," Morgan segued as smoothly as she could, sliding off the settee and stepping into the galley, "Let's get your things washed so we can hang them up."

"Oh," Becca said, looking down at her own hand. "Right."

There was nothing awkward at all, Becca tried to convince herself, about standing in an aisle holding one's underwear while a friend explains that the rope one picked up was previously used for ... recreational purposes. There was nothing wrong with curiosity, after all. Learning things was good.

Even if they were things that made her blush to consider.

At least Morgan had decided to change the topic. Becca was not disappointed in that at all; her curiosity did not need more indulgence at this time.

Morgan moved into the kitchen and rummaged under the counter, coming up with a plastic basin and a bottle labelled Fairy liquid. She set aside the bottle and opened the tap, checking the temperature as she ran water into the basin.

"This really is laundry detergent," Morgan assured her, squirting thick, blue fluid from the bottle into the water. "It's easier to control, in small amounts, in a bottle from washing-up liquid than from one of the ones designed to pour into a washer."

Becca nodded. The identity of the detergent being used on her underthings had not been the most burning question on her mind. She edged past where Lynn was still sitting on the port wall bench, doing her best not to brush against their knees in the aisle, and stopped just short of the kitchen counter. She hesitated.

"Right," Morgan ducked her head, "I'll just give you some space?" She stepped onto the carpeted platform of the companionway and perched in the hatch, motioning Becca into the kitchen.

Becca carefully manoeuvred past the other woman, very aware of Morgan's eyes on her as she washed out her panties and bra. It was ridiculous to be shy about it, she knew. It wasn't as if they were sexy lingerie; white cotton granny panties and a decently supportive beige brassiere weren't some scandalous revelation. Becca rinsed them carefully, then squeezed out the worst of the water.

"Would you like me to take those for you?" Morgan offered. "Or would you rather put on the buoyancy aid and mess with the lifelines yourself?"

Becca felt herself blushing and she took it out on the garments, wringing the fabric over the rectangular sink perhaps harder than was strictly necessary. Eyes averted, she passed the damp fabric to Morgan.

Morgan accepted the things without commenting on either their intimacy or Becca's embarrassment, which she appreciated. As Morgan climbed out of the cabin, Becca moved to the stairs to watch, though she stayed inside the hatch. The way Morgan moved effortlessly over the moulded-in benches and past the wheel at the back of the boat was beautiful. Morgan unhooked one of the vinyl-coated horizontal wires that surrounded the deck from its supporting fencepost. She threaded the free end through the leg holes of Becca's panties and through the shoulder straps of her bra before clipping the cable back to the vertical pole.

"This way, there's no chance of it getting caught in a breeze and falling in," Morgan explained, glancing back to catch Becca staring. Becca blushed and averted her eyes, but she still admired her friend's natural grace as she moved to the other side of the boat. Morgan unhooked the lines, not even seeming to notice the slight motions of the boat on the water. She gathered in Lynn's shirt and swim trunks before returning to the cabin.

Shuffling quickly out of the way to prevent Morgan from having to brush past her, Becca found her back against the bathroom door.

Morgan casually tossed Lynn's swimwear at them.

"Thanks," Lynn said, making a face. They threw the dry garments back at Morgan. "Could you just throw them in my cabin?"

"Fine," Morgan mock-sighed, and opened the door leading back from the kitchen. Becca caught a brief glimpse of a similar set-up of wall-to-wall mattress while Morgan tossed the bundle through.

'Thanks," Lynn said, as Morgan latched the door. They tapped the deck of cards on the heel of their hand. "So, were we going to try poker? Or did you want to talk about rope some more, Becca?"

"Umm," Becca said. She hadn't expected that offer. A small part of her was tempted to just duck into the bathroom and stay there, but she knew she'd have to come out eventually, and a brief escape would just make it harder to face them on her return. She could just say no, of course, try her hand at learning poker. But she was still curious about the rope. "I ... I'm not sure what to ..."

Morgan watched Becca search for words, and frowned. Was the woman interested and just being shy, or was she trying to find a way out of the conversation? Lynn would tell her to ask Becca. Lynn *had* asked Becca. But it wasn't that *easy*. And Becca was looking at *her* now, as if for guidance.

"I'm happy for either one," Morgan tried to re-assure her. "You seemed a bit curious earlier, but I'm not going to shove it down your throat, if you've heard enough."

"I ... don't know how to ask," Becca said, back still pressed hard against the door to the head. She was obviously scared about something, but that wasn't a no. She didn't know *how* to ask, rather than not wanting to ask. Morgan just didn't know how to make it easier for her.

"Come sit down again," Morgan invited, extending a hand. She tried to keep her voice gentle and her movements slow and unthreatening.

Becca accepted the hand and allowed herself to be guided to her former seat on the settee. Tucked into the corner between the forward and star-board cabin walls, Becca looked very small and vulnerable in her borrowed nightdress. *Should* Morgan be encouraging her to learn poker, rather than more rope discussion?

"Becca," Lynn spoke, and their voice was unusu-ally gentle. Becca startled and looked at them. "You look terrified."

"I'm sorry," Becca said, ducking her head between her shoulders reflexively.

"You don't need to be sorry," Lynn said, and their voice was still soft, reassuring. This wasn't a side of Lynn that Morgan usually saw — the dy-namic between them was more dynamically switchy, more playful challenge than this reassur-ing certainty — but she felt herself starting to re-spond to it now. "Your feelings are valid, and you're allowed to have them."

Becca nodded, a tiny thing but there, and her eyes were on Lynn. In this moment, the cargo shorts and faded navy t-shirt they wore did nothing to detract from Lynn's authority.

"How can we help?" Lynn asked softly.

"I don't know." Becca hugged her knees to her chest. "I'm sorry. I don't know."

"I understand," Lynn said. Morgan expected them to pull Becca into a hug, but Lynn stayed still, contained on their own side of the aisle. Lynn sat patiently as Becca shivered, waiting until the tension started to ebb from Becca's neck and shoulders before speaking again.

"You are safe here," Lynn said, voice still soft but unquestionable. Another ripple of tension passed through Becca at the sound, but when that wave passed, it took with it a little more of her pre-existing anxiety. Lynn continued, "Nobody here will hurt you. Not me. Not Morgan. You are safe."

Another nod, as Becca sat huddled in the corner. Lynn nodded back.

"You seemed to indicate that you were interested in learning more about the rope," Lynn said, "but you didn't know what to ask?"

Becca nodded.

"Is it that you don't know what questions to ask, or what would happen if you asked them?" Lynn probed.

"Both?" Becca said, no confidence in her voice.

"What do you think would happen if you did ask?" Lynn prompted. The words could have been teasing, but their tone was anything but. They were providing guidance, Morgan recognised, rather than tempting or challenging Becca to step into the unknown.

"I don't know," Becca whispered, her eyes on the table in front of her.

"Would it help if you did?" Lynn asked.

Becca nodded, still hugging her knees, but the lines of her body not nearly as tense as they had been earlier. "Probably?"

"Morgan," Lynn asked, keeping their tone reassuring even when not addressing Becca directly. "What would happen if Becca said she wanted to know more about rope, but couldn't put together a specific question?"

"I mean," Morgan started. "We've done rope demos before. I could ..."

Becca had tensed up at the word "demos", and Morgan trailed off.

"When you say demo," Lynn asked, and if it were possible for their voice to have gotten any gentler, it did. "What would you be demonstrating? On whom?"

Becca shivered at the last question, and Morgan finally made the connection. Becca might be interested, but somehow she had confused asking questions with leaping in to volunteer as a demo bottom.

"There are some basic ties," Morgan said, watching Becca's response. "Usually I show off one or two of those, or Lynn does. Not on you, I mean, not on an audience member. Unless they want." Morgan was usually *good* with words, but she couldn't seem to find the right ones, couldn't coax Becca to relax.

"It's just ... explanation, and to see how it's done," Morgan promised. "Just a demonstration, not –" a scene, she was going to say, but would that word make any sense to Becca? "Not something super serious and involved."

"Just a demonstration, then," Lynn summarised. "That's what we're offering. Probably demonstrating on me, or else on Morgan." Lynn was nodding their head, and Becca echoed the gesture. "If you asked to see that demonstration," Lynn told her, "we wouldn't expect anything more of you. Does that make sense?"

Becca nodded her head.

"So your choice is this," Lynn said, still slow and gentle. "Would you like me to get out some fresh rope for a demonstration, or would you like to learn how to play poker?" Becca was still looking hesitant, but not as scared as she had, earlier.

"Or," Lynn continued, their voice edging back towards teasing, "would you like to lock yourself in the head for the rest of the night, and see how that works out?"

Becca blushed again and shook her head, but there was a hint of a smile, too, rather than the earlier stark terror. "I'd like to learn a little more," she said.

"Rope, or poker?" Lynn's voice was still gentle, but it was no longer guiding quite as firmly. An invitation, rather than a firm hand between the shoulder blades, Morgan thought.

"Rope, please," Becca mumbled, eyes anywhere but on Lynn and Morgan and her face a deep shade of red.

"Okay, then," Lynn said, approval in their voice. "Morgan?"

Five

"Okay, right. Demo," Morgan repeated. Of *course* Lynn would pass it back to her now. She took a breath and ordered her thoughts. "Lynn, could you get out the rope and stuff?" She looked at Becca. "Umm. Can I get you a drink or anything? Should I put on some tea?" She moved back to the galley to put the kettle on even before Becca had a chance to reply.

"We're out of milk," Lynn reminded her, standing to rearrange the cushions on which they had been sitting. They retrieved the rope bag from the storage area built into the port side settee and put it on the floor before replacing the cushions and sitting back down.

"Maybe something herbal?" Morgan suggested. She knew the ritual of pouring and steeping would help settle her own nerves; she didn't usually *bustle* like this. She had started on the washing-up, for crying out loud. Morgan was usually happy to leave dirty mugs in the sink until Lynn got tired of waiting for her to get around to them, or at least until they had a full meal's worth of dishes. Now, at least, it was something to do with her nervous energy.

Becca was still sitting in the inner corner of the settee, hugging her knees in front of her and watching with wide eyes as Lynn unpacked the rope bag onto the table. For their part, Lynn was keeping their movements slow and deliberate; Morgan appreciated the effort they were making to avoid startling the woman. Becca seemed stretched taut, but it wasn't Lynn setting out the EMT shears or the carbiner of rope that made her jump. That was down to the kettle, announcing it was ready with a piercing whistle.

Morgan offered what she hoped was a reassuring smile, and turned off the flame. "Chamomile?" she asked.

Lynn left the items on the table and returned to their seat against the port wall. "Sounds good," they said. Becca just nodded, adjusting her position so her legs were under the table rather than forming a barrier in front of her.

Morgan transferred teabags from a zippered plastic bag to each of the clean mugs, then added the boiling water. She took the time to put the rest of the tea away before lining up the three mugs on the forward edge of the counter. She wasn't delaying, she told herself; Lynn was always on about how she should clean up as she worked.

Out of excuses, Morgan walked back into the lounge and eased her way onto the starboard settee. Becca's nervous sideways shuffle, so her back was to the forward wall rather than the corner, hurt Morgan's heart but she just passed her friend a warm mug. If Becca needed a bit more space, she could give that to her.

"It's okay," Morgan said quietly. She took a mug for herself and patted the seat to her left, inviting Lynn to join her.

Becca's hands gripped her own mug tightly, eyes focussed on the tea within, but she flinched visibly when Lynn stood.

"Becca?" Morgan asked, reaching out to touch her wrist. "What's the matter?"

"Nothing," Becca mumbled. Morgan could feel the cushion shift as Lynn sat beside her, but her focus was on her friend.

"Are you sure?" Morgan asked. "Can you look at me, hon? We don't have to do this." Becca's shoulders came up around her ears, but she did turn to meet Morgan's gaze.

"It's okay," Becca said, her voice unsteady. Morgan could see tears behind her glasses. 'I said I wanted to ..." She stopped, took a breath, and Morgan could see her trying to get herself under control. "It's nothing. Just a demo. I'm being dumb."

"It's not dumb," Morgan said. "You said you wanted to. And we can. But we don't have to. Do you understand that?"

"I," Becca started. She took another breath, and nodded. "Yes. I understand that."

"Do you still want to go forward?" Morgan asked. Everything in Becca's body language suggested one answer, but she wanted to check, to be sure.

"Yes," Becca said.

Okay, that was not the answer Morgan had expected. Beside her, she heard Lynn put their mug back on the counter.

"Why?" Lynn asked. It was a reasonable question. Morgan let go of Becca's wrist and sat back, trying not to be in the way of the conversation.

Becca knew Lynn wasn't a threat, that her reaction was unreasonable. It was a reasonable question, 'why,' but she wasn't sure she had a reasonable answer for them. Or herself. She didn't even know why Morgan pulling her hand away left her feeling so empty and alone.

"I'm curious?" Becca tried, and it seemed lame to her own ears. Lynn nodded. Was that going to be enough of an answer?

"I can understand curiosity," Lynn said. "What are you curious about, exactly?"

"The ... everything," Becca said. "It's, I mean, it seems to be a thing ..." Lynn nodded, listening, but Becca felt like she was digging herself deeper into a hole. Under the table, Morgan touched her hand lightly; Becca grabbed it as if she were drowning. She felt like she was.

Becca didn't know about rope. Not on people, anyway. But Morgan and Lynn had offered to show her stuff. How it worked. A couple of ties, Morgan had said. So just technique, like learning about knitting or golf or birdwatching.

Becca didn't know about rope, but she knew it was a thing that Morgan liked to do. She liked Morgan. Morgan thought it would be okay to teach her. And this might be the only time she'd ever get to see Morgan. If she said no now, she'd probably never get another chance.

She didn't want to miss that chance to learn, to connect with Morgan that way.

There was no way she could explain that to Lynn.

"It's a new thing to learn," she said. "I like learning new things."

"Okay," Lynn said. "So your words are telling me that you're curious and you want to learn something new. That's fair. So why is your body language screaming that you're terrified?"

"I'm sorry," Becca said. She made an effort to sit up straighter. "I know I'm being unreasonable. I apologise for my reactions." Morgan squeezed her hand under the table. It helped.

"I don't want an apology," Lynn said. "I want to know that you're making a choice to be here. I want to know that you'd feel safe, saying no, because if you're saying yes because you're afraid of the consequences, that's not a yes we should be taking."

"You said you won't hurt me," Becca said. Lynn nodded.

"That's true," they said. "And as long as you know that applies to saying no, as well as if you say yes, I'm happy to help."

"Thank you," Becca said. Morgan's hand, holding hers, was steadying. She did feel better.

"Of course," Lynn said, and turned their attention to their tea. The examination was over, and Becca had apparently passed.

Morgan waited until she was sure Lynn was done and gave Becca time to take a sip of tea before asking, "How are you doing, hon? Do you need anything?" Becca still looked a little wobbly, but a bit steadier than before Lynn had taken her in hand.

"Sugar, maybe?" Becca asked.

"We can do that," Morgan smiled. "It's just behind that sliding door by your head. The white stuff in the empty peanut butter jar. There should already be a spoon in it."

Becca eyed the cabinet door warily, and Morgan stifled a laugh. "I promise there's nothing kinky in that one," she said. "It's just food." Becca blushed and ducked her head, but there was at least a hint of a smile on her face. She got the sugar, sweetened her tea, and passed the jar along to Lynn when they held out a hand for it. Morgan sipped her tea straight, but gave Becca a few more minutes to settle her nerves.

When Becca's tea was half gone and the tension across her shoulders had ebbed, Morgan reached for the carabiner of rope Lynn had left on the table. She removed a single hank and set it on the table just in front of Becca's mug.

"This is rope," Morgan said, slipping into a calm, lecturing cadence. "There are a few varieties one can use. Cotton is an inexpensive choice, and fairly gentle to the skin. Some people like nylon for how silky it feels, though it doesn't hold knots as well, and it's easier to get rope burn from it. What Lynn and I have — and therefore what I'll be using — is hemp. It's a traditional choice, a little harder than cotton, but it softens wonderfully as one uses and washes it."

Becca had tensed up a little when Morgan put the rope directly in front of her, but that wasn't unexpected. She was holding her mug a bit closer to her chest now, and peered at it while Morgan spoke.

"You can touch it," Morgan told her with an encouraging smile. "It won't bite." Becca nodded and fingered the rope gingerly, but didn't respond to the lame attempt at a joke.

"This type is made of several strands twisted together, but other ropes are braided," Morgan went on. "We like the weight and density of this; it's thick enough that it won't compress down and become impossible to untie. There's a friction to it, too, so you can wrap the hemp around itself and it won't slip all over the place, even without a knot."

Becca nodded, seeming to gain a little confidence in examining it as Morgan spoke. It wasn't until Morgan reached out to make a point that she tensed up again, pushing the rope back towards her friend. Slowly, Morgan put two and two together.

"Becca," Morgan said softly, using her name to refocus her attention. "You understand that I'm not going to do anything to you, here, without your explicit permission, right?"

Becca just blinked at her.

"You're allowed to be curious," Morgan said. "You're allowed to explore the rope. You're allowed to watch and ask questions and even play with it yourself. And you don't need to worry that you're going to find yourself tied up without any warning."

"I ..." Becca blushed and shook her head, eyes on the rope and the table. "I'm sorry," she said. "I know you said it was just a demo. But I wasn't sure?"

"No, *I'm* sorry," Morgan said. "It's such a basic rule in kink spaces that I didn't think to tell you specifically. They're very much 'no until somebody says yes' rather than 'go until they say stop.'" She sighed. "If you've been thinking otherwise ... no wonder you've been so on edge."

"I'm sorry," Becca said again, very quietly.

"You didn't do anything wrong," Morgan insisted, and Becca drew in on herself more. Morgan tried to make her tone gentler. "It's my responsibility," she said. "Nobody is mad at you. There's literally no way you could have known." She took a breath, and tried to figure out how far she needed to back up.

"Okay," Morgan said. "The basic rule in any sort of kink space — not just with me and Lynn, but any time you go into a specifically BDSM space — is that if you want somebody to do anything to you, you're going to have to ask them in words. If you

want to touch somebody in any way, you're expected to ask first."

"That's actually a little less true, here at home,"
Lynn put in. "Because you already know Morgan,
we're a bit more comfortable assuming that she's
allowed to touch you casually. If we were meeting
for the first time at a play party or a munch, something like touching your wrist or giving you a hug
would require your permission before trying it."

"Play party?" Becca asked, getting hung up on
the jargon. "Munch?"

"They're specific sorts of get-togethers," Morgan
explained quickly, trying to move on without giving more details that might make Becca more uncomfortable. "But Lynn's right that I should probably ask now. Are you still okay with me touching
your face, your shoulders, your arms, and your
hands?"

"Touching?" Becca asked uncertainly.

Morgan nodded, "Like the way I touched your
hand, under the table. Or the way Lynn touched
your back, as you were boarding *C Shell*."

"That ... you need permission for that?" Becca
sounded confused, or maybe a little overwhelmed
again. Morgan hoped her smile was reassuring.

"In what we call vanilla spaces — in most of the
world — it's just ordinary interaction," Morgan
agreed. "If you told somebody to stop, of course,
you'd expect them to listen. But mostly the rest of
the world is run on a 'yes until I say no' basis."

Becca nodded faintly.

"This is already a little bit beyond the bounds of
a vanilla interaction," Morgan went on. "If I went

to a kink class or demonstration, I would expect the general kink rules to apply to anything that happened there, even if I were just in the audience. And you probably do deserve that level of protection."

"Protection?" Becca asked. "I'm ... I've been okay with what you've done so far?" Morgan nodded.

"So are you comfortable with us continuing the way we have been?" she prompted. "Me and Lynn?"

"I guess so," Becca said. She didn't sound certain, but certainty wasn't something Morgan was getting a lot of, from Becca, tonight.

"Okay, then," Morgan said. "If I intend to go any further, I'll still ask you first. And neither of us is going to hurt you."

"Unless I ask for it?" Becca ventured. Morgan could see how far outside her comfort zone Becca was reaching, and she smiled at the joke.

"Honestly," Lynn said, leaning forward to speak past Morgan, "probably not even then."

Becca looked at them. Her shoulders had gone tight again, and Morgan touched her arm for reassurance.

"Becca," Lynn said gently, "you're trying hard. We can see that. And when something's new and exciting, it can be really tempting to do All The Things. We've seen people get in trouble that way, going too far too fast."

Becca nodded slowly.

"Take it slow," Lynn advised. "Neither of us wants to harm you. And I think that, right now, letting you push into stuff that you think of as 'hurting' ... would do you harm. Does that make sense to you?"

"I guess," Becca said. Morgan wasn't sure the hurt/harm dichotomy was something she was able to grasp, right now, but this was not the time to push it. Not when it was easier to just do neither. Becca took another sip of tea and added, "Thank you."

"You're welcome," Lynn said. "And you're safe here."

Becca nodded again, and seemed a little closer to believing it.

Morgan tapped the rope pointedly. "If you're feeling a bit steadier," she said, "Would you like to move forward?"

Becca blushed and nodded, but still looked much more comfortable than she had before the digression. She didn't flinch when Morgan reclaimed the rope from in front of her.

As Becca watched, Morgan unwound the end of the rope from around the centre of the hank. She used her thumb to anchor the two loose ends against her right palm and glanced over to make sure Becca was following.

"Almost everything we do," Morgan explained, "starts with the rope folded in half." She made a loose fist around the double strand of hemp with her left hand, then pulled the rope through. When she reached the middle, she dropped the ends she had been holding in her right hand and trans-ferred that grip closer to the fold.

"This is called the 'bight'," Morgan explained. "Usually, we start here, and work out from the centre point." She looked at her partner. "Could I have your wrists, please, Lynn?"

Lynn extended both their hands to the centre of the table. To Becca's surprise, they held their wrists almost a hand's span apart, rather than crossing them like victims in the movies.

"So, we're going to lay the bight here, between the wrists, with a fair amount of tail for when we tie it off later." Morgan demonstrated, the loop in the rope extending approximately to the tip of Lynn's ring finger.

"If she were being lazy, rather than trying to impress you," Lynn put in, "she'd ask me to hold the end with the bight."

"Hush you," Morgan laughed, swinging the loose ends of the rope at her partner's bare arm. Becca managed not to giggle.

"*Any*way," Morgan said, "the next step is to wrap the rope around the wrists."

Lynn kept their elbows on the table but lifted their forearms, giving Morgan a good angle at which to work. Morgan coiled the rope several times around their separated wrists, saying nothing about the gap.

"The important thing here is that the ropes lie flat and parallel," she explained. "A nice, even tension is important, but if the ropes cross each other they can dig in and quickly become uncomfortable." She completed four wraps of Lynn's wrists before stopping. "The wider we make this part, the more comfortable it is," Morgan explained. "Again, narrow bands dig in; wide bands distribute the pressure." She smiled encouragingly, "Do you have any questions so far?"

"Umm," Becca said, embarrassed to ask, "isn't it a bit loose?" She blushed. "Like, couldn't they just pull both their hands out of the loops?"

Morgan looked at her work. "Well, uh, I wasn't done yet," she said.

"I'm sorry," Becca said, moving further back against the bench.

"No, no." Morgan shook her head. "You definitely do have a point."

"There is a reason," Lynn said, suppressed laughter in their voice. "I'm sure she'll get to it eventually."

"*Anyway*," Morgan said, taking back control of her lecture. "Four wraps, that's eight strands of rope creating width. At *this* point, we can take the loose end and cross it with the bight end, like this." She interlocked the two double strands of rope like the ribbon on a holiday parcel, one strand going over the gap at the centre and the other below, before cinching a knot tight on the other side.

"You see the way the knot pulls those loose strands together?" Morgan pointed out. The rope that had stretched across the gap between Lynn's wrists was now gathered into a tight bundle between them. The length that had looked excessive had been just enough to curve along the inside of Lynn's wrists and allow room for the knot; there was only a small gap visible between skin and rope.

"Yeah," Becca said. "That's ... How did you know how much space to leave?"

"We *have* done this before," Lynn smiled. "There was a lot of trial and error, at first."

"If it were still too loose," Morgan added, "I could do more wraps in the middle here, to fill the space. Sometimes, you might leave room to do that on purpose; it can be helpful to hold the wrists apart as well as together."

"Once you have the knot done," Morgan looked back to Becca, "you need to check the tension again, like this." She slipped a finger into the gap between rope and Lynn's left wrist. "You want to allow one to two fingers of space, for safety."

"Couldn't ... couldn't they still wiggle out, if it's too loose?" Becca asked. Morgan looked to Lynn.

"If it's too loose, yes." Lynn used their bound hands to brush hair out of their face. "I might be able to wiggle out of this one, but often ... that's not the game we're playing. She's not tied me up because I want to get away, but because I want to be tied up."

Becca nodded slowly. It *almost* made sense.

"Could you put your hands across so she can see for herself?" Morgan prompted, and Lynn stuck their hands across the table obligingly. Becca kept her hands in her lap, peering from a safe distance.

"It's safe to touch," Morgan told her, and Lynn nodded confirmation.

"It's okay," Becca said hurriedly, shifting a bit further back on the bench to give them space. Lynn nodded and withdrew their hands to a more neutral position.

"The other thing we're watching is the temperature of their hands," Morgan said, continuing as if nothing had happened. "If the hands start getting colder, that's a sign circulation might be impaired. Am I missing anything, Lynn?"

"The part where you actually ask me if it's comfortable?" they replied.

"Right," Morgan said, shaking her head. "With Lynn, they would have spoken up because, again, they're familiar with how rope is meant to feel. But I should have asked about any discomfort, numbness, or tingling. Any of that, Lynn?"

"Nope," Lynn replied cheerfully.

Morgan nodded and looked back at Becca. "Sometimes the position in which we tie somebody might be uncomfortable, or become uncomfortable, but that's different from the rope itself causing pain. One of the major risks of rope is that it can cause nerve damage, and the bottom's discomfort is the main warning sign of that."

"Is it dangerous?" Becca asked. It didn't look all that scary, but nerve damage?

"It is," Morgan replied, "but not like you might think. It's true that there are risks. That's why we talk about safety from the first time we pick up the rope, and why we always have these handy." She patted an oddly formed pair of scissors. "On the other hand, *everything* has risks. Crossing a street. Taking a shower. Going out in the sun. We don't just avoid doing those things, though. We take precautions."

"Soapbox, Morgan," Lynn interrupted gently, and Morgan looked abashed.

"Right, sorry. Anyway, yes there are risks. I think it's rewarding enough to do that it's worth the risk, but it's still important to be aware that the risks exist."

Becca nodded. It made some sense, at least.

"So, yeah. This is the double column tie," Morgan concluded. "Any questions?"

Becca looked back at the scissors Morgan had patted when lecturing about safety. "What are those things?" she asked. "I mean, they look like scissors, but there's something weird at the tip." Morgan picked up the shears, and Becca nodded.

"These are Tuff Cuts," Morgan explained. "Which yes, means they are basically scissors. The ambulance service uses them to cut through tough materials, like seatbelts if there was a car accident or jeans if you need to access a wound. They'll even cut through leather or mild steel, but they're meant to be safe to use right up against the body."

Morgan slipped the spade-like tip of the lower blade under the rope around Lynn's wrist.

"That's why the end of the lower blade is flattened like this," she said. "I can slide it right against the skin without worrying about stabbing them, even if the rope were on too tight."

Lynn winced. "Please don't cut the good rope as a demo," they objected.

"If the choice were rope or Lynn's well-being — anybody's well-being, really — I'd cut the rope in a heartbeat," Morgan said, removing the jaws of the scissors from around the rope. "Good hemp is expensive, but people are worth more."

"If this were a planned demo, we'd have some cheap rope on hand," Lynn said, "especially so that we could demonstrate this. But I'm fine, and this is our good rope, and I suspect you already know how to use a pair of scissors."

Becca nodded.

"How are you doing so far?" Morgan asked her, a hand moving out to cover Becca's. "Is this more than you're comfortable hearing?"

Becca shook her head. "No, it's ... interesting," she said. "I'm not sure I'd ever use it, but it's interesting."

Morgan smiled. "I'm glad. I enjoy it, and I don't want you to feel like it's too dark and scary to think about."

Becca blushed a little, and shook her head again.

Morgan tugged the free end of the rope, pulling Lynn's hands back towards her. She untied the knot, and Becca admired her friend's movements as she unwrapped the rope. Morgan's motions were swift and confident, one hand always in place to keep the ends from tangling or flying free to knock Lynn in the face.

Lynn shook out their hands, then took advantage of their freedom to have another sip of tea. Becca echoed the gesture; her tea had gone slightly cold, but the sweetness was comforting. Honestly, so was seeing Lynn and Morgan work together on the demonstration; she had thought rope stuff would be 'dark and scary', as Morgan had put it. It wasn't; Morgan and Lynn were just so *comfortable* together. She was a little sorry it was over.

"Are you interested in seeing another?" Morgan asked. Becca managed not to choke on her tea, but took a moment before responding.

"I ... yeah. I think I would." Becca hesitated, looking between Lynn and Morgan. "What's next?"

"Usually we cover the single column tie," Lynn said, turning to Morgan. "Do you want to model this one, love?"

Morgan shrugged. "Sure. We could do it that way."

Lynn picked up the rope and smoothed it through their hands. Becca saw a couple of kinks untwist as they found the centre again. Lynn held out their left hand, and Morgan half turned to place her right hand in it.

"The double column holds things together," Lynn explained. "Two wrists, for example. A single column wraps around one thing. I'll be using her wrist, again. because it's an easy bit to pass around." Lynn grinned. "It's also a good excuse to hold her hand."

Morgan actually blushed a little when Lynn mentioned holding her hand, which wasn't some-thing Becca was used to seeing from her friend.

Lynn tapped the bony bit on the outside of Morgan's wrist to draw Becca's attention. "We want to start below this point. There's a gap between the arm bones and the hand bones, here." They demonstrated with their finger, drawing a line right around Morgan's wrist, where it would bend. "There are nerves in there that we don't want to compress. We start a bit further onto the arm, and it's fine."

Morgan seemed completely relaxed with Lynn supporting her hand. Two of Lynn's fingers exten-ded along Morgan's wrist, and their thumb held the bight end of the rope against Morgan's palm.

"Again," Lynn explained, beginning to wrap the long end of the rope around Morgan's wrist, "you want the tension gentle, and the lines even." Their motions were a little more deliberate than Morgan's had been, but just as confident. Lynn wrapped the rope around three, then four times before slipping their fingers out of the coils.

"You'll use the bight end, now," they explained, anchoring the now-looser loops of rope to Morgan's wrist with a finger. "Cross it over the rest of these wraps, then run it back under, against her wrist. Then we bring it back up inside the loop it was forming." They did something complicated with the rope that Becca couldn't quite follow, but she didn't want to interrupt.

"Make a loop in the running end, like this," Lynn was still explaining, "then run the bight through it, doubled. Tighten it up, and there's your knot."

Becca just nodded.

"When we leave the bight doubled over like this, we can quickly release it by tugging on the bight end." Lynn grinned at their partner. "If I want her more secure, I can run the loose end here through the loop in the bight, tighten it up, and it might take her a little longer to untie it when my back is turned." Morgan stuck her tongue out at them as they fit actions to words.

"Any questions?" Lynn asked, and Becca looked at the loose cuff Lynn's knot had formed.

"Isn't that going to slide down to the point you said you didn't want pressure, if she moves at all?" Becca asked.

"Probably," Lynn said, "but when it's tied in an open position like this; it's not going to tighten or manage to slip a single rope width in to compress the nerve."

"Would you like to see?" Morgan offered, and Becca nodded even as she shifted slightly backwards on the bench.

"You're okay," Morgan told her, reclaiming her hand from Lynn and resting it on the table between herself and Becca. "You're allowed to be curious. I get that this is kind of new for you."

Becca nodded, peering at the tie. Unlike what Morgan had done for Lynn, the single column didn't seem to be restricting her movements at all. Morgan picked up her mug and had a sip of tea, the loose end of the rope just trailing on the table.

"What does it feel like?" Becca asked hesitantly.

Morgan reached across the table and laid her right hand on Becca's, positioning the rope-wrapped forearm directly in front of the other woman. "You're allowed to touch it," she said. "I'm not going to bite you."

Cautiously, Becca reached out with her left hand and stroked the rope. The fibre was slightly rough under her fingers, and she could feel the indentations where one strand lay against the next. Morgan waited patiently.

"Is it itchy?" Becca asked, and Morgan shook her head.

"Some hemp can be, but this is pretty well conditioned by now."

"It's pretty loose?"

Morgan nodded. "Yeah, Lynn was being nice to me this time." She grinned. "If one of us is going to try to wiggle out of rope, it's generally me. This could actually go a bit tighter before there's any sort of risk, but it's good to err on the safe side for a demo."

"Does it hurt?" Becca asked, though Morgan did seem perfectly comfortable.

"Without pressure on it, like this?" Morgan shrugged. "No more than the cuff of a dress shirt."

"What if somebody pulled on it?" Becca asked.

Morgan passed the loose rope to her. "Go ahead."

Becca bit her lip, but tugged carefully on the cords. Morgan's hand didn't even budge.

"Really?" Morgan asked. "Is that the best you can do?"

Becca blushed and dropped the rope, pulling her hand back.

"Give it here," Lynn sighed, holding out a hand, and Morgan passed the rope over to her left.

"She asked if it was painful, and you didn't give her an answer to that," Lynn said. They yanked the rope, and Morgan's arm was pulled back. "Of course she wasn't going to pull very hard. *She* doesn't want to hurt you."

Morgan recovered from the initial jerk, but Lynn must have been keeping a lot of tension on the line. When they suddenly let go of the rope Morgan lost her balance and almost knocked Becca's drink into her lap.

"I'm sorry," Morgan admitted, when she caught her balance. "Lynn is right." She pushed the rope cuff a little further down, and Becca could just make out a faint imprint of the rope on her skin. "It doesn't hurt; that's the reason we wrap it wide like this."

"It left a mark," Becca said, lightly touching her friend's skin.

"Sort of," Morgan said. "About the same as when I wake up with my weight on sheets that are folded weird."

Becca nodded; she supposed she'd had that happen to her before. And the impressions were already fading. Morgan was watching her face closely, and Becca wasn't sure what she saw there.

"Would you like to try it on, yourself?" Morgan offered, hoping she wasn't pushing too far. Becca was obviously curious, had relaxed while they were doing the demo, but now she tensed up again.

"I ..." Becca stammered, looking back and forth between Lynn and Morgan, her shoulders hunching in on themselves. Morgan kept her posture open; Lynn sat quietly beside her, their hands in their lap.

Finally, Becca's eyes settled on the rope around Morgan's wrist.

"Maybe?" she said, and her voice was small and frightened.

"It's safe to be curious," Morgan reminded her. "And you're allowed to say no, or to say yes."

Becca nodded silently.

"Would you like me to do a single column on your wrist," Morgan made the offer explicit, "just so you can see how it feels?"

Becca bit her lip. Her glance flickered once more to Lynn, who continued to sit quietly, then back to Morgan.

"Yes, please?" she asked, and if her voice was still uncertain, the request was clear.

"I can do that for you," Morgan said, calmly unpicking the knot at her wrist and removing the rope. "Could I have your hand, please?"

Seven

Hesitantly, Becca extended her hand. Morgan took it in hers, and just held it gently for a few moments, her thumb stroking the back reassuringly.

"I'd like you to be less frightened before I begin," Morgan said quietly.

Becca's flinch and reflexive apology were not unexpected, but saddening anyway.

"It's okay. You're not doing anything wrong." Morgan tried to make her tone reassuring. "But would it be okay if we just took a few moments here to breathe, to let yourself relax?"

Becca nodded. Morgan continued to rub the back of her hand with a thumb.

"You wanted to know how it feels," Morgan said quietly, "and I can tell you that it doesn't feel like fear, for me. But if I just rush in, when you're uncertain and scared already, you'll take fear into the experience. Does that make sense?"

Becca nodded a little.

"When somebody puts rope on me," Morgan tried to explain, "it's like an extension of their touch. I'm good when Lynn pulled hard on the rope, because I like it when Lynn pulls hard on me."

Lynn cleared their throat quietly, and Becca jumped. Morgan squeezed her hand reassuringly.

"You seem to have this in hand," Lynn interrupted, though their tone was unusually gentle. "Would you be terribly offended if I went to read my book?"

"Hmm?" Morgan said. "No, sure, go ahead."

Lynn slid along the seat, moving slowly as they extricated themself from the table. Morgan could hear them walk back to the aft cabin, latching the door in the open position before flopping onto their bed.

"I'll be right here if you need me," they called. Morgan nodded acknowledgement, still not sure why Lynn had needed to break her flow to announce their departure. Then she noticed the shift in Becca's posture, a subtle easing of tension around her eyes.

"They weren't going to hurt you," Morgan said quietly. "You're safe here."

"I'm sorry," Becca said, and her shoulders drew up towards her ears as if she heard it as a rebuke, but she didn't pull her hand away.

"It's okay," Morgan repeated. "You're safe. Nobody is upset with you. And you don't have to do anything that's not comfortable for you."

Becca bit her lip and nodded slightly. Morgan continued to rub the back of her hand gently, slow and steady.

"How are you feeling?" Morgan asked. "How can I help you feel more comfortable, right now?"

"I'm sorry," Becca said again. "I know I'm supposed to be comfortable. I know everything is fine and I'm being unreasonable. I just ..." She shook her head. "I'm sorry."

Morgan nodded. "It's not a requirement, you know."

Becca looked at her, startled, and she nodded again.

"You're not required to be comfortable. You're allowed to be scared or anxious or whatever else you're feeling." Morgan squeezed the other woman's hand gently. "You're safe, and I hope you know that. But you're not required to feel calm or comfortable or anything else. You're allowed to tell me to back off, or that you've changed your mind and don't want to do something. But you're also allowed to explore in areas that might not *feel* safe, and ask me to support you in that."

Morgan watched Becca carefully. She realised that she had no idea what Becca did or did not know about kink, or how she felt about it, and didn't want to scare her off by talking about her own experiences, but at the same time ...

"There are times when I deliberately play with things that make me scared and uncomfortable," Morgan said carefully. "With partners I trust to keep me safe, it can be ... a powerful thing to experience, sometimes to overcome, to feel like I survived." She couldn't read Becca's face, and was afraid of guessing wrong.

"With Lynn?" Becca ventured, and Morgan nodded.

"Sometimes with Lynn," she said. "Sometimes with other people. It depends."

"Was that what they meant? When they said that *I* didn't want to hurt you? That *they* would?" Becca's hand in Morgan's had pulled into a half-fist, and her voice sounded as if she were afraid of asking the wrong question, or maybe afraid of the answer she might get. Morgan patted her hand, considering her next words carefully.

"I do trust Lynn a lot. They can do things to me that hurt, and part of me still knows that I'm safe."

"So when you say they wouldn't hurt me?" Becca asked hesitantly.

Morgan nodded. "Mostly, that's because you wouldn't want them to. They wouldn't assume you can trust them that much."

"Trust them?" Becca's eyes flicked back to the aft cabin.

"That's right," Morgan said. She hesitated. Would it make sense to Becca, if she explained that she could let Lynn hurt her without taking harm from it, but that was a relationship they had developed over time? How much information would be too much? She patted Becca's hand gently.

"What I'm trying to say," Morgan settled on, "is that I understand, in a way, wanting to try stuff that's scary or uncomfortable. And I'm not going to tell you that you can't or shouldn't do that. But if you are deliberately asking me to do something that will be challenging for you, I'd like to know that that's what's going on."

"I ..." Becca bit her lip and looked at the table. "I didn't think of it that way?"

"I'm not saying you have to do that," Morgan said. "But if you want to go there with me, if you want to trust me to help get you through a scary or uncomfortable experience, I'm willing to do that for you."

Becca looked up at Morgan, wisps of light brown hair half-hiding her face. "I don't want you to hurt me," she said.

Morgan nodded, "I know. I don't want to hurt you. I want to help you know that you're safe, even if you don't feel safe at the moment."

"I ... is that what I'm asking?" Becca asked.

"I don't know," Morgan said quietly, her hand still on Becca's. "Are you?"

Becca hesitated, chewing her lower lip.

"Do you *want* to ask that of me?" Morgan asked, when Becca hadn't said anything for what seemed like an age.

"Is that allowed?" Becca asked. "I don't ..." She shook her head. "I feel like I don't understand what I'd be asking? Like it's something serious, and bigger than I'm seeing, or like it's part of the kinky sex stuff you do, and ..."

Morgan shook her head and squeezed Becca's hand reassuringly. "It doesn't have to be big or serious or overwhelming. I'm not suggesting anything sexual with you. It's just ... I'm not sure what you need from me, hon. I'm not doing a good job of making you comfortable. I am willing to hold the space if you want to do something that's hard for you. But I don't know how better to express that."

Becca nodded, taking a breath. "I'm … curious?" she said, and her voice made the statement into a question. "I saw it on you. The rope. And I trust you. And I do wonder what it would be like. And … I'm scared, and I'm mad at myself for being scared. So I … want to do it anyway?"

Morgan nodded. "We can do that." She patted Becca's hand once more and reclaimed her own, straightening the length of rope into the double strand with the bight at the centre.

Becca took a breath, and offered her right hand across the table. She *did* trust Morgan, she reminded herself. And her friend had only offered to show her how it felt. Just having it on her wrist. This was something she could handle, she was sure; the fear she felt was not a reflection of reality.

Morgan's grip on Becca's hand, this time, was different from her earlier touch. That had been gentle, careful, reassuring, almost tentative. This was firm and certain. It wasn't aggressive, but there was no doubt in Becca's mind that Morgan was in control. That Becca had *given* her that control.

She tried to meet Morgan's eyes. Managed, for a moment. Morgan smiled at her. Becca ducked her head, but she managed not to pull her hand away.

"You're safe," Morgan reminded her. "This is just a demonstration, just to show you how it feels." A gentle hand stroked from wrist almost to Becca's elbow; Becca suppressed a shiver. "If you don't like it, we can take it off. Okay?"

Becca nodded. This was what she had asked for. This was what she said she wanted.

Morgan's grip shifted, the index finger of her left hand extending along the back of Becca's wrist. She laid the rope across Becca's palm and curled Becca's fingers over it; the rope was soft, though unyielding in Becca's hand.

"Just hold that for now," Morgan told her, and Becca nodded again, gripping the doubled rope tightly.

Morgan guided the rope slowly around Becca's wrist, over her own finger, and back up in a full loop. "Is that too tight?" she asked

The double strand of rope was a distinct pressure against Becca's wrist, but it wasn't uncomfortable. As Morgan had promised, it was no tighter than the cuff of a shirt. Becca shook her head.

"Good," Morgan said, and it felt like praise more than just acknowledgement. Becca felt herself blush.

Morgan laid the next wrap right up against the first, and Becca was surprised to find that she didn't feel them as two distinct strands, but that they blended into the pressure from the first loop. Morgan's movements were firm and certain. Maybe it should have been intimidating, Morgan's confidence, but it was actually comforting. Being able to trust that Morgan knew what she was doing. Watching the rope wrap around her own wrist was a little surreal, but the four wraps were done quickly, and Morgan was searching her face.

"Are you doing okay?" Morgan asked, and Becca nodded wordlessly.

Morgan slipped her finger out of the loops, leaving them looser on Becca's wrist, then used the same finger to hold the rope against her wrist from the outside. Becca took a breath. This was okay. She had seen Lynn do the same thing, with Morgan. It was nothing new or unexpected. She trusted Morgan. There was no reason to be afraid.

Becca just needed to stop being afraid, stop re-acting wrong.

Morgan reached out and touched Becca's cheek lightly. Becca looked at her. She didn't look upset. Concerned, maybe.

"Would you like me to explain as I go?" Morgan offered. "Or would you like to just let yourself ex-perience the sensations?"

"Explain, please?" Becca asked, trying to keep her voice steady. Explanations were good. As long as she could think about it, make sense of it, it was easier to ignore the fear. The fear was dumb. She was smarter than that.

The words would help, though.

Morgan nodded. "Okay. So right now, I'm just holding the rope like this so it doesn't tighten un-evenly while I'm working. I'm going to be wrap-ping the bight end that you're holding around the bundled loops." She reached for the end she had tucked under Becca's fingers. Becca dropped it, and Morgan smiled. The smile felt good.

"The next step is to bring this end across to the other side of the cuff," Morgan explained, manipulating the rope. "Then we pull it through underneath." Morgan left the rope lying across Becca's forearm and touched the inside of her wrist with her right index finger.

Becca managed not to jump at the touch, but it took a few moments for her heart rate to slow again. Morgan waited for her, impossibly patient.

"We usually want to draw something towards us, rather than push from the back," Morgan explained when Becca had stopped blushing. Her finger slipped under the rope, caressing the skin of Becca's inner wrist.

Becca shivered a little, but nodded. Everything was fine. Morgan was being patient with her. She was explaining things. This was something Becca could understand. It was fine.

"So I'm just going to hook the bight here, with my finger, and pull it back with me." Morgan moved slowly, and Becca had time to appreciate the contrast between the finger sliding over her skin and the rope against it. Looking at Morgan earned her an encouraging smile.

"I like to bring the end up through the loop it formed, almost like a half hitch, to control where it pinches the cuff better," Morgan said, pulling the rope through. Becca could feel the friction as rope slid over skin, but it wasn't uncomfortable.

"This wrap will hold the loops open," Morgan explained, releasing the pressure on the back of Becca's wrist in favour of using her left hand to hold the bight, "and now I just need to tie it off with the running end."

Becca nodded. Watching Morgan work was fascinating; Becca had no idea how the other woman managed to be so good at everything she did.

"It's just a half twist here," Morgan explained, pinching a bit of the loose end of the rope and turning it into a loop, "then I can pull the bight halfway through and tighten the knot around it. You see how that works?"

Becca looked at the rope on her wrist, the loops of the knot, and the wide band of cuff. She nodded.

"How does it feel?" Morgan prompted. "Any discomfort, numbness, or tingling?"

"No, none of that," Becca said. It wasn't uncomfortable, but she was very aware of the feel of the rope against her skin. Maybe that was just because of the setting, or the newness, or the fact that Morgan was sitting so close.

"Do you want to try putting some pressure on it?" Morgan suggested, holding the tail end in her fist. "See how it feels that way?"

Becca bit her lip, and started to comply. Her imagination filled in the gap, what it would feel like, what it would *mean* to hit the end of the rope and not be able to move further. She didn't know if she could deal with that. Not now.

But Morgan had asked her to try, to put some pressure on it, just to see how it felt. That wasn't unreasonable. There was no reason to react as if it were a threat.

Becca took a shaky breath, remembering what she had been told.

"I'd ... really rather not?" Becca said. They had said she was allowed to say no. Both Morgan and Lynn had. But she didn't want to hurt Morgan's feelings.

"Fair enough," Morgan said, letting go of the rope entirely. She didn't *look* angry.

"I'm sorry," Becca said anyway, pulling her hand away. Morgan let it go easily, let Becca put a little more distance between them, and Becca hated herself for the pain in Morgan's eyes.

"You don't have to," Morgan said softly. "You never have to. It's okay."

The nicer Morgan was about it, the worse Becca felt. "I'm being unreasonable," she said.

Morgan didn't argue, but instead nodded. "You're not required to be reasonable."

"I'm not?"

Morgan smiled. "You're not. I told you that I was willing to support you in exploring something you found scary." She held out a hand, inviting Becca to take it, but she just couldn't. Not yet. Morgan left her hand in the middle of the table, not for-cing the issue but being there in case Becca changed her mind. Patiently. Patience Becca didn't deserve.

"Part of that," Morgan said, "is understanding that scared *isn't* reasonable, and when you reach the end of how far you want to push ... you're al-lowed to make that choice."

Becca fingered the rope on her right wrist. The idea that being unreasonable might be a reasonable response ... no, that didn't make sense. But Morgan said she was allowed to be unreasonable, anyway. It was a new idea for Becca, and not entirely comfortable. But it also wasn't as if her feelings were giving her a choice.

"You can take the rope off yourself, when you're ready," Morgan said, "or you can ask me to."

"I ... think I want to leave it on for a few, if that's okay?" Becca asked. She wasn't sure she could explain why. She wasn't sure she *understood* why. "I'm just ..."

"Take all the time you need," Morgan said. She removed her extended hand from the table, and Becca felt a pang of guilt for not having accepted the offer of contact. It was unreasonable of her, that rejection.

Morgan said she didn't have to be reasonable.

Becca took a breath, and nodded. She rubbed the rope on her wrist again, and let her fingers follow it down to the running end that Morgan had dropped. Experimentally, she gripped it herself, and tugged.

"How does that feel?" Morgan asked quietly. Becca flushed.

"It's okay," Becca said, not meeting her eyes.

"It doesn't cut in anywhere?" Morgan prompted, and Becca shook her head.

"It's fine," Becca said. "I'm sorry. I know I should have trusted you with it ..." She trailed off and offered her wrist across the table.

Morgan very gently covered Becca's hand with her own, not making any move to touch the rope.

"You're okay," she said. "You don't need to push yourself to make me happy." Morgan smiled sadly. "I was trying to encourage you to explore, not to make you feel threatened or trapped. I'm sorry I missed the mark."

"I know," Becca said. "I'm sorry."

"How are you doing now?" Morgan asked.

"I'm okay, I think," Becca said. "This is ... it's interesting?"

"Are you sorry you tried it?"

Becca shook her head. "I'm sorry I reacted wrong. Thank you for being willing to show me?"

"Of course," Morgan said. "Would you like to try the other side of it? Maybe learn how to do the tie?"

"I could do that?" Becca asked. She remembered what Morgan had said about the risks. "I don't know if I should do that. What if I messed it up and hurt somebody?"

Morgan grinned. "That would be why I usually teach this on a roll of kitchen roll. It's squishy enough that you can see if you're tying too tight, but you're also not going to hurt anybody."

"If you're sure you wouldn't mind," Becca said hesitantly, and Morgan smiled.

"I'd be happy to!" She glanced back at the aft cabin. "Lynn, would you mind grabbing a roll of kitchen roll for us?" she called.

"What?" Lynn asked, emerging from their book.

"Kitchen roll," Morgan repeated. "I want to show Becca how to tie it."

Eight

Lynn sighed, but levered themself off the sleep surface. "You could have gotten it yourself," they pointed out, stepping into the galley and reaching into one of the cabinets under the sink.

"Thank you, Lynn," Morgan said, ignoring their comment. She accepted a roll of paper towel from her partner and passed it to Becca.

"The single column tie is good on anything that's basically a cylinder," Morgan said. She was back in lecture mode now; Becca recognised the cadence and settled in to listen.

Morgan picked up the carabiner from the bench beside her and unhooked a new hank of rope. "Do you remember what the first step is?" she asked, handing the rope to Becca.

"Unwind it and find the centre?" Becca asked, already loosening the rope from its hank.

"Very good," Morgan said, warmly enough that Becca felt a blush start to rise in her cheeks. She copied what she remembered seeing Morgan and Lynn do, feeling the way the bends in the rope untwisted as she pulled it through her loose fist, and the step made a little more sense as something other than a formality.

"This is the bight," Becca offered, as she reached the centre point.

"That's right."

Becca bit her lip and looked at the paper towel roll. She could remember this.

"I let the bight hang off this end," she said uncertainly, laying the rope along the width of the roll, "because I'm going to need it later."

"Yes." Morgan's voice was reassuring, giving Becca space to figure it out while still promising to be there, if she got lost.

"Then I wrap the cords around." Becca began doing so. It took longer than she had expected to make the double strand lie perfectly parallel, but she remembered what Lynn had said. It needed to be even in order not to dig in. "And I pull the bight end under?"

"Almost," Morgan said. Not quite right, then. Becca frowned at the rope, trying to remember.

"Okay, no" she said. "The rope goes over first, then I pull it back under."

"That's right," Morgan said, and Becca tried to wiggle her finger between the paper towel and the wraps of rope.

"And this is why you had your finger along my wrist," she sighed. "I have this too tight, already."

"A little," Morgan admitted.

Becca unwrapped the rope and tried again. Trying to work around having her finger in the loops was awkward because it reduced her to having one working hand. "Do you have a pencil or something?" she asked.

"Sure," Lynn said. They extracted the pen that had been stuck in one of the journals Morgan had moved off the table, then handed the pen to Becca.

"Thank you," Becca said. She tried to hold the pen against the paper towel. It was still a bit awkward, using the web between her thumb and index finger to hold it in place, but not nearly as bad as trying to use her finger as the spacer.

"Okay, so I wrap these loops around, not too tight, and then I ... slip the pen out, and pull the bight end through?"

"Very good," Morgan praised, and it was still hard for Becca to hear. She *knew* she had been making mistakes, so how could it still be 'very good'?

"Okay," Becca said, determined to do better. "Next I bring it up here, on this side of the bend where it goes over the cords?"

"That's the way I do it," Morgan agreed. "Either side is fine, though."

Becca nodded and tried to concentrate on the next step. "I make a loop on the other end of the rope," she said, twisting the rope first one way, then the other.

"That's right. The running end should come out towards the wraps."

Becca corrected her twist, and Morgan smiled.

"Then I pull the bight end halfway through," Becca said, chewing on her lower lip.

"That's right." Morgan was watching everything she did, so she couldn't be screwing up too badly. "Now just snug it up."

Becca pulled the loose end of the loop she had formed around the folded bight. When Lynn and Morgan had done this, it had created a neat, bow-like knot. Her own attempt, however, had the loop going looser rather than tighter, and the cord ends a tangled mess. She looked at the result, then back at Morgan.

"It's okay," Morgan encouraged. "Try again." Becca nodded and untangled the cords back to the point where she had wrapped over and under the loops that formed the cuff.

"Did I at least have it okay this far?" she asked. Morgan looked at the roll of paper towels.

"Yes, that's right," she confirmed.

"Okay. So I form the loop in the long end," Becca said, half to herself. "Then I pull the bight halfway through."

"Yes," Morgan confirmed, watching her work.

"Now I just pull on this end," Becca pulled the loose tail of the rope, "and ... it all falls apart." Morgan frowned at the rope with her.

"Falling apart isn't the desired behaviour," she confirmed. Becca nodded.

"Can you do it?" she asked, offering the roll to Morgan.

"Yes," Morgan said, undoing the mass of not-quite-knot back to the point Becca had before. When her hands formed the loop and pulled the bight halfway through, it seemed effortless; when she pulled the loose end to tighten the knot, the rope politely formed itself into the knot it had refused to give Becca.

"I thought that was what I did," Becca said.

"Yeah," Morgan agreed. She untied the part she had done and handed it back. "Try it again?"

Becca carefully formed the loop, one half twist in the running end of the rope. She looked at Morgan, and the other woman nodded. Becca folded the length with the bight in half, and pulled it through the loop.

"Is this right so far?" she asked.

"Looks good to me," Morgan said. "Lynn?"

Lynn had been sitting at the desk with the journals and computer, their nose buried in a blue paperback. They looked up.

Becca tugged the loose ends harder this time, as if she could trick the rope into becoming a knot. The last loop she had formed still tried to escape off the end of the bight and yielded something that looked more like a tangle than an actual knot. Becca sighed at the mass of rope and started unpicking the snarl she had made.

"Try holding onto the middle of the bight end, this time," Morgan suggested. Lynn moved a bookmark to the pages they had been reading and set the book aside, walking over to stand beside Becca.

Becca felt Lynn looming over her, but they weren't a threat. She knew that. They were only trying to help, because Morgan had asked them to. Everything was fine.

"May I?" Lynn asked, gesturing to the bench beside Becca. She nodded, sliding to her left to make room. Closer to Morgan.

Lynn sat down.

Sitting there, trapped between Morgan and Lynn, Becca was even more acutely aware of what a mess she was making of things.

Rope. She was meant to be focussed on rope.

"Okay," Becca said, trying to calm herself. Getting frustrated was not going to help. "I form the loop here, like this."

Morgan nodded; Becca didn't quite dare look over at Lynn.

"Then I pull the bight through," she said, repeating the step she had done three times already. This time, she held onto the middle of the bight end, as Morgan had suggested. The knot didn't quite fall apart when she tightened it, but it was definitely still more of a mess than a knot.

"I'm not sure what's going on," Morgan said. "You seem to be doing everything the way I did." She shook her head. "You could always end with some other sort of knot."

"I want to do it *right*, though." Becca appreciated how nice Morgan was being about it, but 'nice' and 'right' weren't the same thing.

"I don't know, then," Morgan sighed. "Do you see anything, Lynn?"

"Maybe," Lynn said, and Becca ordered her heart to slow back down. She had known they were there. They were not a threat. "Do it again?"

Dutifully, Becca unpicked the knot and worked through it again. Loop. Bight end. Pull the running end.

"Wait," Lynn said, as she started to tighten the knot. "You're pulling away from yourself. Try pulling the other direction."

When Becca switched from pulling in one direction to pulling the other, the knot completely inverted and undid itself. She tried not to cry.

"Try again," Lynn prompted. "But this time, don't switch directions; just pull the rope towards yourself from the beginning."

Becca finished undoing the knot again. One more time, she went through the steps. Loop. Bight. Pull, this time her arm moving towards Lynn rather than Morgan.

This time, the knot held.

"Excellent!" Morgan beamed. Lynn was quieter.

"Try pulling it the other direction, now," they suggested. "Or directly away from the tie."

Whatever the angle, this knot stayed politely in place, just as Morgan's had when Becca tugged on it.

"That kitchen roll will never escape now!" Morgan grinned, seeming prouder of Becca's work than Becca felt herself. Becca just nodded. She poked the paper towels where the rope pressed into them.

"Is it too tight, though?" she worried. "Would I be hurting somebody?"

Morgan grinned as if it were a joke, but Lynn looked at the paper towels seriously.

"Maybe a little bit tight," they said. "It would be easier if we could ask the kitchen roll how it feels; we can compress fat more safely than muscle, for example." They took the roll from Becca, and tried to work a finger under the rope; they barely managed. "Ideally, it would be a little looser. Would you like to try it again?"

"I want to get it right," Becca said, accepting the paper towels back from Lynn.

"You're still learning," Morgan reminded her, stroking her shoulder gently. Becca shrugged it off.

"If I'm learning, I need to learn it right," she insisted. Wasn't that obvious?

The rope came off the paper towels more easily than it went on, and Becca took a deep breath before starting again.

"The pen helped, but I need to keep it a bit further off," she said, fumbling to maintain a larger gap. "How do I know how far off to hold it?"

"Time and experience," Lynn said quietly. "You're allowed to make errors in learning. You're not going to hurt anybody. That's why we use the kitchen roll."

Becca nodded, wrapping the rope more loosely around paper towel and pen. She manipulated the bight end over and then under the loops before remembering to pull out the pen, and this time the finishing knot came together as intended. She checked her work, then passed it to Lynn.

"That's much better," they said approvingly. "You see how you can get a finger under here without crushing the roll? That's what we want to see." Becca nodded, rubbing the rope still on her own right wrist once more.

"Is that still comfortable?" Morgan asked.

"It's not uncomfortable," Becca said. She was still aware of it, certainly, every time she moved her wrist. But it wasn't unwelcome. It was interesting. "Should it be hurting, after this long?"

"Not at all," Morgan said. "Unless the position itself gets painful, you should be able to wear rope all day without it being uncomfortable."

"All day?" Becca asked. "Have you ... done that?"

"Sure," Morgan said. "There are some harnesses that can go on under your clothes, and nobody who doesn't know what to look for will be the wiser."

"Why would you do that?" It didn't make a lot of sense. Having the rope on her wrist was interesting, as something to try, but wearing it all day? "I mean, what's the point?"

"It can be fun," Morgan said. "Knowing you have a secret under your boring business clothes. Sort of like wearing sexy lingerie to work, except rope."

"I ... have literally never done that," Becca said.

"Really?" Morgan asked. "I find that it can make a boring conference feel much more interesting."

"Really," Becca confirmed. She didn't think she *owned* anything she'd consider sexy lingerie; she certainly wouldn't wear something like that to work.

"Okay," Morgan said, shaking her head. "Well, sometimes there's a sensation element, too. Depending where the knots are, it can provide interesting stimulation when you move."

It took Becca a few moments to try to understand what Morgan meant.

"It's all connected," Morgan explained, "so when you reach for something, it might pull on the rope over your shoulder, but you feel it *everywhere*."

"Oh," said Becca, blushing as the implication of 'everywhere' sank in.

"So there's rope to do something, like tying somebody down, and then there's rope that's just for wearing," Morgan concluded. At least she was treating it like a lecture question, not some sort of come-on.

"Why ..." Becca began, then shook her head. "I'm sorry," she said. "I'm just still not sure why you'd want to tie somebody down?" She blushed. "I mean, if they don't want to be there, shouldn't you just ... let them go?"

"If they didn't want to be there, sure," Morgan said. "But sometimes it's fun not to be able to get away from whatever somebody is doing to you."

"Fun?" Becca asked. "What makes it fun?"

"Situation, context," Morgan said vaguely.

"Lynn said earlier that they had you tied to the mast last night." Becca felt herself blushing, and hated that she couldn't control the reaction. And maybe she shouldn't be asking. But she wanted to understand. "Was *that* fun?"

"Yes," Morgan glanced across Becca, at her partner, and it almost seemed as if her own face was turning pink. "I would say that last night was definitely fun." Lynn grinned back at her.

"What made it fun?" Becca persisted. "It sounds like it would be scary."

"Sometimes scary *is* fun," Morgan said. "Like a roller coaster. The nervousness as you're going up the hill is part of the excitement."

Becca shook her head. Morgan was enthusiastic, but it still wasn't making sense. "I actually don't get roller coasters, either."

"I don't know how to explain it, then." Morgan turned the question around. "What sort of thing do you find fun?"

"Some games, I guess," Becca said, finding it hard to come up with anything. "Like, Scrabble? Trying to put together the best word from what's available, stretching your brain against somebody else's. The role-playing campaign we've been doing, coming up with a way to use my limited spell list to solve a problem."

Morgan nodded, "The challenge aspect I can see. Testing your limits."

Becca nodded.

"And when I ask you to imagine what it would be like if somebody tied you to a mast, can you think of any way that might test your limits?"

Suddenly, this didn't seem like a neutral lecture.

"I hadn't really thought about it," Becca said. It was true. She hadn't. Even if her brain was rushing to fill in the blanks, now.

"Never?" Morgan asked. Becca couldn't tell whether she was curious or teasing.

"I mean," Becca said, reaching for something plausible, "I think most people have had the odd Johnny Depp fantasy?"

"Genderqueer Caribbean pirates?" Morgan licked her lips. "Yes, please." Becca blushed a bit more.

"I guess that's where my mind goes," Becca said. "Tied to the mast by a wicked pirate intent on having his way with you?"

"Tied to a mast, you say?" Morgan slid off the settee and walked around to stand beside Lynn. She grinned and picked up the trailing end of the rope attached to Becca's wrist. With almost two metres of slack line, keeping it loose was easy, but she watched Becca's reactions carefully. For now, with no pressure on the rope, she mostly seemed curious.

With a few quick motions, Morgan attached the end of the rope to the pillar of mast that came up from the floor and through the ceiling of the cabin.

"There!" she said with a flourish. "Now you can tell everybody that you've been tied to a mast by a wicked woman."

Becca's eyes went to the mast, and the knot. She blinked and used her left hand to tug on the rope between her right wrist and the tied end. The knot held. She started to look worried.

"Morgan," Lynn warned, "that's escalating." They shifted back on the settee, giving Becca a little more space.

"It isn't," Morgan argued, "She's perfectly free to move." Lynn put their hand on her wrist, tapped three times with a finger, and Morgan stopped to listen.

Becca reached hesitantly past Lynn to touch the knot on the mast. Lynn stayed very still, but the way Becca was watching them – watching both of them – was a knife in Morgan's heart.

Morgan bit her lip. She hadn't *meant* to escalate. And the only thing she could do now was ... nothing. Nothing to make it better. Try to do nothing to make it worse. Deliberately doing nothing as Becca watched them with wide, frightened eyes. Doing nothing to interfere as Becca moved to untie the knot from the mast.

There was nothing else Morgan could do.

"That's right," Morgan said, as the knot came free. "You're allowed to undo it." Becca's eyes were back on her, her face pale. Morgan made her voice as gentle as she could. "You're perfectly safe. I didn't mean to scare you." Becca nodded.

"Are you a wicked woman, then?" she asked, obviously trying to make a joke out of it. Her voice was still shaky, but she was trying.

Lynn patted Morgan's bum and slipped past her, off the settee. "She certainly is," they said affectionately. Morgan moved into Lynn's former place around the table. Lynn settled back against the port wall with their book.

"Maybe," Morgan said. "I really didn't mean to make you uncomfortable there, though."

"It's okay," Becca said. "Is that really the mast? I was picturing the tall thing coming out the top of the boat."

"Part of it," Morgan said. If Becca wanted to move back to a more neutral topic, she could do that. "The mast extends all the way down to the hull. If it were just stuck on top, it would rip the roof off rather than moving the boat."

Becca reached out to touch the mast, and Morgan smiled.

"Not quite what you imagined being tied to the mast would be like?" she asked.

"Not exactly," Becca agreed, shifting a little on the bench. "It wasn't ... bad?"

"Are you sure?" Morgan asked. "You looked pretty scared there."

"I was," Becca said. "But I didn't *need* to be. Does that even make sense?" Morgan nodded, and she went on. "I ... You let me get out of it, when I needed to."

"Always," Morgan said. "I don't want to hurt you. As scared as you were, it looked like you were being hurt. And I don't want that to happen."

"It was ... I mean, you were ... You weren't mad at me, when I untied it. I wasn't ever really trapped, the way it felt. And I know you say I'm allowed to be unreasonable, but I don't want to be. It wasn't what I had imagined, but it was fine. In the end. It was okay."

"I'm glad," Morgan said, reaching out to touch Becca's hand. She smiled, trying to lighten the mood. "Would you like to tell me what you *were* imagining?"

Becca blushed. "With, umm, Johnny Depp?" she asked.

"Is that whom you were imagining?"

Becca flushed a deeper shade of red. "No."

A smile played around Morgan's lips, but she controlled it. "Oh?" she asked, trying with only limited success to control the impulse to tease her friend. "Then what were you imagining?"

"You," Becca mumbled. Morgan stroked her hand gently. The other woman looked up at her.

"I'm honoured," she said. "Do you want to tell me about that?"

"Do I have to?" Becca asked. Morgan shook her head.

"You don't *have* to do anything that makes you uncomfortable," she said. "But if you can be comfortable enough to tell me about it, I am curious to hear it."

"Okay," Becca said quietly, her eyes on the table. She waited long enough that Morgan was unsure whether she intended to continue. "It's stupid," she warned.

"I very much doubt that," Morgan said quietly. "You don't have to tell me. But I am sure it's not stupid. I like you, and I'm flattered that you might invite me to go there, even in your imagination."

"There wasn't even very much to it," Becca said, blushing. "I mean, Lynn had talked about tying you to the mast last night, and it ... you made them stop talking about it, but it kind of sounded like you enjoyed it." She glanced up at her friend. Morgan nodded.

"I did," she confirmed. "And that made you curious?" Becca nodded, looking at her hands again, her face burning.

"I ... it ..." she shook her head. "I mean, you'd be gentle with me, I think. The way you ... well, you've been very nice to me today. Touching my face, brushing hair out of my eyes, even the way you held my hand when we were walking in the dark. And ... I don't know," Becca said.

"I've tried to be gentle with you," Morgan said. "I don't want to hurt you." Was Becca actually suggesting what it sounded like she was suggesting?

"And ... well ... the rope is interesting. It's not as scary as I thought it would be, I guess? At least not like this." Becca rubbed the parallel strands wrapped around her wrist. "And even doing that, you were ..." She shrugged. "And my brain, well, it's ... it sort of put things together, and ..." She blushed again.

"You don't *have* to tell me," Morgan reminded her, brushing the back of Becca's hand lightly. Becca looked up at her again and Morgan smiled. "But I do wonder what you put together."

"Just, I guess, being up on the deck," Becca said. "You know. The mast at my back, just tied to it, not like ... not loose, like you did, but so I couldn't really move?" She wasn't meeting Morgan's eyes, of course. She was blushing and looking down, but she also hadn't pulled away from Morgan's caress, and ... this really did sound a lot like interest.

"Is that something you'd like to try for real?" Morgan asked, as gently as she could. Becca froze, not moving for several seconds before responding.

"What ... what would happen if I said no?" Becca asked, almost inaudibly.

"Then I would let the topic drop," Morgan told her, watching the other woman's eyes as they roamed across the table, the upholstery, anywhere but at the other people in the room. "And I wouldn't bring it up again, though you would be welcome to."

Becca bit her lip, and her voice was even quieter as she asked, "And if I said yes?"

Nine

Becca was obviously struggling even to ask the question, and Morgan *remembered* that place, the painful push and pull between curiosity and apprehension. It was so *tempting* to try to persuade her, to take the lead and guide her through an experience, to take responsibility away from her so Becca could just *be*.

But still Morgan laid out the harder path.

"'Yes' would be the start of the conversation, not the end," she began. "There are logistics — what exactly we want to do together, what you want to feel, things you don't want to have happen — but also questions you won't know how to answer yet."

"Like what?" Becca asked, looking up at her. Morgan reached out to rest a hand over one of Becca's. She trembled, but did not pull away.

"Things like, 'What does it look like when you're enjoying yourself?' 'What happens when you're not?' 'What helps you feel safe and comfortable after a scene?'"

"Yeah, I don't ..." Becca trailed off, looking scared and lost.

Maybe Morgan should have let Becca take that excuse to talk herself out of it, to pull away, but Morgan shook her head softly.

"You don't know, and that's okay. But it means this is a conversation we would continue having. Before the scene starts, during it, after. Sometimes with words. Sometimes," she looked at their joined hands, "by just gently making a move and seeing how you respond."

Becca blushed a little and pulled away, folded her hands in front of her on the table. Morgan let her go.

"Pulling away is allowed. It's part of the conversation, letting me know it's still a step too far for you." Morgan kept her tone gentle, chose her words carefully. "Can you tell me what worries you most?"

Becca hesitated, staring at her own hands. "I don't want to be afraid of you," she said, glancing up briefly and then back at the table. "This is all new and scary and intriguing and you know what you're doing and I ... I like you. I don't want to be afraid of you."

"Look at me, Becca." Morgan said. She kept her hands to herself, this time, waiting for Becca's chin to come up, slow and trembling, for the wide eyes behind the glasses to meet hers. "I'm not going to hurt you." Firm, sincere ... she hoped it came across as sincere.

Becca glanced away. "You've talked before about whips and ... things," she said. "And I kind of ignored it, because it ... wasn't something you do with just-friends." Her shoulders were hunched up near her ears, now, and she wasn't meeting Morgan's eyes any more. "If we're not just friends ..."

Morgan nodded. This was a line she would need to walk carefully. She didn't want to scare Becca away, but lying to her would be no better.

"I do have whips," Morgan said. "And other things. I never said that I don't hurt people. I have, and I will. People who enjoy it, who want to engage in that sort of play with me." Morgan took a breath. "You've *known* that about me, as you say, and you're right that it wasn't something that was relevant to our friendship. What I'm telling you is that it still isn't. I won't hurt *you*."

Becca looked up at her again, briefly. "But why? What makes *me* special?"

Morgan shook her head, almost laughed. "Because you're sweet and scared and adorable. Because I want to protect you and keep you safe and show you things I think are wonderful and help you see them as wonderful too. Because you don't *want* to be hurt or scared, and I want to connect with *you*, not some random cardboard cut-out of a submissive masochist."

"Oh," Becca said faintly.

"Too much?" Morgan asked. She should have been more careful. Those words hadn't been planned. They had just flowed, without giving her time to judge and weigh their likely impact.

Becca shook her head, almost met Morgan's eyes again. "You won't hurt me?"

The relief flooding Morgan was almost painful. She smiled and reached out to brush Becca's cheek with the back of her hand. "I won't hurt you. I promise."

Becca nodded, looked at the table in front of her. Quietly, she said, "I'd ... like to try it, please. The rope. The mast thing. If that's still okay with you?"

Another gentle caress of the cheek turned into a finger under the chin. Morgan lifted Becca's face until their eyes met. Becca trembled, eyes wide, but let herself be held in place.

"I'd like that very much," Morgan told her.

Becca swallowed hard. "What comes next?" she asked.

Morgan smiled, released her chin, and covered Becca's hands with her own.

"Words," she said. "Words come next. Setting expectations, ground rules."

Becca nodded, eyes still on Morgan's face, not trying to look away.

"How would you describe the scene you were imagining?" Morgan prompted gently. "What happened in it?"

"I was tied to the mast," Becca said.

"Mmhmm," Morgan agreed. "And then what happened?"

Becca hesitated. "I ... don't know," she said. "My brain just stopped there. I guess that's the part where you have your way with me. I don't know. What does happen next?"

"Do you *want* anything to happen next?" Morgan asked. "Or is it enough to just have the experience of being tied there, without something coming after?"

Becca blinked. "Is that allowed?"

"Yes," Morgan said firmly. "That's allowed."

"But then ... what's in it for you?"

"Besides the pleasure of your company, the connection it builds, the way it feels that you're willing to trust me to do something that still scares you?" How could she convey the feelings to somebody who was so completely new? "You're offering me a chance to do something I enjoy doing with somebody I very much like. That's enough. It's more than enough. I don't *want* to take more when you're already giving so much."

Becca nodded and looked away. Morgan gave her some time to process it, waiting until tension had eased from her shoulders before she moved on.

"In order to tie you," Morgan said, "I'll need permission to touch you fairly extensively. Is that okay?"

"I ... yes?" Becca answered.

"Where, and how?" Morgan prompted.

"Gently?" The uncertainty in Becca's voice, that she thought she needed to specify, hurt. "You said you wouldn't hurt me."

"I'm not going to hurt you," Morgan repeated. She made the question more explicit. "Where on your body are you comfortable being touched? Head, neck, torso, arms, legs?"

"I guess?" Becca said.

"How about clothing?" Morgan prompted. "Are you okay in the nightdress? Did you want to wear something special?" She grinned, and risked teasing. "Or nothing at all?"

Becca blushed at that. "The nightgown is fine," she mumbled.

"Okay," Morgan smiled. "Do you have any physical limitations I should know about? Range of motion issues? Epilepsy, or anything that might cause you to have a seizure or lose your balance?"

"No, nothing like that," Becca said. She looked confused, but these were important questions Morgan needed to ask.

"Is there anything else that you know you don't want to have happen?" Morgan asked. "You know I won't hurt you, but is there anything that might make you uncomfortable, things you'd rather avoid?"

"I don't know," Becca said plaintively. "I'm sorry. I'm doing this all wrong, aren't I?"

"You're not," Morgan said firmly. "You're doing fine. I told you there would be questions you couldn't answer yet. It's like ... asking you if there are things you don't eat, before planning dinner. Maybe you don't have any food allergies, and you're open to experimenting ... but if you're coeliac, I need to know that before we just order a pizza. If you can tell me upfront that you hate cabbage, well, I'm not serving coleslaw."

Becca nodded. "That makes sense," she admitted, taking a breath. "I can't think of anything right now. But what if I'm wrong? What if something comes up and I forgot to tell you or I didn't know?"

"That's where 'this being an ongoing conversation' comes in," Morgan smiled. "If we hit something you don't like, or something feels wrong, you can tell me and expect me to work with you to make it better."

Becca nodded hesitantly.

"There's even something called a 'safeword', which is like an emergency stop button. If I hear you say it, then I will immediately stop what I'm doing to help you get back to being okay."

"A safeword?"

"Mmhmm," Morgan confirmed. "I usually use 'red'. It's short, easy to remember, and not likely to just come up in normal conversation."

"And if I say it, what happens?" Becca still looked worried. "Is it like game over, I ruined it, we're done?"

"If you want it to be," Morgan allowed. "If you need it to be, absolutely. Not because you ruined it, but because that's what we need to do to keep you safe." How could she make Becca understand? "But you can also use it to ... just put things on pause, knowing whatever you say next is going to be taken seriously, and I will do what is necessary to keep you safe and help you find your way back to being okay."

Becca took a shaky breath and ran the fingers of her left hand over the rope on her right wrist. Finally, she looked back up at Morgan.

"This is scary," she said before ducking her head again. "I'm scared. And I want to say yes, and I know I'm not supposed to be scared, but it's ..."

"Becca," Morgan interrupted, and waited for the other woman to look at her again. "You are allowed to be scared. It *is* scary, and even when it's exciting and you're eager to do something, it can *still* be scary." She glanced aside at Lynn, who was pointedly reading their book. "For some people, that can be part of the fun."

Becca looked at Lynn, looked back at the table.

"I know," Morgan said softly. "Not for you. Not right now. And I'd like to help you feel less scared; I'd like to show you how it can be. But you're not doing something *wrong* by being scared, and you have the option of saying no, you don't want to do this. But also the option to let yourself do it even though it *is* scary."

Becca nodded, mumbled to the table, "I want to."

"Okay, then," Morgan said. "Will you let me take the rope off your wrist, now, or would you rather do it yourself?"

Becca offered her wrist across the table. Morgan took it gently – Morgan was always gentle with her; there was no need to be anxious – and smiled.

"I know it seems odd, when I'm just going to be tying you up again," she said, her fingers tugging the bight end to release the knot and unwrapping the rope from Becca's wrist. "I just don't want to risk you tripping on a loose end or getting it caught on something, on the deck."

Becca nodded her understanding watching Morgan straighten and re-coil the rope.

"What ..." Becca hesitated to ask the question, but was anxious enough to know she needed to. "What about Lynn? What will they be doing while you, umm ..."

Lynn looked up at the sound of their name.

"Reading their book, I imagine," Morgan said. "But really, whatever they want." The vagueness was not reassuring.

"Lynn will be heading back to their cabin," Lynn said steadily, "and yes, continuing to read their book." They looked at Becca. She tried not to flinch. "You don't need to worry about me," they said. "Morgan's right that by reading my book I'll be doing what I want, but even beyond that ..." Lynn paused, and Becca reminded herself she didn't need to be afraid of them. "Are you concerned about how I'll feel, or about me interacting?" they asked.

"Both?" Becca said, and even in her own ears, her voice sounded small.

"This isn't my scene," Lynn said softly. "It's very much between you and Morgan, and I don't have a place in that. I'm going back to my cabin because it doesn't have a hatch leading up to the mast. You can have your privacy, and you truly don't need to worry about me inserting myself, or even watching."

"And ... you're okay with that?" Becca asked. Lynn nodded.

"It's far from the first time Morgan's played without me," they said gently. "It's part of the whole poly thing, and I don't expect you to understand it, but I hope you can believe me when I say that I'm happy to give you two time together. I love Morgan, and I want her to enjoy herself. I like you, and I hope you can have a good experience with her. But I don't need to be part of that."

Becca nodded uncertainly.

"I promise it's okay," Lynn said. "I told you before that she won't offer you anything that would hurt me if you accepted. That's still true."

Becca nodded again, and Lynn smiled. It was probably meant to be comforting.

"Are you okay?" they asked. "Because if you don't need me, I'm going to take my book back to my cabin and leave you to it."

Becca blushed, but nodded again. Lynn stood, and walked through the kitchen, this time closing the door behind them.

Becca looked at Morgan awkwardly.

"You can still back out," Morgan said. "I'm comfortable with this, and so is Lynn, but you're allowed to not be."

"No," Becca said, taking a breath. "I'm okay. I just ... don't want to accidentally hurt them, or take something that's theirs."

"My time is *mine*, Becca," Morgan said firmly. "I'd like to spend it with you, if you're okay with that."

"Okay," Becca said, glancing around the cabin. "Umm. So. I guess we need to go outside?" Morgan nodded.

"That would seem to be the next step," Morgan agreed, sliding off the bench around the kitchen end of the table. She picked up the Tuff Cuts and the carabiner of rope and put them back in the duffel bag.

"Since we're going back on deck, you'll need your buoyancy aid," Morgan said. She retrieved the bright yellow vest and held it out for Becca before slipping into her own black harness. It took Morgan longer to get into her harness because she had to fasten a pair of straps that passed between her legs. Despite its embarrassing shade, Becca was grateful that her own PFD was just a zipper and three buckles around the front. The nightshirt felt short enough without crotch straps rucking it up.

"Once you're tied to the mast," Morgan went on, "we can take it off again, let you experience the full sensation of the rope against your chest." Becca shivered at the thought, but it wasn't entirely unpleasant. This was what she had asked for, wasn't it? "Until then, though, the rules about buoyancy aids on deck are there for a reason."

"Keeping me safe?" Becca ventured, and Morgan nodded.

"That's always the goal," she said. "Are you ready?" Becca nodded, and Morgan carefully slid back and removed panels from the hatch. She stopped to pick up the duffle bag, then led Becca up the companionway and into the cockpit.

Ten

Most of the light in the cockpit had been spilling over from the cabin. As Morgan replaced the panels and slid the hatch shut, Becca's eyes struggled to adjust to the dimness. The single light at the top of the mast still left the deck as a mass of shadows. At least, Becca supposed, anything they did at the mast wouldn't be terribly visible to somebody glancing out over the water.

"Are you ready for this?" Morgan asked, extending a hand.

"Probably not," Becca admitted, but put her hand in Morgan's and let herself be led over the moulded-in benches, out of the cockpit, and onto the deck.

Morgan's grip was firm, but the pressure drawing Becca along the side deck was gentle. The breeze off the lake was cooler than she would have expected, though the fibreglass deck was still warm and she could feel the texture against her bare feet. They were nearly to the bow when Morgan stopped beside a softly glowing skylight where the cabin roof sloped down to the deck.

"That's the forward cabin down there," Morgan said, "where you'll be sleeping." She stepped up onto the raised area, pulling Becca along behind her. "Don't worry; the roof is sturdy enough. But the mast is back here. Mind your toes."

Becca wasn't sure exactly what she had been imagining; maybe just a vertical wooden post? In front of her, though, a metal rod almost as thick as her forearm seemed to be mounted along the forward side of the much larger metal mast; thick ropes ran from the rear of the mast to angled guides positioned to either side.

"As long as you stay forward of the mast, you'll be fine," Morgan assured her, setting the duffle bag down to its left, "but if you stray back too far and stub your toe, that's not a lot of fun."

Becca nodded, hanging back a little. Actually on the deck, barely lit by the light far above, the mast seemed very large and the deck very small amid a lot of water. She could see the dark mass of island looming off to the side, the unlit nature preserve seeming both distant and empty. Morgan still held her hand, and that contact was some comfort. Morgan looked back at Becca and smiled gently, pulling the other woman up to stand beside her. She slipped an arm around Becca's shoulders, barely perceptible through the thick padding of the PFD.

"It's lovely, isn't it?" Morgan asked, gesturing to the lake and sky even as gentle pressure guided Becca back towards the mast. "This quiet stillness is one of the things I like best about anchoring, rather than staying at a marina." The only sound between her words was a gentle lapping of the lake at the hull of the boat, and Becca could feel it moving slightly beneath her. She nodded.

"I'm not sure if you've ever been up close with a mast before," Morgan said, and Becca shook her head. Morgan smiled gently. "Well, this is the mast itself, here," she indicated the thick post, "and heading astern from it is the boom. The blue canvas is the cover over the mainsail."

Becca reached out hesitantly to touch it, and Morgan nodded encouragement.

"None of this is going to break if you lean on it; it carries most of the force that propels the boat, so nothing you can do will harm it." Morgan indicated the pole mounted on the front of the mast. "The whisker pole is the one piece you might not want to grab; it's only attached at one end, so you *might* be able to knock it out of its socket. It still wouldn't be an issue, but it would take a minute to re-mount and it's not something I'd want to trust my weight to."

"So all I have to do to get a break," Becca tried a joke, "is manage to knock that piece just right?"

"Becca," Morgan said seriously, and her hands on Becca's shoulders were firm as she turned the shorter woman to face her. "If you need a break, all you need to do is tell me."

Becca looked away, scanning the deck rather than meeting Morgan's gaze. "I was joking?" she offered lamely.

Morgan's finger was gentle but irresistible as she used it to raise Becca's chin, forcing the eye contact. "I know," she said, "but I'm not."

Becca nodded awkwardly, and Morgan moved her finger to stroke Becca's cheek. It took effort not to move away, but Becca didn't *want* to. This was where she wanted to be. Even if it was A Lot.

"You're okay," Morgan assured her. "You're still allowed to back out, you know."

Becca nodded. "I know," she said, glancing briefly at Morgan's face. She didn't look upset. How was Morgan always so patient with her? "I don't really want to? I'm sorry I made a dumb joke."

"It's okay," Morgan said again. "You didn't do anything wrong. It just needed to be said, when you raised the point. Okay?"

"Okay," Becca said. Her gaze followed the ropes from the mast, and she reached for the opportunity of a more neutral topic. "Where do those ropes go?"

"Those are the sheets for the mainsail. They come down through the guides here, on the deck, and similar ones further back, so we can control the sails mostly from the cockpit," Morgan explained. "That can be important, with a small crew, especially when we run into weather."

"Sheets?" Becca asked. "Like the sail itself?"

"The lines on a boat that control the sail are called sheets," Morgan said. "I'm not sure why that's the term, but it helps distinguish them from the other lines we use, like for docking." She grinned and indicated the duffle bag she had set alongside the guide for the sheets. "Technically speaking, the only ropes on this deck are in that bag, there."

Becca blushed, looking at the bag. "Umm. I guess that's why we're up here?" she ventured.

Morgan smiled, "Yes, I suppose that is why we're up here. Though I do enjoy just spending the time with you, too." Carefully, she transferred Becca's hand to the mast, giving her something to hold for balance. "Is that your way of telling me to get on with it?"

Becca's blush deepened, and she gripped the main sheet tightly. "I mean ... I guess?" she said.

"Well, then," Morgan grinned at her, encouraged by this small initiative. Keeping her movements slow, she knelt beside the rope bag and unzipped it. She watched Becca's reactions as she worked, selecting twelve metres of the 8mm hemp and freeing the rope from its hank. Keeping her movements predictable, Morgan found the ends and pulled the rope through a loose fist to find the bight. Becca seemed to do better when she knew what was happening, so Morgan stuck exactly to what she had demonstrated in the cabin. She could see Becca's chest move with her breathing, a little fast, but the other woman's eyes were on Morgan's hands rather than searching the deck for an escape route.

Without standing again, Morgan crossed the short distance between her and Becca. Gently, she moved her right hand to rest on the outside of Becca's left knee, inside the nightdress but just above the hem. She felt her friend tense up, and waited a few breaths to give her time to process the sensation before asking, "How are you doing?"

"I'm okay," Becca said, and if her voice was shaky and her knuckles white around the main-sheet, it was still her choice to say. Morgan smiled, sliding her hand several centimetres higher, and Becca caught her breath. "Can you ..." she struggled with the words, "what ... what's going to ..."

Morgan sat back, maintaining the gentle contact, and looked up at Becca's face. "What am I going to do, here?" she prompted. Becca nodded tightly.

"I'm going to start with a double column tie on your thighs, here," Morgan said, a gentle squeeze on 'here'. "Just like you saw on Lynn's wrists. I'm going to keep your legs a bit apart like this, for balance, because it's important that you feel safe here. Once that's done, that's when I'll ask you to shuffle over so the whisker pole is at your back. The centre of the tie will go back to the mast, at which point you'll be nice and secure."

"Why ..." Becca took another shaky breath. "Why so high? Or so low? Or ..."

It took Morgan a moment to parse the question, hear the real concern prompting it. "Do you need me to take my hand off your leg?" she asked, as gently as she could.

"I ..." Becca hesitated. "I don't know?" Morgan could feel her shaking under her hand, but listened carefully to her words. "Just ... why?"

Morgan nodded. "If you need me to back off, you can tell me at any time. As for why here ..." Morgan paused a moment to order her thoughts. "If I were restraining your ankles or calves, any loss of balance would put a lot of pressure on your knees, all at once. If I were any lower on your thighs," she probed down to the hollow at the back of Becca's knee, brushing the tendons to either side, "I'd be putting pressure on the tendons, here."

Becca nodded slowly, not quite meeting Morgan's eyes but clearly working to process the information.

"The most important thing here is to keep you safe," Morgan said. "Any higher on the thigh, of course, and I'd worry more about the femoral artery. Even here, I'm going to keep it fairly loose."

Becca hadn't expected Morgan's hand under her nightgown. It was okay; Morgan wasn't doing anything bad. But it was scary and sudden and ... it was part of keeping her safe. Morgan was always trying to keep her safe.

Becca nodded again, trying to take it all in. The words at least provided one anchor point of logic she could follow. Morgan's hand, warm against her thigh was another point of stability. The rope — no, the sheet — from the mast was another anchor point, the thick rope firm in her grip. She clung to these things, trying to make them enough to hold on to. She could do this.

"Are you okay to go forward?" Morgan asked, and Becca nodded again. She watched Morgan move slowly, clearly trying to be non-threatening, and reminded herself she was safe. As the double strand of rope was pressed against her thigh, Morgan's hand holding it in place, Becca reminded herself that she *did* know what to expect. This was the same thing she had seen Morgan do with Lynn's wrists, and that hadn't been frightening.

That also hadn't been on her thighs, alone, in the darkness.

The rope was rough as Morgan passed it around her legs, but not uncomfortable. Morgan's hands were confident, her touch reassuring as she smoothed the rope into even, parallel bands. Becca gripped the mainsheet, closed her eyes, and tried to concentrate on the memory of the demonstration in the cosy cabin. That was right. Think about the technique, the demonstration, not the hands moving under the hem of her borrowed nightshirt. Not the knowledge that her panties were hanging off the back of the boat rather than providing her even minimal protection.

The steady, anchoring pressure of Morgan's hand against Becca's leg receded. Becca felt the tension on the top and bottom ropes shift against her legs as Morgan twisted the ends together. She took careful, deliberate breaths as Morgan passed the bight end between Becca's thighs and the longer end between her knees. Becca clung to the sheet as Morgan's arms wrapped around her legs, and she braced herself for the sudden jerk of tension as Morgan knotted the rope on the other side.

"You're doing so well," Morgan told her, her voice nothing but praise.

Becca didn't feel like she was doing well. She was doing her best. Morgan said she was doing well. She closed her eyes and took another breath.

"That's right," Morgan said, and Becca both felt and heard the other woman move around behind her. Morgan cinched up the second half of the knot, and the pressure of multiple strands of rope pulled Becca's legs closer together. Becca shifted her feet a little, adjusting her balance.

"You're doing just fine," Morgan assured her, voice gentle. Was it deliberate, the way her words helped Becca track her position on the deck? Morgan was beside her again, a hand back on Becca's thigh, and it was surprising how much that point of contact helped.

"I'm just going to wrap this a few more times around the centre," Morgan told her. She reached through for the rope, as she had before, but this time Morgan's hand brushed the skin of Becca's inner thighs.

Suddenly, it was all too much. The touch, the rope, the moistness between her legs. That wasn't right. What if Morgan noticed that reaction?

"No," Becca said hastily. "Wait ..." Her mind raced, but more words refused to come.

"I heard no," Morgan said, her own voice calm and steady. Confident. She abandoned the rope pulled partway through, but left her hand on the outside of Becca's leg. "What do you need?"

Becca struggled to get her thoughts in order. She knew she was being ridiculous. Morgan's hand had made contact this time because her legs were closer together, now. That was all. She tried to master her reaction.

"I'm sorry," was all Becca managed to say.

"Do you need me to back off?" Morgan offered, voice still gentle, hand already lighter against Becca's leg.

"No, please?" Becca felt herself on the edge of panic. She was only barely holding on *with* Morgan's support. Offending her friend, or making her pull away, would just make everything worse. "Don't leave me?"

"It's okay," Morgan told her, and her hand remained warm against Becca's skin. "You're safe. I'm right here with you."

Becca took a few shaky breaths, struggling to get herself back under control. Morgan gave her that time, patient with her. Gentle. It was okay.

"Can you tell me what's wrong, hon?" Morgan asked. Becca shook her head helplessly.

Morgan nodded, taking Becca's left hand with her free one before removing the hand on her leg. She stood up, standing directly in front of Becca. Slowly, she reached out and brushed tears from Becca's cheek with a gentle finger. Becca couldn't meet her eyes.

"I'm not going to hurt you," Morgan said, squeezing her hand gently. "But I'm not a mind reader. I need to know what's going on, Becca."

Becca just shook her head. "I'm being dumb," she mumbled, looking at the deck. "It's nothing."

"It's not dumb," Morgan was insistent, and very much *there*, in her space. Becca took half a step backwards, shifting at the last moment as the rope on the deck found its way under her foot. Morgan's grip on her hand tightened, and she moved her other hand to steady Becca's shoulder. The contact helped Becca keep her balance, but did not decrease the intensity at all.

"I can't," Becca said, unable to keep her voice from shaking.

"You don't have to," Morgan told her. "You're safe. Let me help keep you safe. Tell me what you can't do."

"I don't ..." Becca shook her head. "I'm just ... reacting wrong."

"You're allowed to react," Morgan said. "You're allowed to feel whatever you feel. It's really okay." Her eyes searched Becca's face. "Would you like me to untie you, now? I promise it's okay to say yes."

The thought of Morgan's hands between her legs again, even to untie her, had Becca shaking her head. "I don't ... we were going to do a thing?" she said, grasping for something she could understand. If not comfort, at least the *predictability* of their prior agreement.

Morgan's voice was a little firmer, now, demanding more than coaxing. "In that case, I need you to tell me what happened, what made things go not-okay. You need to help me keep you safe."

Becca looked down. "I'm sorry," she said.

"When you're ready," Morgan prompted. Patient, but uncompromising.

Becca didn't *want* to tell her. Didn't want her to know. Didn't want to lie to her.

She needed to help Morgan keep her safe.

Becca's mind raced, but only went in useless circles.

Morgan was still watching her, still waiting for an explanation.

"Your hand on the rope," Becca tried, still struggling some with the words. "When it brushed so close ..."

Morgan nodded encouragingly. Becca felt herself blush.

"I don't ..." she said, and still couldn't put together a working sentence. "I felt ... something," she admitted, "but I don't *want* to."

"Something?" Morgan asked.

Becca watched her put it together, the words and the blush and the things she could not say.

"Oh, sweetheart," Morgan said, pulling her into a hug. Becca didn't resist, but found herself clinging to the dark-haired woman. "It's okay. Really it is."

Becca fought back tears. There was no reason to be crying.

"It's absolutely normal to become aroused with bondage," Morgan told her, rubbing her back gently. "Especially working around the thighs like that. I'm never going to be offended by that."

"But I don't *want* to," Becca said, and the tears refused to stay out of her voice.

"You don't have to," Morgan assured her, and she was certain in a way Becca couldn't even imagine being. "Bodies do what they do. You're the one who makes the decision what to do about it, or what not to do about it."

Becca nodded shakily.

"You're allowed to be aroused and choose not to do anything about it," Morgan said. "I wasn't intending to take this in a more sexual direction. That would have involved a lot more discussion, and you making a decision that you wanted to go there with me." Morgan tapped Becca's head lightly. "You, not part of your body that doesn't even have a brain."

Becca nodded and hugged back convulsively. "Thank you," she said.

Morgan kissed her cheek gently, and moved back out of the hug. A gentle hand wiped away the tears still on Becca's face, and she asked, "Feeling better?"

Becca nodded. She still clung to Morgan's hand, and Morgan squeezed it gently.

"Are you sure you want to keep going?" Morgan asked, and Becca nodded again, more firmly.

"Okay, then," Morgan said, and sank back to the deck, releasing Becca's hand and moving her grip to Becca's calf. "I'm going to be a little more careful, but do tell me if it gets overwhelming again."

Becca nodded, and took hold of the mainsheet again, for balance. 'More careful' apparently meant that Morgan was pushing the ends of the rope through from front to back and picking them up on the other side, rather than pulling them through in her hand.

Becca was distinctly aware of the texture of the rope against her inner thighs, the way pressure on the rope sent vibrations through the whole tie as Morgan filled the gap by wrapping the outer coils together. It was easier, though, knowing that Morgan was not going to push further than this.

She forced herself to breathe, and tried to focus on the feel of the rope rather than worrying about what might happen next. Even the necessary jerk as Morgan tied off the last knot was just sensation, and the mast's support helped keep Becca steady.

Morgan squeezed Becca's ankle and smiled when Becca looked down at her. "How are you doing?" she asked.

"It's ... very interesting," Becca said, only blushing a little. She shifted her weight from foot to foot, but the mass of rope between her legs meant that even moving them closer together was no longer an option.

"Any discomfort, numbness, or tingling?" Morgan asked, and Becca remembered the questions from the discussion inside. She shook her head.

"In that case," Morgan grinned up at her, "are you ready to be tied to the mast?"

Was she? Becca took a breath. That was what she had asked for. What she had wanted. What she did want.

Becca nodded.

With a final reassuring squeeze to Becca's ankle, Morgan returned to the duffle bag. Becca watched her take out another hank of rope. Morgan stood up and walked over to stand in front of Becca. Gently, she took both Becca's hands in her own

"May I take your glasses, now?" Morgan asked quietly. Her glasses? She supposed it made sense. Becca nodded.

Moving slowly, Morgan removed them from Becca's face. She folded the arms inward and tucked the eyeglasses into her blouse. Becca smiled shakily, and Morgan smiled back.

"That's right," Morgan said, guiding Becca into position against the mast. "Just over here, now, back to the mast. You're doing fine."

Eleven

Without her glasses, Becca's world narrowed. There was Morgan, directly in front of her, and nothing beyond but an indistinct blur of light and shadow. The whisker pole was hard and solid against her back, even through the PFD. With only a single layer of nightgown between skin and mast, the metal was cool against her bum. Becca was acutely aware of Morgan in front of her, the way one of Morgan's hands was able to hold both of hers. A small bubble of fear rose within her.

Morgan must have seen something in her face. "What's wrong?" she asked, watching Becca's eyes.

Becca fought the urge to look away. "Trapped?" she managed, just the single word, but it was enough.

"Only as much as you want to be," Morgan said. A half-step back gave Becca more room to breathe, and Morgan squeezed her hands gently. "Do you remember how to get out of this, Becca?"

"Ask you," Becca mumbled, and was rewarded with Morgan's smile.

"That's right."

They were still so close together that looking down left Becca staring at Morgan's chest. Morgan's breasts were framed and separated by the thick black harness she wore. And they weren't an appropriate place to be looking.

Becca quickly shifted her gaze to the other woman's shoulder. There was a small brand tag sewn on the right side of the harness, only a little blurry without her glasses, and Becca forced herself to focus on that.

Morgan reached out to brush hair from Becca's face, tucking a stray wisp of it behind her ear. "I'm on your side here."

Becca mumbled something Morgan couldn't quite make out.

"What was that, hon?"

Becca blushed and shook her head.

Morgan stroked her face again, keeping her touch light. "Tell me," she insisted gently. Becca had been far too close to the edge to ignore anything she said.

Becca blushed more deeply. "On my side," she mumbled again, "right in front of me, behind me ...." She ducked her head, trying to hide behind her hair.

Morgan grinned and ran her hand lightly down Becca's left arm, from shoulder to wrist. Becca shivered under her touch, and Morgan watched the blush spread from her face down her chest.

"Is that such a bad thing?" Morgan asked.

Becca shook her head, blush deepening, eyes locked on Morgan's shoulder rather than her face.

"You *could* tell me to back off," Morgan teased gently, "but you're not doing that. You're blushing and hiding your face, but your words keep saying 'yes, go on'." She leaned in to plant a quick kiss on Becca's cheek, gone almost before the other wo-man noticed. "And you can trust me to listen to your words."

Becca just stood there, blushing and trembling, with both her hands caught in Morgan's left and her back against the mast. It was a powerfully erotic vision. Or it would have been, if Morgan weren't so afraid of hurting her. The amount of trust Becca was handing her was breathtaking, but she was *so* close to breaking.

Deliberately, Morgan reined in her reaction a little more, letting go of Becca's hands and patting her face reassuringly.

"You're no more trapped than you want to be," she said again, sinking back down to the deck. She concentrated on joining the new rope to the run-ning end of the one around Becca's legs. "Are you ready to move on?"

Ready to move on? Becca took a breath and nodded. She wasn't sure what to do with her hands, without Morgan holding them in front of her. With the mast directly behind her, she couldn't reach out for the mainsheet. She clasped her hands in front of her, thumbs rubbing over one another nervously.

She could hear Morgan moving behind her, felt the tension as the other woman wrapped the end of the ropes around the mast. The rope on her thighs tugged her further back, closer against the metal post. Becca took another breath and tried not to resist.

She could feel Morgan push a bundle of rope between her legs. Push, not reach in to pull it through. Going easy on her. Trying not to scare her.

There was no reason to be scared.

Morgan's arms stretched around the outside of her legs, grabbing the rope bundle. She pulled it back between Becca's knees, then away. Around the mast again, probably. Then the rope, pushed between her thighs again, and back between the knees. Repetition. Simple. Becca tried to relax into the pattern of it.

After several more passes, and a few more minutes to interact with the mast rather than Becca's legs, Morgan sat back on her heels.

"How does that feel?" she asked. "All nice and secure?"

Becca shuffled her feet on the deck. She had maybe a centimetre or two of motion, forwards or to the side, before the rope stopped her.

"Okay, I guess," she said. "I'm not uncomfortable?"

Morgan nodded. She stood up and moved right back in front of Becca. Very close. "How about now?"

Oh. So Morgan *did* know how her nearness was affecting Becca, and she was *enjoying* it. Becca felt her blush returning, and a flip-flopping in her stomach that wasn't quite fear. She tried to look down, found herself accidentally staring at Morgan's chest again.

"Umm." she said, wishing her face didn't betray her quite so easily. "Maybe a bit more uncomfortable?"

Morgan grinned and brushed away the hair that had fallen in Becca's face again. Her blush really was adorable.

"Now, since you're all nice and tied up, and not likely to fall off the deck, shall we get this buoyancy aid off you?" Morgan's finger trailed along the vee of the yellow buoyancy aid's neckline. Becca swallowed hard, and Morgan waited for her to find the words she needed.

"Are you flirting with me, right now?" Becca's voice trembled.

Morgan blinked. How was this even a question?

"Yes," Morgan said. "I am very aggressively flirting with you right now. I am teasing you and enjoying watching you blush and squirm, but you can tell me to back off and I will."

"Okay," Becca said.

Morgan smiled, but she kept her voice a little gentler as she asked, "You're okay with me flirting with you? Or with taking off the buoyancy aid?"

Becca just nodded, blushing harder. Morgan waited for her to elaborate, but she just ducked her head, hiding behind her hair and fidgeting with her hands.

"Both?" Morgan asked, and Becca nodded again.

Morgan stepped closer, watching Becca's face for signs she was going too far. She placed Becca's left hand on Morgan's own right shoulder, just outside the harness strap, then moved Becca's right hand to Morgan's left shoulder. With Becca's hands thus out of the way, Morgan slowly unbuckled the bottom-most fastener on Becca's buoyancy aid.

Becca squirmed a little, but the rope held her thighs to the mast. She wasn't going anywhere. She couldn't meet Morgan's eyes, but she also didn't remove her hands from Morgan's shoulders or say no.

Morgan kept her eyes on Becca's face, her fingers finding the sides of the second buckle, squeezing them in. She could feel Becca's hands tighten on her shoulders as the second buckle fell open.

"I'm not going to hurt you," Morgan whispered, even as her hands reached for the final buckle on the front of Becca's buoyancy aid. "You can stop me if you need to." Becca nodded, and Morgan unfastened the buckle.

The sound of the zipper's slider moving down and the teeth separating was distinctive on the quiet deck. Morgan paused, waiting for Becca to relax at least a tiny bit.

"You're okay with me flirting with you," Morgan said, watching Becca's face carefully. "Are you still okay with me touching your upper body? Your shoulders, your arms, your torso?"

She had asked this inside, but Becca had been calmer there. The woman refused to ask her to back off, so she needed to check in, to make sure she wasn't pushing too hard.

Becca nodded.

"Am I allowed to touch your face?" Morgan continued. "Brush your hair?" Another nod. "Your breasts?" Becca ducked her head, blushing again, but she still nodded.

"Are you more scared right now, or excited?" Morgan asked.

"I ... don't know?" Becca said, her voice nearly lost in the darkness.

Morgan brushed the back of a hand against Becca's cheek. "You'll be okay," she promised, and moved her hands to the padded shoulders of the buoyancy aid. Positioning her thumbs to lightly caress Becca's collarbone, Morgan slowly traced the edges of the buoyancy aid's neckline. She reached the now-open zipper, and the sides of the buoyancy aid parted easily.

Gently, Morgan removed Becca's left hand from her shoulder and guided it through the arm hole, then the right. Only the friction between Becca's back and the mast still held the buoyancy aid up, and Morgan leaned in, one hand to either side of Becca, to get a better grip on it.

The way Becca got blushy and shy with Morgan's arms around her, even for such a mundane purpose, was irresistible. Morgan gave her a quick kiss on the nose before pulling the buoyancy aid free.

She tossed it carefully to the deck beside the rope bag and returned her attention to Becca.

"Are you doing okay?" Morgan whispered in her ear, and Becca nodded.

Becca crossed her arms over her chest, shivering slightly as Morgan pulled back. It wasn't so much that she was cold, but the sudden absence of nylon and foam padding had her feeling very exposed. The speculative way Morgan looked at her just made her blush harder, and she found herself hiding her face behind her hands.

Morgan grinned, and her voice turned teasing. "Are you being all shy now, Becca?" Becca blushed harder, but in a way the teasing was easier to take than the gentle reminders that she could stop if she needed to. It was uncomfortable, sure, but it wasn't the same temptation to run away from something she wanted.

"And what would you do," Morgan teased, "If I took those hands away? If they were all tied up and you couldn't hide behind them any more?"

Becca could only squirm, covering her face and trying to will the blush away. It didn't work.

"Would you be okay with that?" Morgan asked, and her tone had shifted. Back to the friend who was on *her* side, regardless.

Becca nodded.

"I need a verbal yes or no on this one, Becca," Morgan insisted quietly.

"Okay," Becca managed, still hiding behind her hands.

She could hear Morgan moving aside, rumma-ging in the bag for more rope, stepping back in front of her. Felt Morgan's hand grasp her wrist firmly, pulling it away from her face.

"Wait," Becca whimpered, back pressed hard against the mast. Morgan stopped.

"I heard wait," Morgan said quietly. "What's go-ing on?"

Becca shook her head, tried to pull her hand free. Morgan let it go easily. She looked concerned, not angry.

"Can you tell me what's wrong, hon?" she asked quietly.

"I'm scared," Becca said, hugging herself with her arms.

"I know," Morgan told her. "How can I help?"

"I'm scared," Becca said again, "and it's *wrong*."

"It's okay," Morgan told her. "You're allowed to be scared, and you're allowed to ask for help with it. How can I help?" Becca chewed her lower lip, trying to think.

"I don't know," she said. "I don't know what's go-ing to happen. And I know I'm meant to trust you. But I ..." she shook her head.

Morgan nodded. "I'm hearing that you're scared because you don't know what's going to happen next," she said.

"Yeah," Becca whispered. That was part of it.

"Would it help if I laid it out for you?" Morgan offered. "Or do you just need me to back off?"

"Can we try it?" Becca asked. She didn't want to stop now. But she didn't know if she could con-tinue.

Morgan nodded.

"We can do that," she said. "So, I said I was going to take your hands away?"

Becca nodded shyly. She had said that. It had sounded good at the time, before it was all too much.

"What I'm thinking is a double column, to hold your wrists together, and then tying them to the mast over your head for a little while," Morgan said patiently. "Then I can say nice things to you, and you can blush and squirm all you want, but you won't be able to cover your face."

Becca blushed, and her hands rose to her face again.

"Yes," Morgan grinned. "Exactly like that."

Becca blushed harder.

"If I leave them above your head too long," Morgan went on, "they might get uncomfortable. So while they're up there, I'll go ahead and tie your torso to the mast, so you are nice and secure. Then I can reposition your hands, and tie them lower in front of you. Does that sound okay?"

"It sounds like a lot," Becca said. Morgan nodded.

"It is a lot. We can take it slow," she promised. "If you get uncomfortable, you can always stop it. Or we can discuss and change it now. But you asked me to tell you what I had planned, and that's what I was thinking."

Becca nodded, "Are you going to be teasing me again?" she asked.

Morgan grinned. "Oh, definitely," she said. "Watching you squirm is *fun*." Becca hid her face again.

"Okay," she said.

Morgan's touch was gentle as she pulled Becca's hands away from her face. Becca blushed harder, but didn't try to fight it. She was still smiling as Becca ducked her head, trying to get what shelter she could behind stray strands of hair.

Morgan moved Becca's hands to the waist strap of her own harness, one to either side of where the chest straps met over her navel.

"You can keep your hands there," Morgan instructed.

Becca nodded, very aware of how low on her friend her hands were resting, but doing as she was told. She stared at the buckle between her hands, trying not to think about it. Morgan had already said she wouldn't move it in a more sexual direction. She could trust that.

Morgan's hands were gentle, but they moved too fast for Becca to follow each step. She recognised the stages, at least. Morgan coiling the rope around both wrists, a hand always between Becca's face and the loose ends as she pulled them around. Wrapping the rope between Becca's wrists. The quick tug as Morgan cinched them together in the middle. She brought bight and loose end together, on top of Becca's wrists, and tied them off. It was done.

"You can let go now," Morgan said, taking a step back, and Becca blushed, pulling her hands away from the buckle. Morgan reached out to brush the hair off Becca's face and tuck it behind her ear. "Has anybody told you how cute it is when you blush like that?" Morgan asked.

Becca felt her blush deepen, and her joined hands automatically began to move towards her face. They hadn't moved far, however, before they came up short. Morgan was holding the loose end of the rope in a low fist, and Becca couldn't raise her hands any further.

"That's right," Morgan said, and her voice was somewhere between gentle and teasing. "You can't hide it any more. Though it's adorable when you try." Becca's face was burning, but not being able to move her hands … wasn't as bad as she had feared. It felt helpless, and embarrassing, but she knew Morgan wasn't going to hurt her.

"Of course," Morgan teased, "If you really want your hands up higher, I can work with that." She stepped forward, a gentle grip on Becca's arms guiding them up until the rope between her wrists was almost resting on top of her head.

"Still comfortable?" Morgan asked, and waited for Becca's nod before stepping to the side of the mast to tie off the rope that would hold Becca's wrists firmly out of her way. She stood there for a moment, just watching, and Becca didn't feel any less self-conscious under her gaze.

"Morgan?" Becca asked quietly.

"Yeah?"

"Am I doing this okay?" The question sounded stupid even in Becca's ears, but it was the one that had her on edge.

Morgan smiled and her hand on Becca's cheek was gentle. "You're doing *so* well. Are you feeling okay?" Becca shrugged.

"I'm nervous. I'm afraid that I'm going to do something wrong and disappoint you."

"Oh, sweetheart," Morgan said, "you are so very far from disappointing me right now." Another gentle pat on the cheek, and the look that travelled from Becca's bare toes against the deck to her wrists tied back to the mast left the woman feeling very naked despite the nightgown that covered her. "Besides," Morgan said, her tone turning teasing again, "one of the lovely things about bondage is that you can't do anything wrong. You can't really do anything at all."

Becca blushed and wiggled, but Morgan was right; she really wasn't going anywhere.

"Though it truly is adorable when you try," Morgan said, and Becca blushed even harder than before.

Morgan moved close, her hand tracing along the neckline of Becca's borrowed nightgown before gliding down over her breasts and down her sides to the waist.

"You remember what I said was coming next?" she asked, and Becca nodded. "You're still doing a bit of wiggling," Morgan noted. "And how much easier will it be to stay still with your torso anchored firmly?" Becca said nothing, but the blush still on her face and the way she looked aside answered for her.

"You stay right there," Morgan instructed, turning back to the bag for another length of rope. "Not that I suppose you have a choice."

Twelve

Becca watched from the mast. The hank of rope Morgan grabbed this time seemed larger, which she supposed made sense; her body was a lot thicker around than her wrists were. She almost managed to meet Morgan's gaze as the other woman stepped back towards her, looking aside at the last moment. Morgan stroked her cheek again, turning Becca's face to meet her eyes when she continued shy.

"How are you doing?" she asked, reaching up to touch Becca's hands. "Are your hands still feeling okay?" Morgan's own fingers felt hot against the skin; Becca's heart was pounding in her chest, but she *knew* she was safe with Morgan. Wasn't she? Becca nodded.

"Okay," Morgan said. "I'm going to work relatively quickly here. Tell me if your hands start going funny, or if you need me to slow down what I'm doing."

"Is this ... dangerous?" Becca asked. She knew she was supposed to trust Morgan; she *did* trust Morgan, but she still had to ask the question.

Morgan stopped what she was doing and met Becca's eyes.

"Not particularly," Morgan said, and the calm certainty in her voice eased some of Becca's fear. "It's just that hands can go to sleep when you hold them up for too long, and it can be uncomfortable when the feeling gets back into them." Becca nodded; that made sense. She knew the feeling of a foot falling asleep, and the pins and needles of returning sensation weren't pleasant.

"Thank you," Becca said.

"Of course," Morgan said, and there was no teasing in her voice this time. "Any time you have questions, or you're not sure of something, you can ask me. Especially if it's about safety." Becca nodded again; Morgan smiled and patted her shoulder before stepping to the side of the mast. The hand Morgan passed behind Becca's back, between her and the whisker pole, was warm and gentle.

"What I'm doing here," she explained, even as she pulled rope into position under Becca's breasts, "Is just another single column tie." Becca tried to pay attention to her friend's words, but the pressure of twisted hemp through a single layer of cotton knit was distracting. She could feel the friction of the rope being pulled between her back and the mast, but she made the effort to focus on Morgan's words.

"You can do a lot with just the two ties you learned tonight," Morgan was saying. Becca nodded. This was just an educational demonstration, she reminded herself, not anything more ... intimate.

Morgan continued wrapping rope around Becca's torso, laying each double strand perfectly against the ones before. Becca lost count of how many times Morgan pulled rope behind her, around her stomach, and back behind. With her hands restrained, she couldn't reach down to count the strands by feel, but she was sure it was more than four.

"You doing okay?" Morgan asked, her rope hand against Becca's lower back. "I'm nearly done with this part."

"Yeah," Becca said. The pressure of the rope over her ribcage was gentle, but she was aware of its presence with every breath. "Tell me I'm safe?"

"You're safe," Morgan smiled and touched Becca's face gently. "A bit tied up, but perfectly safe."

"Thank you," Becca breathed. It didn't make sense that just hearing the words would make a difference, but whether or not it made sense, it *helped*.

"Always," Morgan said. "Are you ready to go on?" Becca nodded.

Morgan's hands were gentle as she pulled rope away from Becca's back. She threaded the tail up along Becca's spine and out the top of the wraps, pulling slowly. The friction of rope against fabric pulled Becca's nightgown up with it until she could feel the night air against her bare bum. She bit her lip and considered saying something, but by the time Morgan had finished knotting the rope, the hem had fallen back into place. Maybe Morgan hadn't noticed, Becca hoped. Certainly it hadn't been deliberate. Everything was fine.

"How's your breathing?" Morgan asked, as she cinched the knot tight.

"Okay?" Becca said. Should it be different?

"I'd like you to take a deep breath in for me," Morgan said, and Becca complied. Her lungs filled with air, her chest expanded, and she felt the pressure of the rope tighten against her.

Oh. That was why.

"How does that feel?" Morgan asked again. "Any trouble?"

"No, it's fine," Becca said. It had been a little scary at first, feeling the limits the rope enforced, but it hadn't really restricted her breathing at all.

"Good." Morgan did something else behind the mast. "Just a quick half hitch right now; I'll come back to this," she promised. "Right now, I'm going to move your hands."

Becca felt more than saw Morgan beside her, reaching up to where Becca's hands were tied. She felt warm fingers brushing her hands as they worked on the knots, and then Morgan's hand was on the rope between Becca's wrists, guiding them down in front of her and rubbing them gently. It was only with the heat of Morgan's hands around hers that Becca realised they had gone a little bit cool.

"How's that feel?" Morgan asked, still cupping Becca's hands in her own.

"Okay," Becca said. "Better?"

Morgan nodded. "Good." She smiled, and the smile turned teasing. "Don't think you're getting your hands back just yet, though," she cautioned. "I like the way you squirm when you can't hide behind them."

Becca blushed again, looking away. Morgan just grinned and kissed her cheek. With one hand on the rope extending from Becca's wrists and the other on Becca's hip for balance, Morgan lowered herself into a crouch in front of the bound woman.

Becca could feel how careful Morgan was being as she passed the rope between her legs, wrapping around the mass of bundled hemp between her thighs without touching the skin to either side. Even the steady downward pressure was gentle; Morgan tightened the tie slowly until Becca's arms were straight. The rope between Becca's wrists held her hands together almost demurely in front of her.

"Comfortable?" Morgan asked, and Becca nodded despite the blush she couldn't seem to get under control. "Good," Morgan pronounced, finishing the knot and securing the ends.

Becca tried lifting her hands, even though she knew it would be useless. They were well and truly stuck, but the way the motion transferred along the ropes to her thighs made her blush a little more deeply. Morgan stood back up and patted her shoulder.

"I'm just going to do the torso a little more securely," Morgan informed her. The pressure holding Becca back against the mast released for a moment, and Becca slumped a little. A gentle hand on her shoulder corrected her posture before Morgan tightened the rope again. Becca was drawn back, steady pressure pulling her into position. She felt hands and rope slide between herself and the mast several times before Morgan was satisfied.

"There we go," Morgan said, standing back to survey Becca. "How does that feel? Any discomfort, numbness, or tingling?" Becca shook her head.

"No, it feels okay that way," she confirmed.

"Any movement, worries that you might do something wrong?" Morgan grinned.

Becca recognised her earlier stupid comment, and burned with shame. Morgan might be teasing, but Becca had said something dumb and Morgan wouldn't forget.

"I'm sorry," she said, looking at the deck. Morgan touched her cheek and her hand was gentle, but Becca couldn't keep herself from flinching at the contact.

"Hey, now," Morgan said quietly. "None of that." Becca nodded; she needed to do better, to get control of her reactions.

"I'm sorry," Becca whispered miserably.

"You're all tied up and safe here," Morgan reminded her, "If you can't do anything, then you can't do anything wrong, remember?"

Morgan had said that before. Her feelings might be all wrong, but as long as she didn't *do* anything, she'd be safe. If she just followed Morgan's lead, just did what Morgan said, she'd be fine. Becca nodded.

"It's okay," Morgan promised. "You haven't done anything wrong. It's safe."

"Okay," Becca said, not daring to argue, but Morgan was wrong. She might not have *done* anything yet, but she shouldn't be *reacting* like this. She *knew* it was safe, and all she needed to do was hold on to that knowledge.

"That's right," Morgan said, her voice persuasive. "You're safe. You can stop trying to control everything, stop trying to think your way through. Just let it go and let yourself feel."

Morgan kept her words gentle, but there were tears in Becca's eyes and she was pressed back against the mast as if she were desperate to get away. Becca's distress was obvious, but Morgan had no idea what had happened.

"It's safe," she promised, resting a hand gently below Becca's collarbone. "Really, it's okay." Becca's eyes were wide and frightened, and she couldn't meet Morgan's for long.

"You're safe," Morgan repeated, trying to keep her voice reassuring. "Everything is fine. Can you take a breath for me?" She felt the shakiness of Becca's breathing under her hand. "That's right. Another breath. There's a good girl."

"I'm sorry," Becca was clearly struggling for words. "I shouldn't."

"You're allowed to be scared," Morgan reminded her. "You can be scared even when you know you're safe. And when you know you're safe, you can let yourself feel the fear without being caught in it. Does that make sense?"

Becca just stared at her, body trembling.

"It's okay," Morgan said again, searching for ways to help Becca relax, snippets of memory that had calmed her before. "Take a breath. That's right. You're safe. You're not doing anything wrong. I'm right here with you." She was rewarded with a tiny nod.

"You're safe," Morgan repeated. Maybe if she said it enough, Becca would be able to believe it. "You have all the control you need to keep yourself safe." Another tiny nod. Morgan took a breath. "Are you okay with my hand on you here, still?"

"Yeah," Becca said, and it was small and shaky, but it was a word rather than the frozen panic Morgan had seen a moment before.

"Okay," Morgan said slowly. Her hand remained gentle on Becca's chest, holding that point of contact. "You're safe. I see that I pushed too hard there, and I'm sorry. It's never my intent to hurt you."

"I know," Becca whispered. Morgan could see the tension across her shoulders, and her own ached in sympathy.

"What I'd like to do," Morgan said quietly, "is move my hand to your shoulder, and gently rub your shoulders and the back of your neck to help you relax. Would that be okay?"

"Okay," Becca repeated. Morgan kept her motions slow, sliding her hand from Becca's chest to her shoulder and kneading very gently.

"How are you doing?" she asked.

"Not okay," Becca admitted, as Morgan's hand moved to rub the back of her neck. "Scared."

"You know you're safe?" Morgan asked quietly.

"Yeah," Becca replied.

"And you're still scared," Morgan filled in. "And that's okay." She continued rubbing, feeling the other woman's muscles slowly release some of their tension.

"It can be interesting, sometimes," Morgan suggested, "to notice how it feels to be both scared and safe at the same time."

"Is ... that a thing?" Becca asked.

"What do you think?"

"I ... don't know?" Becca's voice was hesitant, feeling her way through unfamiliar territory. "I ... my reaction is wrong. Fight or flight ... when safe?"

Morgan watched Becca's face shift as the cognitive gears started to mesh. Yes. This was how she'd be able to get Becca back to stable ground. She just needed to choose her words very carefully.

"Your reaction is normal," Morgan corrected, rubbing more firmly as she felt Becca's trapezius respond to the massage. "But that's one of the interesting things about being tied down like this. You don't have to worry about fight or flight because you can't do either. You know you're safe, or you wouldn't be here with me. So you can let yourself feel the way your body responds to the fear without having to do anything about it."

Becca nodded slowly. Morgan waited, giving her time to process the idea, to move back to the analytical mode where she felt safe. It was all she could do, holding the space while Becca struggled with the ideas.

"Are you feeling a bit better?" Morgan asked finally.

"A bit, yeah," Becca said.

"Would you like me to untie you now?" Morgan offered. "Have you had enough?"

"I ... don't know," Becca hesitated. "I ... don't want to lose. I don't want to feel like I'm running away. I'm safe. I can ... I think I can deal with this?"

Morgan looked at her; Becca was still shaking a little and Morgan considered using her own veto to end the scene. Becca had trusted her to come this far, though, and *her* choice was to persist. Morgan had promised her all the control she needed. Stopping now just ... didn't seem like it would be fair to her.

"Do you have any idea how impressive you are?" Morgan asked. Becca blushed and shook her head.

"I'm not," she protested. "I freaked out over nothing."

"Becca," Morgan said, moving a hand to her cheek, "you were scared. And you let me help you through it. That's huge."

"But I shouldn't have *been* scared," Becca objected.

"But you were," Morgan said. "And that you trusted me anyway is a very great honour."

Becca blushed and looked aside, but Morgan lifted her face back up to meet her eyes.

"You're still all tied up, my dear," Morgan said, watching the response carefully. "You can't evade being told you're wonderful that easily." Becca just blushed a deeper shade of red, and Morgan grinned. It was going to be okay.

"I'm not, though," Becca tried to deny it.

"Mhmm," Morgan said, "but I say you are. And all you can do is stand there and take it." Morgan considered asking Becca to repeat the words of her own praise, but she remembered how hard it had been when Lynn did that to her. More intensity was not what either of them needed right now.

Becca shook her head, and Morgan allowed the woman to move away from her hand in doing so. She stepped back and looked Becca up and down before moving over to the rope bag again. Eyes still on Becca, she removed the rainbow plaid picnic mat and set it on the deck for later.

"I'm afraid, my dear," she let her tone slip towards teasing, keeping it playful, "that you are my prisoner, and if I want to say lovely things to you, I can do that." She watched Becca's eyes, softening her tone slightly as she reminded her, "You do know how to get out of this. You're no more trapped than you choose to be. But as long as we're still playing this game, I can be nice to you and there's nothing you can do to stop me."

Becca bit her lower lip and nodded, still blushing.

"And you don't get to tell yourself, either, that I'm just saying things to make you blush," Morgan continued, teasing again. "Pretty as it is when you get all shy and try to hide your face, every word I say is true." She reached out to touch Becca's face again, stroking a very warm cheek with the back of her hand.

"You're absolutely safe," Morgan told her, letting the hand trail down the side of Becca's neck, "and absolutely vulnerable." Her hand reached Becca's shoulder, and she continued stroking down the outside of her arm, noticing the goosebumps under her fingertips. "And feeling both at once, feeling my touch and knowing that I intend to both tease you and keep you safe ... how does *that* feel?"

Becca shivered, and Morgan took the woman's bound hands between her own, checking the temperature as well as giving comfort. The hands were the same temperature as the flesh above the rope, so that was good. She raised her hand to stroke along Becca's collarbone again, lightly over the curve of her breast, then down to the rope holding her to the mast. Becca wiggled under her hand as she traced the path back up, brushing ever so lightly over the nipple that was clearly visible through the single layer of nightdress. Becca tensed up as she did so, though whether it was fear or excitement was hard to tell.

"Too much?" Morgan asked, her hand still on the upper surface of Becca's breast.

"A little," Becca said in a small voice. "I'm sorry."

"Hey now," Morgan objected gently. "You're allowed to tell me no."

Becca nodded.

"Do you need me to keep my hands off your breasts, or just leave your nipples alone?"

"Nipples," Becca managed, her face hot.

"I can do that," Morgan promised, then leaned in to kiss Becca's flaming cheek. When she pulled back, both hands had moved into position to caress the tops of Becca's breasts. Becca wiggled a little inside the rope that held her to the mast, and Morgan grinned. "Comfy?"

Becca nodded and Morgan smiled, some of her own tension relaxing.

"Good," Morgan said sincerely, gazing into Becca's eyes until the other woman blushed again and looked away. Gently, Morgan stroked a line up to Becca's shoulders, fingers curling behind to massage gently.

"This is rope," Morgan said softly, and her voice now was neither teasing nor lecturing. "This mix of safety and nervousness, this not being able to move and not needing to. This connection." She caught Becca's eyes again, and thought she saw understanding. "This is rope."

They stood like that for several moments, Morgan's hands gentle on Becca's shoulders, giving her space to feel with no demands on her.

"And this is the part," Morgan said quietly, shifting her arms into a hug around Becca's body, "where I start to untie you." She worked the knot free single-handed and began unwrapping the single column she had placed around the mast, keeping one arm around Becca, her body still pressing the woman gently against the pole.

"I'm right here with you," she reminded her friend, beginning to undo the wraps around her torso, one hand guiding the loose end and the other gentle on Becca's shoulder. "Let yourself breathe."

Morgan slowly uncoiled the last wrap of rope from beneath Becca's breasts. She knew from experience how it felt, the contrast between the comfortable firmness of the rope and the freedom it left behind, but she reminded herself that it was all new to Becca. Morgan kept one hand on her friend's shoulder, an undemanding contact while Becca took a few shaky breaths.

"Still safe," Morgan reminded her, smiling gently. Only when Becca nodded did Morgan remove her hand and loosely re-coil the rope.

Morgan lay the coil aside and crouched on the deck. A gentle hand stroked Becca's calf, giving the woman time to accept the touch, then Morgan released the rope holding Becca's wrists in place.

"Are you doing okay?" she asked, taking Becca's hands in hers. Becca nodded, and Morgan moved both of her friend's hands to her left before beginning to untie the knot between her wrists. Slowly, Morgan unwound the rope, caressing Becca's wrists with every pass. Becca blushed a little, and Morgan smiled.

"You're so pretty when you blush like that," she said, taking advantage of these last moments with Becca's hands held away from her face. "And even cuter when you squirm," she teased. Becca's helpless reaction to even minor compliments was adorable, and Morgan couldn't resist.

"This isn't fair," Becca mumbled.

"Not at all," Morgan agreed. "Thank you for trusting me enough to let me tease you like this."

She finished removing the rope and rubbed the skin where it had been. Morgan smiled up at Becca. "How is this feeling?"

"Okay," Becca said, reclaiming her hands and shaking them out. "It felt okay the whole time, honestly."

Morgan nodded and retrieved the buoyancy aid from the deck before standing again. She threaded the back of the it between Becca and the mast, then helped the other woman insert her arms through the holes.

"Of course, you're pretty when you're not blushing, too," Morgan commented as she lined up the zipper at the front of the buoyancy aid. As expected, Becca hid behind her hands at that comment, leaving Morgan room to zip up the front fastener.

"Not that not-blushing seems to last very long, any more," Morgan mused, using her hands to press Becca's arms down and kissing her very pink cheek. Becca blushed harder, and Morgan gave her a quick hug before fastening the three buckles on the front of the buoyancy aid. She patted Becca's hip just below the edge of the foam filled vest, maintaining that contact as she knelt on the deck beside her friend. Untying the thigh rope to release Becca from the mast took only a moment, but the next bit would be more delicate.

"You remember this part," Morgan said, carefully pulling the rope between Becca's knees. "I'm going to be as careful as I can, but there may be some contact between your legs. Are you okay with that?" Becca nodded tensely, and Morgan squeezed her hip for reassurance.

"Can you put your hands on my shoulders, to help keep your balance?" Morgan invited.

Becca leaned forward a little, and the tension in her grip revealed anxiety she hadn't admitted in words.

"I'm not going to take this anywhere you don't want to go," Morgan promised. She untied the knot, carefully keeping her hands to the outside of Becca's legs as she pulled the rope through. Even the friction of hemp against skin made Becca shiver, and Morgan paused to check in with her friend.

"I'm okay," Becca said. "It's just ... sensation. It's interesting."

Morgan nodded, "That's right. It *is* interesting. And you're allowed to feel whatever you feel, without judgement." She continued to unwrap rope from the centre of the tie, then loosed the final knot and unwrapped the coils from around Becca's legs. Morgan quickly chained the rope for washing, then she reached up to take Becca's hands in her own.

"How are you feeling?" Morgan asked, drawing Becca with her in a sideways shuffle to where she had lain the picnic mat on the deck.

"I'm okay," Becca said. She still sounded a little shaky, but she allowed Morgan to pull her down to sit on the mat beside her. "Did I ... was I ... okay?"

Morgan smiled and brushed hair off Becca's face. "You did wonderfully. But it's not about satisfying me. I want to know about your experience."

Becca let herself be pulled into a hug. Morgan held her gently, waiting for the other woman to relax against her before stroking her hair softly. "What was it like for you?"

Becca took a shaky breath and leaned into the hug, hiding her face against Morgan's shoulder. "It was ... a lot," she said.

"Overwhelming?" Morgan suggested, and Becca nodded.

"Overwhelming," she agreed. "Terrifying. But also ... the way you were there?" she shook her head, trying to find the right words. "Like, even when I was terrified, you stayed with me and reminded me how to get out of it? You helped me get through it."

"I did the very best I could," Morgan said, acutely aware of how limited her best had been. "It was my honour, you trusting me to do that." She continued stroking Becca's hair, her hand continuing down onto the back of the buoyancy aid.

For several minutes it was enough just to hold her gently, to maintain that connection, but eventually Morgan felt Becca shift in her arms. She released the pressure of the hug, and Becca pulled away a little.

"If I'd been planning ahead," Morgan admitted, "I would have had snacks and water up here, to let us take a bit longer to decompress. As it is ... do you feel up to heading back to the cabin, hon?"

"Okay," Becca acquiesced.

Morgan returned Becca's glasses, stroking the woman's hair but letting her put them on herself. She led Becca back along the side deck and into the cockpit. The other things on the deck could wait for later; right now, her attention belonged on Becca.

Thirteen

Morgan removed the panels from the hatch and let Becca precede her down the companionway, then used a gentle hand to guide her back onto the settee around the table.

"Would you like more tea?" Morgan offered, taking three chocolate covered digestive biscuits from a tin. She set them on a piece of kitchen roll in front of Becca without asking. "Chamomile again?"

"Yes, please?" Becca agreed. Morgan put the kettle on. While it heated, she opened the door to Lynn's cabin.

Lynn looked up from their reading. "Did you have fun?"

"It got a bit intense," Morgan said, keeping her voice quiet enough not to carry. "It's okay. It was good. But could I ask you to fetch the things in, please?"

Lynn put aside their book. "Whatever you need," they said. "How's she doing?"

"A little shaky, still," Morgan admitted. "I think she's okay. But I do want to focus on her right now." Lynn nodded.

"How are *you* doing?" they asked, swinging their legs off the edge of the sleep surface. Morgan backed away far enough to give them room to stand.

"I'll be okay," she said, listening for the tea kettle. Lynn stepped forward and pulled her into a tight hug. Morgan allowed herself the luxury of a moment to just melt into their support.

"I know you *will* be," they said. "How are you now?"

"Better now," Morgan said. "Thank you, *cariad*. I'm going to get back to her now."

Lynn nodded, following her back into the galley just long enough to pull on their own harness before heading out on deck.

"Is Lynn okay?" Becca asked. She had barely nibbled the edge of one of her biscuits.

"They're fine," Morgan assured her, turning off the hob as the kettle began to whistle. "Why do you ask?" She put teabags in two mugs before pouring the water over them.

"They just walked out onto the deck," Becca said. "I worried they were mad?"

Morgan carried the mugs over to the table and set both of them in front of Becca before nudging the other woman to move over and let her slide in. Becca shifted obligingly.

"They're not mad," Morgan said. "I just asked them to do me a favour, is all." She gently tried putting her arm around Becca's shoulder. Becca froze for a moment, long enough for Morgan to start to worry, before letting herself relax into the touch.

"Okay," Becca said. "Is it my fault? That you couldn't do it yourself?" Morgan laughed.

"I'm sure Lynn would tell you that my leaving things where they don't belong is something that long predates your arrival."

"But is it my fault *this* time?" Becca seemed determined to worry. Morgan rubbed her shoulder reassuringly.

"They might have been more willing to indulge me this time, so I could spend time with you," she allowed. "That's a good thing, and it's a courtesy I return when we're visiting people who are special to them."

Becca nodded. Morgan held her quietly as the tea cooled, enjoying the feeling of the woman slowly relaxing against her. It wasn't until Lynn returned to the cabin that Becca startled upright again.

Lynn surveyed the room as they descended the companionway, then put the rope bag on the bench at the chart table.

"Would you two like some privacy?" they offered.

"No, it's okay," Becca said quickly, sitting up straight. "We weren't doing anything!"

Lynn nodded and refilled the kettle to make themself a drink. "Just sitting together doing nothing can be important, too," they said. "And you're allowed to have privacy for it, if you prefer."

Morgan let Becca pull away, trying not to be frustrated by the reaction. Lynn had done her a favour, and hadn't done anything wrong. It was just that Becca had been starting to relax, and now she was on edge again.

"You're okay," she said quietly, covering Becca's hand with her own, willing her to calm. "It's a real question. They'll go back to their cabin, if we want, or we can have the pleasure of their company."

Becca nodded, but didn't say anything. Lynn quietly poured boiling water onto a mint teabag and waited to be told what they were doing. They looked at Morgan.

"What would you prefer?" Morgan asked Becca, rubbing the back of her hand soothingly. Becca did not seem soothed.

"I, well, you should," Becca fumbled for words. "They're your partner. I don't want to interfere."

"You're not interfering," Lynn said, deciding the matter by bringing their mug to the end of the table. "I'm the one who risks interfering with *your* connection with Morgan, right now."

Becca shifted, uncomfortably aware that she was physically between Lynn and Morgan when she didn't want to come between them at all. "I'm sorry," she said.

"It's okay," Morgan said, beside her. "I'm still right here with you."

"But you should," objected Becca vaguely. "But Lynn ... "

"Lynn is also right here," Lynn noted, and there was over a metre between them and Becca, but she still felt their presence, intense and close. "Lynn is not a threat to you. You haven't done anything wrong. You're fine."

"I'm sorry," Becca said again. She didn't feel fine. "I'm ... it's ..." She couldn't find the words to catch her balance.

"Take your time," Morgan said, squeezing her hand gently. "It's okay." Becca nodded and took a breath "Eat your biscuits."

Becca nibbled the edge of a cookie obediently before asking, "Why?"

"It will help you relax," Morgan said, and Becca blinked.

"Really?" She took another small bite. "How?"

"Carbs, mostly," Morgan said, taking a bite of her own. "The way I heard it, your body has competing systems: fight-or-flight, and rest-and-digest. When you eat something, especially something carb heavy, you tell your body that it's time for the second one, that it's safe to relax and eat food."

Becca nodded. She'd heard of fight or flight, of course, and had certainly felt it earlier. "That's interesting," she said. "Is that why you keep pushing tea on me?"

Morgan laughed, "I mean, we're also British. There are certain standards to uphold."

"For my part," Lynn offered, "it was part of my decision to make hot chocolate earlier. Carbs, the steadiness of drinking, and I've heard that chocolate is especially good, though I'm not sure of the science on that." They shrugged. "It's something I like, when I'm anxious or upset, and I hoped it would work for you, too."

"Thank you," Becca said. "Thank you for looking out for me." Maybe it was the cookies working, or maybe just the conversation, but she was starting to feel a little better.

"As much as we can," Morgan said. "How are you feeling, now?"

"I'm okay," Becca said, and it wasn't quite a lie. "I guess your mind control cookies are working?"

Morgan laughed again, "Excellent. All part of my wicked plan." Lynn smiled.

"Speaking of wicked plans," they said to Morgan, "I presume you'll be in your own cabin tonight, with Becca?" Becca froze, and the cookie in her mouth turned to dust.

"Well, that rather depends on Becca," Morgan said easily. "Has my wicked plan to worm my way into your affections and your bed worked?"

"I ..." Becca stammered, "if you want?" She tried to keep her voice steady, but it refused to obey her. "It's your room."

Morgan turned to look at her, seeming surprised by Becca's hesitation. "Are you okay?" she asked.

"I'm fine," Becca lied.

"You are," Morgan agreed, "whether you say yes or no. Talk to me, hon?"

"I thought you were going to sleep with Lynn," Becca mumbled to the table.

"I was," Morgan said. "I thought, when we arranged that, that you would be less comfortable sleeping with me."

"And now?" Becca asked, feeling her cheeks burn. "I ..." she looked at Lynn in appeal, "We didn't do anything. I'm not trying to ... anything."

"You're okay," Lynn's voice was quiet, and they kept their hands on their mug of mint tea. "I trust Morgan. I believe that you didn't do anything wrong." Becca nodded anxiously, and watched Lynn sip their tea. "What you did wasn't 'nothing', though. Even without knowing details, I can guess that it was an emotionally intense experience, and quiet time together after that is important."

Becca blushed again. Morgan was still holding her hand, close beside her, and Lynn was at the kitchen end of the bench. She didn't want to reject Morgan and make her feel bad, but she didn't want to pull Morgan out of her partner's bed, either. Becca shook her head. She didn't even know what Morgan would *expect* if they shared a bed. And she really *hadn't* been trying to do anything.

"It's okay," Morgan said. "It really is. I'm not going to force you into something you don't want."

"I know," Becca said faintly.

"I can sleep with Lynn, if that will make you more comfortable," Morgan said. "I'd like to spend some time just cuddling you and telling you you're lovely and safe," she grinned as Becca hid behind her hands, but didn't interfere, "but we can do that out here."

"I'm sorry," Becca said, still sheltering behind her hands. Morgan slipped an arm around her shoulders, and Becca let herself be pulled against the other woman. It took several moments before she could relax more than that.

"It's okay," Morgan reminded her. "You're safe." She hugged gently.

"I'm sorry," Becca sighed, and Morgan finally felt some of the tension go out of her shoulders.

"It's okay," Morgan said again, rubbing her shoulder gently. She didn't have any good options, and she ached at knowing that whatever she did would probably result in people getting hurt. Given how close to the edge she had been skating with Becca, on deck, she would be shocked if there weren't an after-reaction in the night. On the other hand, forcing herself into the bed of somebody who didn't want her there .... "We can do what makes you most comfortable."

Becca nodded, and this time the tone of "I'm sorry" was grateful, as if she were accepting a concession she didn't think she deserved.

"You're welcome," Morgan said gently, amused that she was starting to distinguish between the different meanings Canadians gave the word. Or maybe it was just Becca. Either way, her increasing comfort was what Morgan needed to hear. She shifted Becca's mug slightly towards her and the other woman took a sip.

"Right, sorry," Becca took the words as a correction. "Thank you."

"You're welcome," Morgan said again. "You can expect that of me, you know. Concern for your comfort. I'll mess up sometimes, and do things that make you uncomfortable, but I really will never intend to hurt you."

Becca blushed a little. "You seemed to enjoy making me uncomfortable, when you had me all tied up," she said.

"What do you mean?" Morgan asked. Becca blushed more, turning her face to shelter against Morgan's shoulder.

"Teasing me," she mumbled. "You said you liked seeing me blush and squirm." Morgan laughed softly.

"That's a little different," she said. "At least I hope it was. How do you feel when I tell you you're lovely, and that I enjoy being allowed to hold you like this?" Becca raised her hands, hiding behind them a little, but didn't pull away from her place on Morgan's shoulder.

"Embarrassed?" she said. "Blushy."

"Mhmm," Morgan said. "But are you hurt by it? Scared?"

"Maybe a little scared," Becca admitted. Morgan frowned to herself; that was not what she had expected.

"What's scary about it, hon?" she prodded.

"I don't know," Becca said. "The ... feeling like I don't deserve it? Not knowing why you're saying it or what you expect of me?"

"Uncertainty?" Morgan suggested, and Becca nodded.

"Yeah. Uncertainty, and not knowing what comes next, and being afraid that I'm doing it wrong."

"Mmm," Morgan said, turning the information over in her head. "If I'm telling you that I enjoy watching you blush and squirm, doesn't that indicate that you are doing it right?"

"I don't know." Becca buried her face against Morgan's shoulder. Morgan rubbed her back gently.

"I mean, I would love it if my words could help convince you that you're lovely and wonderful and clever and strong," Morgan said, meaning every word. "But I know it's hard to hear, and just listening to it can be a lot."

Becca pressed closer, hiding her face and holding on to Morgan as she was hit with the challenging words, but Morgan could feel her nod.

"So I can understand why that feels a little scary," Morgan went on, stroking her back reassuringly. "I wonder, though, if it can feel good, at the same time?" Becca peeked up at her face, and Morgan smiled.

"You remember what I said, about feeling different things at the same time?" Morgan said, and Becca nodded. "So you might feel a bit uncertain, but still feel good to know I really do think well of you. Maybe a little nervous, but knowing that I'm not going to make you go somewhere you really don't want to go?"

"Maybe?" Becca said, still hiding.

Morgan stroked her back steadily. "And I hope that the fact that you stay with me even when I'm teasing you is because you know you can trust me to back off if you tell me to."

Becca nodded. "I was ... a little surprised by that?" she said, unconfidence making everything a question.

"Oh?" Morgan prompted.

Becca nodded, "Even when I was being unreasonable," she began. "Well, I mean, every time was unreasonable, so ..." she trailed off. "I'm sorry."

"Hey now," Morgan said, squeezing her shoulder. She had been doing so well. "Whenever you feel like you need me to back off, it's reasonable for you to ask me to back off."

Becca nodded, "But I shouldn't have felt that way."

"You're allowed to feel what you feel," Morgan insisted. "And when you tell me honestly what that is, I am able to keep my promise not to hurt you."

"Thank you?" Becca said.

"Always." Morgan hugged her close. She was rewarded by feeling the other woman relax into her, and for a while the silence was enough.

Finally, Morgan reached up to stroke Becca's hair gently. "It's getting late, hon," she said. "What do you want to do about bed?"

Becca pulled away reluctantly, but Morgan was right. "I'll go," she said, sitting up and looking around.

Lynn was still there, sitting at the end of the bench. Becca had forgotten them, and they'd been there the whole time.

"I'm sorry," Becca said.

Lynn shook their head. "You're fine," they said. "I enjoyed watching you relax a bit. It's actually really nice, being allowed to witness your connection like that."

Becca blushed and shook her head, "It's not ..."

"Could you do me a favour, Becca?" Lynn asked, and Becca froze.

"Sure?" she said, cautiously.

"Would you please try to stop insulting my partner by diminishing what you've done together?"

"I wasn't," Becca flushed. She turned to look at Morgan. "Was I doing that?"

"It's okay," Morgan said.

"I get it," Lynn said. "You're anxious and you don't want to step on any toes. But I keep telling you that nothing you've done with Morgan impinges on her relationship with me." They sighed. "But saying it was nothing, denying the comfort that I saw you take in her ... it doesn't help anybody."

Becca nodded, "I'm sorry." She shifted uncomfortably on the bench, still blocked in by Morgan's presence beside her. "I should just ... go." Morgan laid a delaying hand on her arm.

"It's okay," she said. "You don't have to rush off immediately. You haven't done anything wrong." Becca bit her lip and shook her head.

"And you don't have to sleep alone, either," Lynn pointed out. Morgan started to say something, but they persisted. "Morgan has *offered* to share her cabin with you. You're allowed to accept that. It's not going to hurt me, and it might benefit you."

"I ..." Becca looked around the cabin frantically. Lynn at one end of the bench. Morgan beside her. "Could you let me out, please? I need to use the bathroom."

Morgan nodded, recognising Becca's need to get away even if the excuse was transparent. She slid off the settee and stepped against the door to the bow cabin, making room for Becca to pass. Becca squeezed out and scurried to the tiny heads cubicle. Morgan sat back down and looked at her partner.

"You're pushing her pretty hard," she said. Lynn nodded.

"I don't want her hurting you," they said. "It's not fair to you. And it's not fair to her, either."

Morgan sighed. "I know. But there's really nothing I can do. If she doesn't trust me ..."

Lynn reached out for her hand, and Morgan stretched across the table to take theirs. They squeezed gently. "I don't think it's that she doesn't trust you," they said. "I saw the way she was hiding against you, rather than pulling away. But she's scared, and I don't think there's much more you can do for her as long as she's refusing to ask you for comfort."

"You're not helping," Morgan said. Lynn shrugged.

"I tried. She's not stupid, but I don't think she realises how much it hurts you when she says stuff like that."

"That doesn't matter," Morgan said. Lynn squeezed her hand.

"I think it does," they said. "And I think Becca would, too, if you gave her a chance." In the silence that followed, both of them could hear the toilet being pumped. Lynn gave her hand another squeeze as water ran in the head. It ended a full minute and a half before Becca emerged from the cubicle; Morgan could imagine the struggle it had taken the other woman to open the door.

"I'm going to just go to bed?" Becca said hesitantly. Morgan stayed where she was on the settee and nodded.

"Would you like company?" she asked, as non-threateningly as possible. Becca shook her head.

"You should be with your partner," she said. Morgan nodded acceptance.

"If you change your mind," she said, "if you need anything in the night? Don't hesitate to ask us."

Becca nodded. Her eyes flicked from Morgan to Lynn, and then to the door of the aft cabin.

"Seriously," Morgan pressed. "The door will be closed, but if you need *anything*, please just knock." Becca nodded mutely.

"We mean it," Lynn put in. "Don't hesitate."

Becca nodded again, taking another step towards the bow cabin. Nobody interfered with her. She hesitated and turned to face her hosts.

"Umm, goodnight?" she said awkwardly.

Morgan nodded. "Would you like a hug?" she offered. Becca took a step back, pressing against the door to the cabin as she gave Morgan room to exit the bench, and nodded. Morgan squeezed out into the aisle and wrapped her arms around Becca.

Becca was tempted to just melt into the hug. Feeling Morgan hold her, warm and supportive, just felt safe and *right*. It was so tempting to believe them, to just take the offer of being held and knowing she was safe, and curling up together for the night. Almost, she began to form the words.

"Goodnight, Becca," Lynn said. "Sleep well. But remember what we said."

Becca hugged her friend back tightly. "Goodnight, Morgan," she said as she let go. "Goodnight, Lynn. Thank you." She slipped into the bow cabin and latched the door behind her.

Fourteen

That was it. She was safe; she could relax now. Morgan and Lynn would stay on the other side of the door; she did trust them that far. She should feel safer, then, relieved to have made it to the privacy of the cabin, happy that Morgan had respected her decision to sleep alone. Becca climbed onto the sleep surface and tried to untangle the nest of sheets. Morgan's sheets. Should she have requested clean sheets? It was probably fine; it wasn't as if she washed her own sheets every night. So why was she hung up on the fact that the sheets that had touched Morgan were now offered to wrap around her?

This was ridiculous. If she were going to worry about Morgan's things touching her, she should be worrying about the fact that the very nightgown she had been wearing all night was Morgan's.

This wasn't helping. She straightened the sheets and settled in, gazing up at the skylight.

Lynn had been wrong, when they were teasing earlier. She couldn't actually see the base of the mast from the cabin. The light from high on the mast glowed on the tinted square of plastic, but she had only her memory of the activities at the mast, not a visual reminder. Becca rolled onto her side, hugging herself, and closed her eyes.

In the other room, she could hear quiet voices, and the fading sounds of Lynn and Morgan moving around. She could imagine them heading back to Lynn's cabin and ... she deliberately stopped imagining.

It had been a long day, she guessed, so it made sense that she was having trouble unwinding. The excitement of getting ready to meet Morgan, a day of exploring the island ... her mind kept coming back to the mast, but darn it, most of the day hadn't been about that. They had just hung out, laughed together. The hike up the lighthouse trail, and Morgan insisting on exploring the base of the lighthouse even though it was closed. The picnic with bread and cheese and sausage rolls picked up at the island bakery. Fresh raspberries growing wild by the trail. Morgan leaning forward to pick a bit of leaf from her hair. Had Morgan really been flirting with her all day? The text message had said she was. Becca reached out to where she had bundled her phone into her clothing in the corner of the sleep surface.

Her phone was at 12%; three hours' charge left. That wasn't good, and she had left her charger in her car.

Would Morgan and Lynn have a spare charger? If they'd already gone to bed, she shouldn't bother them. She didn't want to wake them, making noise by moving about.

Quietly, Becca opened the door to her cabin.

The main room was dim, with only a small light illuminating the desk by the bathroom near all the dials and switches. Lynn's laptop was still on that table, but Becca also saw a USB hub with an un-used cable. She tiptoed over and checked the con-nector. It did fit her phone; with a sense of relief, Becca plugged it in.

Something was on the seat that belonged to the desk. In the dim light, Becca recognised the rope bag that Lynn had brought back to the cabin. The rope Morgan had crocheted hung from the handle by a carabiner. The rest was presumably inside.

Not wanting to touch Morgan's things, Becca perched on the end of the bench along the same wall as the desk, just within range of the USB cable.

Still restless, Becca checked e-mail and caught up with chat messages. It had been a slow day; Thursdays usually were. Morgan had been with her all day, and everybody else would have been at work. Louise had posted a couple of comics in the memes channel, but there was nothing that needed a reply.

Becca eyed the door to Lynn's cabin, but she had already found the charger she needed. The sheet thing was silly, and she'd feel stupid raising it after everybody had gone to bed anyway. If she was going to object to that, she should have said something before lying down the first time. As for the ... restlessness ... she felt, well, there was nothing they could do for that. There was absolutely no reason to bother them.

Right. She had intended to review what Morgan had said about flirting, so she could get it out of her head.

```
<Becca> They seem to think you
        were flirting with me,
        today?
<Morgan> Well, yeah.
<Morgan> It's fine that you
         weren't interested,
         but I was *definitely*
         flirting.
<Becca> 
<Morgan> How does *that* make
         your head explode?
```

Becca shook her head. It still didn't make sense. None of it made any sense. Why would Morgan have been flirting with her? She *knew* she wasn't interesting. Morgan and Lynn sailed the world, lining up contracts for work, managing everything for themselves in exotic countries. Becca couldn't even deal with being unexpectedly stuck on an island in her own province, where everybody spoke her language and all she needed to do was be on time to catch the damned ferry home.

And Morgan had a relationship already. More than one, actually; Becca remembered her missing game sessions on account of a chance to visit one of her other partners. There was no way Morgan could be interested in her *that* way. Part of her tried to imagine what it might be like, to be a reason Morgan would miss the weekly game, but she stamped it down firmly. That just wasn't how things worked in the real world.

But Lynn thought Morgan fancied her.

Becca thought about how much Morgan had tried to take care of her, all the times the other woman had leaned closer, had touched her hand or stroked her arm. The way she had listened, even just about game stuff and wondering what Erin would pull on their characters next session. The way she had listened when Becca got upset over nothing, and tried to fix things even when the only thing wrong had been Becca's reactions.

They did have a relationship, though. They were friends. All of that could just be friendship. There was no reason to imagine Morgan might want more. Friends look out for one another, after all. They had gotten on well, and maybe Morgan touched everybody that much. Or at least all her friends.

She tried to remember if she did it with Lynn, and couldn't quite. Becca thought it might have been less, but she couldn't actually remember. She tried to remember how much contact Morgan had had with Lynn, when she was demonstrating the rope, but her mind kept slipping back to how Morgan's hands looked, handling the rope, pulling it tight, and how it had felt when Morgan pulled the rope against *her*.

What would it have been like if she had accepted Morgan's offer to spend the night with her?

Of course, Morgan had been clear that she didn't intend to get sexual with Becca. That should have been a relief; Becca had never thought of Morgan in those terms before today. But those touches, the gentleness and the insistence on holding her attention, almost made Becca want more, even if she didn't know what that would look like.

And Morgan had been *willing* to show her the ropes, to show her how they worked. The demonstration on Lynn, the way she let her own wrist be used as an example. How carefully she had walked Becca through trying it herself. The way she didn't get mad even when Becca panicked over nothing. The patience when Becca had struggled with the paper towel.

And then there was Lynn.

Lynn, who had been nothing but kind since they came into the cabin to apologise. Who kept telling her that nothing she did with Morgan was wrong, even when the memory of it made Becca blush. Who made hot chocolate and helped her with a knot. Lynn, who still made Becca nervous, and who had the best claim on Morgan's time.

A noise from the rear cabin interrupted Becca's thoughts. She considered making a run for her own room, but there wasn't time. The door started to open, and there was Lynn.

Lynn, who apparently needed a trip to the bathroom in the middle of the night. Becca sat very still, hoping maybe Lynn wouldn't notice her in the dim light.

It almost worked.

Lynn had reached the door to the bathroom, even had their hand on the handle, before they glanced over. "Oh!" they said. "Are you okay?"

Becca ducked her head sheepishly. "Yeah," she said. "I just ... my phone needed charging?" Lynn nodded.

"Did you find what you needed?" they asked, still a bit muzzy from sleep.

"There was a cable at the desk," Becca said. "Do you mind?" It was a bit late to ask, but she was at a loss as to what else to say.

"No, that's fine," Lynn said. "Look, Becca, I need to ..." They gestured at the bathroom door. "We can talk when I'm out, okay?"

"It's okay," Becca said hurriedly. "We don't need to."

"We can, though," Lynn said again, before letting themself into the room.

Becca took the opportunity to escape back to the front cabin and shut the door while Lynn was busy with other business. She curled up under the covers and hoped they would just go back to bed. She heard the bathroom door open and footsteps in the cabin, but she stayed quiet under the sheets until the sound receded.

Eventually, she slept.

Becca woke with the square of sunshine from the skylight directly on her face. Pulling the sheets over her head only provided minimal respite, and a chance to reflect that her apartment did not feature a skylight. She rummaged through her memories, and found herself blushing at what she found.

Had she really done that?

She glanced down at the pink nightgown she was wearing.

"Sleep. Relax. *recharge*. Love."

This was definitely not a nightgown she owned. Her memories were checking out, and Relaxed was not exactly how she was feeling. She peeked out of the sheets and looked around the triangular bunk.

There were her clothes, in the corner of the sleep surface, where the wall met the cabinet. She probably should have hung them the night before, but she had been a little distracted. She started to sort them out, to pull them on, when she realised that her underthings were still hanging off the deck.

Well. She guessed she was wearing the night-gown a while longer. This wasn't embarrassing at all, in the cold light of day, she tried to lie to herself. She sighed. Summoning what courage she could, she opened the door to the main cabin and made herself step though. Lynn was in the kitchen, working over the stove.

Of course it was Lynn. Though maybe Morgan would have been worse? Becca sighed; perhaps awkward was unavoidable, here.

"Good morning, Lynn," Becca said, and slipped into the bench surround around the table, taking the same place she had occupied the night before. Lynn looked up from a pan of ... were they cooking beans? Was it that late in the day?

"Good morning, Becca," Lynn reached into the oven, using tongs to flip half-toasted bread under the broiler. "Are you feeling any better?"

"I'm okay," Becca said. How much of a fool must Lynn think her?

"You disappeared pretty quickly last night," they said neutrally. Becca blushed and ducked her head.

"I'm sorry," she mumbled at the table.

Lynn let the apology pass, retrieving a stack of three plates from the cabinet behind the stove. "Would you like some breakfast?" they offered.

"I'm okay, thank you," Becca mumbled. They nodded and dished themself some beans and toast, carrying their food to the table before turning and retrieving Becca's phone from the desk. They passed it to her before sitting down on the bench.

Becca unlocked the phone and tried to find an excuse to lose herself in it while Lynn ate. No new e-mail in the "Primary" tab; nothing much had happened in chat. She glanced at Lynn cautiously.

Lynn ate their beans and toast, giving Becca time to calm herself. They waited until Becca stopped pretending to be engrossed in her phone before speaking again.

"We were worried about you," they said, when Becca glanced at them again. Becca blushed and looked back down at the table, but Lynn continued. "Did you sleep okay? I was surprised to see you up in the night."

Becca shrugged. "It took a while?" she said. Lynn nodded.

"Was anything bothering you?" they asked, and Becca flinched. It took real effort not to reach out and rest a hand on her arm, but the chance that would make things better rather than worse seemed vanishingly slim.

"I'm sorry about last night," Becca said, and Lynn frowned.

"Why?" they asked. Becca shrugged.

"I was out of line," the woman said. "I ... did a lot of things I probably shouldn't."

Lynn chose their words carefully. It should really be Morgan having this conversation, but Morgan had still been asleep when they slipped out of bed, and they hadn't wanted to wake her. She'd had a hard night, herself, dealing with her own reactions to how far she had pushed and to Becca's withdrawal from her. But at least Lynn had been able to be there for her, holding her close and rubbing her back, reminding her that she had done her best and that everybody was okay.

But Becca had been alone, and there was no guarantee that she *had* been okay. Lynn had done everything they could. They had told her not to hesitate to knock on the door. They had offered to talk to her when they were done in the head. But she had disappeared back to the bow cabin instead of accepting the offer. Should Lynn have knocked, insisted, or roused Morgan to do so? At the end of the day, they had to let the woman make her own decisions, even if they *knew* they were the wrong ones.

"Do you regret what happened last night?" Lynn asked carefully.

"I ..." Becca began. "I was out of line." Lynn nodded noncommittally.

"I don't think you were out of line," Lynn said. "But I'm less worried about what you did than about what happened *to* you." Becca looked up, surprised, but Lynn nodded seriously. "Morgan was in tears last night, worried that she had hurt you, had made you go further than you actually wanted to go. I'm asking if she was right."

"No!" Becca cried. "Not at all! Morgan was lovely, she was ..." she blushed, "a lot more than I deserved. She took the time, and put up with me. *She* didn't do anything wrong!"

"Did I?" Lynn asked evenly.

"No," Becca shook her head. "You've been nothing but kind. Neither of you did anything wrong."

"You didn't, either," Lynn said. Becca shook her head, not accepting the reassurance, so Lynn amended it. "Okay, you did one thing wrong."

Becca looked at them.

"We told you to knock if you needed anything," Lynn reminded her.

"I'm sorry," Becca said, abashed. "I thought you said it was okay that I used the charger."

"That's not what I mean." Lynn kept their hands to themself by force of will. "Can you honestly tell me that you weren't feeling this way when I caught you up last night? Hurting and afraid you did something wrong?"

"That's not something being wrong," Becca said. "That's just *me* being wrong. My reactions, my brain. Not something I can ask you to fix." She fidgeted with her phone. "What could you have done, even if I *had* bothered you?"

"Honestly," Lynn mopped bean sauce from their plate with a bit of toast, "I would have been tempted to shove you in the cabin with Morgan and hold the door shut until you two talked." They chewed thoughtfully. "Still might be the best course, actually." Late, they noticed the way Becca had pulled back in on herself, and sighed.

"Umm," Becca said hesitantly, eyes wide and arms close to her body. "Red?" Lynn blinked.

"I heard red," Lynn confirmed, the same structure they used between themself and Morgan. "Can you tell me what's wrong?"

Becca shook her head, clearly still struggling. "I'm sorry," she said. "Please don't force me?"

"I was joking," Lynn said, deliberately keeping their voice gentle. "I wasn't going to actually do it."

"I'm sorry," Becca hunched in on herself, shoulders around her ears. "I shouldn't have said ..."

"It got my attention," Lynn said. They hadn't expected a safeword from Becca, hadn't thought they were enough of a threat to need one. "I'm sorry I frightened you. That was not my intent. You did well to draw it to my attention."

"You're not mad?" Becca asked, looking at Lynn from under her hair. Lynn blinked again.

"No, I'm not mad," they said. "I'll never get angry at somebody using a safeword properly."

"But was that," Becca fumbled, "It's not proper when, outside, I mean, context?"

"Context," Lynn said gently. "You were scared?"
Becca nodded.

"You needed me to stop?"
Another nod.

"You trusted that my intent was not to harm you?"
She nodded again, more hesitantly.

"That's the context you need," Lynn said firmly. "You didn't try to make a joke of it, or do it just to jerk me around. You used it to ask for help, and that's absolutely right."

Becca nodded once more, her eyes still a little too wide. Maybe it was just that she had washed off her make-up before bed, but she looked very pale and vulnerable against the blue cushions of the settee. The effect was not lessened by the night-dress she had borrowed, the pink one that Morgan never wore unless it was the last clean thing in her closet, and her sleep-mussed hair.

This wasn't the first time Lynn had breakfasted with Morgan's other lovers, but usually Morgan was either there with them or the other person had been the one to let her sleep. The awkward-ness this time, with Becca actively afraid of them and unresolved tensions between Becca and Morgan, was unique in their experience.

It was not a novelty Lynn was enjoying.

"I can see that you're struggling," they contin-ued. "I want to help. Is there anything I can do?"

Becca shifted uncomfortably, blushing and mumbling something at the table.

"I didn't catch that," Lynn said. Becca blushed deeper, but glanced up at them.

"I was going to get dressed," she said, "but my, um, underthings are still hanging outside. And I'm not supposed to go up there without supervision."

"Ah," Lynn said, nodding. This was something they could do. "Would you like me to grab them in for you?"

"If you don't mind," Becca said, still blushing. "I'm sorry."

"It's no trouble," Lynn assured her, depositing their dishes at the sink as they moved toward the hatch. Removing the panels and pushing it open was muscle memory by now; unclipping the life-lines long enough to retrieve the bra and knickers took only a moment. They casually kicked the base of the starboard bench and storage locker, and took a moment to enjoy the midmorning sunshine before they returned to the cabin. Morgan should be nearly awake by now, anyway.

Becca's face was still a bit pink when Lynn returned to the cabin, and Lynn handed her the garments without further comment.

"Thank you," Becca said. "I'll just ..." she gestured at the cabin door. Lynn nodded.

"Of course," they said, and Becca slipped away. They headed back to their own cabin.

Morgan was sitting up in bed when Lynn opened the door.

"I heard thumping on deck," she said. "Is everything okay?"

"Sorry," Lynn said. "I was hoping it would wake you, but I didn't want to worry you or, well, draw attention to it."

"Is Becca up, then?"

"Yeah," Lynn confirmed.

"How's she doing?"

"Struggling," Lynn sighed "She didn't have a great night, either, I think." Morgan nodded.

"I should have ..."

"She wouldn't have let you," Lynn interrupted. They sat on the edge of the sleep surface and patted the space beside them.

Morgan untangled herself from sheets and moved over to lean against them. Lynn stroked her hair.

"You didn't do anything wrong," they said. "I asked her. And she only had good things to say about you, how gentle you were. You did the best you could possibly do, and she appreciates that."

"That's quite the chat to have over breakfast," Morgan said. Lynn smiled.

"She didn't even get as far as breakfast," they said. "She did ask me to get her things from the deck, though; she might be more comfortable once she's dressed."

"Does that mean there's actually enough food left for me, this time?" Morgan teased, calling back to the hot chocolate from the night before. Lynn tousled her hair.

"Come on, love. If Becca can deal with somebody she's afraid of, first thing in the morning, you can at least be there to comfort her."

"Is she afraid of me?" Morgan worried.

"She's afraid of *me*," Lynn corrected.

"But you didn't do anything to her!"

Lynn shrugged, "She barely knows me, and I do have a habit of asking her to consider hard questions."

"Like what?"

"Like how she feels about the fact that you fancy her," Lynn said, and Morgan blushed.

"You didn't!" she said. Lynn grinned and pushed open the door, stepping back into the galley.

"You do, though, don't you?"

"That's not the point," Morgan said, following her partner into the main cabin. Becca hadn't re-emerged from her cabin yet, so that was a small mercy. "If she's not interested ..."

"Do you really think last night was somebody who 'wasn't interested'?" Lynn laughed. "And I thought Becca was oblivious." They re-ignited the hob to heat the beans remaining in the pan, and extracted four more pieces of bread to go under the grill. Morgan just blushed and sputtered a bit until they shooed her into the dining area.

"She could have just been curious," Morgan said, trying to get her complexion back under control.

"Mhmm," Lynn stirred beans, checked the toast. "Intellectual curiosity always leads me to ask somebody to tie me to a mast."

The door to the bow cabin had begun to open, but stopped partway. Lynn moderated their tone.

"Come on out, Becca," they said. "It's okay; I'll stop teasing." Morgan turned to look forward.

Morgan watched Becca slip into the main cabin. The woman had clearly overheard some of what Lynn had said; stood with her back to the cabin door, she looked ready to bolt at any moment. Becca was blushing madly and her eyes were glued to the floor, and Morgan had to admit to herself that Lynn was right about her attraction. Morgan smiled and patted the seat beside her. Becca was a dear friend and she didn't want to make her un-comfortable, but seeing her there with a slightly rumpled t-shirt skimming her curves and dark jeans outlining her legs? Yes, Morgan fancied her. She could only hope Lynn was also right about it being mutual.

"Come sit down," Morgan invited. Becca slipped onto the settee nearest the cabin door. She glanced between Morgan and Lynn anxiously.

"Are you sure you don't want any, Becca?" Lynn asked from the galley. They flipped the toast and had begun portioning out the last of the beans. When Becca shook her head, Lynn scraped the rest of the beans onto Morgan's plate.

"Are you positive?" Morgan pressed. Becca shook her head again. Morgan accepted the plate of toast and beans from her partner and slid along the settee to be closer to her friend. Becca shifted a little uneasily, but didn't object to the closer prox-imity. Morgan scooped a forkful of beans onto her toast and gave her friend time to relax.

"Are you trying to do the carbs for calm thing again?" Becca asked, after Morgan had taken a few bites. Morgan chewed and swallowed.

"Not consciously," she said. "Though it's not ne-cessarily a bad idea." Morgan took another bite of her breakfast. "Are you not hungry? Or do you not care for beans?"

"I mean, it's a bit odd for breakfast?" Becca ven-tured.

"It might be a cultural difference," Morgan al-lowed. "Can we offer you something else? Even just some toast?"

Becca glanced at Lynn, who had started washing out the pan. "If it wouldn't be too much trouble?" she asked. "I don't want to put you out."

"It's no trouble," Lynn assured her. "What would you like?"

"Just some toast, if you don't mind?"

Lynn nodded easily and slipped bread under the grill. "Butter? Jam? Marmite?"

"Jam, please?"

Lynn flipped the toast in the oven, then removed the section of countertop and fished out a jar of strawberry jam from the recessed refrigerator. They passed it to Morgan, who passed it on to Becca, taking the opportunity to brush her hand while making the transfer. Becca looked at her; Morgan returned a smile before going back to her plate of beans.

Lynn put the fresh toast on a plate and buttered it before carrying it from the galley to Becca and returning to sit at the nav desk. They waited until Becca had finished her first piece before asking, "Are you feeling any better?"

Becca looked up at them and nodded; her entire posture seemed more comfortable than it had been. "I am, thank you." She blushed a little, but only looked away briefly. "And thank you for earlier, too."

"Of course," Lynn said. "I'm sorry I hadn't thought to offer you something different for breakfast."

"It's okay," Becca said. "I shouldn't be so picky. I'm sorry."

"You're fine," Morgan said, brushing Becca's arm. Lynn grinned to see how quickly Becca re-oriented, the shy smile as she met Morgan's eyes briefly before returning to her toast. It was still a fragile thing, but they were sure it was there. They just hoped Morgan wouldn't get hurt.

"So what's the plan for today?" Lynn asked, when the two women had finished their breakfasts. "I know you hadn't planned to be out overnight, Becca. Do you have anything you need to do today?"

"Not particularly," Becca said. "I mean, I definitely need to get back to my hotel, so I can check out tomorrow, but there's nothing more urgent than that."

"We do need to get more milk," Morgan said, "and we should probably do the laundry, if things are falling out of the hamper and assaulting guests." Becca blushed, but Morgan just grinned at her. "Not that I regret what came of that." Becca blushed a deeper shade of red and hid her face. Lynn nodded, and moved on before Morgan could get sidetracked with teasing Becca.

"Is there a grocery store on the island?" they asked, flipping open their laptop.

"Not really," Morgan said. "There's the bakery, and they do have milk and a few other things, but the prices are high; it's meant to cater to unprepared tourists, I think, with that you're-a-moron markup." Lynn nodded.

"It wouldn't be a bad idea to hit a pump-out station and refill the water tanks, anyway," Lynn said. "If we can find a transient slip on the mainland, that might be ideal." They pulled up one of the slip-booking websites they and Morgan usually used. At the table, Morgan continued to flirt with Becca.

"Is there any reason you need to take the ferry back?" she asked, stroking Becca's arm.

"My car is at the ferry terminal," Becca said, a little uncertain.

"I mean, I invited you back to the boat, but we've been anchored the whole time you've been here," Morgan explained. "It's not really the full experience?"

"It's okay," Becca said, clearly misunderstanding Morgan's intent. "You don't have to ... I mean, you've done so much for me ..."

"Logistically," Lynn put in, "we'd need to get a cab for groceries, anyway. Buying at the marina has the same sort of poor-planning markup that tourist destinations do. If you wanted to sail with us, we could have the cab drop you at your car before continuing to the grocery."

"But that's silly," Becca objected, taking the bait. "If we're going to my car anyway, it would make more sense for me to drive from there, to get the shopping done." Morgan shot Lynn a grateful look, and they grinned back.

"So you will sail with us?" Morgan asked hopefully.

"If you want me to," Becca said. "I don't want to impose any more than I already have."

"I want you to," Morgan said. "I enjoy spending time with you. Sailing away with you would be a lovely fantasy." The last line had Becca looking a little nervous, Lynn noticed.

"If you want us to," they said, "we will absolutely take you back to the island so you can catch the ferry home, as you had planned." They waited for Becca to nod before continuing explicitly, "You're not trapped here. We would enjoy your company for the afternoon; we would love to take you sailing. Your offer to drive to the grocery was generous. But you're not obligated to do that." Becca nodded again.

"I'm sorry," Becca said. "I was being stupid."

"Morgan was being enthusiastic," Lynn corrected. "And I love her dearly, but she can be A Lot when she gets a plan in her head."

"I'm right here," Morgan objected.

"And I'm not wrong," Lynn said. Morgan conceded the point.

"I promise I have no intention of abducting you and forcing you to live out my wildest cabin-boy fantasies," Morgan said, and the example was so over the top that even Becca had to grin. She blushed and ducked her head.

"Unless you were into that," Lynn couldn't resist teasing. Becca blushed deeper.

"I mean, I'm only on holiday until the end of the week," she mumbled. Morgan laughed and stroked her hair.

"Erin would notice you missing at Saturday's game anyway," she said. "If I ever do get to abduct you, we'll have to put much more consideration into the scheduling." Lynn wondered briefly how much their partner was kidding, but Becca seemed to accept it as a joke. Lynn went back to searching for a marina with a free slip on no notice, only paying half attention to the two women.

"I think I'd like that," Becca said. "The sailing, I mean. Not the abduction." Morgan nodded.

"I should probably get dressed, then," she said, sliding along the bench seat to exit the galley end rather than push past Becca. "I forgot to grab anything before going to sleep in Lynn's cabin, so ..." Becca nodded as Morgan slipped into the bow cabin where she had slept the night before.

Sixteen

Lynn finished booking a transient slip for the next night at the municipal marina. Check-in began at noon, but there was no need to arrive that early. As long as they got there before the office closed, they would have time to get a restroom key; it would be nice to be able to grab a shower with un-limited hot water.

Their reverie was broken by a soft sound of clinking plates. They looked over to see Becca stacking dishes at the table.

"You don't have to do that," they said, trying not to startle her. Becca flinched anyway.

"Do you mind?" she asked. "I'd like to be able to do *something*." Lynn nodded; they supposed it might have felt awkward, sitting silent at the table

"If it makes you happy," they said.

"It's just, I'm a guest here." Becca shifted into the aisle and picked up the dishes, carrying them back to the galley. "And I don't think I've been a very good one." She seemed uneasy, walking past Lynn, but they let it go.

"You're fine," they said. "We're pleased to have you. But if it will really make you happy to do the washing-up, far be it from me to interfere." That, at least, got an awkward grin from Becca. They turned to face her as she worked, but maintained their seat at the nav desk.

Lynn was actually fairly impressed that Becca remembered where to find the washing-up liquid, though her movements in reaching for it were tentative. Did she expect Lynn to object? If Becca could convince Morgan that volunteering for washing-up duty was a good way to relax, Lynn would be ... well, shocked, honestly. They'd been with Morgan long enough to know what to expect from her. It occurred to them that a lot of Becca's hesitation around them was probably simply a function of not knowing what to expect from *them*.

Becca ran water into the basin that Lynn had left upturned in the sink, swishing washing-up liquid into it and mopping the plates and cutlery with a dishcloth before propping them on the towel where Lynn had left the pan and their own plate to dry. She was looking around the cabin for any stray dishes — or, Lynn supposed, any further excuse to avoid direct interaction — when Morgan emerged from her cabin.

Lynn watched the smile break across Becca's face, and shook their head. They'd been watching both her and Morgan do the "she couldn't be interested" dance around each other since she ar rived, but it was blazingly obvious to anybody with eyes. They hoped they hadn't been that oblivious when they were first courting Cailean, though part of them suspected they had.

"Becca's taken your turn with the dishes," they said aloud. "I think she felt a bit at loose ends. If you'd like to take her up on deck and get the cover off the mainsail, that would be lovely."

"Sure," Morgan said, walking between them to retrieve her Spinlock from the pegs near the companionway and holding out the yellow buoyancy aid to Becca. Becca, interestingly, blushed and hid behind her hair even as she accepted the buoyancy aid and put it on.

"It's fine," Morgan said. Becca's blush was adorable, and she couldn't help teasing, "I'll leave the rope bag inside, this time." Becca flushed deeper red, and hid behind her hands until Morgan gently pushed them down. "It's okay," she said again, less teasing. "You don't have to come up on deck at all, if you don't want to, or you could stay in the cockpit." She reached out to brush Becca's face with her fingers. "I wouldn't manoeuvre you into a situation like that without warning." Becca glanced at Lynn, perhaps for confirmation.

"Oh, she'd do it to me in a heartbeat," they grinned. "But I'm reasonably confident she can tell us apart. You're safe." Morgan thwapped them upside the head gently.

"Only because you enjoy it," she said, making sure Becca had the context she needed.

"I never claimed otherwise," Lynn laughed. Becca looked amused, rather than intimidated, so Morgan let it go.

"It's probably better if you leave your shoes in the cabin," Morgan suggested, glancing at the hiking sandals Becca was wearing. "It's a little easier to balance when you can feel the deck through your feet."

"Okay," Becca said. She unbuckled the sandals and kicked them off. Morgan felt a little guilty about how much she enjoyed watching Becca bend over for them and walk them back to the bow cabin. The view as Becca returned was even nicer, especially the adorable way she blushed a little under Morgan's interested gaze. Morgan grinned and led the other woman up the companionway to the cockpit.

Becca did better when invited to think rather than feel, Morgan remembered, so she took time to point out some of the basic boat anatomy that surrounded them. She started with the rope clutches on the cabin roof, to either side of the hatch.

"You remember all the lines coming off the mast, last night. Most of them run back to here," Morgan explained. She traced the lines through the clutches and around appropriate winches. "Set up like this, with a bit of preparation, either of us could handle the boat alone. Which is a good thing, when we're at sea, but less of an issue today." She led the way along the side deck, the breeze carrying her hair off her face, and let Becca choose to follow. It was understandable that the woman might be a bit anxious, approaching the mast again after last night. Morgan didn't want to force the issue.

Becca did follow, though, one hand on the low lifelines beside her, looking distinctly uncomfortable at their lack of support.

"Wait," Morgan said, walking back to her and steadying her with a hand on her shoulder. "You notice those are a bit wobbly?" Becca nodded. "They're good to stop you if you're sliding on deck, but if you want something to grab, that's what these rails on the coach roof are meant for."

"They're a bit low," Becca said doubtfully, looking at them. The teak rails were solid and well secured, but they were mounted on the low roof of the internal cabins and didn't even come up to knee level. Morgan nodded understandingly.

"We normally only need them in rough weather, when it's good to stay low, anyway," she said. "You'll be fine just walking normally, on a day like today."

"If you say so?" Becca said. "I still feel like I'd rather have *something* to hold."

"You *could* hold my hand." Morgan grinned, half-teasing. Becca blushed and ducked her head.

"That would be nice," she admitted. Morgan took her hand and stepped onto the coach roof. She provided a steadying grip as Becca stepped up, but tried to stay alert for any hesitation as she led the way forward.

"The cover here protects the sail from both rain and sunlight," Morgan explained, her non-Becca hand on the blue canvas cover over the mainsail as she walked towards the bow. "But we need to take it off to raise the sails again." Becca nodded, and if her eyes drifted a little lower on the mast, Morgan was willing not to call attention to it. Morgan unzipped the cover from the forward side of the mast, working the flap out from behind the whisker pole, and began folding it back towards the stern of the boat. The motion recalled Becca's attention.

"How can I help?" she asked. Morgan smiled.

"You see the toggles along the bottom of the boom?" Morgan motioned to the horizontal spar extending to aft, in case Becca didn't remember where the boom was. Becca looked, and nodded. "If you could just unfasten them as I come to them, that would be a great help." The fact that she got to admire the way Becca filled out her jeans, as she stooped to reach the underside of the boom, was simply a bonus.

By the time Morgan had folded the sail cover back on itself and removed it from the boom entirely, Lynn had made a good start on the other chores. They had hauled the dinghy out of the water; *bash* was hanging from the davits off the back of the boat. Lynn themself was sprawled half over the roof to the left of the companionway. Their attention was on the lines threaded through the clutch, adjusting the tension carefully.

Morgan walked back and flopped onto the port bench, shoving the sail cover under the edge of the bimini canopy that protected the hatch area. She invited Becca to sit beside her, extending an arm along the back of the bench. Becca curled her legs under herself, leaning against Morgan comfortably.

"I'm still going to want Morgan to haul on the halyard when we raise the sail," Lynn warned, smiling back at the two women. "Just because I *can* do this single-handed doesn't mean it's the best idea."

"I'm sorry?" asked Becca.

"No," Morgan said, hugging her around the shoulder. "I'm the one they think would be slacking, if they don't keep on my case."

"Would you?" Becca wondered.

"I mean, if the alternative were cuddling you?" Morgan grinned. "It would be awfully tempting. But I also promised to take you sailing, which will work better with the sails actually up."

"Can I help?" Becca offered, but Morgan shook her head, sliding out from behind the other woman.

"Honestly, you'll be safer if you wait back in the cockpit," she said, kissing Becca on the forehead. "I'll take you back up to the top after the sails are set, okay?"

"Sure," Becca said, sliding along the bench to the corner Morgan had abandoned.

Morgan disappeared around the side of the blue canvas awning, and Becca waited for her to re-appear through the slightly cloudy plastic windows in front. She watched Morgan return to the mast alone.

"You'll be able to see her better if you move over behind the wheel," Lynn offered, extending a hand to help Becca up. Becca looked uncertainly at the lines across the cockpit, but accepted the hand, placing her feet carefully.

"It's okay," Lynn told her. "Worst case, you kick the lines and I have to recoil them again. We're not under any sort of time pressure, here." Becca nodded, still choosing her path cautiously, and was grateful of the balancing pressure of Lynn's hand.

"Should all the lines be bunched up like that?" she asked. Around the cockpit were various empty spools mounted on the deck, but for some reason Lynn had chosen to have everything in front of clamps on the cabin roof.

"It makes them easy to grab, where I need them," Lynn said, "instead of having to leap all over the cockpit after them." They guided her to the seat behind the boat's wheel, just in front of where the dinghy was hanging.

"Okay," Becca said. The invitation to move closer to the stern of the boat, rather than stay near the cabin wall, had also taken Becca further from the confusing mass of ropes.

"I'll need to move different lines on and off the winches here," Lynn explained further, though their attention was on Morgan's progress forward. Becca didn't blame them at all; the way Morgan moved was a pleasure to watch, and Lynn had been right that it was easier to see past the awning from her current perch.

"Are you ready?" Morgan shouted back, from the mast. Lynn returned their attention to the line they were holding, wrapping it around a spool on the cabin roof.

"Whenever you are," they agreed. Morgan leaned towards the mast — Becca reminded herself firmly that there was no reason to blush, watching her motions — and took hold of one of the lines that ran up its side.

Morgan hauled back hard, directly away from the mast and towards the side of the boat. For a moment, Becca worried that she'd fall off the side of the cabin roof, or even off the side of the boat, but she should have had more faith in her friend. Morgan pulled back, waited for Lynn to pull in the end of the line they had wrapped around the spool, then pulled again. Even from her place at the stern, Becca could see that it was hard physical work, and she understood why Morgan hadn't wanted her in the way.

And that's all she would have been, wasn't it? In the way.

Becca hugged herself, watching the two work smoothly together, watching the sail slowly rise under their attentions. Morgan's part seemed to require more and more force, and Lynn was beginning to struggle with their end, even though the rope was wrapped several times around the spool.

"Could you grab that winch handle for me, please, Becca?" they asked, pointing at a wall. It took Becca a moment to recognise that there was a pocket formed into the fibreglass wall, and a metal tool sticking out. She stepped over to it and pulled it out.

"This?" she asked, offering it to Lynn.

"That's the one," Lynn approved, manoeuvring the star-shaped protrusion on one side of it into the hole on top of the spool. The metal bar of the tool now extended to the side, giving them more leverage as they used one hand to crank the line in while the other still held the tail. Guessing she wasn't needed any more, Becca returned to the place she had been assigned behind the wheel.

The sail was three quarters of the way up the mast, now, and Morgan was just watching it rise. She caught Becca's eyes on her and waved for her to come forward. Becca looked at Lynn, but they were still concentrating on cranking the spool, getting the sail the rest of the way up, Becca hesitated long enough that Morgan walked back.

"What's wrong?" Morgan asked, balanced on the edge of the cockpit.

"You told me to stay back here?" Becca said.

"Well, yeah," Morgan said, "but ..." she shook her head. "Never mind." She reached out to brush Becca's loose hair with a hand, and Becca was mildly embarrassed that her fingers caught in a tangle. "Do we need the jib out, Lynn, do you think?" Lynn looked back at them, faintly amused.

"I suppose we don't *need* it," they said, adjusting the tension on the sail. "I did tell Becca we're in no hurry. But I am going to start suspecting that you're deliberately making this slower than we need to be." They locked the line they had been winding in the cleat at the top of the spool; a quick glance showed Becca that the sail was fully up.

"I mean," Morgan blushed a little, looking at the deck. "Do you blame me?" Lynn grinned.

"I don't have to blame you, to tease you for it," they said, walking over to tousle Morgan's hair. Morgan blushed a little more and batted at Lynn's arm ineffectually. Lynn grinned at Becca.

"She's cute when you get her off balance," they opined.

It was different, Becca thought, to have Morgan be the one blushing for a change. The fact that Lynn was teasing about Morgan wanting to spend time with *her* took a little longer to register, but when it did, Becca felt an echo of the same colour rising in her own cheeks.

"I guess?" she said. Lynn looked at her.

"Am I making you uncomfortable again?" they asked.

"I'm, uh," Becca stammered. Lynn nodded as if it were an answer.

"I can't promise I'll stop teasing her in front of you," they said, claiming the end of the starboard bench and turning to face Becca. "It's fun to watch her get flustered, and it's cute the way she flails. But I don't want to make you uncomfortable." Becca nodded.

"I'm sorry," she said. She really didn't mean to interfere in their relationship. Clearly, it was good for them. Why should *her* feelings matter?

"Your comfort is important," they said. "I'm not going to hurt you. Not because Morgan would pre-vent me, though she would. But you don't have to hide behind her in order to be safe."

"I know," Becca said. "I'm sorry. I didn't mean to imply ..."

"It's okay," Lynn promised. "You're not doing anything wrong."

"Other than literally all my reactions?" Becca said wryly. Lynn shook their head.

"It's not your fault that I keep forgetting how things are going to look to you," they said. "Most of our social circle is this lovely queer/poly/kinky/geeky subculture, so I don't even notice some of the stuff *until* you react."

"Yeah," Becca looked around the boat. "I don't really belong here, I know." She'd considered Morgan a friend, but beyond the Saturday afternoon games, they really didn't share many of the same social circles.

"That's not what I said," Lynn said sharply, "and it's not what I meant." Their tone drew Becca's attention. Were they annoyed with her?

"I know we're in no hurry," Morgan interrupted, moving between them and laying a hand on Lynn's shoulder. "But do you think we should maybe raise the anchor at some point?" Lynn flushed, but nodded.

"Can you do that?" they asked.

"I could," Morgan said, "but I'd rather you do it, right now. Can you give Becca and me a bit of space?"

"Of course," Lynn said. "I'm sorry." They turned back to Becca. "You're welcome here. It feels like you belong, which is why I make the mistake. I'm sorry if that was unclear." They waited until Becca nodded before heading to the front of the boat.

Seventeen

"I'm glad you're here," Morgan said, stepping up to work with the lines on the cabin roof. Becca watched her move lines off and on the spool, but didn't have the prerequisites to understand what was going on. That might be a fair summary of this entire visit, she thought wryly.

"I told you I'd take you back topside, once the sails were set," Morgan continued. "That was why I was trying to wave you forward."

"I'm sorry," Becca said, but Morgan shook her head. She wrapped another line around the spool on the other side of the hatch

"No, you're right. I wasn't clear." Morgan said, though most of her attention was on her work. The boat began moving and she smiled back at Becca. "Are you doing okay?"

"Yeah, I'm fine," Becca said.

"You really are," Morgan agreed. Forward, Becca could hear the clank of heavy chain being wound back into the boat, but Morgan paid no attention to it. She walked further back in the cockpit, still holding the two lines she had wrapped around separate spools, and rested one hand on the steering wheel in front of Becca.

"Am I in the way?" Becca worried.

"No, you're fine," Morgan smiled. "What we're doing now is trying to sail off the anchor, rather than using the motor to position us over it. That means sailing directly into the wind, which takes tacking."

"Why?" Becca asked.

"Lynn would accuse me of wanting to show off for you," Morgan grinned. "But they're not here and, to let you in on a secret, they like showing off too."

"Okay," Becca said, "but why do you have to sail into the wind?"

"Oh!" Morgan said. "Well, we set the anchor so it would dig in when the wind moved the boat on the water." She looked at Becca, but Becca shook her head.

"I'm sorry," Becca said. "I'm still lost."

"Okay, have you noticed that the whole time you've been here, the wind has come off the bow?"

"I hadn't," Becca admitted.

"Okay," Morgan said. She paused a moment, clearly trying to figure out how far back Becca needed her to go. "So, parking a boat isn't like parking a car. When you park a car, the tires have contact with the ground and you're pretty much not going anywhere."

"Right," Becca said, trying to keep up. "But a boat is floating, so the wind could push it over the water, even with the sails down?"

"That's right," Morgan said, hauling on one line while she loosened the other. Above her, the sail swung. "A lot of the point of the sail isn't to make the boat go, but to make it go the direction you want." She waited until Becca nodded before continuing. "Without a sail up, like we were all night, the boat will swing around until the pointy end is facing the wind, because aerodynamics."

"That makes sense," Becca said. She hadn't actually considered it before, but it should have been obvious.

"When we drop the anchor, we give it a fair amount of chain," Morgan continued, and the on-going sound of chain being pulled back into the boat was undeniable confirmation. "It doesn't go straight down; we actually want it on an angle, so the anchor is pulling sideways and digging in to the bottom."

"So it's not like a balloon weight, or something," Becca said.

"Right. Even with a balloon weight, it prevents the balloon from going up, but not so much from going sideways," Morgan agreed. "When it was explained to me, I was told that we don't get to stick the boat to the bottom with magnets, we actually have to wrap it around something." She adjusted the lines again, and the sail swung the other way.

"Okay, so if you have it on an angle to anchor, and you're trying to sail towards it now," Becca tried to work it out. She knew she wasn't stupid, even if Morgan was amazing. "So you want a shallower angle so it lifts more easily?"

"That's right," Morgan smiled.

Becca felt the boat rock forward a little bit, then settle back.

"And that's the anchor up," Morgan concluded. The chain clanking continued; Becca supposed it was just getting the anchor through the water, now. Morgan adjusted the sails again and turned the wheel slightly.

"You're sure I'm not in the way?" Becca worried again. "Should you be behind the wheel, if you're driving?"

"Not really," Morgan said. "Actually, if you could handle the wheel for a minute, that would be great."

"What do you want me to do?"

"You see this compass, just through the centre of the wheel?" Morgan pointed it out.

"Yes," Becca said. It was a large, black dome and she was a bit embarrassed not to have noticed it before.

"Just keep it pointing in the same direction," Morgan said. "It's a bit easier than trying to go by 'just head away from the island,' and there's a sandbar if we try to skirt it too closely." She adjusted tension on the sails once more, then secured both lines in the cleats on top of their spools.

"But what if I mess up and wreck your boat?" Becca worried.

"You'll be fine." Morgan walked over and hugged her, more confident in Becca's competence than she was herself. "It's not that difficult. I just need to duck below for a minute, and Lynn will be back soon." The sound of the chain reeling in had already fallen silent.

"Okay," Becca said dubiously. Morgan kissed her forehead and disappeared down the cabin hatch.

Becca focused on the compass position, though the wheel really didn't need much in the way of attention. She was still relieved when Lynn came back, ducking low to avoid the boom.

"How are you doing?" they asked. "Did you have a good talk?"

"I guess?" Becca said, her eyes still on the compass. It wasn't actually doing anything, but what if it did? "She explained how anchors work, anyway, then left me holding the wheel while she went inside for a minute." Lynn laughed.

"Typical Morgan," they said. "I leave you alone for a heart to heart, and she gets sidetracked turning it into a lesson."

"Would you like the wheel?" Becca offered hopefully. "I really don't have any idea what I'm doing, other than keeping it pointed south."

"You're doing fine, I'm sure," Lynn assured her. "We're going far enough south to avoid the sandbar, then we'll loop around the island and head back north."

"Okay," Becca said, still worried.

"I'll take it if it will make you more comfortable," Lynn offered. "But it's not because you're doing a bad job."

"Would you, please?" Becca asked, not quite pleading, and Lynn smiled.

"Of course," they said, walking over to stand beside Becca and resting one hand on the wheel. "I have the wheel. You're free."

"Thank you!" Becca let go and quickly moved to the bench along the left side of the cockpit. Lynn moved easily onto the seat she had vacated, behind the wheel.

"You're welcome," Lynn said, looking faintly amused at how quickly Becca dropped the responsibility. Becca blushed and looked awkwardly at the floor.

"I just, I feel like I didn't know what I was doing," she said. "And I don't want to mess it up."

"Steering the boat?" Lynn asked. "Or in general?" Becca blinked and looked at them.

"I meant steering the boat," she said. "But yeah, I guess it's true in general, too. You know what you're doing. Morgan knows what she's doing. And I'm just ... along for the ride." Lynn nodded, their hand light on the wheel.

"She does come across confident," they said. "And with the sailing, yes, we have been doing this for a while. Probably long enough to know what's safe to trust to a new person and what's not, really." The last sentence seemed a bit pointed, and Becca shifted uncomfortably.

"In general, though," Lynn continued, "I'm not sure Morgan is nearly as skilled as she'd like you to believe."

"But the thing at the mast," Becca said, blushing to discuss it but pushing forwards despite her reaction. It wasn't as if Lynn didn't *know* what had happened, anyway, and this was more than Becca could make sense of on her own. Maybe talking to somebody else would help. "She knew exactly what she was doing, took the time to explain it to me, changed it when I needed her to ... and I was just useless."

"I can understand how it felt that way," Lynn said, and their tone was serious. "And I wasn't there, but I think you're misunderstanding some-thing important."

"What's that?" Becca asked.

"What Morgan was doing, when she took you up to the mast, wasn't rope, not really." Lynn was watching Becca now, though the compass wasn't straying from its assigned position. "In the cabin, what she was showing you was rope, was tech-nique and ideas. But from the point she asked if you wanted to go up on deck with her ... in a real sense, what Morgan was doing wasn't rope, but Becca."

"What do you mean?"

"I wasn't there," Lynn said again. "So I'm guess-ing. But it's very much an educated guess; I saw her shift, even in the cabin, when she offered. Waiting for you to say no, hoping you'd say yes."

"But I did say yes," Becca said. Lynn smiled.

"Yes, you did. But I don't think she'd expected you to."

"Did I do the wrong thing?" Becca asked.

"No, not at all." Lynn sighed. "I'm explaining this poorly, and I apologise. And maybe this is a conversation you should be having with Morgan.

But she's really not good at showing weakness or uncertainty, and my teasing her to show you she's not this awesome god-like person has the opposite effect."

"I'm sorry," Becca said. She wasn't sure what she had done, but it was probably down to her just re-acting wrong to everything.

"Morgan knows how to do rope," Lynn tried again. "Like the sailing, she's had practice. But when she decided to engage in a scene, rather than just a demonstration, it stopped being about the rope, and it started being about her partner."

"You were still downstairs, though," Becca objected.

"I meant you," Lynn said, and Becca blushed. It didn't help when they continued, "And don't tell me that you weren't doing anything. At least in that scene, you were her partner."

"I don't understand," Becca said. Why did Lynn keep insisting that something had happened? She looked back at the cabin hatch. What was taking Morgan so long, anyway?

"You said she explained things to you, adjusted to your comfort level?"

"Yeah," Becca said. Lynn was obviously trying to make the explanation clear, but Becca re-membered Morgan's intensity on the deck, Morgan's explanation that "*this* is rope."

"At that moment, in that scene, those were the important things," Lynn insisted. "Not how to wrap the ropes and tie the knots; that, she knows how to do. But how to make it good for you, how to help you understand what was going on. How to honour your fear, but still leave room for you to choose to back out or go forward."

"She ... she did all that," Becca admitted. Lynn nodded.

"I believe you," they said. "Though you might want to tell her that, at some point. She was extremely concerned that she had made mistakes in that, and hurt you."

"But she was so certain," Becca objected. She didn't disbelieve Lynn, but it also didn't fit with what she had seen.

"She does that," Lynn said. "And that's part of my point. She wants you to feel safe, so she does her best to let you believe that she has perfect control, that she can *keep* you perfectly safe. And a lot of that is an imperfect attempt to perform a role, rather than the hyper competence you seem to be seeing."

"You don't think I'm hyper competent?" Morgan sounded amused, but Becca jumped; she hadn't seen the other woman emerge from the cabin. Lynn was unperturbed.

"I don't," they said. "And neither do you. I saw you last night, remember?" Morgan blushed a little and peered forward, turning her face away from Lynn and Becca to check the sail.

"You seemed perfect to me," Becca offered. Morgan shook her head.

"'Perfect' would have warned you before I put my hands between your legs. 'Perfect' would have been telling you what was going to happen without you even needing to say anything. 'Perfect' wouldn't have *scared* you like that." The pain in

Morgan's voice was surprising, and the intensity of her self-recrimination.

"But," Becca managed. She took a breath. "My reactions were just wrong. It wasn't you who did anything."

"But what I was *trying* to do was show you a good time," Morgan said. "Your reactions were the point, helping you feel good about what was happening, but I kept making you feel unsafe and," she shook her head, started again, then stopped. "So yeah, I guess Lynn is right. Last night, I wasn't hyper competent. I was barely competent at all."

It was Becca's turn, now, to reach out and try to give comfort. She touched her friend's arm gently. "I don't feel that way," she said.

"That's what I was trying to explain," Lynn put in. "Becca is overwhelmed and intimidated because we both seem to know what we're doing, and she doesn't."

"I've been trying to explain things," Morgan said, but Lynn shook their head.

"You have, yes," Lynn said, looking directly at their partner. "And I know you well enough to know that 'explaining things' is one of the ways you try to convince yourself and others that you still have control, when you're feeling insecure." Morgan looked away. She glanced at Becca briefly, then focussed on the lines wrapped around the spools flanking the cabin hatch. Lynn still wasn't done. "And it doesn't just affect Becca; it hurts you, too."

"Do we have to do this here?" Morgan asked plaintively.

"I think we do, yes," Lynn said. "Because this *is* something that affects Becca, but she isn't in a position to call you on it, herself." Becca wished she could melt into the deck, to give Morgan the privacy she clearly wanted.

"Becca's been seeing you as perfect and overwhelming and a little unapproachable," Lynn continued, "which is one heck of a crush, but probably not the best position for going forward."

Becca blushed and shook her head. A crush? She didn't *think* she had a crush on Morgan. Though, come to think of it, she wasn't sure what having a crush *would* feel like. Maybe Lynn was right?

"Is that true?" Morgan asked. "Am I that overwhelming and unapproachable, for you?"

"You're my friend," Becca fumbled for words that would make her feel better. "And you're awesome, and better than me in every way, and I don't know why you bother spending time on me. But I'm glad you do."

"That sounded a lot like a yes," Morgan said softly. Becca shook her head.

"Sure, it's a bit overwhelming, trying to keep up with you, sometimes," she said. "But that's only because you're awesome, and it's worth trying to keep up with you, even if I'm not good enough."

"But you *are* good enough," Morgan insisted. "I'm sorry I make you feel that way. I'm just ... I have different skills than you do, but that doesn't make them better."

"This part," Lynn interrupted quietly, "doesn't have to be done here." When Morgan looked at them, they nodded. "This is a conversation you need to have with Becca, but I don't think I need to be here for it. Why don't you let me steer the boat, and you two can talk on the deck."

"Is that okay with you?" Morgan asked Becca, extending a hand. Becca took it.

"Okay," she said.

The sail was set to starboard, so Morgan led Becca carefully along the port side of the deck. Having Becca's hand in hers was pleasant, as always, but she worried about the way Becca seemed to be holding back. Was it just the unfamiliarity of the boat or, as Lynn had suggested, was it something *she* was doing to make Becca uncomfortable?

"Be careful of the boom, when walking along the deck," she warned Becca. "When we're underway, like this, it may come around to catch the wind, hard enough to knock you off."

"Okay," Becca said, and Morgan cursed herself. She was over-explaining again. No wonder Becca was overwhelmed.

"It will be okay, once we get forward of the mast," Morgan continued. She just couldn't seem to stop. "I'm sorry. I'm just ... I want you to have the information you need to stay safe."

"I appreciate it," Becca said. "Thank you for taking care of me."

"I do my best," Morgan said sincerely. She led Becca forward to the space between the mast and the skylight from her cabin. "I should have brought the picnic mat. Do you mind if I go back for it?"

"I ... sure?" Becca said, seeming a bit be-wildered, and Morgan moved swiftly back towards the stern.

"That was fast?" Lynn asked, as she returned to view. "You forgot Becca."

"I forgot the picnic mat," Morgan explained, ducking back into the cabin. This time, she thought to grab bottles of water and the container with the remaining butter tarts, too. Passing through the cockpit again, she paused long enough to shove a butter tart at Lynn.

"You're a dork." Lynn said, taking the pastry. "And I love you. Now go and actually talk to Becca. You two are cute together, and I want this to work out."

"I love you, too," Morgan said. "And thank you. Wish me luck."

"I wish you the courage to have the conversa-tion you need," Lynn said.

"Yes, oh wise mentor," Morgan rolled her eyes, but she was glad of Lynn's support. Forming a new relationship didn't require Lynn's approval, but Lynn did know her well enough that their advice was worth heeding.

Eighteen

Becca looked a little lost, standing alone in the space before the mast. She smiled when she saw Morgan coming, and Morgan waved. Lynn was right, she realised. She really was a dork.

"Hold these a second?" Morgan said, passing the water bottles and plastic container to Becca before spreading the picnic mat on the deck.

Becca was still just standing there, looking bewildered, when Morgan had finished spreading the rainbow-checked fleece across the decking and took back the food and water.

"I'm sorry," Morgan said. "I'm doing a bad job of being less pushy and overwhelming, aren't I? Come sit down." She patted the mat beside her. Becca sat down gingerly near its edge.

"I didn't say you were pushy," Becca said, fingering the fleece of the picnic mat. "I don't ... I like you, I like spending time with you, even if you are so much better than I am."

"I'm not, though," Morgan said. "I know how to sail, and I know how to do macrame on people, but that's just ... that's not something that's relevant in your life, so you never needed to learn it."

"Yeah, but you can do everything I can, *plus* the sailing and the rope and the travel and ... everything."

"I doubt that," Morgan said. "I ... I'm not even sure what you do at work all day, to be honest."

"It's just an office job," Becca said. "Maintaining the network, resetting passwords ... so many password resets. Dealing with rollout issues, when there's an upgrade. Just boring, mundane stuff."

"It only feels boring and mundane because you've been doing it for years, though," Morgan said. "The stuff you think is so impressive is stuff I've done for years."

"It's different, though," Becca argued. "There were classes. High school, university, work. Just doing the next thing I'm supposed to be doing. It's not like the stuff you know."

"I've made some different decisions about what I've learned," Morgan admitted. "But there are classes for that, too. None of it is stuff you couldn't decide to learn. We saw that last night, with the kitchen roll."

"Can I learn it?" Becca just refused to accept what Morgan was telling her. "I didn't even get it right on the paper towels."

"Not your first time, no." Morgan said, reaching out to take Becca's hand. "But you did get it." Becca nodded grudgingly.

"Eventually," she admitted. "But I'm no good at it."

"Not yet," Morgan said. She decided to risk some gentle teasing. "If you did want to get better at it, I'd be happy to give you more opportunities to practise." Becca blushed and looked at the picnic mat.

"On the paper towels?" she asked.

"That's one option," Morgan said, watching her friend's reaction carefully. "It's not the only one."

"Are you teasing me?" Becca asked, looking at Morgan uncertainly.

"Only a little," Morgan smiled. "It's a real invitation."

"Why?" Becca asked, her eyes wide and vulnerable behind her glasses.

"Because I like you," Morgan said gently, trying not to scare her. "Because bottoming for rope is something I enjoy doing with people I like." Morgan wasn't sure how to read Becca's reaction, the way Becca's hand squeezed hers but her eyes returned to the picnic mat. She tried to be reassuring. "It's not something I'd ask you to do, if you're not interested. And if you'd rather stick with kitchen roll, that's okay, too."

"I don't want to hurt you," Becca said, stroking the picnic mat anxiously. "I *think* I remember the safety stuff, but what if I make a mistake?"

"Then it would be a good thing you were practising on somebody who knows how it's supposed to feel," Morgan said. She reached out to touch Becca's very red cheek. "Mistakes happen in learning. The point isn't to be perfect, but to let yourself play with it."

"I don't know," Becca hesitated.

"And that's okay, too," Morgan said. "The offer is open, if you want to take me up on it later. And I'm not going to push it, if you're not interested."

"I'm not ... uninterested." Becca blushed. "It's ... umm. It's an interesting thing to learn." Morgan grinned and decided she could risk teasing a little further.

"If you want more experience from the other side," she offered, "we could do that, too." Becca's blush deepened.

"You'd ... really want to do that again?" Becca asked. "But I messed it up. Lynn said you were worried, afterwards."

"I was worried that I'd hurt you," Morgan said. "And yeah, if you decide to let me tie you again, we'll know more things we should discuss first. But you didn't mess it up."

"It felt like I messed it up," Becca said. Morgan nodded.

"It felt like I messed it up, too," she admitted. "I did worry that I had hurt you, and you'd be afraid of me and never want to do anything like that again, and ..." Morgan trailed off.

"That's not how it felt to me," Becca said. "I felt like you knew exactly what you were doing, what *we* were doing, and all I needed to do was follow along ... and I wasn't doing that right."

"I wanted you to feel safe and comfortable," Morgan said. "I was trying to show you something I enjoyed, and it didn't feel like I was able to make you enjoy it." Becca nodded.

"If I ... didn't enjoy it?" Becca asked. "Could we still be friends?"

"Of course we could!" Morgan gripped Becca's hand tighter. "How could you think otherwise?"

Becca flinched, and Morgan immediately regretted her emphasis.

"I don't know," Becca said. "It ... I don't understand why you're friends with me in the first place! How could I possibly know what it would take for you to stop?"

"Becca," Morgan said firmly, trying to keep her voice gentle, "I like you. I like you a very great deal. I do not want to lose your friendship. I'd love to have more than that. But if you don't like what happened, I need you to tell me. It's not going to make me like you less."

"I ... I don't know if I liked it, if that makes sense?" Becca said. "It was ... it was a lot. I didn't *dislike* it? But I'd need to try it again, I think, to know if it were something I did like?" Morgan reached out to brush a bit of hair off her face, and she didn't move away.

"It makes sense to me," she said softly. "You're allowed to not like it, you know."

"I know," Becca said. "It's ... thank you for allowing me to be scared?" Morgan smiled.

"You're allowed to feel what you feel," she said. "I keep telling you that."

"Yeah, you do," Becca said, and returned the smile. "I'm a bit slow, sometimes."

"It will make you easier to catch, if you ever do run away," Morgan laughed, but she noticed Becca tense up. "I'm teasing you. You're safe." Becca nodded uncertainly.

"Don't do that to me, please?" she asked, a little shakily. "I don't ... I can't ..." Morgan didn't like the way her breath was catching as she searched for the words.

"I won't," Morgan promised, still trying to piece together what she was promising not to do. "You have a lot of trouble with the idea of being trapped, don't you?" she tried. "Not being able to get away?" Becca nodded.

"I'm sorry," she said, and she sounded near tears.

"It's okay," Morgan said. "You're not the only one. I should have you talk with Niamh, some time."

"Who's Niamh?" Becca asked. "Why do I need to talk to her?" Her voice was still shaky, and her tone asked, "Do I have to?'

"She's a friend," Morgan said. "She doesn't do well with 'trapped' either." She smiled, trying to be reassuring. "You don't have to talk to her. She might be a good resource, is all, in figuring out how to navigate those feelings."

"Okay," Becca said, but it was a more passive acceptance than Morgan liked.

"For right now, what I can promise," Morgan said, "is that a safeword will always work with me."

"Always?" Becca asked. "Aren't they just for ... when you're doing stuff?" Morgan shook her head.

"That's one way to use them," she said, "But you've seen me use a safeword with Lynn, outside of a scene. You saw it work. And I promise it will work for you, too."

"Okay," Becca said slowly, and Morgan could see her calming as she accepted the truth.

"If I am pushing hard enough that you feel trapped or scared, all you need to do is tell me to back off," Morgan promised. "Lynn's right when they say I can be pushy, but I don't want to hurt you. Especially not accidentally."

"But on purpose?" Becca worried.

Morgan shook her head. "Not unless you really wanted me to." It was important that Becca understand this, but it was so hard to get through to her. "Wanted for your own reasons. Not just because you thought you should, or wanted to make me happy, or something like that. It's ... not something I can see being comfortable doing with you any time soon."

"Why not?" Becca asked. She sounded honestly curious. Morgan tried to find a safe way to word it, and couldn't find one.

"Because I don't trust you to be able to say no to me, yet," she said. "Because I've watched you say yes when you're scared and I haven't been sure that I should believe it. Because with a hug, or even with tying you up, I have a level of control that I don't with something that's intended to cause pain." She shook her head. "I'm not even sure it makes sense, when you think about it logically, but I still feel like it's different, like it's not somewhere I want to go with you, yet. So I'm not going to."

"I ..." Becca started, but she didn't finish the sentence.

"You get to say no, Becca," Morgan said quietly, "but so do I. Just because I've done and enjoyed something with other people doesn't mean I want to do it with you. Okay?"

"I'm sorry," Becca said.

"It's okay," Morgan said. "A lot of people forget that, forget that the top gets to say no, too."

"Okay," Becca said.

"So can we just accept that I don't want to hurt you?" Morgan asked.

"Yeah," Becca said, looking at the deck. "I'm sorry."

"It's okay," Morgan said, and smiled. "There's lots of stuff I would like to do with you."

"Like what?" Becca looked up.

"Like sit on the deck in the sunshine and eat butter tarts," Morgan said, opening the box. "Does that sound like something you could enjoy sharing with me?" Becca blushed.

"Yeah, it does," she said, and took a butter tart from the box. Morgan smiled and took the last one, nibbling at it quietly. Just sitting there with Becca, nothing special required of them, was really nice.

She was seriously going to owe Lynn after this, and it would be more than worth it.

Morgan watched contentedly as Becca finished the butter tart, watched her lick her fingers clean and look around.

"How are you doing?" Morgan asked.

"I'm okay," Becca said. "This is nice. Thank you for the butter tart."

"Thank you for sharing it with me," Morgan said, brushing Becca's cheek with her fingers. Becca blushed a little, for no apparent reason, and Morgan smiled.

"I'm ... you're welcome?" Becca said. Morgan used the same hand to brush a stray bit of hair away from Becca's face.

"I brought a brush up with me," Morgan offered. "Would you like me to brush your hair for you?"

"I can do it," Becca said, looking a little embarrassed. Morgan nodded and passed over the brush, watching the other woman work through the tangles.

"You have lovely hair," Morgan tried again.

"Thank you?" Becca said, seeming confused. "It's nothing special."

"You're special," Morgan said. "That means your hair is, too."

Becca blushed and looked down at the mat, but kept brushing her hair. Morgan admired the way the sun caught almost reddish highlights from the smooth brown strands and smiled at the way the wind pulled it away from where Becca was trying to smooth it in place.

"Thank you," Becca said, passing back the brush.

"My pleasure," Morgan smiled. "I'd love to braid it for you, if you'll let me."

"You ... would?" Becca asked. Morgan smiled at her.

"Only if you're willing," she said, remembering to leave Becca room to feel like she could escape.

"I'm ... that would be very nice?" Becca said, her voice hesitant and a little confused.

"Can you move over and sit in front of me?" Morgan asked her to move, rather than risking chasing her across the deck. Becca shuffled over, sitting with her back to Morgan. Morgan placed a gentle hand on Becca's shoulder, but there was tension under it.

"You seem nervous," Morgan said. "Can you tell me why that is?" Becca shrugged her shoulders, but they didn't relax all the way.

"I don't know," she said. "This situation? It hasn't happened to me before, and I'm not sure why you want to do it or what you expect from me, and I'm afraid I'll do it wrong." Morgan nodded and slowly stroked the brush through Becca's straight, brown hair. There was a reflexive flinch, but Becca didn't actually move away, so Morgan continued.

"You're not used to people flirting with you?" Morgan asked.

"Is that what's happening?" Becca asked. She sounded honestly bewildered.

"It is," Morgan said carefully, brushing slowly and steadily. "Offering to brush your hair for you was part of flirting with you, too. And you rejected that, and it was fine."

"I did?" Becca asked. Morgan's soothing words were not having the intended effect.

"Yes," Morgan split the hair near the crown of Becca's head into three sections, keeping her motions gentle and predictable. "You said you'd rather do it yourself than let me, and that was fine."

"I … didn't realise?" Becca said. "I'm sorry. I didn't mean to reject you."

"It's okay," Morgan assured her, starting the braid. "You're allowed to say 'no' or 'let's do this instead'. And I still got to watch you brush this lovely hair." Becca blushed and tried to duck her head. "Are you okay?" Morgan asked, as her grip on the hair brought Becca up short.

"Yeah," Becca said. "Just embarrassed."

"Why?" Morgan smiled at the back of her head. "Because I like watching you?"

"Maybe?" Becca said. Even from behind, Morgan could see the way she was blushing.

"I don't mean to embarrass you," Morgan said. "You're safe here, with me." She gathered more hair from further down on Becca's scalp and incorporated it into the braid.

"I just …" Becca paused, looking for words. "Flirting?" she said.

"Yes," Morgan tried to keep her tone reassuring. "This, brushing your hair, braiding it, is a reason to be near you, to touch you in a way that's not scary, to build that feeling of connection."

"Why?" Becca asked.

"Because I like you," Morgan said. "Because I value your friendship. Because I want to build a closer relationship with you."

"Oh," Becca said.

"Are you okay with that idea?" Morgan asked.

"I'm ..." Becca tried. "This is nice. I like being close to you. Even if I don't understand what you're doing."

"I'm braiding your hair," Morgan said, a smile in her voice. "And maybe getting you used to the idea that my teasing and flirting can feel good." Becca blushed, but her head still wasn't going anywhere; that was an unintended benefit of the hair-braiding. "And I'm enjoying watching you get shy and flustered, too."

"That's not fair," Becca complained, covering her face with her hands.

"Not one little bit," Morgan agreed, continuing the braid down her back. "And it can feel good, despite being unfair, can't it?"

"Maybe?" Becca's words were slightly muffled by her hands. Morgan tied off the end of the braid with a black elastic.

"You're safe with me," Morgan said, a gentle hand on Becca's shoulder again, slipped in between the padding of the buoyancy aid and the woman's shirt. "Even when I'm teasing you, even when you hide behind your hands and don't know how to deal with my flirting, you're still safe."

"I know," Becca said. "I just ... this sort of thing doesn't *happen* to me."

"It's happening now," Morgan pointed out.

"But it doesn't make sense," Becca complained. "I'm boring and plain and I react wrong and I can't possibly be worth the trouble!"

"You are fascinating and adorable and very much worth the effort of reminding you so," Morgan said. Becca wasn't quite pulling away, not yet, but her muscles were tense under Morgan's hand.

Nineteen

"Becca, please," Morgan said. "I *like* you. Why is that so hard to believe?"

"It just doesn't make sense," Becca said, turning to face her. "This doesn't *happen* to me. Other people are interesting and fun and make connections and flirt and ..." She shook her head. "I just ... it's not something that happens to me."

"What would it mean, if it did happen to you?" Morgan asked gently. Becca shook her head again.

"I don't know," she said. "It just doesn't, okay?"

"It's not okay," Morgan said softly. "It's not okay, because you're dismissing something that is currently happening and pretending it isn't." She sighed. "It would be okay if you were rejecting me because you're not interested. I know how to deal with that. But this rejecting yourself on my behalf? I can't be okay with that. This is my friend you're running down, somebody I care about very much."

"I'm sorry," Becca said, looking down at the picnic mat between them.

"*Are* my attentions unwelcome?" Morgan asked the question explicitly. "You're allowed to tell me you're not interested, that I need to stop flirting with you. But so far, every time I've asked if I should back off, you haven't wanted me to."

"I don't," Becca said, looking up only briefly. "I ... I don't want to lose your friendship. I like being with you."

"And is that all you want, friendship?" Morgan asked.

"I don't know," Becca said. "What else is there? What would it mean if I wanted more? I ... I'm not used to feeling this way, and it's confusing and scary and I don't want to hurt you but I don't know what to do, to not."

"As if you were back in high school?" Morgan asked sympathetically. Becca shook her head.

"I never felt this way in high school." she said.

"What, no crushes on a cute guy?" Morgan teased gently. "Or a girl?" Becca shook her head again.

"I mean, I knew I was supposed to. I thought about it, I guess. Like this guy might not be awful, if I had to be with somebody. But it wasn't something I really wanted. Nothing like ..." she waved her hands vaguely. "I want to do stuff with you. Even if it seems scary, but I know you like it, I kind of want to at least try it? Because if you like it, then it can't be that bad?" Becca shook her head again, fingers running over the fleece of the picnic mat. "I know. It's stupid. I'm just being stupid."

Morgan put her hand over Becca's, and Becca looked up at her.

"You're not stupid," Morgan said firmly. "It's not stupid, and neither are you." Becca tried to look away, but Morgan moved her other hand up to her friend's cheek, holding her gaze. "I get that it's scary for you. But I care about you. I would like to explore a relationship with you that includes more than what is usually included in friendship. But your friendship matters to me, very much, and I don't want to lose that for anything."

"What does that even mean?" Becca asked. "What would 'more than friendship' look like? I don't know *anything*."

"I don't know, either," Morgan said quietly. "There's not some relationship-shaped stencil that we have to conform to. We can see what works for us, what feels good, what's comfortable or not-comfortable-but-in-a-fun-way, and we can make our relationship out of that."

"I don't know," Becca said again, but it was uncertainty in her voice rather than rejection. "I know you don't want to have a sexual relationship with me, at least ..."

"How did you decide that?" Morgan asked, confused.

"You said it last night, that you didn't intend to go there with me," Becca said, not sounding any less confused than Morgan felt. "Not that I blame you. I'm not ..." She gestured to herself with a shrug.

"Becca," Morgan said, "that's not what I said. I didn't say I didn't *want* a sexual relationship with you; I said I wasn't going to *do* anything sexual."

"Is there a difference?" Becca asked.

"Yeah, there is." How could she explain the difference between wanting and doing, if Becca didn't already understand? "Last night, it would absolutely not have been appropriate for me to push things in a more sexual direction. You were scared and already at the edge of what you could share with me. I don't want to force you into anything you're not making a free choice to do. Last night, you couldn't have done that."

"But I ..." Becca's eyes were a little too wide, a little too frightened, and Morgan was already being as gentle as she could.

"We don't have to go there," Morgan said with as much quiet sincerity as she could muster. "We don't *ever* have to go there. I like you. I don't want to scare you or make you do something you don't want to do."

"What if I just don't know?" Becca said. "I don't ... I don't know."

"That's okay," Morgan said. "You don't have to know. There's no contract to sign. I'm not asking you to agree to anything that will bind you later."

"I mean," Becca blushed, looking at the mast. Morgan smiled.

"I certainly *can* bind you later," Morgan teased gently. "But you remember the way that works, don't you? That you can stop me when you need to. That when you're scared or confused, I will help you get back to being okay." Becca nodded, taking a deliberate breath.

"It's hard to believe," she said. "It's hard to believe I did that. Hard to believe I wanted it. Hard to believe you ..." She trailed into another blush.

"Hard to believe I what?" Morgan asked.

"Hard to believe you wanted to, I guess," Becca offered. "Hard to believe you still want to, after ..." She waved a hand vaguely.

"After you honoured me with your trust?" Morgan suggested. "After you went places with me that challenged you, and trusted me to help you find your way back?"

"I was going to say 'after I messed up everything,'" Becca mumbled.

"But that's not what happened," Morgan said. "I don't want to push you somewhere you don't want to go. But I do want to invite you to explore with me. Does that make any sense?"

"Almost?" Becca said. "But ... you already know everything, you've done everything, you have all the experience. I just ... I'm the one who doesn't know anything."

"Becca, sweetheart," Morgan said. "It's not about things I've done. It's about the connection with the person I'm doing things *with*. I've done things that were fun with one person, but not so much with somebody else, and that's normal. There are things that I do with Cátia that I'd never do with Lynn, and vice versa. If you want to explore what we can enjoy together? It will be as much a discovery for me as it is for you, because that connection is what matters."

"I just ... I don't want to hold you back?" Becca said, the anxiety in her voice turning it into a question.

"You won't," Morgan said. "I want to build something with you, but that doesn't mean tearing down what I already have. I value my connection with Lynn, my connection with Cátia, and those are separate from anything we might build." She moved her hand to brush a wisp of hair that had already escaped the braid off Becca's face. "Does that make sense to you, hon?"

"I think so," Becca said.

"And I guess I should ask," Morgan said. "Are you okay exploring a relationship with me, knowing that other people are also important to me?"

"I'm ... what does that mean for me?" Becca asked. "I don't know how this works. Do I need to know these people? Have a relationship with them?"

"Well, since you're currently in Lynn's home, you should probably know them," Morgan smiled. "And having a friendly relationship with them would be preferable."

"But I mean, because they're involved with you," Becca said. "And if I were involved with you. What would that mean for us? For them and me?"

"Okay," Morgan said carefully, "this is an answer that's different for different people. But for us, a relationship isn't transitive. Just because I love you or want to play with you doesn't mean any of my other partners would, or oblige you to do anything with them, okay?" Becca nodded.

"So we're just … it's okay that Lynn is a little scary, and I don't even know Cátia?"

"It's okay," Morgan said, "though it would be nicer if you felt a bit easier around Lynn. You're *allowed* to find them a little scary, but you don't *need* to, if that makes sense."

"It does," Becca said. "And I know I shouldn't be. But they're awesome and you're awesome and you're awesome together and I'm just on the edge here and … I don't know."

"You don't have to be on the edge," Morgan said. "You can come closer."

"But I don't want to come between you two," Becca said. Morgan nodded.

"I appreciate that," she said. "But honestly? That's my responsibility, not yours. My relationship with Lynn, and what it takes to keep it healthy, is between me and them."

"What is my responsibility, then?" Becca asked. "I don't want to mess it up."

"Our relationship, yours and mine, gets to be half your responsibility," Morgan told her. "Beyond that? The hardest part might be understanding that sometimes I will be spending time on those other relationships, and they matter to me just as much as you do. And that can be hard, sometimes."

"It … sounds like it," Becca said. "But also sort of not? Like, it's not like any relationships are 24/7 access? People have jobs and friends and hobbies."

"That's true," Morgan said. "I don't know. It's a relationship style that works for me, but I know it bothers some people. I would like you in my life, but I don't want to make you uncomfortable with that aspect of being in my life."

"Just uncomfortable in other ways?" Becca asked. Morgan thought the woman was blushing again, a little bit, and she grinned.

"If by uncomfortable you mean blushy and squirmy and not sure why you're still enjoying this, but you are?" she agreed. "Absolutely." Becca was definitely blushing now, but she nodded too.

"I ... maybe?" she said, looking at the blanket, glancing up at Morgan shyly. "I don't really know what you want with me. I don't really know what I want. But being in your life sounds nicer than not, even if I am just on the margins."

"You don't have to hang back at the margins unless that's where you're most comfortable." Morgan smiled, "I did invite you to come closer." She patted the picnic blanket beside her. Becca ducked her head but shifted a little closer, red face contrasted against the yellow buoyancy aid. Morgan reached out to put an arm around her, and Becca leaned into it gratefully.

"It's not that I want to be on the margins," she mumbled, her face against Morgan's shoulder. "I just ... I'm not sure what's deeper in?"

"It's okay," Morgan promised quietly. "We can explore it together, as you're ready. And only as much faster as you can enjoy."

Becca seemed content with that, letting herself relax against Morgan. They sat quietly for some time, just enjoying the breeze and the sunshine and being together.

Eventually, of course, it had to end. Morgan's stomach complained audibly about the time since breakfast, and Becca shifted in her half-doze, pulling away to stretch. She glanced back at Morgan, found herself blushing, and looked at the deck. Morgan laughed and pulled her back into a hug. Becca only felt a little awkward as she hugged back, taking comfort in Morgan's arms around her.

"We should probably head back and see how Lynn is doing," Morgan said, standing up. She started folding the picnic blanket.

Becca nodded and awkwardly looked around for something useful to do. She picked up the plastic box that had held the butter tarts, and also the untouched water bottles.

"They're going to be okay with this?" Becca asked, still a little nervous.

"They will," Morgan said. "I promise." She finished folding the blanket and stood up. "Let's go, sweetheart." Becca blushed, but followed her ... friend? something more? She followed Morgan along the side deck to the cockpit

Lynn was still seated comfortably behind the wheel. They looked up at Morgan's return and smiled.

"Did you two figure out what's going on between you?" they asked. Becca thought they might be teasing Morgan, but she wasn't sure. Lynn did have a right to know.

"Nope," Morgan said cheerfully, shoving the picnic blanket under the bimini, on top of the sail cover. "But we can figure the details out as we go."

Becca hesitated at the edge of the cockpit. Morgan turned and took the plastic box and water bottles, but full hands were not why Becca hesitated to move into the space.

"Have you at least decided whether there's something to decide the details *of*?" Lynn asked. They didn't seem worried, just interested. It was okay. Morgan had promised it would be okay.

"Yeah," Morgan said. She turned to where Becca was still hesitating and offered a hand for balance. "Come on, hon. It's fine. Just step on the seats."

"If you're sure," Becca said, trying not to shy away from Lynn as she stepped down into the cockpit.

"I'm certain," Morgan said, looking at her. "You don't need to be on the edges," she said more quietly. "You're welcome to come closer." Becca nodded, glancing at Lynn and resisting the urge to hide behind Morgan.

"I like your hair, Becca," Lynn said. "Did Morgan do as well with words as she did with the hairbrush?" Becca blushed and ducked her head.

"It was ... something," she mumbled.

"Well, that's better than when you were insisting it was 'nothing'," Lynn allowed with a smile. "How do you feel about it?" Becca hesitated, took half a step backwards, and Morgan slipped an arm around her shoulders.

"I don't think she knows yet, *cariad*," Morgan answered for her. "We talked, but it was ... exploratory. There's space to try things, even without knowing where we're going or how far." Lynn nodded.

"Sounds like a good talk," they said. "And I can see how that would be a little scary. Or is it me?" Becca looked at the deck, and Lynn gentled their tone slightly. "Are you anxious around me because you don't get to dismiss it as nothing, any more?"

"Maybe?" Becca said in a small voice. Lynn nodded.

"Do you want to talk about that?" they asked.

"Not really," Becca whispered. Only Morgan's arm around her shoulders prevented her from pulling back further. She leaned into Morgan instead, hiding her face on the other woman's shoulder.

"I didn't catch that," Lynn said softly, but Morgan shook her head.

"Not right now," she said, holding Becca gently. "She knows you're not going to hurt her. I've told her you're okay with it. Just give her feelings a little time to catch up with what she knows, okay?" Lynn looked between the two women.

"Okay," Lynn said. "I'm really not a threat to you, though. I hope you do know that."

"I know," Becca said to Morgan's shoulder. "I'm sorry. I know I'm being dumb, here." Lynn sighed. Becca clung tighter to Morgan. Everything she said was wrong, and she was just upsetting people.

"You're a little overwhelmed," Morgan said protectively, "but you're not dumb."

"Becca, could you look at me for a moment, please? There's something I need you to understand." Becca looked up; Lynn was still sitting behind the wheel of the boat, their hands resting lightly on it. "I am happy to hear that you and

Morgan are going to explore the possibility of a relationship. I love her; I like you. You two are adorable together." Becca looked at their face, at their hands still on the wheel. Nothing in their posture looked threatening; they seemed sincere.

"I want you both to be happy," Lynn continued. "I understand that you are scared and overwhelmed by this, but I'm not. This isn't my first rodeo."

"I'm trying," Becca offered. It didn't feel like nearly enough. "I don't want to do anything wrong."

"You will, though," Lynn said frankly; Becca flinched. They nodded. "You will. So will I. So will Morgan. We're all of us just human. And when we're human, sometimes people get hurt. Morgan is glaring at me right now because she's afraid I'm going to scare you and screw up a relationship she very much wants." Becca looked at Morgan; Morgan quickly shifted her gaze off the stern of the deck, but Lynn had been telling the truth.

"I'm not trying to intimidate you," Lynn continued. "I think you can handle the truth. But there's a chance that I've misjudged and you're too scared right now to hear it. I hope not. I'm trying to support you as much as I can. And I'm not perfect, either. All I can do is hope trying's enough to matter."

"I'm doing my best," Morgan said. "I don't want to scare you away. It was hard enough getting you this close." Becca looked up at her uncertainly, and she smiled. "I'm teasing you, hon. It's okay."

"I'm not trying to be difficult," Becca said.

"I know," Morgan kissed her forehead. "Just ... have a seat and try to relax?"

"You might need to let her go, for that, love," Lynn said, sounding amused. Morgan blushed a little. She used her arm to guide Becca to sit on one of the benches lining the cockpit, but Becca saw her turn and stick out her tongue at Lynn. Lynn just laughed.

Twenty

"Do you want to watch the helm for a few while I pop below and make tea?" Lynn offered.

"Still no milk," Morgan reminded them, moving over to the wheel.

Lynn shook their head. "Okay, point. But I do need a drink. Should I grab you some water?"

"We didn't open these two, earlier," Becca offered, finding the bottles Morgan had taken from her.

Lynn picked one up. "They're a bit warm," they said, "and I still need to go below. If I don't stow the picnic mat back in the rope bag, it won't be there the next time we need it. Is there anything I can get you?"

"Could you take the hairbrush down, too, *cariad*?" Morgan asked. Lynn nodded and looked at Becca.

"Do you need anything?" they asked again. "Cold water? A snack?" They looked at her more closely. "You're actually looking a bit pink. Is that just Morgan making you blush all the time, or did you get a bit too much sun, yesterday?"

"I had sunblock yesterday," Becca said, "And my foundation had an SPF value."

"But nothing today?" Lynn asked. Becca shook her head, and Lynn frowned.

"We do have sunscreen, you know," they said. They shook their red hair away from their face. "I'd be fried to a crisp without it. You could have asked for some."

"I didn't want to be any trouble," Becca protested feebly.

"Keeping you safe and healthy isn't 'being any trouble'," Lynn said firmly. "I'll bring it up. And also a fresh bottle of water. You've already had enough sun that you probably need it." Becca nodded meekly.

"They can be a bit protective, sometimes," Morgan said, as Lynn disappeared down the hatch. "But it's okay. I'd be happy to help you apply the sunscreen."

"I mean, it's just my arms and face," Becca said, feeling herself blush. Morgan grinned.

"So does that mean you won't let me put it on you?" she asked, "or that it's okay if I do?"

"I guess, if you want," Becca said. Her braided hair refused to fall forward to cover her face, and she wondered briefly if that had been part of Morgan's plan.

"I would very much like to," Morgan said, and the grin on her face made Becca shift uncomfortably. Morgan's grin slipped a little, and she spoke more gently. "Could you come over here, please, sweetheart?"

"Okay," Becca said hesitantly, walking over to stand beside her, in the space between the rear bench and the wheel. Morgan reached up to brush her face, very gently.

"You can say no," Morgan said. "You always get to say no, if you need to."

"I don't want to say no," Becca said. "I just don't know what I'd be saying yes *to*."

"And that's scary," Morgan finished. Becca nodded.

"I know I shouldn't be, but I keep feeling like I'm in over my head."

"And all you can do is trust the buoyancy aid to work," Morgan extended the metaphor.

"Pretty much," Becca agreed, staring at the deck. Morgan stroked her finger along Becca's cheek, under her chin, lifting Becca's face to meet her eyes.

"I've tested the buoyancy aids," she said, "and you're allowed to test me."

"It's okay," Becca said, looking aside at the stern bench. "I trust you." Morgan smiled.

"As long as you trust me enough to say 'no' when you need to," she said, letting go of Becca's face. Becca shifted awkwardly, but nodded.

"I'm trying to," she promised. "But it's ... you know what parents always used to say? 'Ignore them and they'll go away, but if you let them know they're getting to you, they'll only make it worse?'" Morgan nodded.

"I remember that," Lynn said, having returned to the deck while Becca had been distracted. "And I remember it was a lie then. Abusive assholes are going to be abusive assholes, and it's not your fault that they are. No matter who tells you otherwise." They approached Morgan from the opposite side, reaching past their partner to hand Becca a sealed water bottle. It was cold in Becca's hand, moisture already condensing on the outside. "Have a drink."

"Lynn's right," Morgan said. "More importantly, if you let me know what's bothering you, I can make it *better*. I don't *want* to make it worse, and you don't have to spend time with anybody who would." She accepted a white and blue tube of sunblock from Lynn along with another water bottle. "You have the helm, Lynn?"

"I have the helm," Lynn smiled. "You two can go be adorable again." Morgan laughed and nudged Becca ahead of her, further forward in the cockpit, nearly to the cabin hatch. Morgan claimed the corner, sitting with her back to the cabin wall and one leg up on the bench.

"Sit down, hon," Morgan urged. "Or would you rather stand?" Becca sat awkwardly on the bench, facing her, back to Lynn and the wheel.

"You ... really want to do this?" Becca asked. Morgan smiled.

"Only if you feel okay about it," she said. "Will you give me your arm?" She held out a hand, wait-ing. Hesitantly, Becca put her hand in Morgan's, trying to steady her nerves. It wasn't as if she didn't know what was going to happen. Morgan was going to apply sunblock to her arm. There was no reason to be anxious about that.

Morgan's grip on her hand was firm, and the line of white cream she squirted onto Becca's arm was cool, but her touch was gentle. Fingers smeared the sunblock over Becca's forearm, up to just under the edge of the t-shirt sleeve. Morgan's palm warmed the cream, rubbing it up and down Becca's arm, spreading the ghostly sheen of titanium dioxide over the skin.

"You're okay," Morgan said, though Becca couldn't meet her eyes. "How does this feel?"

It felt strangely intimate, Morgan holding her hand, just rubbing her arm. There was nothing improper about it, Becca knew. Morgan's hand was barely going high enough to get under the edge of her shirt sleeve.

"It's okay," Becca said, her eyes on Morgan's hand as it rubbed the sunblock into her skin. Morgan turned her hand over, exposing the paler underside of Becca's arm, and continued. It almost felt like a gentle massage.

"Are you sure?" Morgan asked quietly. "It's okay to tell me if it isn't."

"I want it to be okay," Becca said. "Do I get a choice?"

"You might not get a choice in how you feel, but you get a choice in what we do," Morgan confirmed, letting go of Becca's arm. "Do you want to give me your other arm?" Becca took a breath.

"I do," she said, putting her other hand in Morgan's. Morgan smiled and stroked the back of her arm gently, then dispensed another line of white cream.

It was easier this time, maybe because Becca had made the choice herself. There was still an intimacy to it, but it wasn't as scary. And it wasn't as if intimacy with Morgan was something Becca wanted to *avoid*. She blushed at the thought.

"Something on your mind, hon?" Morgan asked, her tone lightly teasing. Becca blushed harder and Morgan grinned.

"No," Becca said, unable to stop blushing. "It's nothing."

"Honestly?" Morgan asked.

"It's just ... thinking," Becca said hesitantly. "About the way it feels, the way it makes me feel."

"How *does* it make you feel?" Morgan asked. Her hand was still on Becca's arm, unmoving now but very much *present*.

"Embarrassed," Becca tried, reaching for the right words. "Vulnerable. Connected?"

"Is that a bad feeling?" Morgan asked quietly. Becca shook her head.

"No, it's good," she said. "Just not ... easy."

"I can understand that," Morgan said. She squeezed some of the sunblock onto her fingers and reached up to stroke Becca's face. Her fingers were gentle over Becca's temple as she moved up to trace along the hairline. She stroked down along Becca's cheek and cupped the shell of her ear. Becca shivered. "Too much?" Morgan asked.

"Not ... yet?" Becca said. She thought she was okay. Maybe. "It might be," she admitted.

Morgan nodded. One of the reasons Becca was so hesitant to tell her when to stop, she was realising, was that the other woman didn't know. She could see the way Becca tensed up sometimes, but Becca wasn't recognising it in herself. She kept her eyes on Becca's face and squeezed more sunscreen onto her own fingers.

"All you need to do is tell me," Morgan said, caressing the curve of Becca's cheek. She drew her fingers over cheekbones and down along the jawline, spreading a thin layer of the protective cream. "Are you doing okay?" Becca blushed and tried to look down, but Morgan's fingers under her chin held her in place.

"I ... think so?" Becca said, shifting awkwardly where she sat. "I'm .... You're ..." She blushed again.

"Yessss?" Morgan drew out the word teasingly, but she didn't reach for Becca's face again. There was plenty of room behind Becca for her to pull away, but so far she had made no attempt to do so. Her only resistance was the blushing and squirm-ing, both of which were heartbreakingly adorable. Morgan wondered if she knew.

"The touch is very ..." Becca trailed off. She tried the sentence again. "It feels ..."

"Gentle?" Morgan suggested. "Safe? Taking care of you?"

"Intimate," Becca blurted. Morgan's hand prevented her from looking away, but she screwed her eyes shut. Morgan reached out to touch her other cheek, stroking cream onto it, gentle but persistent.

"That may not be an accident," Morgan admitted, trying to keep her voice light, trying not to scare Becca any more than she could avoid. "How do you feel about that?"

"It's scary," Becca said, opening her eyes a crack. "It's nice. It feels ... special. But it's A Lot."

"It is," Morgan agreed, applying the sunblock to the other side of her face. "Do you need a break?"

"I ..." Becca said. "Yeah. Yeah, I do."

"Thank you for telling me," Morgan said, offering the tube of sunscreen. "Would you like to do your own neck?" Becca blinked at her but accepted the tube.

"That," she started, "yeah. That would be good." She took a shaky breath and dispensed sunscreen into her hand, rubbing it down the column of her neck and over her throat. Morgan allowed herself to at least enjoy the view. Since the view included Becca *not* slowly failing to stave off a breakdown, this was some consolation indeed.

Becca turned away slightly when it came time to rub the sunscreen onto her chest, a bit shy even though her t-shirt's v neckline was not cut particularly low. Morgan grinned.

"Feeling better?" she asked, and Becca nodded.

"Yeah, I am," she said. "Thank you." She handed back the sunscreen.

"Whatever you need," Morgan said. She dabbed a bit of sunscreen onto Becca's nose and laughed as the other woman scrunched it. "Would you like to turn around so I can do your back?"

"I get to keep my shirt, right?" Becca asked, turning the rest of the way to face the stern.

"Absolutely," Morgan said. "Could you lift up your braid, please?" Becca hesitated a moment before reaching back to comply. "Is this okay?" Morgan asked.

"Yeah," Becca said, and Morgan could hear the blush in the other woman's voice. She smiled to herself and applied a line of sunscreen right along the spine, from neckline to hairline. Becca flinched and her shoulders lifted halfway.

"Are you okay?" Morgan asked. Becca took a breath and nodded.

"Yeah," she said. "It's just a bit cold." That might even have been true; the skin on Becca's face and neck was warm and pink, and not entirely from the sun.

"Mmmm," Morgan teased. "I'm sure I can warm you up." Even from behind, she could see Becca's skin get redder, and the way she ducked her head as if to hide her face. No refusal, no pulling away, just the adorable shyness. "You okay with this?" Morgan asked again.

"Yeah," Becca said. Morgan smiled and used both thumbs to spread the sunblock, starting at the centre line and spreading outward. Palms and fingers resting lightly on Becca's shoulders, Morgan gently drew the layer of sunscreen along the hairline, then stroked down to distribute it over the back of her neck. She limited herself to areas Becca hadn't already covered, but carefully extended the coverage onto the bits of shoulder and back that weren't protected by Becca's top.

"Still okay?" Morgan asked, extending her fingers under the neckline of the shirt.

"I think so," Becca said, not sounding entirely certain. "How far are you going?"

"Just this far," Morgan said. "Maybe five centimetres. Just far enough that if your top shifts as you move, you'll still be protected." Becca nodded, and Morgan added a little more cream to her fingers. "You can let go of the braid now."

Slowly, Morgan distributed the sunscreen across the top of Becca's shoulders and her upper back, taking advantage of the opportunity to rub tense muscles as she worked in the sunscreen. Slowly, Becca relaxed, so by the time Morgan was satisfied with the coverage, Becca was comfortably leaning back against her chest. Morgan smiled. She could see Lynn watching from the helm, an indulgent smile on their face, but they didn't say anything to break the moment.

The trip back to the mainland took several hours at their leisurely cruising pace. Becca actually seemed to have drifted off to sleep, still resting against Morgan. It made sense; from what Lynn had said, she had had a long night. Morgan was happy just to hold her, listening to her breathing and watching her chest rise and fall.

The weather held lovely, with a following wind. Between the thermal mass of the lake and the stiff breeze that propelled them, temperatures on the boat remained pleasantly cooler than the raging summer the forecast had predicted further inland.

Twenty-One

Becca drifted slowly back to consciousness with the sound of wind on the sail, only becoming aware of Morgan's arms supporting her when the other woman spoke.

"Did you sleep well?" Morgan asked. Becca blushed and struggled to sit upright, pulling away from Morgan. How long had she been out?

"I'm sorry," she said quickly. "I didn't mean to fall asleep on you." Literally on her, Becca realised, and her blush deepened.

"It's fine," Morgan said, reaching out to touch Becca's arm again. "Really. It's an honour that you trusted me enough to sleep." Becca looked back to the wheel, but Lynn just smiled at her.

"You needed the rest," they said. "If I'd needed Morgan for something, we'd have woken you, but she's right. It was fine."

"I'm sorry," Becca said again, and Morgan nodded.

"Are you hungry?" she asked, changing the topic. "There's bread and cheese left, or we can take over the wheel and let Lynn put together something that actually tastes good."

"It's likely to just be leftover pasta salad or some sandwiches," Lynn warned. "It's a lovely day, but it's rather warm and I'd rather not turn on the hob."

"We?" Becca asked nervously.

"I'll steer," Morgan promised, "if you just sit beside me and keep company?"

"I think I can manage that." Becca tried a smile. It felt surprisingly natural.

Lynn's idea of a 'simple' pasta salad was lemony and basilful, and studded with bits of onion, cucumber, and cherry tomato. Olives and feta cheese rounded out the flavours, and each bite was a little different. If this was what Lynn called 'just leftovers', she could see why Morgan was happy to abide by their dietary restrictions when on board.

Becca had slept away the remainder of the morning, it seemed, but it was a lovely afternoon to be on the water. Although the mooring behind the island had been isolated, the number of boats they saw increased as they approached the mainland. To Becca's surprise, Morgan and Lynn took the sails down before entering the marina, switching to a motor she hadn't realised the boat had.

"Oh, yes," Morgan said. She was still at the wheel after lunch; Lynn was moving between the uprights that supported the lifelines around the deck. At each, they carefully adjusted the height of a white cylindrical bumper, adjusting them so their bottoms hung just above the waterline. "The motor itself is behind the stairs down into the cabin."

"But why?" Becca asked. "Isn't this a sailboat?" Morgan smiled.

"It is," she said, "But the wind is not exactly the most obedient of servants. In the close confines of a marina, between the wind, the current, and the wakes from the other boats? It's safer to use the motor, just to give us that much more control."

"One thing, though," Lynn said, returning to the cockpit. "Docking is a tricky business, even with the motor. We like you. We value you. We want you here. But we really need you to stay out of the way and let us concentrate until we're docked, okay?"

"I'm sorry," Becca said.

"It's okay," Lynn said, lowering themself to the seat across the cockpit from Becca. "You haven't done anything wrong. Nobody thinks you would deliberately do anything wrong. And I'm telling you now so you don't think we're mad at you when it's just that we need to pay attention to docking in a strange place."

"Okay," Becca said faintly.

"You're okay tucked up in the corner like that," Morgan offered. "Or if you'd rather go below, you can do that."

"You'll have a better view up above," Lynn offered. Becca nodded and hunkered down in the corner where the bench met the cabin wall.

To the left of the boat, Becca could see the ferry dock. Morgan steered right, towards a place where a wall seemed to cut through the lake and separate it from the marina. As Morgan adjusted the angle of approach, what had looked like a single continuous barrier resolved into two, slightly offset, with a corridor to pass between them.

Morgan guided the boat through the corridor, rounding the end of the wall closer to shore to enter the marina. The whole set-up reminded Becca of the entrance to the bathroom at Walton's department store. It made sense, she supposed; in both cases the designers wanted to shelter the interior without making people stop to open a door.

Lynn had moved forward again, maybe a third of the way to the front of the boat, and was steadying themself with their left hand while holding a thick line in their right.

"Which slip are we in?" Morgan called over the noise of the engine and wind. Lynn looked back at her.

"Any of the transient slips are fine," they shouted back. "They have three hours' free dockage, which is nice. We can finish registering after we're docked."

"Fair enough," Morgan said, and surveyed the line of slips near the shore, cutting the speed to almost nothing. She glanced back at the flag flying from the rear of the boat, a solid red one with the Union Jack in the upper left corner, and back at the water. "I'm going to back her in," she told Lynn. Lynn nodded.

It didn't seem, to Becca, much different from parking a car. The individual slips were defined by strips of floating dock, almost like the lines delineating parking spaces, and the way Morgan motored past before shifting to reverse and turning to try to ease into the space was similar. She seemed to be approaching at an angle, though, rather than lining up parallel with the side of the parking space.

Of course, Becca didn't have a passenger step out of the side of the car to stop it, when she was driving. As Lynn stepped onto the dock and quickly wrapped one of the lines they were holding around a T-shaped metal bit protruding from its edge, Becca realised that a boat lacked the brakes her car had. Or the friction between road and tires. Suddenly the fact that the boat was barely moving made sense. She watched the line pull taut and the boat strain against it. Inertia swung the front of the boat towards the dock with the single line acting as a pivot point. Morgan cut the engine.

It wasn't until the bow had swung in on its own that Lynn walked to the end of the side dock and tied off the second line. White rubber bumpers nestled between the side of the boat and the wood of the dock. Becca wondered whether she was safe to move, yet; she stirred a little, but Morgan held up a hand.

"Soon," Morgan said. "We just need to secure the stern lines." Becca nodded and stayed put.

The docks floating to either side were fairly narrow, but they joined a wider walkway behind the boat. Lynn finished securing the front of the boat and walked towards the stern. Morgan tossed them two more lines, each attached to a rear corner of the boat. Lynn moved efficiently, tying them off to t-shaped cleats at the edge of the main walkway.

"Was that it?" Becca asked hesitantly. Morgan grinned at her.

"Pretty boring, you think?" she asked.

"No," Becca said. She hadn't meant to cause offence. "That's not what I meant."

"It's okay," Morgan said. "Boring dockings are good dockings. I can't blame you for not being able to see the way the current and the wind affected things. Not being able to see them easily is what makes the process so stressful." She walked over and kissed Becca's forehead. "Besides, this one was pretty easy. Trying to tie up at an unprotected fuel dock, with a dozen other boats already tied off, just ahead of a big storm? *That's* exciting."

"I think I'll take the boring one, thank you!" Becca assured her. Morgan laughed.

"Could you get the other spring line, please?" Lynn called. They had untied the first rope, for some reason, and were moving it to a tee further along the side dock.

"Of course," Morgan called back. To Becca, she said, "Just sit tight a few more minutes," and she headed forward. She was almost exactly at the new point where Lynn was tying the first line they had secured when she bent to attach a new rope to the side of the deck. Becca watched her pass it to Lynn, then Lynn took *that* line back to where they had tied the first one. The two ropes crossed in an X off the side of the boat. Becca stayed in her corner. She might be useless with boat stuff, but at least she could stay out of the way. She was still feeling useless when Morgan came to sit beside her.

Morgan looked over the docking lines. It wasn't that she didn't trust Lynn to do their work, but experience and training both told her to double-check anything safety-critical. It didn't matter that it was a nice day, or that it had been Lynn who had pulled her into sailing and they knew it better than she did: the habit was ingrained.

Satisfied that the boat was secure, Morgan looked back at Becca. She had been sitting in the corner between the bench and cabin wall, and her knees were pulled up to her chest.

"Are you doing okay?" Morgan asked, sitting on the bench beside her.

"Sure," Becca said. "I'm sorry I'm so useless."

"You're not useless, hon," Morgan tried to explain. "It's just docking. You did fine." Becca nodded, but she did not seem convinced. Morgan continued, "I guess you'll be glad to get off the boat?"

"I guess," Becca said. "At least I'll be out of your way."

"You're not in the way." Morgan reached out and touched Becca's knee. "Honestly. I've loved having you here. I've enjoyed your company. I'm excited about what we discussed on deck." Becca blushed, and Morgan smiled.

"Really?" Becca asked.

"Really," Morgan promised. "Come on. You might feel better, back on solid ground."

In theory, 'getting back on solid ground' should have been easy. The boat sat placidly with its bumpers against the dock. This should be easy.

Certainly Lynn hadn't had any trouble when they stepped off the side of a moving boat to stop it. Morgan, similarly, swung over the lines around the deck and hopped down to the side dock with no trouble at all. When Becca tried it, however, she was quickly reminded that while Morgan and Lynn lived on the boat full time, everything about it was new to her.

Sure, the boat was nice and close to the dock. There was less than a metre of space, horizontally, between the edge of the deck and the floating strip of dock.

The deck was higher, though; Lynn had stepped down onto it, and Morgan did everything gracefully, but the more Becca looked at it, the bigger a step it seemed to be.

"I ... don't suppose I could just stay on the boat forever?" Becca tried to make a joke out of it. Morgan laughed, turning back to her.

"Much as I'd love to have you," she said, "I thought you wanted to get home."

"I guess," Becca said. She didn't want to look stupid, but looking stupid for asking was better than not asking and looking stupider. "How do I get off this thing?"

"Very carefully," Morgan said with a grin.

"Carefully," Becca repeated. "That doesn't help very much." Morgan looked back at her, finally seeming to recognise how worried Becca was.

"It's okay. It will be fine." Morgan's voice had slipped into its 'reassuring' tone again, but Becca did not feel reassured. "We're always careful, but you can do this."

"You just hopped off like it was nothing," Becca said.

"She hopped off like she's been doing this for years," Lynn corrected, coming up beside their partner.

"You're allowed to not know things," Morgan agreed. "You're allowed to take time to learn."

"Okay. Well. If I'm going to learn this," Becca took a deliberate breath, "what do I do?"

"It's safest to board or disembark from the middle of the boat," Lynn said, walking along the dock to the space between where the side lines were tied. Becca followed along on the deck. "That's right. You see the shrouds, there?"

"The what?" Becca asked.

"Those cables from the mast," Morgan clarified. "You can grab them for balance."

Becca nodded and took hold of one. It felt firmer under her hand than she had thought it would, like a rigid rod rather than a flexible cable.

"Okay," she said. "What next?"

"Have you ever done any rock climbing?" Morgan asked.

"No," Becca said. "You're the one with all the interesting hobbies."

"I only tried it the once," Morgan said. "I have more interesting uses for rope." Becca blushed, and she grinned. "But in rock-climbing, they talk about keeping three points of contact at all times. Like, you have two hands and two feet, and as long as three of those are anchored, you're safe."

"Okay," Becca said, still clinging to the shroud.

"So what you're going to do is step over the life-lines, one leg at a time," Morgan encouraged her. Becca grabbed the cable with her other hand.

"That's right," Lynn said.

Becca swung one foot over the cables that fenced off the sides of the boat. Her toes curled over the strip of wood that defined the edge of the deck.

"Now the other one," Lynn encouraged. "You're safe. We're both here for you." Both heels hanging off the edge of the deck, Becca looked back nervously.

"It's okay," Morgan promised. "Just step down, now." Becca reached back with a foot, but there was nothing under it.

"You can shift your grip lower on the shrouds," Lynn said. "Just like that, yes. And now step back."

If the floating dock rocked a little as Becca's second foot hit it, she was too relieved to notice. Lynn's hand on her shoulder steadied her before Morgan pulled her into a hug.

"You did it!" Morgan said.

"Err, yeah." Becca looked at the dock, embarrassed. It was nothing for them, so why make a big deal out of her success? Morgan kissed her on the cheek.

"This may be the wrong time to ask," Lynn said, "but did you leave anything on the boat?" Becca checked her pockets. Keys, wallet, cell phone.

"No, I think I have everything," she said.

"Shoes, perhaps?" Lynn suggested. Becca looked down at her feet, bare against the wooden dock.

"Err, yeah," she said, eyeing the boat distrustfully. "I left them in Morgan's room."

"Would you like me to get them for you?" Lynn offered. "I could take the buoyancy aid, as well, if you like." Becca had almost forgotten she was wearing it. Exactly how stupid was she, today?

"I'm sorry," she said. She shrugged out of the PFD and handed it to Lynn, not meeting their eyes.

"You don't need to be sorry," Lynn corrected. "It was good for you to keep it on during the transfer, but you should be fine, now." They grabbed the shrouds with one hand and pulled themself onto the boat, then disappeared below.

"How are we going to handle the errands?" Morgan asked when Lynn got back.

"I'm open to options," they said, handing Becca her footwear. "What were you thinking?"

"Well, we need to get Becca's car, first," Morgan said. "After that, Becca, are you still comfortable driving to the grocery and laundrette?"

"Sure," Becca said, putting on her sandals. "No problem." She still seemed more subdued than Morgan would have liked, but maybe she'd relax once they were away from the boat.

"I'll finish getting us registered, then," Lynn offered. "I think we can wait on fuel and pump-out until we're ready to leave. If we stay over two nights, they'll do the pump-out for free."

"That's definitely worth waiting, then," Morgan agreed. She offered Becca her arm with an extravagant gesture. "Shall we, milady?"

Twenty-Two

From the marina parking lot, a paved promenade led all the way back to the ferry terminal. A gentle kilometre's stroll, with Morgan beside her and solid ground beneath her feet was lovely. Even the heat of the late afternoon sun on Becca's shoulders was pleasant, though the company was even better.

Probably the nicest part of the walk was sharing the time with Morgan and not having to do anything. Everything on the boat had felt at the same time rushed and also static, like nothing would ever change and yet everything was changing at once. The simple fifteen minute walk was just more space than Becca had felt like she had for days.

The pearl-blue Kia was still waiting patiently for Becca's return — she had been a little worried it would be towed overnight, but apparently fate had at least spared her that much. She opened the passenger side door and cleared a few papers off the seat, making room for Morgan before she walked around to the driver's side.

"It's still so strange to get in on this side, and not have a wheel in front of me," Morgan commented, fastening her seatbelt.

"Really?" Becca asked. "Oh, right. You do drive on the other side of the road, don't you?"

"Yeah," Morgan said. "Not that I drove much at all, but the habit of getting in on the left, when you're the passenger, is almost a reflex."

"That makes sense," Becca said. The car was a bit stuffy, so she rolled down the windows rather than turning on the air conditioner. "Where did you want to go first?"

"Probably groceries?" Morgan suggested. "We'd have to go back to the boat to get laundry, and we'd have to take groceries back to the boat, so that seems a better order to do it."

"Did you bring the grocery list?" Becca asked. She hadn't seen Morgan grab anything.

"There's a reason we do it on the cloud," Morgan grinned, pulling out her phone. "It's a shared spreadsheet; either Lynn or I can update it, and it's less likely to be forgotten on the table when we need it."

"That's actually a really good idea," Becca admitted. "I'm not sure why I didn't think of that."

"Force of habit, I imagine," Morgan said. "I don't know how many times I had to text Lynn and ask them to take a photo of the list, before we came up with this." Becca nodded, considering the route.

"So I'm not actually from here," Becca warned, "But I saw a Walton's that sells food, almost across from my hotel, and a budget grocery store about a block from there. Or do you know where you want to go?"

"I doubt it makes much of a difference," Morgan said. "Local is better, though."

"Well, they're both chains," Becca said, "But I think the budget one tends to do the locally-owned-and-operated thing."

"Sounds reasonable," Morgan said. "Are you okay with that?"

"Sure," Becca said. "I just want to make you happy."

"Oh, you do," Morgan said warmly, covering Bacca's hand on the wheel with her own. Becca's heart beat faster, and she felt her face heat up.

"I meant with where to shop," she mumbled.

"That's fine, too," Morgan said, but removed her hand. Becca took another breath to steady herself before starting the vehicle. She needed to focus on driving, not the way Morgan's touch made her heart race.

Becca pulled out of the ferry dock parking lot, onto Erie. It was only a few minutes before she spotted the store she had remembered, its neon green sign distinctive in the small strip mall; she turned onto Pulford and then left into the parking lot.

Allegedly as part of the store's commitment to "lowering food prices", the shopping carts were chained together with a coin lock system. Becca fished a loonie out of her pocket and inserted it into the slot, popping a cart free for them to use. She backed it out of the line of carts, and offered it to Morgan.

"Trying to keep my hands where you can see them?" Morgan asked. Becca blushed; she was sure Morgan was teasing, but she had also hoped that part wouldn't be obvious.

"Just giving you control," Becca said, trying to return the teasing in kind. "Over the cart, I mean."

"Of course you do," Morgan laughed, guiding the cart into the store.

The height of summer meant the produce area, just inside the door, was overflowing with fresh local vegetables and fruits. Even only four hours south of her home, Becca noticed a difference in the peaches; she thought more of those at home were imported, and the ones here seemed to be a little less apple-hard than what she could get at home. Morgan grabbed a clamshell packet of thyme and a small bag each of potatoes and apples, but then she added cherries as well as peaches to the cart

"So you have a list," Becca said, "but you ignore it?"

"Not ignore, really," Morgan objected. "I just embellish a little." She took her time looking over the other options, eventually adding a cucumber, a head of lettuce, and a bunch of tomatoes on the vine to the cart.

With the way the boat fridge was recessed under the counter, a 4L bag of milk wouldn't have been practical; a spill could be catastrophic. The 2L car-ton with the screw top that Morgan picked out made much more sense. The eggs were right next to the milk, along the back wall, but they had to turn down an aisle to access the refrigerator cases that held the cheese.

Looping back up the next aisle, with the canned goods, Morgan added some more of the baked beans she and Lynn apparently considered a breakfast food. Coconut milk, a bag of lentils, and a few boxes of flavoured rice joined the other items in the cart.

The frozen pie crust was harder to select than Becca had expected — the first one she picked up had contained lard, but looking more carefully revealed an almost identical box with a light blue banner under the brand name that was "all vegetable".

In all, the groceries only really filled four bags, including the four Coffee Crisp bars they added from the candy display at the check-out. With the limited storage space on the boat, that seemed logical; buying in bulk only made sense when one could store in bulk.

"I suppose, since we have frozen stuff, we can't really stop for supper," Becca said. "I should have thought of that before we went in."

"Would you like to get something after we pick up the laundry?" Morgan asked.

"That would be nice," Becca said, taking the bags from the cart and putting them in the hatchback. "What about Lynn, though?"

"Already texting them," Morgan said, eyes on her phone. "Do you know if there's anything we can grab them on the way back to the marina? I think I saw a sub shop."

"There's that," Becca said. "Or do they like burgers? There's a Humphrey's right across the road. I accidentally got one of their veggie burgers, once, and it was good."

"How do you accidentally get a veggie burger?" Morgan asked. "But yeah, they say a burger would be fine. Would you like me to return the cart?"

"Sure," Becca said, arranging the grocery bags so they wouldn't shift. When Morgan got back, handing Becca the coin she had used to unlock the cart, Becca explained, "My aunt is mostly vegetarian. We confused the burgers on the tray, so I had a bite before realising that I had ordered onions on mine, and that burger didn't have any."

"And you couldn't tell from the flavour?"

"Not without a beef one, side by side," Becca said. "Do you know what Lynn likes on a burger, by the way? This place makes them to order, with the toppings you like."

"Well, what do they have?" Morgan asked. Becca shrugged.

"They have a lot," she said. "I don't remember them all. Maybe we can find a list online?"

"Or I could just walk over there and go in," Morgan said.

"I can drive," Becca objected. "It's on the way."

"Don't be silly," Morgan said. "It's less than a block; it would take more time to get in and out of the car than I'd save." She leaned in and kissed Becca's cheek. "You can pick me up there, okay?"

"If you want," Becca said, blushing. She really shouldn't be reacting to every little thing Morgan did like this, she thought, but the thought didn't seem to make a difference. She closed the hatchback and climbed into the driver's seat

Morgan had been right about the walk; she was already inside when Becca pulled into a parking spot in front of the restaurant. Humphrey's was less busy than Becca had expected, until she looked at the clock. Somehow it had gotten onto seven in the evening without her noticing. Morgan returned to the vehicle with a brown bag in her hand.

"Did you know that the poutine here is vegetarian?" Morgan asked, as she climbed into the vehicle.

"I hadn't, no," Becca said. "Did you get them some?"

"I did," Morgan said. Becca started the vehicle and turned back onto Erie, heading south to the marina.

Becca helped Morgan carry the grocery bags back to the boat, but she stayed on the floating dock and passed them to Morgan rather than trying to climb over the lifelines again. Morgan popped below to deliver Lynn's food to them, and came up with a large drawstring bag. She passed it over to Becca, and went below for another. Becca recognised this one from the closet in Morgan's cabin.

"Thank you for driving," Morgan said, as they carried the bags back to the waiting car. "We really did leave this longer than we should have."

"It's okay," Becca said.

"Not that I'm entirely sorry," Morgan said. "I mean, imagine how different things would have been if the rope hadn't just fallen at your feet and gotten you all curious." Becca blushed crimson.

"I really did think it was some sort of crafts project," she objected. "It would have been okay to ask, if it had been a crafts project."

"Mhmm," Morgan said. "I believe you. Poor, innocent Becca, waylaid by wayward laundry and a wicked woman." Becca blushed and shook her head.

"I should have just ... left it," she said. "Put it back in the closet or something? I shouldn't have pried." They were almost back to the vehicle, but Morgan stopped and touched Becca's arm.

"Do you really wish you had done that?" Morgan asked softly.

"I ..." Becca said. She looked at Morgan. "I'm sorry. I .... No. No, I don't." Morgan nodded, and Becca could see her relax a little. She hadn't realised that Morgan might be nervous; she had seemed so confident with everything they did.

"I'm glad," Morgan said. "I never want to hurt you. And I know you're not always comfortable. And I worry about that, sometimes. About making you do things you didn't want to do, about taking things too far."

"But you haven't," Becca said. Every step of the way, Morgan had told her she could stop. How could she question whether Becca wished it had never happened? And was the public parking lot of a marina the best place to discuss it? She fished out her key fob and unlocked the doors to the Kia. "You've been ... you're wonderful."

"Thank you," Morgan said, hitching the laundry bag back over her shoulder and continuing to the car. "I do try."

"Thank you for that," Becca said. She opened the hatchback and stowed the laundry bag, "You really are .... I mean, I don't think I could have done any of this, with anybody else." Morgan smiled, but put her own laundry bag in the cargo area before reaching out to brush Becca's arm again.

"You really are something special," she said. "I don't know if you understand how special you are. Like, I can do rope with lots of people, and it's just rope. But with you ... well, it's not a trivial thing for me, the hope I have to build a relationship with you. And I know that doesn't obligate you to any-thing, but ... " She trailed off, and shrugged. "I'm sorry. The important thing is that, however I might feel, it doesn't obligate you to anything. We can explore the possibilities of a relationship at the rate that's right for you." Becca nodded.

"We should probably get to the laundromat," she said, though she didn't really want to pull away. "It's getting kind of late."

"Right," Morgan said, though her grin seemed a little less confident than usual. "That's a good idea. Feelings are hard; laundry is easier."

"And supper," Becca said, climbing into the driver's seat. Morgan let herself into the passenger side and fastened her seatbelt. "Do you want to just go to Humphrey's while the laundry is running?"

"Can we do that?" Morgan asked. "Leave the laundrette while our things are running?"

"I don't see why not," Becca said. She pulled out onto Robson Road, then headed north on Erie. "The Humphrey's is right in the same strip mall, and the machines lock when in use. As long as we're back by the time the cycle ends, it should be fine."

"So no getting lost in each other's eyes over custom-made burgers and poutine?" Morgan joked.

"I can set a timer on my phone, if you wanted to do that," Becca suggested. It was a little easier to tease back when eyes-on-the-road gave her an excuse not to look directly at Morgan. It would have been nice to see Morgan being the one getting flustered, but Becca knew she'd never be the one to accomplish that. She pulled into the strip mall parking lot before looking at Morgan again.

"Maybe we *should* do that," Morgan said, and Becca was the one blushing. She mumbled something and ducked inside the laundromat to fetch one of the wheeled metal laundry baskets.

At $5.50 each, the large steel front-load machines were significantly more expensive than the standard white top-loaders. There was enough laundry, though, that the two drawstring bags completely filled three of the giant machines.

Becca helped Morgan sort the darks into one and the lights into another. Morgan handled most of the underwear and delicates herself. She zipped the crocheted lengths of rope into pillowcases before adding them to the delicates load. As a last step, the laundry bags themselves were tossed in with the darks.

After withdrawing two twenties from the laundromat's ATM and changing them for coins, Morgan measured laundry powder into the drums and slammed the washing machine doors.

"The sign says not to leave machines unattended when in use," Morgan pointed out. "Are you sure we shouldn't wait until after the washing is done before we go across for dinner?"

"If you're more comfortable, I can wait," Becca said. "Though I'm not sure what to do while the cycle is running, in that case."

"I seem to recall somebody mentioned eye-gazing," Morgan said playfully. Becca blushed and looked aside. She needed to remember not to even try to tease Morgan, in the future. There was clearly no chance that she'd win.

Morgan reached out and gently took Becca's chin in her hand, turning her face so she had to meet Morgan's eyes. Becca blushed, and Morgan leaned in to kiss her nose quickly.

"You're adorable when you get all shy like that," Morgan told her. Becca just blushed harder.

"Can we ... maybe not?" Becca asked. "At least not in the middle of the laundromat?"

"Of course," Morgan said. She let Becca's chin go, stroking her cheek as her hand moved away. "I didn't mean to make you uncomfortable."

"Yes, you did," Becca said, reaching out to touch Morgan's arm. It wasn't that she didn't want the connection; it was just that the setting seemed a bit public for anything so overt. "You enjoy making me uncomfortable, and watching me deal with it, and making sure it's okay."

"I mean," Morgan admitted, "I do like teasing you." Becca nodded.

"And you have to know that's not *comfortable*, even if it's not bad." Becca took Morgan's hand and squeezed it gently. The taller woman nodded.

"I don't want it to be bad for you, I guess I should have said." She found a pair of uncomfortable chairs and led Becca over to them. "I care about you."

"I care about you, too," Becca said. "It's not bad, exactly. I'm just not sure how to take it, sometimes." Morgan smiled.

"Take it as a token of affection?" she suggested. "I love you. I love seeing you react to things I do. It makes me feel like I matter to you, too."

"You ... love me?" Becca asked. Morgan bit her lip.

"Is it too soon to say that?" she asked. "I'm sorry. I'm trying not to pressure you."

"But you ..." Becca tried to put words to her confusion. "But you have other people who are better than I am, already. I mean, Lynn, and was it Katya?"

"Cátia," Morgan said, correcting her pronunciation. "And yes, I love them, and they mean the world to me. But that doesn't mean that I can't love you, as well."

"But why would you?" Becca said. "It doesn't make sense."

"I don't know that love ever makes sense, Becca," Morgan sighed. "And if you decide you don't actually want to be involved with me, well, I'm an adult and I will get over it. I don't want to lose your friendship. But also ... seeing you hurt hurts me, the same way I hurt when Lynn does, or when Cátia does. Seeing you delight in something new is delightful. And the word I have for that is 'love', so I just ... used it."

"I ..." Becca said, still trying to process it. "I ... it's a lot to take in," she said. Morgan nodded.

"I know," she said. "I really don't want to spook you, or scare you off, or make everything get so serious so fast. It doesn't have to be, you know. Serious, I mean. It can just be silly and casual and a bit of fun, if you want." Morgan actually seemed as nervous as Becca felt, which she hadn't thought possible.

"I'm not sure I could handle silliness or a bit of fun," Becca said. "I don't know. I don't know how to do serious, This hasn't happened to me before, somebody being interested. But ... I think I love you, too?" Morgan nodded.

The washers shifted into their high speed spin cycle. Becca stood up.

"And thus the universe," Morgan said wryly, "demonstrates its disregard for grand declarations of love, calling us back to the demands of the real world."

"I kind of like being in the real world with you," Becca said. "It's nice. Even when it's just groceries or laundry or something."

"I like spending the time with you, too," Morgan said. She moved the darks from the washer drum into the basket and rolled that over to the dryers. "Though if you can convince me to love laundry, I think Lynn will submit you for canonisation." Becca laughed, and started moving the delicates into another laundry basket.

"What do you want to do with these bags of rope?" she asked. "Can they go in the dryer?"

"Better if they don't," Morgan said. "Is there somewhere we can hang them in the car?"

"We could drape them over the back seat, I guess," Becca said. Morgan nodded.

"Would you mind doing that? Morgan asked. "I have coins for the dryers, but you're the one with car keys."

"Okay," Becca said. She took the damp pillow-cases out into the hot summer evening and opened the rear door. She unzipped the pillow-cases and crawled half into the back seat, her arms full of wet rope.

One crocheted chain at a time, she laid the hemp over the back of the bench seats, trying to make sure they were spaced widely enough to be able to dry properly. The car was probably hot enough inside to bake them, but she turned the key in the ignition and lowered both rear windows a bit to try to get more air circulation. She and Morgan were just inside the laundromat, after all, so there wasn't much risk to it. The empty pillow-cases she took back inside with her; Morgan was still loading dryers.

"Thank you, hon," Morgan said, taking the pillowcases and tossing them into the dryer with the light coloured items. "It shouldn't be too long; these dryers seem to run hot." Becca nodded.

"I sort of feel a bit weird," she confided, "having the rope displayed like that to anybody who looks in the car windows." Morgan smiled.

"Remember your thought, when the one hank fell at your feet?" she asked. "That it was some sort of crafts project?" Becca nodded, blushing a little, and Morgan continued, "Well, anybody just passing by the car isn't going to have any more idea what it's really for than you did."

"I guess," Becca said. "But what if they do?"

"If they do," Morgan grinned, "If they know exactly what sort of use that rope is put to? It's because they're into it, too."

"Umm," Becca said. It made sense, but ...

"So if somebody comments on the rope and asks for your number," Morgan said, grinning, "you can know what to expect if you give it to them." Becca was pretty sure she was just teasing, but she felt her face going red anyway.

The dryers only took about half an hour, and helping Morgan fold the laundry was a comfortably mundane task. Maybe it should have been weird, handling Morgan's panties or learning what sort of underwear Lynn preferred. Becca thought it would have been, if this were some romantic comedy, but it wasn't like that at all. She was just working side by side with a woman she had known for years before they ever met, somebody who was just comfortable to be around. At least when she wasn't actively trying to make Becca blush.

Twenty-Three

Morgan took charge of sorting the laundry back into the bags. Other than being a bit larger, many of Lynn's things weren't that different from something Morgan might wear.

"It's not as if we don't borrow back and forth, either," Morgan said, when Becca mentioned it. "It's cosy, sometimes, deliberately stealing their shirt against the cold. It's like they're holding me, even if they're asleep below."

"It sounds nice," Becca admitted. "Though I think I'm glad I didn't have that image in my head, when I borrowed your nightgown." Morgan grinned.

"Oh?" she said, and her tone was definitely teasing now. "You don't *like* the idea of my hands stroking over your skin, everywhere the nightdress touched you?" Becca blushed crimson. Morgan laughed and reached out to caress her flaming cheek.

"I ... umm." Becca stammered. "I seem to recall your hands doing a lot of stroking. I mean, without relying on the nightgown." Morgan laughed again.

"Not nearly as much as I'd like to do, in the future," she said. And then she waited, watching Becca's face. Becca took a breath.

"That's not supposed to sound scary, is it?" she asked. If she knew her reactions were wrong, maybe she could just ignore them.

"I don't want to scare you," Morgan said, "but if it does, I'd like to know about it."

"I know it's just supposed to be sexy and exciting and stuff," Becca said. She looked at the bags of laundry, cinched at the tops and already in the wheeled basket to return to the car.

"Is that what's scary about it?" Morgan asked softly.

"Maybe," Becca said. "I know I'm just reacting wrong. I'm sorry."

"Your reactions aren't wrong," Morgan said. "They're yours. And they may not be reactions you enjoy, but they're still your feelings, and your feelings matter to me. Very much."

"I don't," Becca began, "I mean, I like the idea. I like it when you touch me, and the nightgown, well ..." She trailed off, blushing. "That image, of it touching me," she blushed again. "It's not bad, exactly. It's just also scary." Morgan nodded.

"Out of control?" she offered. "Not sure you can stop it?" Becca nodded, and Morgan suggested, "Not entirely sure you can keep yourself safe?"

"That, yeah," Becca said. "I think that's it, really. Like, I feel like I don't know what's going on, and even if I know the right answer for this step, well, I don't really know where it's going to go next. Or if I want to go there." Morgan nodded.

"Do you want to take the laundry back to the car?" she asked, changing the topic. Becca looked at her in surprise, and Morgan smiled. "I think you already know what I need to say to that. That we can take it slow, that we don't have to go anywhere you don't want to go. And you know all that, and it's still scary, so telling you again isn't going to magically make you feel better."

"I," Becca said. "Yeah. I do know that." She grasped the upright on the wheeled laundry basket and started guiding it towards the laundromat's entrance.

"I'll tell you again, any time you need to hear it," Morgan promised, walking beside her. "I am more than willing to give you all the control you need, in order to feel safe with me."

"Even if I don't know how much that is?" Becca asked. She fished the key fob out of her pocket and unlocked the vehicle.

"Even if," Morgan confirmed. "And I'll give you the time, too, to figure it out." She lifted the hatchback, and moved first one, then the other bag of clean laundry into the cargo area. "You did a good job with the rope. Thank you."

"It's good enough?" Becca asked. "I know it would be better if it were hanging free, but I did my best."

"It's perfect," Morgan assured her. "Are you okay walking to the Humphrey's?" It was in the same strip mall, freestanding in the middle of the parking lot.

"Sure," Becca said.. "Just give me a moment to return the basket."

Morgan had been in the Humphrey's earlier, of course, to get Lynn's veggie burger. The selection of toppings had been impressive, but the seating was typical fast food — tables anchored to the floor and metal chairs with the H of Humphrey's cut out of the backrests. The burger place was co-located with a chicken and ribs restaurant, though, so she suggested that alternative.

"Since we don't have to be back in time to get laundry out of the machines," she suggested, "shall we try the Rotisserie and Grill? Take the time to sit down?"

"If they're still open," Becca said. "It's already after nine."

Morgan smiled and brushed her back with a hand. "The sign says they're open until ten-thirty," she pointed out. "That's plenty of time to get some eye-gazing in."

Becca blushed and walked a bit faster, opening the door and holding it for Morgan without meeting her eyes.

Late as it was, the restaurant wasn't busy. Morgan scanned the small seating area— half of the building was given over to the Humphrey's after all — and noticed the perfect spot.

"For two?" the hostess asked as Becca followed Morgan into the foyer. Morgan smiled at her, putting on the charm.

"If you please," she said. "Could we sit at one of those booths at the back?" The hostess glanced over; all three of the half-circular booths were unoccupied.

"Sure," she said. "Just follow me." She led them past a handful of other tables — only two occupied, one with a young family just finishing their meal and another with an older couple chatting over pie. The hostess left them with two menus and the promise that their server would be with them shortly.

When the restaurant's sub-heading had promised chicken and ribs, it hadn't been understating the case. The entrée section of the menu consisted almost entirely of chicken, ribs, chicken and ribs, or one offering of chicken and broiled shrimp. There was one veggie burger on the menu, Morgan noticed, but this might not be the best place to bring Lynn. Tonight, though, was just her and Becca.

Becca was right about the time, though. Morgan took a moment away from admiring the other woman to send a quick message to her other partner.

```
<Morgan> It looks like we'll
         be out late.  We had
         to babysit the washers
         at the laundrette,
         and, well, there's a
         sit-down
         restaurant . . .
```

```
<Lynn> Take your time, love.
       I'll be here when you
       get home
<Morgan> Love you
<Lynn> Love you, too.  Now pay
       attention to Becca.
       I'll be fine
```

"Is everything okay?" Becca asked. Morgan looked up at her and smiled.

"Oh, yes," she said. "I just needed to let Lynn know we'd be out late."

"Oh," Becca said. She shifted awkwardly in her seat. "What did they say?" Morgan grinned.

"To stop bothering them and pay attention to you." Morgan reached out to stroke Becca's arm lightly; the other woman shivered.

"Really?" she asked. Morgan nodded and held out the phone so she could read it. Becca read the text, but Morgan wasn't sure she relaxed much. Not that there was really anything she could do about it.

"Is there anything on the menu that you can re-commend?" Morgan asked instead.

"I usually get the double leg dinner," Becca said. "The fries are good, but so is the Caesar salad."

"Do you want to get one, and I'll get the other, and we can share?" Morgan suggested. Becca blushed a little — Becca blushing was always cute, even if Morgan had no idea what she was thinking to cause it, this time — and nodded.

The server's arrival wasn't very fast, but sitting beside Becca was enough of a pleasure that

Morgan didn't mind. It was pretty late, after all; only the one server seemed to be working, and there were people with delivery bags coming in and out of the store. Morgan got the half chicken dinner, both a leg and a breast, with chips and lemonade, though she did have to correct 'chips' to 'fries' in order for the young woman taking the order to understand that she wasn't looking for a packet of crisps. She let Becca order her own double leg dinner with salad and pop.

Sharing the chips and salad gave Morgan enough excuse to slide closer to Becca on the bench. Throughout the meal, she took advantage of little opportunities to touch Becca's hand, catch her eyes, brush her hair out of her face.

"Morgan?" Becca asked at one point.

"Yes?" Morgan said with a smile.

"Are you, umm, flirting with me?" Becca asked. She sounded so uncertain that Morgan wanted to laugh.

"Yes, dear," Morgan said instead, brushing Becca's cheek and gently turning her face until she met Morgan's eyes. "I am flirting with you. Are you okay with that?" Becca nodded, blushing and looking at the table between their plates. Greatly daring, Morgan leaned in to kiss her cheek; the blush deepend to a shade that almost illuminated the table, but Becca made no move to pull away. "I like you very much," Morgan said, holding her hand. "And these little affectionate gestures, this flirting, is how I demonstrate that."

"I like you, too," Becca said. "But I don't, I mean, I wouldn't know how to do the ... how to show it like you do," she finished lamely. Morgan shook her head.

"At the moment, it's enough that you not run screaming," she teased gently. "I love you. I don't need you to jump through silly hoops to show you care about me. The flirting comes naturally to me; if it doesn't from you, it wouldn't be the same."

"So, I don't disappoint you?" Becca asked, looking up, her eyes anxious.

"Sweetheart," Morgan said, "you are so far from disappointing me that you have no idea." She pulled Becca into a hug and kissed her forehead. "I love you, not some cardboard cut-out of an ideal lover. The way you feel, the way you react, is what's important to me."

"I just worry," Becca said. "I don't want to do this wrong. I want to be good enough. I don't want to hurt you."

"I love you too," Morgan said. "The only way you could hurt me would be to not tell me things I need to know, especially things where you'd get hurt for me not knowing." Becca nodded.

"So, umm, tomorrow is Saturday," Becca said, an obvious attempt to change the subject. "Are you looking forward to the game?"

"The game?" Morgan pretended not to remember their regularly scheduled roleplaying session. "Were you going to come over and learn to play strip poker? Or was I meant to come to your hotel room for private lessons?"

Becca blushed and batted at her. "The game with Erin and them."

"I'm not sure Erin would want to play strip poker with us," Morgan said. "I think she's straight. And her husband might object, even if she weren't."

"The roleplaying game," Becca clarified, and then she took a breath. Her voice was less confident as she asked, "Can you stop joking about strip poker, please?"

"Of course," Morgan said. "I'm sorry I distressed you. I was just kidding around. I'd never make you play, if you didn't want to."

"I'm sorry," Becca said. She looked so sad, as if she were the one who had done something wrong. "I knew it was just a joke. I'm just reacting wrong. Again."

"Stop that," Morgan said, and Becca flinched at her tone. Morgan made an effort to gentle it. "Your feelings are valid. When I go too far, telling me is exactly the right thing to do. Okay?"

"Okay," Becca said, but she still seemed subdued.

"We took down those green dragons last session, right?" Morgan recalled her attention to the game. "There were a couple of emeralds in their hoard, I think."

"Yeah," Becca said. "I called dibs on those for the Ring of Gygax. I've been hoping to craft it ever since I found the formula in that ancient tome, two quest-lines back."

"How's that going to work?" Morgan asked. "Are they just like spell components, so they get consumed?"

"Not exactly," Becca explained, settling into the topic. "Erin says that to craft the ring itself, I'd need profession: goldsmith. Otherwise, I'll need to work with an NPC to incorporate the magic into the metal and the stones."

The rest of the meal, Morgan kept the topic on the game and their characters. She still took advantage of each opportunity to touch her friend, to build the connection, and slowly she saw Becca relax again.

It was tempting, when dinner was over, to make a comment about walking Becca home, then staying the night. It was very tempting, but Morgan wasn't entirely sure Becca would say no to her, if she needed to, and that wasn't a risk she wanted to take right now. Not when a stupid joke had upset her so much. Not when they'd be apart the next day, and she might not see Becca again before they had to leave.

Morgan let Becca drive her home, and help carry the bags to the boat. Lynn came up without being asked and swung the bags over the lifelines to carry them below. Morgan walked back to the carpark with Becca.

"You're sure you don't want to stay another night?" she invited. Becca shook her head.

"I have my own room," she said, "with my own things. And if I stay with you, I might be too distracted to make it to the game, tomorrow."

"Would that be such a bad thing?" Morgan asked.

Becca blushed. "We have a responsibility to the others," she said. "Louise and Gabrielle and Erin."

"I care more about you," Morgan said.

"I care about you, too," Becca said. "But we made a commitment." She leaned in then, surprising Morgan as their lips met.

It was the first time Becca had initiated a kiss, and Morgan had to make a real effort not to escalate, not to pull her closer and explore her mouth with her tongue, to just accept it. She couldn't afford to frighten Becca right now, not when it was so late and Becca was leaving and they didn't even have solid plans for when they would meet again. She yearned for more, but Morgan returned the kiss as chastely as it was offered, and then watched Becca get into the car and drive away.

Twenty-Four

Watching Becca drive away from the marina for her own hotel room had been hard, but Becca had pointed out that they couldn't just skip the weekly gaming session to spend more time together. They both had a responsibility to Erin, Louise, and Gabrielle. While Erin might be able to work around one of her players missing a week, half the party being MIA did not a workable session make.

Becca did have a point, too; they had just spent two days mostly in one another's company, and New Relationship Energy aside, it was reasonable to slow down a little. Even if Morgan didn't want to.

She had missed Becca that night, of course, but the relative calm of being able to just curl up against Lynn as they read their book was its own satisfaction, and one she never wanted to lose. She'd even persuaded Lynn to read bits of it aloud, and if Morgan hadn't quite been able to follow the intricacies of why Peter Pan and Captain Hook were trapped in a cave system, it had been the connection that mattered.

Morgan had even managed to drag Lynn off the boat for a couple of hours, this morning. Together, they had found a place for lunch with both eggplant parmesan on the menu and the patience to answer Lynn's questions about the source of the rennet for the parmesan. They had gotten back to the boat in plenty of time for the game. The game with Becca.

Morgan connected to the voice chat and logged into the Polyhedra website. Across the table, Lynn had their work laptop open and their bullet journal with project notes beside them. Becca, Gabrielle, and Erin were already connected, and Louise logged on a moment after Morgan did.

The previous session had mostly been navigating through a large forest; a few bad navigation checks had resulted in the party running straight into a pair of young green dragons. While all four of them had survived (and the dragons had not), it had not been a simple thing. Torra, Gabrielle's cleric, had used the last of her spells. If Morgan's own Ecaeris Nightthorn hadn't been able to substitute four hours of trance for eight of sleep, they might have had to risk the night with nobody standing watch. This session, thankfully, began with their arrival at the free city of Cloixtal.

Cloixtal, as Erin described it, was a bustling city, with a multi-racial marketplace. Jorinn, the dragonborn fighter Louise played, was able to upgrade her armour and found a smith who was capable of reforging her family's ancestral sword. Gabrielle, always the party mum, took care of selling loot and stocking up on potions and trail rations as well as restocking her spell components. By the time it was Morgan's turn, half of her wished they could just be in combat again, rather than role-playing each haggled transaction. The other half, though, had an idea.

"Okay, you've gotten your extra rope and refilled your poisoner's kit," Erin said. "Is there anything else you'd like to do, while you're in the market?"

"Actually, yes," Morgan said. "Can I see where Breena is?" Breena was Becca's wizard character, but as a rock gnome she was only a metre tall, and fairly easy to lose in a crowd of larger people.

"I'm at the jeweller's stall, over here," Becca volunteered, helpfully wiggling the icon for her character on the screen. "I took my share of the gems from the last adventure, before Torra sold the rest, and I need to talk to the jeweller about making a custom ring."

"She's pretty well hidden," Erin said. "Roll perception." Morgan clicked the proper section of her character sheet.

"Sixteen," she said aloud, though Erin would have seen it on her screen as well.

"That's a pass," Erin said. "After a few minutes of looking around, you see Breena sitting just inside the jeweller's shop, on the far side of the tables that extend into the marketplace. Breena is talking to an elderly gnome inside the shop, and a human apprentice is watching the tables outside." The battle map on the web site allowed people to place their characters relative to one another and the landscape, but it was the dungeon master's descriptions that made it come alive.

"I'm going to sneak over there," Morgan said, "walking casually to hide myself in the crowd. I'll stop at the booth next door and look at whatever they're selling."

"Okay," Erin said. "You get as far as the tables without anybody noticing anything, and you examine the leather goods being sold there. Do you go further?"

"Is there any cover further into the jeweller's shop?" Morgan asked.

"Not very much," Erin said. "There are fabric-draped tables and glass cases. Hiding would be almost impossible."

"That's what, a DC twenty?" Morgan asked.

"Make it twenty-five," Erin said, adjusting the difficulty check upwards. "The shop is designed not to provide cover for thieves." Morgan looked at her character sheet.

"I have plus nine to stealth," she said. "I'm going to try it."

"Fine," Erin sighed. "But the apprentice is meant to be watching the space, so you'll roll at disadvantage."

"You already increased the difficulty for that," Morgan objected.

"You don't *have* to sneak in and steal from the shop where your friend is trying to negotiate a deal," Erin suggested pointedly.

"Fine," Morgan said, and clicked to roll two dice. The software automatically discarded the nineteen she had rolled, but the lower of the two was still a seventeen. "Seventeen plus nine. Twenty-six," she said.

"Tell me how you're making this work," Erin said.

Morgan could hear aggravation in the dungeon master's voice already, but this was going to be good.

"While the apprentice is helping another customer," Morgan said, "I slip under the black velvet fabric that drapes the table. Moving from shadow to shadow, I silently make my way to the curtain hanging beside the door behind the jeweller. I use my bonus action to hide."

"Of course you do," Erin sighed. "Becca, what's your passive perception?"

"Eleven," Becca said. Morgan's roll far exceeded that.

"Okay," Erin said. "You miraculously disappear into the shadows of the well-guarded shop, with nobody the wiser. I presume you're going to steal something?"

"You could say that," Morgan grinned, though none of the other players could see it. She clicked her sleight-of-hand skill to roll the 20-sided die. 25, the Polyhedra site reported; she had managed a perfect roll, a natural twenty, even before her plus five from dexterity. "I'm going to steal a kiss from Breena."

"You ... wait, what?" Erin demanded.

"I rolled a natural twenty, so automatic success, and I'm going to steal a kiss." Morgan repeated. "From Becca. I mean Breena."

Across the table, Lynn looked up from their work. Over the voice connection, both Gabrielle and Louise chimed in, though Becca didn't say a word.

"I thought you weren't allowing PvP," Louise complained.

Player versus player combat could lead to a tense game, and many dungeon masters chose to disallow it. Given that Louise's dragonborn character could have pounded Morgan's wood elf into paste if the characters had come to blows, Morgan was generally in favour of Louise opposing PvP combat.

"I'm not sure it's exactly a combat action," Gabrielle chimed in, "which means you don't auto-crit on a skill check. But it is sort of a consent issue. What the heck, Morgan?"

Gabrielle played the cleric, so it would have made sense in character as well as out, if Torra Blesseddelver had been present in the shop. Which she wasn't. Hers wasn't really the important reaction, anyway. So far, Becca hadn't said anything. Neither had Erin, for that matter, at least not on the rules issue.

"A natural twenty?" the DM said finally, as Morgan heard a ding in her messaging app. The notification was from Becca, but Erin was still speaking in her role as the dungeon master. "You're right; let's go with this critical success theory." Gabrielle started to say something else, but

Erin spoke over her. "You manage to steal a kiss from the gnomish wizard. Your high level of stealth and excellent roll combine to create the perfect crime. Breena's lifetime supply of kisses is reduced by one, and nobody is any the wiser. Neither Breena nor the jeweller notice, and you escape the shop without incident."

"That's not exactly the sort of success I had in mind," Morgan complained. Lynn could only hear Morgan's side of the conversation, of course, but they were paying attention now. Morgan waved in a way intended to convey that she would explain later, and she opened the text message from Becca.

```
<Becca> Are you . . . flirting
          with me right now?
```

Morgan shook her head and typed back a reply.

```
<Morgan> Yes.  I am definitely
          flirting with you
          right now.  I am
          teasing you and
          enjoying imagining you
          blush and squirm
```

"It may not be the success you intended," Erin said. There was no compromise in her voice. "It is, however, a successful theft by sleight of hand, which is what you rolled. You steal the kiss and you exit the shop." She really seemed not to appreciate the cleverness of Morgan's move.

```
<Morgan> Though apparently
          you're not the only
```

```
          one who missed that I
          was flirting
```

"Beyond that, Louise's point about PvP is relevant," Erin said, sounding actually angry. "As is Gabrielle's about consent, and for the same reason. PvP isn't just about combat against another character, but anything that removes their agency."

Morgan rolled her eyes. If Becca was okay with it, why were the other three making it into a big deal?

```
        <Becca> Yeah, she messaged me
                asking if I was okay
        <Morgan> What did you say?
        <Becca> I told her it's okay
```

"If Becca's okay with it," Morgan tried to argue, "why is it an issue?"

"*Is* Becca okay with it, though?" Louise asked.

"Did you even *ask* her, first?" Gabrielle demanded.

"Because you don't *know* if Becca's okay with it," Erin said, speaking over the other two. "No more than we do. Because you brought this out of left field. You've upset the entire party – if Becca actually *is* okay with what just happened, she's the only one – and I expect you to know better than to pull this sort of nonsense at my table."

"It's okay," Becca said in the voice chat, though she didn't sound terribly confident. With the other three so upset, this was hardly a surprise. "It's not that big a deal."

"Yeah, it really kind of is," Gabrielle said, and her voice was much gentler with Becca than it had been with Morgan. At least there was that much; Morgan was more confident of her own ability to withstand being yelled at than Becca's.

Erin sighed. "Look. I know it's early, but I think I need to call the game at this point. I don't think anybody is really in a great headspace to continue right now. I'm certainly not. And I want to talk to Becca privately before I make any ... well, before I decide that I know what's been going on here. Because obviously I don't have the information I need to moderate whatever the heck *that* was."

"That's ... probably the best decision," Gabrielle said. "We'll pick up here next week?"

"Anything else you need to do in the marketplace, message me," Erin said. "We'll work it out between sessions."

"I have two weeks until the smith is done with my sword," Louise offered. "Are we just doing downtime offscreen, until then?"

"That's probably reasonable," Erin said. "Seriously, though, we'll work it out in text chat before next week."

"Okay," Louise said.

"Sure," Gabrielle agreed.

"I guess," Morgan said. "For what it's worth, I'm sorry I upset people."

"Yes, well, we'll talk about that later," Erin said. She did not sound mollified, but the bloop sound from the chat program indicated that she had already left the main voice channel.

When Morgan looked at the window, she saw that both Becca and Erin were now in the private DM-Corner voice channel; Erin must have moved her over. Two more bloops accompanied Gabrielle's and Louise's departures, leaving Morgan alone in chat. She disconnected and removed her headset.

```
<Morgan> Are you okay?
<Becca> Yeah.  I already told
        Erin it was okay
<Becca> In text
<Morgan> They're worried about
        you
<Morgan> Should I be worried
        about you?
<Becca> No, it's okay
```

"Do you want to tell me what that was about?" Lynn asked.

"Apparently, I wasn't as clever as I thought I was," Morgan said, typing her reply to Becca.

```
<Morgan> Are you sure?  I
        didn't want to make
        you uncomfortable.  I
        just thought it would
        be fun
<Becca> I guess?
<Becca> I mean, I like you
<Becca> but Breena gets
        nervous around big
        people sometimes,
        still
```

```
<Becca> and Ecaeris Nightthorn
        is kinda scary?
```

"What did you do, Morgan?" Lynn asked.

Morgan typed one more message to Becca before answering Lynn's question.

```
<Morgan> Well, rogue?  A
         little bit of
         assassination and
         poisoning go with the
         territory
<Becca> That might be my point
```

"Well, I play a rogue in this game, right?" Morgan said. Lynn nodded. "And, well, there wasn't much going on, so I decided to steal a kiss from Becca's character."

```
<Morgan> Maybe there aren't
         enough rogues in her
         life
<Becca> I think the quotation
        was 'scoundrels'
<Becca> And Breena isn't
        exactly Princess Leia
```

"Mmmhmmm," Lynn said. At least *they* didn't sound surprised. "I take it that didn't go over well."

"Yeah, not exactly," Morgan said.

"How upset is she?" Lynn asked.

"She doesn't seem to be, is the thing," Morgan said. She pulled up the text conversation on her phone and passed it to Lynn. "It's everybody else."

```
<Morgan> I won't do it again,
         if you're
         uncomfortable with it.
         Or Ecaeris won't
<Morgan> Though I did have
         this idea for a scene
         where Ecaeris
         confesses what she did
         and offers to give it
         back
<Becca> 😳
<Morgan> What do you think?
```

"*I* think you need to back off, until you have something with more nonverbals than text," Lynn opined, reading the conversation on the phone. Morgan reclaimed the device from her partner and rolled her eyes. "But yeah. She seems more upset that it was out of character than that you stole a kiss."

"Erin dragged her into a private voice chat, too," Morgan looked back at the game's dedicated chat server. "So there's that."

```
<Morgan> How's it going with
         Erin, anyway?
<Becca> Okay.  I don't think
        she's going to kick
        you out of the game
<Morgan> Was that a real
         possibility?
```

"And apparently it was a bigger deal than I thought," Morgan told Lynn, blinking.

"Oh?" Lynn said. Morgan passed the phone back, and they looked at it. "Ah. Ouch."

```
<Becca> I don't know.  I
        guess?
<Becca> I'm sorry
<Becca> She said she'll talk
        to you, but she wanted
        to make sure I was
        okay, first
<Morgan> It's okay.
<Morgan> I am in favour of
         making sure you are
         okay
```

"So am I," Lynn said aloud. "So you're ended early for the day, then?"

"Yeah," Morgan said, half her attention still on the screen. "Erin was really upset. She called it until she could talk to Becca and, I guess, settle down."

```
<Morgan> Lynn says they are,
         too
<Becca> I am
<Becca> It was just kind of a
        surprise
<Becca> and, ummm
```

"Would you like to maybe do something for supper, then?" Lynn asked. "Together? Or is Becca still afraid of me?"

"I don't think she's actually afraid of you." Morgan said. "Just a bit overwhelmed by everything."

```
<Morgan> *listens*
<Becca> Erin says if we want
        to do that thing . . .
<Becca> with giving the kiss
        back?
<Morgan> Yesssss?
<Becca> that we need to run it
        by her first 😳
<Becca> and that she's not
        running _that_ sort of
        game 😳
```

Morgan laughed, and felt tension she hadn't realised she'd been carrying relax out of her shoulders.

```
<Morgan> You actually _asked_
         her about that?
<Becca> well, yeah?
<Becca> was I not supposed to?
<Becca> I'm sorry
<Morgan> You're wonderful
<Becca> 😳
```

Wait, are you actually volunteering to leave the boat twice in one day?" Morgan asked, finally processing what Lynn had said.

"Hey, I'm not that bad," Lynn objected.

"Yeah, you kind of are, *cariad*," Morgan said.

"Well, we *could* just get a pizza delivered to the marina," Lynn said. "But I was thinking we could go back to that Italian place? They were good."

That was often the way it was, with Lynn; review sites made finding tasty vegetarian food relatively simple, but it was the people who had made the difference in their willingness to return. There had been enough incidents in the past with people who objected to 'their sort' – whatever those people had decided Lynn's sort was – that they could be hesitant to try new places. With unknown venues, there was always a looming threat of random bigots ruining their evening out. The fact that they did it anyway, sailing all over the world with nothing familiar in each new port, was one of the things Morgan loved about them.

"The Italian place was nice," was all Morgan said aloud. "Would you like me to ask Becca?"

"Yeah, that would be good," Lynn agreed. "If you think it's a good idea."

```
<Morgan> Are you doing
         anything this evening?
<Becca> I need to pack
<Becca> Checkout is at eleven,
         tomorrow, and it's a
         four hour drive to get
         home
<Morgan> Would you like to
         come to dinner with me
         and Lynn?
<Becca> and Lynn?
<Morgan> Yeah, you remember
         them?  Red hair,
         sidecut, about my
         height?
<Becca> Yes, I know, but . . .
```

The app continued to report 'Becca is typing' for some time.

```
<Morgan> You're allowed to say
         'no', you know
<Becca> I know.  I don't want
        to say no
<Becca> I just . . . don't
        know what's expected?
<Morgan> There's a nice
         Italian place, I think
         it's local, where we
         had lunch
<Morgan> I went with the
         blackened chicken, at
         lunch, but the pizzas
         looked good, too
```

"Are you deliberately being obtuse, love?" Lynn asked, still holding Morgan's phone.

"Not really," Morgan said. "I don't know what she's trying to ask, and if that's the wrong answer, maybe it will get her to ask the right question?"

"I'm willing to bet it's a poly dynamics issue," Lynn said. "Are you forgetting how new she is to this stuff?"

"But I told her on the deck that it wasn't transit-ive, that being involved with me didn't mean she'd be romantically involved with you."

"Mhmm," Lynn said. "And now you're inviting her to dinner with both of us. Do you see how that might be confusing?"

"I guess," Morgan said. According to the chat app, Becca was still typing.

```
<Morgan> I mean, I know it's
         not a romantic dinner
         date
<Morgan> Though I would like
         to do that with you,
         some time
<Morgan> But this is
         just . . . getting
         together and chatting
         after the game
<Becca> And Lynn's okay with
        it?
<Morgan> They suggested it
<Becca> Oh
```

"Let me know what you two decide." Lynn passed Morgan's phone back to her again.

```
<Becca> I guess that could be
        good.  Yeah
<Becca> Do you two need a
        ride?
<Morgan> It's okay; we can
         walk
<Becca> It's no trouble
```

"Do we want a ride?" Morgan asked. "She's offering." Lynn rubbed the bridge of their nose.

"I was hoping for a situation where she's *not* trapped in an enclosed space with us," they said. "But it is pretty hot out there."

"Her car isn't that small," Morgan offered. "And it does have air conditioning."

"Whereas it's about an hour's walk, if we go straight there," Lynn supplied. They had detoured a fair bit, that morning, through the main shopping area of town. "Yeah, if she's willing, a ride would be good."

```
<Morgan> If you don't mind
<Becca> I don't.  When should
        I pick you up?
<Morgan> How's the packing
        going?
<Becca> I may not have started
        yet >.<
<Becca> I can do it after
        dinner
<Morgan> Whenever works for
        you, then
<Becca> Give me half an hour?
<Morgan> Of course.  We'll
        meet you in the
        carpark?
<Becca> Okay
```

Twenty-Five

Morgan spent most of the half hour trying to decide what to wear. She had told Becca it wasn't a romantic dinner date, and that was true, but at the same time she wanted to look good. Just not too dressy. Or too casual. She settled on black leggings and a slightly low-cut red tunic top with cutwork roses embroidered around the neckline.

Lynn would have been perfectly happy wearing their black 'If it were easy to understand, we wouldn't call it code' t-shirt over khakis, but Morgan managed to talk them into at least dressing up as far as a dark green plaid shirt with actual buttons. They did add several pin-back slogan badges to express their own personality, but Lynn was Lynn, and Morgan loved them. Even the silly bits.

Morgan spotted Becca's pearl blue Kia in the parking lot even before they made it off the dock, and picked up the pace; Lynn let her lead the way. Becca got out of the vehicle as she approached, and Morgan pulled her into a hug.

"How are you doing?" Morgan asked, after she had let Becca go. "Really?"

"I'm okay," Becca said. "I think Erin was more upset than I was. Has she spoken to you, yet?"

"Not yet," Morgan said. "I should probably be grateful. She wasn't mad at you, was she?"

"No," Becca said. "More worried, I think. And I sort of had to explain stuff, like, that we had gotten on so well when we met up, and you probably thought I'd be okay with it."

"Yeah. Were you?"

"I mean, Breena would have been a bit taken aback. It's not something she's ever done." Becca thought for a moment. "Maybe I should make you write to her father, asking for permission to court her. That would be in character, and probably count as running it by Erin." Since the dungeon master was responsible for playing all the characters in the world other than those run by the players, including Breena's fictional father, this did make some degree of sense.

"Is that a thing in gnomish society?" Morgan asked. "A poor wood elf like Ecaeris would have no way of knowing this."

"It could be!" Becca said, opening the side door of her vehicle. "Where did you two want to sit?"

"What's most comfortable for you?" Lynn asked.

"Umm," Becca said. "You two should probably sit together. Is the back seat okay?"

"I really don't mind if you want her beside you in the front seat," Lynn said.

"No, it's fine," Becca said. "How far are we going, anyway? Do you have the address?"

"It's up at Wilkinson, I think," Morgan offered. "The place is called Duilio's?" Becca punched the name into her phone.

"Oh, yeah, that should only be about nine minutes," Becca said. "I think I could survive that long without Morgan beside me."

"So could I," Lynn pointed out, but they did slide across to the right hand side of the vehicle, leaving room for Morgan on the bench seat beside them.

Sitting directly behind the driver's head did make it awkward for Morgan to have a conversation with Becca, but she was right about it being a short trip. Morgan supposed her flirting could wait for ten minutes. They drove past a variety of other restaurants on Erie Street, both chains and local, but Becca didn't question the choice of destination. Soon enough, they pulled into the parking lot in front of Duilio's.

The entrance stood out from the rest of the building; the doors reached the pavement in front, but a narrow garden buffered the main walls of the building from passing traffic. Stone brick columns flanked the door, reaching to twice its height. Above the charcoal-grey canopy, a single script D alluded to the name of the place.

"This looks nice," Becca said once she had backed into a parking space. She sounded concerned.

"It's not too expensive," Morgan said, guessing at the cause.

"Besides," Lynn put in, "We're the ones who invited you, therefore we get to pay for it." That was news to Morgan, but she wasn't going to argue.

"I can pay for my own," Becca objected.

"You could," Lynn agreed. They nudged Morgan to open the door. "But this time, we've got it."

"Are you okay with that?" Morgan asked, opening the door and stepping out of the vehicle. "We're not trying to make you uncomfortable."

"I guess," Becca said. "If you're sure."

"I am," Lynn said, and Morgan noticed they were leaving her out of it. "We invited you, we picked the restaurant, and we can afford it." They slid out of the vehicle and smiled. "Besides," they said, "you did save us a significant walk, and I'm grateful for that. Even if I did use more sense in selecting my footwear than Morgan did." Morgan blushed; her low heels might have been less suited to hiking than Lynn's trainers, but they were still perfectly sensible.

"I don't mind," Becca said, but this additional excuse seemed enough for her to accept the deal as fair. Lynn didn't think they were as good with people as Morgan was, but they really didn't give themself enough credit. "You look really good today, Morgan."

"She always looks good," Lynn agreed. "Today, though, she wouldn't even let *me* come out looking like a slob." They dropped their voice to a stage whisper. "I think I managed to sneak the pins past her, though."

"You both look nice," Becca said. "May I read your buttons, Lynn?"

"That's why I wear them," they said. Becca moved closer, further into Lynn's space than Morgan had seen her voluntarily go before. She peered at the calligraphy on the round pins.

Morgan hadn't actually checked which ones Lynn had chosen from their extensive collection, today. She moved in beside Becca and started to read along with her. The choices, of course, were typical Lynn: "A computer is a genie that can grant any wish. The catch is that you must express your wish exactly, in binary", warned one. "There are 10 kinds of people, those who are comfortable with binary, and those who aren't", said another. A third suggested, "The heck with top and bottom – I want relationships with strangeness and charm"; that one was a quarky choice. Morgan really wished, though, that Lynn had left "I'm much cuter on my knees" at home. Becca blushed when she came to it.

"We should probably head into the restaurant," Morgan said quickly. She supposed she should be grateful it wasn't the one that said, "Now that I have you at my mercy, what do I do next?"

The restaurant's interior was a little less imposing than the outside. The server led them to a booth with brown vinyl seats and fabric padding on the backrests. Lynn slid in first, with their back to the entrance. They really were making an effort to make Becca comfortable. Morgan slid over to the window on the facing bench, leaving Becca with a choice of positions.

The outcome hadn't been in question, really. Becca slid in beside Morgan and the server dropped off a basket of bread along with three copies of the menu. A few minutes reviewing those – the dinner options were somewhat different from those at lunch – provided a little space for Becca to recover from any lingering embarrassment.

"Did you want to get a pizza?" Morgan asked. Or does one of the entrées look tempting?"

"We could get a pizza," Becca agreed. "Lynn doesn't eat meat, right?"

"That's right," Lynn said. "Don't let that limit you, though. Order what you want."

"I was thinking the Mediterranean one looked good?" Becca suggested.

"Tomato sauce, red peppers, red onions, sun-dried tomatoes, feta, kalamata olives?" Morgan read, once she had found the pizza section of her own menu. "Yeah, that sounds good. Lynn?"

"Suits me," they said. "Should we add an appetizer or two? I'm not sure how big their pizzas are." Morgan flipped back to the first pages of the menu.

"Not much for you, here," she said, making a face. "Spinach-artichoke dip, red pepper dip, or bruschetta."

"Bruschetta," Lynn said. "It's too hot for a cheesy melty dip."

"Okay," Morgan said. "Do you want anything else, Becca?" Becca glanced at Lynn.

"We could do the Chef's Trio," she suggested hesitantly. "It has the bruschetta, and the roasted red pepper dip and the spinach and artichoke dip."

"That works," Lynn said. "I didn't mean to restrict your choices. I was just saying I can't do hot cheese in this weather."

"Okay," Becca said. Morgan reached out and took her hand.

"We could also just get another pizza," Morgan suggested. "The Margherita, if you're worried about being able to share with Lynn."

"Basil is good," Becca said. "I just ... I don't want to make things bad for Lynn."

"Are you talking about dinner now, or in general?" Lynn asked. Becca blushed.

"Maybe both?" she said. Lynn nodded.

"How about you trust me to speak up, if I need something?" they suggested. "Can you do that?"

"I don't know," Becca said. "I can try?" Lynn nodded.

"Trying is good. Talking to one of us when you're worried is another option." Becca nodded.

"I get that you're new to this," Morgan said. "You're allowed to not know things."

"You're allowed to ask, and I promise I won't lie to you about whether you're getting close to something that makes me uncomfortable," Lynn said. "There's nothing worse than thinking everything is fine, and then being blind-sided by something that wasn't." They spoke from experience, Morgan knew, but this wasn't really the time to go into it. More important that Becca not gain the same experience.

The server's return interrupted the discussion. Morgan took the responsibility of speaking for the table, and asked about pizza size.

"Well, they're meant to be for one person," the young man told her. "But most people end up taking some home, if that helps. Or you could order a larger one, from the take-out menu."

"That does help," Morgan told him. "We'll have the Chef's Trio to start, then we'll share the Margherita and the Mediterranean pizzas among us. Does that sound good?"

"Sounds reasonable to me," he said, taking down the order. "Worst case, you'll have room for dessert."

"That's never a terrible thing," Morgan agreed. He flipped his order pad closed and walked away.

"Are you two staying in the area for a while?" Becca asked when he had gone.

"No," Morgan said. "We do actually work, sometimes."

"I'm sorry," Becca said. "I thought you did that from the boat. Like, remotely?"

"We do," Lynn confirmed, shooting Morgan a look. "But we also attend industry conferences, sometimes, and there's one in Toronto in about a week."

"That may have been my main excuse for us to come up this way," Morgan admitted.

"If you just need to get to Toronto, I could give you a ride," Becca offered, blushing. "I live just on the other side of it." Imagining four hours in the car beside Becca, Morgan wished it were a real option.

"It might be four hours for you, but it will be several days in the boat," Morgan said. "And I can't ask Lynn to do the lift locks alone."

"Oh," said Becca, looking away. "I'm sorry. I hadn't realised."

"It's fine," Lynn said. "It was a kind offer, and there's no reason you *should* have known." Becca looked back at them; Lynn smiled. "Remember the bit where we promised to let you know if you were overstepping? This is what that looks like. Nobody is mad; we're just having to say no."

"I'm sorry," Becca said. "I don't want to make your life more difficult." Lynn nodded.

"I forgive you," they said. "But also, you didn't make it difficult. Just because somebody says no doesn't mean the question was wrong." Becca nodded slowly.

"If you're closer to Toronto," Morgan suggested, "maybe we could do something one night? Maybe get dinner?" Becca looked at Lynn, but Morgan shook her head. "Not as a group, I mean. Just you and me." She batted her eyelashes at Becca in an attempt at over-the-top seduction. Becca blushed, but she couldn't suppress a giggle. She was even cuter giggling than when flustered; Morgan would need to do more of this.

"I mean, I was off this week, so work is going to be busy," Becca said. "But yeah. I'd like that. If it's okay." She glanced at Lynn again, a bit more nervously.

"It's okay," Lynn assured her. "It's ... look. You know how you worry about not interfering with my relationship with Morgan?" Becca nodded.

"Okay; so can you believe I'd give the same courtesy to Cátia, in her relationship with Morgan?" Becca nodded again.

"I can see that," she said. "I guess that would be pretty important, when she has to split her time between you."

"Love is infinite," Lynn quoted, "but time is not. We actually have a shared calendar, on the cloud, to help manage it. Though realistically, when we're *in* Portugal, or when Cátia's visiting, more of Morgan's free time is spent with her."

"Is that fair to you?" Becca worried. Lynn smiled.

"Is it fair to Cátia that I have most of Morgan's time between visits?" They shook their head. "Sometimes it's less about what's fair in theory, and more about what works for us."

"I can see that," Becca said. "It must be hard."

"I'm not going to speak for Morgan," Lynn said. "I know how much I miss Cailean, when we're not together, and I'm grateful for the way she picks up the slack when I'm with him. It's a balancing act, making space for one another, but it's important." The appetizers arrived, and Lynn took a piece of bruschetta.

"I can see that," Becca said. She dipped a piece of flatbread in the green-flecked dip.

"But what I'm trying to get at," Lynn said, "is that if I can make space for Cátia, if Morgan rearranges her schedule to give me more time with Cailean, if you are trying so very hard not to step on my toes ... why wouldn't you expect the same courtesy from me, in your relationship with Morgan?"

"But I don't," Becca started. Morgan laid a hand on her knee, and Becca looked at her. "We don't," Becca tried again. "I mean, I'm not even sure what our relationship *is*," she said.

"I don't pretend to know, either," Lynn said. "But I do know that it's important to Morgan, and that's enough for me." Becca looked between the two of them; Morgan squeezed her knee gently.

"It's okay," Morgan said quietly. "We're still figuring things out, and that's okay. But you don't need to hang back on the edges. There's room for you here." She could see the tension in Becca's posture, but there was nothing more she could do to help the woman understand.

"I don't want to hurt you," Lynn said. "I don't want to frighten you. And, to be clear, you don't need a reason to tell Morgan you don't want to go on a date with her." Morgan nodded, but Lynn kept their eyes focussed on Becca's face. "But I don't want to be the reason for you to turn it down. Is that clear?"

"Yes," Becca said meekly. "It's clear." Lynn nodded, but Morgan could see a little of their pain at the way Becca had pulled in on herself. They were trying so hard, but Becca was also doing her best, and they just weren't connecting. It hurt to watch them, but there was nothing Morgan could do to make it better. Some things just took time.

"So now that you have Lynn's permission," she tried to make a joke out of it, "would you like to do something together, next weekend?"

"Friday night?" Becca suggested. "I work in the city, so I'd be down there anyway. And I don't think

Erin would appreciate us skipping next week, after what happened today."

"I don't think we're scheduled to make it to Toronto until Friday," Morgan said. "It might be cutting it close, depending what time we get out of the canal."

"Would you want to go out after the game again, like this?" Becca suggested. "I mean, all of us?" Lynn smiled; they seemed surprised to be included, but Morgan very much appreciated Becca making the effort.

"I'd really enjoy that," Morgan said. "Then maybe we could do something alone, on Sunday or Monday night?" Becca blushed, and nodded.

"I'd like that," she said. She took some more of the flatbread, trying the red pepper dip this time.

"We can work out the details online," Morgan said, spreading spinach dip thickly on a piece of bread. "Where you'd like to go, that sort of thing."

"Do you want to do the touristy things, Saturday?" Becca asked. "The game usually ends around six. I could be in Toronto by seven, I think."

"Do you have a laptop?" Lynn asked, and Becca blinked.

"Well, I didn't bring it with me to supper, but yeah," she said. "That's how I was playing at the hotel. I mean, I'm not sure gaming from the business centre would have been appreciated." Lynn nodded.

"If you came in earlier in the day, you could log in from the *C Shell*," they suggested.

"Do you have enough bandwidth for that?" Becca asked uncertainly. "We use voice chat."

"That's the reason we try to rent a transient slip, for Saturdays," Morgan said. "The marina Wi-Fi is generally better than our satellite connection."

"As always," Lynn pointed out, "You're allowed to say no to us. You don't need to make excuses."

"I'm not trying to make excuses," Becca objected, and Lynn nodded their acceptance of that. Morgan chose to keep her mouth shut and just enjoy the hot dip; the air conditioning in the restaurant was strong enough that she enjoyed its warmth and richness.

"What would you recommend, if we wanted to do touristy stuff?" Lynn asked. "Either with you or on our own."

"Well, the Tower is right by the lake," Becca said. "If you get a day pass for the bus, that opens up a lot. I know the Science Centre is meant for kids, but I still like it. Then there's the Museum, and the Art Gallery, of course."

Lynn kept her chatting about basic sightseeing destinations until the pizza arrived, and Morgan was pleased to see the conversation slowly wear away Becca's anxiety.

Two pizzas had been the right choice. Each pie was the size of a full dinner plate. Morgan took a slice of each and watched Becca do the same. Lynn helped themself to a slice of the Mediterranean.

"Don't you like the margherita?" Becca worried.

"It looks lovely, but I can only eat one slice at a time," Lynn said. "Besides, if you're unwilling to take more than your fair share of Morgan, when she's all shiny and new and exciting?" They grinned. "I figure I can trust you not to leave me without a crumb of the other pizza." Becca glanced aside at Morgan, and Morgan covered her hand with her own.

"Lynn is a much more trusting soul when you're here," Morgan said. Lynn laughed.

"Only because I know perfectly well that you *will* take the last piece without a second thought," they retorted. Becca looked between the two of them, and Morgan patted her hand.

"It's okay," she said. "We're fine." Lynn nodded.

"It's just playful teasing," they confirmed. "Besides, with a new partner to impress, I'm sure Morgan will be on her best behaviour." Becca blushed a bit, and Morgan stuck out her tongue at Lynn.

"I'll do my best to keep her in line," Becca said valiantly, "but she *is* a rogue, you know. She could steal the mozzarella off my pie without me being any the wiser."

"You really do need a higher perception," Morgan agreed. "I can't believe Erin pulled out that 'successful theft means nobody notices anything' line."

"Maybe stealing kisses should be a charisma check?" Lynn suggested.

"I mean, bards do tend to be played that way, more," Becca agreed. "Flirty and all."

"That's why you didn't see it coming from Ecaeris," Morgan said. If she was making it up on the spot, nobody needed to know. "Maybe she's been stalking you for months, casing out the boundaries of your affection, planning the kiss-heist for ages in order to pull it off perfectly." Becca blushed, but she also looked uncomfortable for some reason. Morgan asked, "What's wrong?"

"Were you?" Becca asked. "I mean, the bit with saying you could take me home, even with the way I misunderstood it. Was that something you planned?" Morgan squeezed her hand gently, but Becca pulled away.

"Becca, no," Morgan said, though she moved her hand out of Becca's space. She hadn't meant to be a threat. "I mean, yes, I've liked you for ages, and you're adorable, and I can't imagine not want-ing to mean something to you. And you know I was flirting with you, Thursday, before you ever no-ticed. But I told you that night. It was fine that you weren't into it. The idea that I'd try to trick you or force you ..." Morgan trailed off. "I wouldn't. I would never hurt you like that." She looked to Lynn for support, but Lynn shook their head slightly. They were staying out of this one. Which was probably wise.

"I'm sorry," Becca said, pulling in on herself.

"Sweetheart," Morgan tried again, "it's okay. I care about you. I want what's best for you. I'd want that even if you decided that what's best for you isn't me."

"I don't," Becca began, but didn't finish the thought. "It's just what you said about Ecaeris planning things for so long." Morgan nodded.

"Ecaeris is a character," Morgan said, trying des-perately to make her understand. "Before today's session, I wouldn't have had any thought that she'd do anything of the sort, because it wouldn't have been right for *us*. But now that it's happened, well, I can retcon anything that happened in her head, outside of the game actions." Becca nodded slowly. Lynn quietly helped themself to a slice of margherita pizza.

"I, okay," Becca said. "That makes a bit of sense." Morgan nodded encouragingly.

"You didn't like how sudden it was. I mean, nobody did," Morgan admitted. "So if it's just the culmination of something Ecaeris has been planning for months, that might work better in the story we're building together?"

"Because, as a rogue, the whole stealth thing is just how she knows how to get things she wants?" Becca asked.

"Yeah, exactly," Morgan said. "And it still didn't work. I mean, she got the kiss, but she didn't get your attention, and that's what she really wanted."

"Breena's attention," Becca said.

"Pardon me?" Morgan asked.

"You didn't get Breena's attention," Becca said shyly. "It definitely got mine." She reached out for Morgan's hand, and Morgan felt half the tension go out of her as she took it.

"But yeah," Morgan said. "If she's been planning for months, and she got her kiss but it wasn't everything she had hoped for, well, assuming Erin lets us get away with it, a heartfelt scene at the campfire, where she confesses to Breena, might work really well."

"I mean," Becca said, blushing deeply and looking at the place where their hands were together on the table, "even if Erin won't let us do it in game, she can't stop us from doing it in private."

"Would you want to?" Morgan asked, trying not to get her hopes up too far. Becca's blush deepened as she nodded.

"Maybe even more than just, uh, talking," Becca suggested, her cheeks crimson. "Maybe, well, Erin says she's not running *that* sort of game, but what happens off camera stays off camera, you know?"

"Are you comfortable with that?" Morgan asked carefully. Becca shook her head.

"Not comfortable, no," she said slowly, like she was feeling out the ideas as she went. "I don't ... I don't know what's expected. I don't know how to relationship. And I want a relationship with you. But I'm not sure how. And, well, with Breena, it's like you said. She's just a character. And if it goes wrong with her, we can just back it up, retcon it, make it didn't happen?" Morgan squeezed her hand gently, and Becca squeezed back.

"That sounds like a really good idea," Morgan said. "I don't want to hurt you. If Ecaeris is far enough from me that we can make mistakes and you don't hate me forever, that sounds like a really good thing to me."

"I couldn't hate you," Becca said. "I'd just be scared of you. And I don't want to be scared of you." Morgan half-turned on the bench seat, reaching out her free hand to stroke Becca's cheek.

"I don't want you to be afraid of me," she said. "I don't want you to ever feel like you need to be afraid of me." Becca looked back at her, and she could see tears behind the other woman's glasses.

"Ecaeris can be scary," Becca said. "She's a rogue. Like you said, a bit of assassination and poisoning go with the territory."

"Not for you, though," Morgan said. "Must protect adorable gnome cinnamon bun wizard."

"Cinnamon bun?" Becca questioned.

"Mhmm," Morgan said. "You've seen the meme, right? 'Beautiful cinnamon bun too pure, too good for this world'?" Becca blushed.

"No," she said. "But she does her share, doesn't she? I mean, I know she's still small and squishy, but wizards are like that. And her spell list isn't bad, at this point. She helped with those dragons."

"Not what I mean, love," Morgan said. "It's not that she isn't a deadly foe — at level eleven, the party could take over any of the towns we served in our first year of gaming without raising a sweat."

"So how is she too pure for this world?" Becca asked.

"Probably her innocence," Lynn suggested. Morgan nodded agreement.

"The way I'll be flirting outrageously, and you'll be all, 'are you flirting with me?'" Morgan agreed.

"That's not Breena, though," Becca objected. "It's me."

"Maybe you're the cinnamon roll, then," Morgan said, leaning in to kiss her cheek. "You're certainly sweet enough." Becca blushed and Morgan added, "And yes, I am flirting with you, right now."

"Thanks for clearing that up," Becca mumbled.

"Does it help?" Morgan asked. Maybe there was a chance it would at least remove some of the Becca's constant uncertainty.

"It kinda does," Becca admitted, blushing. Replacing uncertainty and hesitation with blushes was definitely a good trade; Morgan made a note to flirt more explicitly in the future.

Twenty-Six

The pizzas slowly disappeared as they spoke, and the light outside was fading. The server came back to recommend the tiramisu, and the party took him up on it.

"We're going to want to leave fairly early in the morning," Lynn said. "We'd like to make it to Erieau before sunset. Even if we did hit it on the way west, it's still a mostly unknown harbour for us."

"I should probably leave fairly early, too," Becca admitted. "So I won't get to see you before you set off?" She looked so sad.

"Probably not, no," Lynn said. Morgan was glad they were doing the talking, now; there was a lump in her own throat. "But you'll come see us at the marina, on Saturday? Either for the game, or after it?"

'I will," Becca said. "If you're sure it's okay, I can come down before the game." Lynn nodded.

"So we'll have a few days in Toronto," they said. "We might be able to do a couple of weeks, even. But have you given any thought to what happens after that?" Becca shook her head, and her hand tightened on Morgan's. Morgan squeezed back reassuringly.

"I ... I mean, I have work, and home, and responsibilities," she said. "I can't ..." Morgan shook her head.

"I wouldn't ask you to, sweetheart," she said. "You have your own life to live, even as we're part of one another's."

"How does it work?" Becca asked, looking from Morgan to Lynn and back. "With your other lovers, I mean?"

"A lot of time online," Lynn said. "What you suggested with Ecaeris and Breena? It's not that different from what Cailean and I do, sometimes. Though ours involves less dice, maybe."

"I'm not intending to roll-to-fondle," Morgan objected.

"Roll for initiative?" Becca suggested, glancing sideways at her. Morgan licked her lips.

"I usually just take that, where you're concerned," she said.

"So far, anyway," Becca said. "Maybe Breena isn't quite so innocent as you think, though?"

"Ohhhh?" Morgan invited. "Do tell."

"Entangle is only a first level spell," Becca said. "And Mage Hand is a cantrip, so I can cast it all day long."

"Mage hand is non-combat and not very strong," Morgan objected. "It couldn't hold me."

"Would it need to?" Becca asked. "Or would it be enough that it can just reach you, anywhere within a 30 foot radius? Stroking, caressing, drawing the rope over your skin while you're not looking." She was blushing, but the ideas were ... well, Morgan felt a bit of a blush rising in her own cheeks. Becca glanced across the table at Lynn. "Maybe Lynn could help me come up with ideas?"

"I'm sure I could help you come up with something," Lynn laughed, and Morgan saw mischief in their eyes. Yes, her Ecaeris might very well be in trouble, if Lynn was going to be feeding Becca ideas. She couldn't wait.

"The role playing will help," Morgan said. "But we also, well, visit when we can. It's never often enough or long enough, it feels like, but it's something."

"Yeah," Becca said, clearly thinking. The confidence she had when speaking about playing with Breena was gone. "What you said, on the boat. About having to plan ahead if you were going to kidnap me. Umm. The thing with cabin boy fantasies?"

"Yes?" Morgan said.

"Is that, umm, something you'd want to do?" she asked hesitantly.

"Of course it is," Morgan said. "If you were into it."

"Probably not an actual abduction scene," Lynn cautioned.

"Aww," Morgan mock-pouted. "Why not?" Lynn looked at her seriously.

"Do you remember that hunt, at Forest Park?" they asked. "The pursuit and take-down scene? How that felt?"

"Yeah." Morgan did remember; it had been where she met Lynn, and also one of the hottest scenes she had ever had the pleasure of experiencing. "Running, looking over my shoulder, trying to avoid the hunters even while knowing it was futile? Yeah, I remember." Lynn nodded.

"I thought so," they said. "You remember how it felt for you. Now forget it." They turned their attention to Becca, and it was only then that Morgan became aware of the other woman's reaction.

"Becca," Lynn said steadily, "take a breath. That's right. You're safe. Morgan is not going to do anything to hurt you. She's not going to deliberately frighten you."

Morgan reached out to stroke Becca's hair, but the other woman flinched away. She lowered her hand slowly.

"I'm sorry," Morgan said. "I wouldn't ..."

"Morgan gets enthusiastic," Lynn said when she trailed off. Their voice was still steady and all their attention was focussed on Becca. "There are things she enjoys that you probably won't. There are things she enjoys that I don't. And vice versa. You know the golden rule?"

"Do unto others as you would have them do unto you?" Becca said uncertainly. Lynn nodded.

"That's the one," they confirmed. "It doesn't apply here." Becca blinked, and Lynn nodded. "What you want done to you might not be what somebody else wants done to them, and that's okay."

"But I don't want anything done to me!" Becca said.

"Not even rope?" Morgan asked quietly. Had she broken that, too?

"I mean," Becca blushed and looked at the table. "Nothing bad."

"That's an example," Lynn said. "There are people for whom rope bondage is terrifying. And if you enjoy it, that's okay. You can enjoy it, and they can avoid it. And you can both be all right."

"Sure," Becca said. "But that's a random somebody. Not someone I'm supposed to be, umm, in a relationship with?"

"Morgan?" Lynn passed the question back to her, and Morgan took a breath.

"I love you," she said to start. "I don't want to hurt you. I don't want to make you do anything you hate. I care about your well-being."

"But I care about yours," Becca said. "I don't want to not give you things you need." Morgan nodded.

"I appreciate that," she said. "But look. Do you like curry?"

"Umm, I guess?" Becca looked confused.

"But you didn't have curry tonight. This restaurant doesn't even serve curry. Does that mean we shouldn't have come here?"

"That's silly," Becca objected. "No restaurant serves everything, and the ones that try aren't very good. The pizza here was excellent. The tiramisu is awesome. It's more than enough food." She poked the last bite of her dessert with a fork.

"Exactly," Morgan said. "Just because you like curry doesn't mean you need it at every meal. Just because I like stuff you don't want to try doesn't mean I don't enjoy the stuff we do together."

"But I don't want you to miss out," Becca said.

"I don't want to miss out on what I can build with you," Morgan said, not taking her eyes off Becca. Was it too soon to try reaching out again? "If you're trying to do stuff you hate, it will make neither of us happy. And it will be at the expense of things where we could build something that's good for us." She reached out with her fork and stole a tiny bit of the remaining tiramisu from Becca's plate. "I'd rather have awesome tiramisu than bad curry, any day."

"Am I tiramisu?" Becca asked. Morgan smiled.

"You're awesome," she said, reaching out and stroking Becca's cheek. Becca blushed, but she leaned into the touch.

"I'd like to see you again, though," Becca said, looking into Morgan's eyes. "Even after Toronto. I'm sorry if I used the wrong word."

"You didn't do anything wrong," Morgan said, gazing back. "I just got carried away. I'm sorry. I don't want to do anything you don't want."

"You do though," Becca glanced away. "And I ... why would you want to be involved with some-body who can't keep up with you?"

"Because it's not a race," Morgan said. "Remember the lighthouse on the island?"

"Sort of," Becca said. "We didn't get very close to it?" Her tone wondered whether she was forgetting something.

"Yeah. It was kind of a let-down, not being able to go up it or even get very close," Morgan agreed. "So getting there faster, with somebody who could keep up, as you put it, wouldn't have been an advantage."

"Was it a bad choice?" Becca asked. She had been the one to pore over maps and visitors' guides, before the visit, and she had suggested the lighthouse trail. Morgan wouldn't have had the patience.

"It was not," Morgan said firmly. "I enjoyed the walk, and I enjoyed the time with you. That's what it's about. Not trying to go as fast as we can or as far as we can, but finding the raspberries off to the side of the trail, picking the leaves out of your hair when you didn't quite duck under the branches, looking for pebbles on the beach. It's not about keeping up; it's about travelling together."

"I wish I could travel with you," Becca said wistfully. Morgan smiled.

"No, you don't," she said sadly. "At least, not for long. But I'd love to have you visit."

"Is that a real option?" Becca asked. "I mean, I've already booked all my vacation time for this year, and I don't think my mum would appreciate me skipping Christmas to run off on a sailboat, but maybe next year?"

"I have Cátia visiting, the last two weeks of December," Morgan said. She pulled out her phone. "Oh, and Lynn has Cailean scheduled to visit in mid-February."

"That might actually work for Becca, too, though," Lynn said. "I mean, assuming you can stay in your own cabin, Morgan." Becca blushed,

"I'm sorry," she said. "I didn't mean to kick her out of her own bed. I didn't want to be any trouble."

"Becca," Lynn interrupted her, "it's fine. It was fine. Everything is fine." Becca nodded, and Lynn continued, "It was okay for you to want your own space. It's okay to continue to want your own space. What I'm talking about now is strictly the practical considerations, if you and Cailean were to visit at the same time."

"Okay," Becca said slowly. Lynn nodded.

"One of the things I'm thinking," they said, "is that you might worry less about poor-Lynn-being-left-out if I do have my pup there with me, at the same time."

"Pup?" Becca asked.

"Don't worry about it," Morgan said, trying to reassure her, but Becca looked more worried rather than less.

"Yes, pup," Lynn said. "That's part of the rela-tionship I have with Cailean, that he takes on the part of a puppy and I'm his handler."

"Is that ...?" Becca began. "I mean," she blushed, "it's not like when we were all kids and playing at being a dog or a kitty, is it?"

"It can be," Lynn smiled. "I mean, it means more to him than just a child's game, and to me, but it's not that different in terms of what you're likely to actually see, if you're there when he is."

"So it's not, like, a sex thing?" Becca asked.

"Was being tied to the mast a sex thing?" Lynn countered. Becca blushed, and they nodded. "Much of what makes it sexual or not is personal to the people participating. I don't have standing to answer it for Cailean, and I don't think you really want to be asking me about my sex life while we're sitting in a nice restaurant."

"Umm, no," Becca blushed. "I probably really do not need to know that." Lynn nodded.

"If you really want to know," they said, "ask me in private and I might be willing to discuss it with you. But if what you're trying to ask is about what you might expect to see? Playing fetch or a pat on the head is more likely than a wild orgy on the deck."

"We actually have a disappointing lack of deck orgies," Morgan put in. "Yes, that's a joke," she added, when Becca turned to her. "Though it is one of the less pleasant assumptions Cátia's family has voiced about us."

"I'm sorry," said Becca.

"I am, too," Morgan said. "There's a reason she spends Christmas with us. Though it took a while to convince her that she wasn't required to spend a religious and family holiday with a family that uses their religion to treat her like garbage."

"And that we really did want her with us," Lynn added. "Which might be something Becca can relate to."

Becca blushed. "My family is fine," she said.

"Good," Lynn said. If they had reservations, they didn't voice them. "But you're still welcome with us."

"Just not over Christmas," Becca said.

"Not this year, anyway," Morgan agreed. "Because you have plans, already. How does February look for you? Maybe the middle two weeks?"

"That doesn't really seem like the nicest time to be on a boat," Becca said. "It's a bit cold?"

"Well, it's a bad time to be on a boat in Canada," Morgan allowed. "We're planning to stay on this side of the Atlantic, this year, but a bit further south."

"Cailean will be flying into Hato Airport," Lynn clarified. "Not all of the islands down there are terribly welcoming to our sort, but Curaçao is fine."

"You mean, umm, rope and pups and stuff?" Becca asked.

"I mean queer," Lynn said flatly. "Some of the lovely islands down there that want your tourist dollars? Not all of them are as bad as Barbados, but still."

"What's wrong with Barbados?" Becca asked. "Olivia went there on her honeymoon and she was all on about the sea turtles and the beaches and the hospitality."

"She's straight, isn't she?" Lynn asked.

"Well, yeah," Becca said. "What does that have to do with it?"

"Barbados is one of the islands where homosexuality is illegal," Morgan said quietly. She took Becca's hand again.

"Illegal? Like, they don't allow gay marriage yet?" Becca asked.

"Illegal," Lynn said, "like life in prison for being gay."

"That's," Becca started, and shook her head. "That's obscene."

"That's a really good reason to be careful where we stop," Lynn said.

"It's not generally enforced," Morgan put in, "but it's still on the books."

"And you can imagine how safe that makes the streets, in terms of crimes being committed against queer folks," Lynn said. "If our existence is illegal, well, how much protection do you think we're going to get?"

"So, I guess I shouldn't plan a trip to Barbados?" Becca said.

"Not with Morgan, anyway," Lynn confirmed. "The tourist areas might be safe enough. But if it comes down to a question of law," they shrugged.

"Curaçao is great, though," Morgan said. "Aruba and St. Maarten, too. They're all Dutch. The other half of St. Martin is French, which is also fine. Saint-Barthélemy, Martinique, Guadeloupe, we have options. And then the American territories and even the British Virgin Islands aren't bad." Becca nodded, still taking it all in.

"I mean, I see tourist ads, you know, hear the song. Aruba, Jamaica ooh I want to take ya? Bermuda, Bahama come on pretty mama?"

"Aruba is lovely," Lynn said. "Jamaica is ... getting better. You know Time magazine named it the most homophobic place on earth, in 2006?"

"I didn't," Becca said. "That's ... not what the Beach Boys told me."

"Given that their ideal was two girls for every boy," Morgan said, trying to lighten the mood, "You'd think they'd be looking for places it was safe for the girls to hook up."

"Bermuda is pretty okay," Lynn said. "Bahamas isn't actively illegal, any more. But it's something where we don't take a lot of chances, you know?" Becca nodded.

"Yeah, I definitely want you two to stay safe," she said. Lynn looked at her.

"Has it occurred to you, yet," they asked, "that this applies to you, too?" Becca blinked.

"That's," she began. "Umm. Yeah. I guess that is a thing."

"I'm guessing your previous partners have been men?" Lynn suggested gently. Becca shook her head.

"I haven't had previous partners," she said. She looked at Morgan. "This is all new to me." Morgan squeezed her hand.

"Ah," Lynn said. Morgan had thought they knew, but maybe she hadn't actually mentioned it to them. "I guess it might not have come up for you, then."

"I mean, we covered it in school," Becca blushed. "The basics I mean. Umm, mostly safer sex."

"You did?" Lynn blinked. "I didn't think you were that much younger than we are."

"I'm thirty-eight," Becca said. That was a year older than Morgan, though a little younger than Lynn.

"Section 28 was never a thing, here," Morgan reminded them.

"Section 28?" Becca asked, looking between them. Morgan noticed the server hanging back, trying to decide whether to interrupt the conversation, and waved him over.

"We'll just take the bill," Morgan told him, as he cleared away the plates. Once he was gone, she addressed Becca's question.

"Section 28 was a law to prevent local education authorities from promoting homosexuality in schools," she said. "And by 'promote', apparently, they meant 'prevent queer kids who come out from being bullied relentlessly', let alone 'provide information about safer sex practices'."

"That's," Becca shook her head. "I'm sorry. I'm sorry that happened to you."

"It wasn't me," Morgan said. "I wasn't that brave. I saw what happened to them and I kept my head down."

"I can't imagine you not being brave," Becca said.

"I wasn't, though," Morgan remembered. "I was a scared kid in a system I knew wouldn't protect me. So I didn't stand up for Mary and Frances. I tried dating the boys. It didn't go well, but I tried to do what was expected of me." Lynn reached across the table to take the hand Becca wasn't already holding. Morgan sat up straighter. She had her partners' support, here and now, and it had been a long time since high school. "I'm not doing that any more," she said decisively.

"I love you," Becca said. "I'm sorry that happened. I can't even imagine."

"I'm glad you can't," Morgan said. "I don't want you to be able to imagine it. And this is not the conversation I wanted to be having on our last night together." The server brought the bill to the table; Lynn let go of her hand to deal with it.

"It's just for a week, though, right?" Becca said. "You'll be in Toronto, and we'll get together then?"

"We will," Morgan promised. "And then maybe in February? If you're okay with sharing space with Cailean, that is." Becca blushed and nodded.

"I hope so," she said. "I'll put in for the vacation time as soon as I get back on Monday." Morgan smiled.

"What are you going to tell your co-workers, if they ask?" she wondered.

"They won't," Becca said. "I mean, nobody outside of HR even really sees the application, and they don't know me well enough to care."

"And if they ask about your holiday in general?" Morgan asked. "Are you going to tell them about the wicked woman you met, and all the terribly naughty things you did together?" Becca blushed.

"I'll tell them about the wonderful woman I met," she said. "Maybe that you took me sailing. They'll be jealous." Morgan smiled.

"I'm glad it's not something you need to hide," she said.

Twenty-Seven

Becca woke up alone, but at least her bags were packed. That was the important thing, right?

After dinner, Lynn had basically shoved Morgan into the front passenger seat before she had a chance to object. She could have asked if Morgan would have liked to come back to the hotel. But Becca needed to pack, in order to check out in the morning, and she assumed Morgan had things that needed doing on the boat. She hadn't asked.

She had driven Lynn and Morgan back to the marina. Lynn had thanked her for the ride and gone ahead to the boat, pointedly leaving her alone with Morgan. She could have asked if they could spare Morgan for the night, she could have asked Morgan even then, and maybe Morgan would have texted her partner and ... well, speculation was useless.

The Kia hadn't been the best place to say good-bye. The console between them had tried to act as chaperone, and the gear shift made its own point about leaning over for a kiss. The open parking lot was no better; she wanted at least a modicum of privacy. Like her own hotel room, but she needed to get back to it and pack, not be distracted with Morgan and, well, she had no idea what would have happened if she had taken Morgan back to her room.

Morgan hadn't asked; Becca hadn't invited her. There had been one long kiss in the parking lot, a kiss that left her shaking and breathless with its intensity. Even the memory of it was enough to raise a blush in Becca's cheeks. And then Morgan had walked away, back to her partner, back to her boat. And Becca hadn't said anything at all.

Becca picked up her phone from the bedside table. The messaging app showed two private alerts; Becca's heart skipped a beat.

The first was just an @everyone from Erin, on the RPG server, reminding everybody to wish Louise a happy birthday. Becca dutifully added her birthday wishes before moving on to the second.

<Morgan> Good morning,
sweetheart

Becca checked the timestamp quickly. Only twelve minutes ago. Okay. She wasn't too late, probably.

<Becca> Good morning, Morgan
<Morgan> How did you sleep?

```
<Becca> Okay.  But I woke up
        alone
<Becca> I miss you.  I wish
        you were here
<Morgan> I do, too,
         sweetheart.  But I
         didn't want to
         pressure you
```

It was still early. Maybe there would be time to
sneak in a few minutes before they both had to go?
But no, that would be foolish. What difference
would a few minutes make, other than to require
another painful goodbye?

```
<Becca> When are you leaving?
<Morgan> As soon as we've had
         breakfast.  It's only
         about 45 nm, but it's
         better to arrive early
         at the anchorage so we
         can get settled in
         daylight
<Becca> 45 nanometres?  Isn't
        that less than a
        millimetre?
<Morgan> 😂
<Morgan> Nautical miles,
         sweetheart
<Becca> Oh.  Is that far?
<Morgan> Seven or eight hours,
         if the weather is good
<Becca> Oh
<Becca> I'll be home, by then
```

```
<Morgan> I never said sailing
            was a fast way to
            travel, sweetheart
<Becca> I guess
```

Reluctantly, Becca put down the phone and got dressed. She shoved her nightgown in the outer pocket of her suitcase, and took her suitcase out to the car.

```
<Morgan> We're casting off,
            now.  Travel safely.
            Let us know when
            you're home
```

Becca walked back into the hotel and forced down some breakfast. Not eating wouldn't help, and if she could imagine sharing a fresh Belgian waffle with Morgan, well, there would be times in the future.

It would only be a week. Six days. Next Saturday, before the game.

It felt like forever.

Turning out of the parking lot, Becca turned left onto Erie, though everything in her wanted to turn right, towards the marina. She knew Morgan and Lynn had already left, but she ached with the fantasy that Morgan would still be there, where she had seen her last. She blinked back tears and concentrated on the road.

That was the laundromat to her right, where they had spent Friday night, the Humphrey's and the Rotisserie and Grill. The grocery store, also on the right, only a block later. They were open – it was midmorning on a Sunday, after all – but they'd feel empty without Morgan. There was no point in stopping, in lingering over the memories. She drove north along Erie, approaching Duilio's and steeling herself to drive past. None of these places held anything for her but memories, and she wasn't a child or some romance-novel heroine, to fall apart over just the reminder of places they had spent time together.

She wasn't.

She refused to be.

Past Duilio's, the distance between buildings increased. The city passed into farmland, another town, and Erie turned into Highway 77. Fields flanked the highway here, and if the road wasn't empty, Becca still still felt isolated. Morgan's absence beside her was a nagging emptiness, and Becca irrationally felt as if she were alone in the world. Alone in the Kia, anyway.

The sun climbed in the sky, a hot summer day developing outside the air conditioned cabin, and Becca merged onto the 401. One advantage of leaving relatively early in the morning was that traffic heading back towards the city was not yet heavy. Past Kelso, a sign for Humphrey's Hamburgers lured her from the highway. She hoped Lynn had enjoyed the veggie burger and the poutine; she had never thought to ask. She had no idea what Morgan would have liked on a burger, either, she realised. It distracted her enough that the crew member at the topping station had to call her order twice before she answered.

Becca's own preference was tzatziki, tomato slices, and lettuce, with pickles on the side. The crew member assembled the burger and set it on the tray beside a side order split between fries and onion rings. Becca filled her cup with pop at the fountain and carried the tray to an empty corner seat. Even before unwrapping the burger, she pulled out her phone.

<Becca> How are you two doing?

She had no idea whether they'd have a signal, or if they'd be too busy to respond. She made herself unwrap the burger and take a bite. The food was excellent, but she nearly dropped it in her haste to pick up the phone when it dinged the sound of an incoming message.

```
<Morgan> We're doing well.
         We've just came around
         the peninsula with the
         national park
<Becca> Do you have far to go,
        still?
<Morgan> Yeah, we're less than
         halfway to the
         anchorage, according
         to Lynn's charted
         route, and GPS agrees
         with them
<Morgan> What about you?  Are
         you home already?
<Becca> No, not yet.  I
        stopped for lunch.
        Humphrey's
```

```
<Morgan> Nice.  Get me
         something?
<Becca> I would if I could,
         Morgan.  I miss you so
         much
<Morgan> I miss you too,
         sweetheart
<Becca> Does it always hurt
         this much?  Leaving?
<Morgan> Every time.  But the
         times between are
         worth it
```

Becca ate her lunch and bussed the trash. She refilled her drink for the drive and placed the plastic restaurant tray neatly atop the trash receptacle.

It was only midafternoon when Becca got home. She tried not to think of the extra hours before bed as ones she could have spent in the morning, with Morgan. She might be home, but Morgan and Lynn were still sailing. She wouldn't have wanted to make them late to arrive at the anchorage, especially after Morgan explained that best practice for anchoring included diving to check how the anchor was set.

She wanted Morgan with her. She wanted Morgan and Lynn safe. She couldn't have everything, so she'd have to settle for what was possible. A week ago, she hadn't had a relationship at all, and now she had Morgan, whatever that relationship was. Girlfriend didn't seem right. They were adults, not girls, but 'womanfriend' just sounded silly. She wasn't sure they were partners, at least not the way Lynn and Morgan were. Lovers seemed like it might involve prerequisites Becca hadn't yet fulfilled, though they did love one another.

```
<Morgan> Does it matter what
         you call it?
<Becca> Sort of?  I feel
        weird, not having
        words for it
<Becca> And Lynn.  I mean, I
        know I don't have a
        thing with them.  But
        it feels different
        from just a friend?  I
        don't know
<Morgan> For Lynn, the word
         you want might be
         metamour
<Morgan> As for me?  I'm happy
         with whatever makes
         you comfortable,
         sweetheart.  I'm not
         going to police your
         terms
<Becca> So I could call you a
        cabbage, and you
        wouldn't mind?
<Morgan> A cabbage?  😂
<Becca> *blush* I think I
        learned it in French
        class.  Chou, as a
```

                      thing you call your
                      sweetheart
<Morgan>
<Morgan> As long as it's not
                      'snookums'
<Becca> Eww. Yeah
<Becca> Can I just use
                      'sweetheart', do you
                      think? Like, "Morgan
                      is my sweetheart.'
<Morgan> If it makes you
                      happy, love

Twenty-Eight

The question of how to talk about Morgan didn't actually come up, on Monday. As predicted, the amount of work on Becca's desk was double what it should have been. Patty had been supposed to cover for her, on new calls, but somehow everything that had come in on the line that was forwarded to Patty had ended up in Becca's voice mailbox. Possibly a glitch; possibly Patty avoiding work. Either way, it was Becca's job to follow up with apologies for the delay.

Olivia had tried to do her part, e-mailing a client with updates about an ongoing project. Unfortunately, the client had responded by e-mail to *Becca's* address, and apparently not followed up with Olivia even in the face of Becca's out-of-office reply. At least the project Sean had been meant to finalise had gone smoothly.

Tuesday, Becca had a little more time to breathe. It helped that some of the contacts Patty had forwarded to her voicemail box had solved the problems themselves before Becca could get back to them. This was less work for her, even if it wasn't great for their customer satisfaction ratings. Becca still took lunch at her desk, but at least she had enough time for a private web search or two.

Spending time with Morgan had been lovely, and the promise of Curaçao was enticing, but Becca couldn't shake a feeling of embarrassment at how badly she had handled the transfer into the dinghy. If only there were some way to get better at that, without embarrassing herself in front of Morgan again. She supposed she could ask Lynn to help her figure it out. They'd probably do it, but she couldn't imagine Morgan not also being there. "Hey, I'd like some alone time with your partner, don't ask why" didn't seem the sort of thing she wanted to say to her sweetheart.

Some sort of formal class would be easiest; that way she'd know there weren't any weird gaps in her knowledge that might bite her later. The idea of such a thing — dinghy lessons seemed awfully specific — seemed a long shot, but it was worth at least looking. Becca typed dinghy lessons Toronto into her favourite search engine.

The first hit was a map to the Sailing and Canoe Club, with adult lessons starting in August. Tuesday and Thursday evenings, they were offered. That would be after Morgan and Lynn left. She didn't want to think about it — waiting until Saturday felt bad enough — but having something to do, to get better at being a match for Morgan, that could be worth it. Especially if she kept it a secret, so Morgan would be expecting her to be useless around the boat again and maybe she wouldn't be?

Becca entered her credit card details to reserve a space in the class, then turned back to her real work. One of the people Patty hadn't helped had tried to solve the issue alone, and now everything was twice as complicated. Becca was trying to track down misapplied settings across half a dozen control panels, and she needed to get hold of the client to figure out what they had *thought* they were doing.

Each night, of course, there were text conversations with Morgan. The Wi-Fi wasn't always strong enough to support a voice call; having spent two nights in a marina already that week, it made sense that they were choosing to anchor for free rather than pay for a slip. Becca understood the logic, even the need, but it didn't make missing the sound of Morgan's voice easier.

Mornings would start with a text; Morgan's "Good morning, sweetheart," on Sunday hadn't been an isolated occurrence. Monday, Becca had woken to another. Tuesday, she had managed to beat Morgan to it, though Morgan got the first word in, again, on Wednesday. It was a silly way to compete, Becca knew, but it felt good.

```
<Becca> Good morning,
        sweetheart
```

It still felt a bit odd, calling Morgan 'sweetheart'. *Having* a sweetheart felt odd. But it was nice.

```
<Morgan> Good morning, Becca
<Becca> How did you sleep?
<Morgan> Could have been
        worse.  We were up
        early to check in at
        the locks.  If we
        weren't paid and
        registered by seven,
        we'd have to wait
        until Saturday to do
        the transit
<Becca> But it's only
        Thursday, now?
<Morgan> I'm quite aware of
        that, sweetheart.  I'm
        not the one who sets
        the lockage schedules
<Becca> I'm sorry
<Becca> When will you start
        through?
<Morgan> It will be a while.
        At least we don't have
        to hire extra crew,
        this time
<Becca> This time?
<Morgan> Yeah, going upbound
        they require three
        people.  Back
```

                downbound, they'll
                allow us to do it
                ourselves
        <Morgan> Should you be getting
                ready for work,
                sweetheart?

She really should, but other mornings had been
all "good morning, sweetheart; the anchorage was
nice and we're looking forward to an easy sail to
our next point."

        <Becca> Probably. But I worry
                about you
        <Morgan> Everything is fine.
                It's very hurry-up-
                and-wait, right now
        <Morgan> They've said it will
                be at least one before
                we can start, and
                we'll be transiting
                with whatever other
                pleasure craft show up
                before seven, I guess
        <Becca> That's kind of a long
                wait
        <Morgan> Yeah. They're pretty
                clear that they're
                really here for the
                commercial traffic,
                and we should be
                grateful they take us
                through at all
        <Becca> So nice of them

<Morgan> I know, right?
<Morgan> But you still need to
         get ready for work.
         Shower first, or
         breakfast?
<Becca> Shower, I guess
<Becca> Why?
<Morgan> So I know when I'm
         supposed to be
         imagining you naked,
         all wet and slippery
         with soap
<Becca> 😳

Becca did get her shower, though it was probably not just the hot water turning her skin pink. She knew Morgan couldn't actually see her, was probably just teasing her about imagining her naked, but she couldn't get the idea out of her head, even as she towelled herself dry.

It took effort not to bother Morgan for updates over breakfast or when she got to work, but Becca didn't want to be too clingy. It was bad enough that she felt this way; she didn't need to act on it. At least the workload was settling back down to its normal level. She finally managed to straighten out the account for that one problem client.

Becca still had no idea how they had gone along for months after their site upgrade without noticing a problem, then suddenly had it become an emergency that required breaking *all* the settings while she was on vacation. Murphy's Law in action, she supposed. She found that she no longer cared how it had happened. She had finally gotten the site sorted; as long as they would leave her alone, she was satisfied with that.

There was a department meeting at noon, previewing new features that would be in the late August rollout and some of the promotions they'd be pushing for back-to-school. Sam had bought pizza for the team, to make up for missing their lunch, but it was still after one before Becca got back to her desk.

```
<Becca> How are you doing?
<Morgan> Still waiting
<Becca> Didn't they say one?
<Morgan> At least one.  We
        have the radio on us
<Morgan> Need to be able to
        cast off whenever
        they're ready for us,
        too, so we can't even
        tie in to dock power
<Morgan> Aren't you meant to
        be at work?
<Becca> I am
<Becca> I just got out of a
        meeting
<Morgan> Stop worrying about
        us, sweetheart.
        Everything is fine
<Becca> Okay
<Becca> Let me know when you
        start moving, though?
<Morgan> I will
```

Becca tried to focus on her work, though she kept her phone propped against the monitor on her desk, just in case Morgan messaged. It was almost quarter to four when she actually did.

```
<Morgan> We finally got the
         go-ahead
<Becca> It's late.  How long
        will it take?
<Morgan> Could be up to twelve
         hours, the handbook
         says, though I think
         it was closer to
         eight, going up
<Becca> That will be after
        dark.  I thought you
        weren't supposed to be
        sailing after dark
<Morgan> There are lights over
         the locks.  We'll tie
         up as soon as we're
         through
<Morgan> And we're doing it
         under power, rather
         than sail
<Becca> Like in the marina?
<Morgan> Yeah, for the same
         reason.  Tight
         conditions, need the
         control
<Morgan> I need to go, love
<Morgan> If I'm slow
         responding tonight,
```

```
                    don't worry.  I'll
                    reply when I can
        <Becca> I love you
        <Morgan> I love you, too
```

"Something wrong?" Olivia asked, from the next cubicle over. Becca hastily shoved her phone back in a pocket.

"Oh, no," she said. "Just catching up with somebody." She could feel herself blushing, and Olivia only looked more curious.

"Oh?" she asked.

"Yeah," Becca said. "Some friends of mine are going through the Welland Canal, and I asked them to update me. Apparently it will be late before they get out."

"Friends?" Olivia asked. "Or a *friend*? People don't usually start blushing over their friends' travel arrangements."

"They're both my friends," Becca said, "but, umm, Morgan might be something special, yeah."

"Oh? Somebody you met on vacation?" Becca nodded and Olivia grinned eagerly. "Tell me about him."

"Her," Becca corrected, her blush deepening. "She, uh, well, we've known each other for years, online."

"Mmhmmm," Olivia said, drawing out the sound. "Yup, we all get blushy and shy about people we've known for years. Perfectly normal."

"We might have gotten, umm, closer, over the course of a visit," Becca admitted, trying to get her cheeks under control before somebody else noticed.

"Mmm," Olivia said. "So I gathered." She smiled. "I'm glad you've found somebody, hon. I worried about you."

Becca left her phone in her pocket for the rest of the day. It was only a few more hours, and she didn't want to get in trouble for slacking off on company time. She could live without constantly checking on Morgan. She and Lynn would be busy on the boat, doing whatever it was they did in locks. The phone would vibrate against her leg if she got a message, anyway.

The phone remained still.

Becca sent another "How are you doing?" message while waiting on the train platform at Union Station. There was no immediate reply and the train was too crowded with commuters to have room to look at her phone. Three stops later, she was finally able to move her hands away from her sides enough to check messages, but there was still nothing. This was fine, she told herself. Morgan had warned her they would be busy.

Becca had retrieved her car and was waiting behind what seemed like every other commuter on the planet to leave the parking lot before her phone vibrated with what might be an incoming message. Just when she couldn't spare a hand to check it. Even if there was a red light. She knew better.

Becca disciplined herself to drive all the way home before checking messages, but she pulled out the phone as soon as she had parked.

    <Morgan> We're doing okay. A
             bit tired
    <Becca> Why tired? *worries*
    <Morgan> It's okay. It's
             just, you remember how
             much fun docking was?
    <Becca> I don't remember a lot
            of fun, but yeah
    <Morgan> Well, 'fun'
    <Morgan> So at each lock we
             have to tie up to the
             side with these extra
             long lines they gave
             us
    <Morgan> Then they start
             draining it, so we
             sink to the level of
             the next lock
    <Morgan> We cast off from the
             wall, proceed towards
             the next lock, and go
             through the whole
             thing again
    <Becca> That sounds like a lot
            of work
    <Morgan> Yeah. Lynn and I
             have been switching
             off between lines and
             piloting, but it still
             feels like A Lot

<Morgan> We'd just come out of
        Lock 4 when I messaged
        you. We're waiting
        for Lock 3, now
<Becca> Will you be okay?
<Morgan> We'll be fine. I
        promise
<Becca> Is it a long wait?
<Morgan> Hard to say. We
        still need to yield to
        freighters
<Morgan> Locks 6, 5, and 4
        were all connected,
        but there's a bit of
        space before Lock 3
<Becca> So you're going
        backwards?
<Morgan> That's the way
        they're numbered. How
        was your day?
<Becca> It was fine. I got
        that one account
        straightened out,
        started setup for a
        newer client, ate
        pizza and heard what
        marketing is promising
        people we'll be able
        to do, next month
<Becca> I'm boring
<Morgan> You're lovely. And
        boring sounds good,
        right now

```
<Morgan> I'm sorry,
         sweetheart.   The L/A
         light has started
         flashing. We need to
         go
<Morgan> Love you
<Becca> I love you, too
```

Becca surveyed the contents of her refrigerator before deciding to order a pizza. She kept looking back at her phone. There were a few more sporadic messages, but if the entire lock transit was like docking and undocking, she could under-stand why Morgan didn't have a lot of time for her.

At least things were going well, even if delays were unpredictable and updates infrequent. She tried to remind herself that each lock brought them closer to Toronto. It helped a little. So did the pizza, and pulling up videos about transiting the Welland Canal that other people had posted to the Internet. The fact that it was after dark, approach-ing Becca's bedtime, and they were still waiting for Lock 2 did not help at all.

```
<Morgan> You should sleep.
         Everything will be
         fine
<Becca> I worry
<Morgan> I know, sweetheart,
         but you missing sleep
         won't do us any good
<Becca> I guess
```

```
<Becca> Promise to message
         when you get through
         safely?
<Morgan> I don't want to wake
         you
<Becca> Please?
<Morgan> If it will make you
         feel better.  Now
         sleep.  I promise
         everything will be
         fine
```

Friday morning, Becca woke to the message,

```
<Morgan> We're through.  We're
         just going to eat
         something quick, then
         fall into bed
<Morgan> If I don't catch you
         before work, tomorrow,
         I love you and have a
         great day
```

The time stamp reported that it had arrived after one in the morning; Becca had slept through it.

```
<Becca> I love you, too
<Becca> Thank you for
         messaging
<Becca> Whenever you get this:
         Good morning,
         sweetheart
```

She waited a few minutes for a reply, but wasn't surprised when none came. They must both have been exhausted.

Around eleven, she felt the phone vibrate against her leg. It would probably be Morgan telling her everything was fine and laughing at her for being worried.

She snuck it out for a glance, just to confirm.

```
<Morgan> Good morning,
         sweetheart
<Morgan> I can say that.  It's
         not noon yet
<Becca> You can 😆
<Becca> I'm working.  Talk at
        lunch
<Morgan> Sure thing,
         sweetheart
```

The hour until lunch took several hours to pass, but finally Becca was able to use her phone without guilt.

```
<Becca> How are you doing?
<Morgan> We're fine.  Glad to
         be through
<Becca> Did you get enough
        sleep?
<Morgan> Yes, sweetheart.
         We're fine
```

<pre>
<Morgan> I'd offer voice, but
         we only just cast off
         from the marina
<Becca> I love you
<Becca> I'm not sure where I'd
        take it, anyway. I'm
        still at my desk
<Morgan> Fair enough
</pre>

Becca tried to control her eagerness, but couldn't help messaging,

<pre>
<Becca> So you'll be arriving
        tonight?
<Morgan> Looks like. Lynn's
         booked a slip at the
         Island Marina
<Becca> On the island?
<Morgan> Yeah. Why?
<Becca> Just that it's a ferry
        ride to get over
        there, and I might not
        have the best luck
        with ferries
<Morgan> I don't know. I
         think my luck with
         your ferries turned
         out to be pretty good
</pre>

<pre>
<Becca> </pre>
<pre>
<Morgan> Yes, exactly </pre>

Olivia passed, returning to her own desk with lunch. She looked from Becca's face to the phone in her hand and asked, "Morgan, again?"

"Yeah," Becca admitted. "I'm on lunch, though. It's allowed." Olivia smiled and shook her head.

"I wasn't planning to tell Sam on you," she said. "I remember that stage, anyway. So in love that nothing else matters."

"I'm getting my work done," Becca said defensively. Olivia held up a hand.

"I never said you weren't," she said. "I meant emotionally. Wanting to connect in every spare moment."

"Okay, yeah." Becca looked down. "I'm sorry."

"It's fine," Olivia said. "I'll stop interrupting your conversation, now."

"Thanks," Becca mumbled. She looked back at the phone. Morgan's emoji was still smirking at her.

```
<Becca> Any idea what time
        you'll be getting in?
<Becca> Do you need anything,
        tonight?
<Morgan> Hard to say.
         Shouldn't be more than
         five or six hours
<Becca> That's around the time
        I get off work.  Would
        you like me to come
        over?
<Morgan> We're pretty tired,
         sweetheart
<Becca> So no?
```

```
<Morgan> I do!
<Morgan> Just don't expect
         much of us, okay?
<Becca> I just want to see you
<Becca> I promise I'll be
        careful of the ferry
        schedule, this time
<Morgan> I mean, you don't
         have to
<Morgan> I do still have that
         nightgown you can
         borrow . . .
<Becca> 😳
<Becca> I thought you said you
        weren't up for much?
<Morgan> What can I say?
<Morgan> You inspire me
<Becca> 😳
<Becca> Is Lynn okay with me
        maybe spending the
        night?
```

The response wasn't immediate. That was good. Becca would feel better knowing Morgan had actually asked. She spent the time logging onto the ferry service web site and pre-booking a ticket. Spending the night or not, she'd at least get to *see* Morgan,

```
<Morgan> They say it's fine as
         long as I sleep in my
         own cabin, this time
<Becca> 😳 😳 😳
```

```
<Morgan> So if you're okay
         with that . . . 😏
<Becca> I'll see you tonight
             😳
```

Becca slipped her phone back into her pocket and finished booking her ticket. This time, she was determined, there was no way she was missing the boat.